"Don't let go, Seth. Reel him in!"

Ben helped the boy hold the fishing pole as Mary ran over to watch her brother.

Together, Ben and Seth alternately tugged and reeled until the trout was safely on shore. Once the catch was secure, Seth grinned wide and held the fish up high.

"Look! I caught one!" the boy crowed.

He laughed out loud, and Caroline could only stare at him in wonder. It was the first time she'd heard such a happy sound come from the boy.

Ben turned and looked at Caroline from over his shoulder. His eyes twinkled with merriment as he pushed his black felt hat back on his head. Then he did something that both startled and delighted her. He winked and mouthed a single word to her.

Victory!

Caroline nodded, unable to contain a smile of satisfaction. Yes, she couldn't agree more. They'd had a great triumph today. Both children were happy. So was Caroline. Because, for a short time, she'd been able to pretend that this was her *familye*.

Leigh Bale is a *Publishers Weekly* bestselling author. She is the winner of the prestigious Golden Heart® Award and was a finalist for the Gayle Wilson Award of Excellence and the Booksellers' Best Award. The daughter of a retired US forest ranger, she holds a BA in history. Married in 1981 to the love of her life, Leigh and her professor husband have two children and two grandkids. You can reach her at leighbale.com.

Marie E. Bast grew up on a farm in northern Illinois. In the solitude of country life, she often read or made up stories. She earned a BA, an MBA and an MA in general theology and enjoyed a career with the federal government, but characters kept whispering her name. She retired and now pursues her passion of full-time writing. Marie loves walking, golfing with her husband of twenty-seven years and baking. Visit Marie at mariebastauthor.com and mariebast.blogspot.com.

LEIGH BALE

Her Amish Chaperone

&

MARIE E. BAST

The Amish Baker's Rival

LOVE INSPIRED

INSPIRATIONAL ROMANCE

LOVE INSPIRED®
INSPIRATIONAL ROMANCE

ISBN-13: 978-1-335-46293-0

Her Amish Chaperone and The Amish Baker's Rival

Copyright © 2022 by Harlequin Enterprises ULC

Her Amish Chaperone
First published in 2020. This edition published in 2022.
Copyright © 2020 by Lora Lee Bale

The Amish Baker's Rival
First published in 2020. This edition published in 2022.
Copyright © 2020 by Marie Elizabeth Bast

Recycling programs
for this product may
not exist in your area.

For questions and comments about the quality of this book, please contact us
at CustomerService@Harlequin.com.

Harlequin Enterprises ULC
22 Adelaide St. West, 41st Floor
Toronto, Ontario M5H 4E3, Canada
www.LoveInspired.com

Printed in U.S.A.

CONTENTS

HER AMISH CHAPERONE

Leigh Bale

This book is dedicated to
Shana Asaro, Melissa Endlich and Diane Parkinson.
Thank you for supporting and believing in me.
You transformed my heart and mind
and made me a better writer.

Peace I leave with you, my peace I give unto you:
not as the world giveth, give I unto you.
Let not your heart be troubled, neither let it be afraid.
—*John* 14:27

Chapter One

Caroline Schwartz didn't dare take her eyes off her feet. If she did, she knew she'd fall flat on her face. At the age of nineteen, she should be able to run past this crosswalk on Main Street without even thinking about it. But after the buggy accident that nearly took her life, it was amazing she could walk at all.

Thankfully, there wasn't much traffic in the sleepy farming town of Riverton, Colorado. Caroline's progress was slow. She gripped the handles of her elbow crutches and inched forward, taking several shuffling steps. The plastic sack of pencils and notepads she'd just purchased from the general store swung easily from her fingers. Pressing her tongue against the roof of her mouth, she concentrated on every step and vowed she would one day do this again without the aid of crutches.

Ignoring her aching muscles and joints, she lifted her feet higher. The black asphalt emanated heat she could feel even through her plain Amish shoes. But she didn't mind. At least it wasn't snowing. She welcomed the dry August sunshine that beat down on her white organdy prayer *kapp*.

The accident last January had crushed her pelvis and broken both her legs. And what had followed had been a long, depressing winter. She'd spent several months in the hospital with her legs and hips in traction, followed by weeks of excruciating physical therapy. The doctors hadn't given her much hope of walking again, but she'd proved them wrong. Ignoring the screaming pain, she'd diligently pushed herself to stand and move her legs. Finally, she'd graduated to elbow crutches. And walking across the street today on her own power was a tremendous victory. It meant she could resume her teaching assignment at the Amish school next month and wouldn't be a burden on her *familye* any longer.

It meant freedom and independence.

The narrow sidewalk extended past the general store but ended just a few feet beyond the post office. If she could make it there, her aunt Hannah would help her to the buggy. Caroline had insisted on walking to the store alone today, but she was tired now and desperately needed to sit down.

The sudden blaring of a horn startled her and she jerked her head up. Two glass headlights and the shiny silver grill of a brand-new black pickup truck stood no more than twenty inches away. She lifted her gaze higher and saw Rand Henbury glaring at her from behind the tinted windshield. Rand was the eighteen-year-old son of the richest *Englisch* rancher in the area. Two of his *Englisch* friends sat in the truck beside him.

Vroom! Vroom!

Rand revved the engine impatiently and honked the horn again. In her haste to get out of the way, Caroline lost her balance and tumbled to the ground in a giant heap. Her crutches clattered around her and she cried out as small rocks dug into her knees and the palms of her hands. As she struggled to push herself up, she heard Rand and his friends' raucous laughter.

A feeling of absolute fear coursed through Caroline's veins. The night of the buggy accident rushed over her in dizzying horror. With perfect clarity, she recalled every sickening sound of smashing wood and the screeching of her broken horse. When help finally arrived, the poor animal had to be put down. And when she'd awoken in the hospital, Caroline had been beyond grateful they didn't shoot people, because her body was just as shattered.

Not twenty minutes before the car struck her buggy, she'd seen the driver yelling and throwing things in the general store. Such a temper was alien to Caroline and her Amish people. They were pacifists, adhering to Jesus Christ's teachings to turn the other cheek no matter what. She'd hurried to her buggy and was on her way home when the man had come upon her in his car. Because he'd been in a drunken rage, he'd been driving too fast and couldn't stop his vehicle in time. But Caroline had learned firsthand why anger and violence were to be shunned. And even though it had happened eight months earlier, it felt like it was happening all over again. Right now.

"Schtopp! Waard e bissel."

She heard the *Deitsch* words behind her but couldn't turn to see who was speaking. Strong hands lifted her and she stared into the face of Benjamin Yoder, her Amish bishop's recalcitrant nephew from Iowa. As she faced her rescuer, Caroline wasn't sure if she should be grateful or even more frightened.

Rumor haunted Ben's name. Hushed whispers claimed he had killed a man seven years earlier. That was why he'd moved here to Colorado. To escape his dark past. And though he was a member in good standing of the *Gmay*, her Amish community here in Riverton, she couldn't trust him. Not ever.

"I have you. It'll be all right now." His deep voice sounded soft, sympathetic and soothing.

He spoke in *Deitsch*, the language of their people. And as he carried her across the street, Caroline felt absolutely safe in his arms. Then she reminded herself who he was and who she was—and she wanted away from him as fast as possible.

With her out of the road, Rand revved the engine of his truck and surged forward. The vehicle accelerated, disappearing around the corner with a squealing of brakes and a smattering of gravel.

Breathing hard, Caroline had no choice but to wrap her arms around Ben's neck. He carried her as if she were light as a baby bird. Beneath her hands, she felt the bunching of his solid muscles and remembered all the stories that surrounded his name.

Violent! Killer!

He was everything Caroline loathed. She'd heard all the gossip. Standing at six feet four inches tall, Ben weighed around two hundred pounds, all of it muscle. He was large and strong and Bishop Yoder called him Big Ben, with good reason. Though everyone in their Amish community kept their distance, the men included Ben in their work projects because he had the strength and stamina of three men. But he never complained. In fact, he was inordinately quiet and kept mostly to himself. He'd become an asset to their *Gmay*, especially when they were building a new house or barn. But just like the drunk driver who had struck Caroline's buggy and almost killed her, she believed Ben had a foul temper. And she wanted nothing to do with a man like him. No, nothing at all.

As Ben reached the sidewalk, she caught his open expression. He was ruggedly handsome, with a lean jaw and blunt, stubborn chin. His nose was slightly crooked, as if it had been broken before. Though she was almost as afraid of this man as she was of Rand Henbury, she saw nothing in Ben's gaze but sympathy and concern.

"Please don't tell the bishop about this. Please!" she whispered to him, fearing she might be deemed incapable and lose her teaching position at the Amish school.

Ben met her gaze, a sober expression on his face. And then he did something that caused her to catch her breath. He winked.

"As you wish. Don't worry. It'll be our little secret," he said.

She stared at him, stunned from the top of her head to the tips of her toes. Did he really mean it?

"Caroline!" Aunt Hannah called.

Too late! Aunt Hannah and Sarah Yoder, the bishop's wife, came running out of the post office. Cliff Packer, the town's *Englisch* postmaster, joined them. No doubt they'd all seen what had happened. There would be no way to keep it secret now.

"Geht es dir gut?" Sarah asked.

"*Ja,* I'm all right. There's nothing to worry about," Caroline reassured them all, but her voice wobbled slightly.

"What happened?" Aunt Hannah asked.

Caroline tapped Ben's sturdy shoulder. "Please, put me down."

He did so, setting her on a wooden bench. As he drew

his large hands away, she was cognizant of his promise. Too many people had seen what had happened to keep it private, but she was impressed that Ben had been willing to try. And though she knew he was prone to violence, she wondered if he was a man of his word.

He stood back, not saying anything. His straw hat shaded his clean-shaven face, and she could no longer see his expression. He looped his thumbs through the black suspenders crisscrossing his blue chambray shirt, looking like the very tall, plain Amish man he was. And yet, Caroline sensed there was so much more to Ben Yoder than what she'd been told. Though her senses were on high alert, her curiosity demanded she know more about his past. To understand what was behind his quiet exterior. What had made him angry enough to kill another human being? But she wouldn't ask. For one thing, it wasn't her business. And for another, never again could she take chances with her life. She wanted away from Ben. And fast.

"Can we please go home now?" she asked her aunt.

Hannah picked up the two crutches, her face creased with a stern frown. "Of course. I told you it was too soon for you to go traipsing off around town on your own. You should have let me accompany you to the store. I don't see how you'll be able to teach school this year. You still need lots of help."

The scolding stung. But Caroline knew her aunt meant well. Hannah was a kind woman and her words stemmed from fear, not cruelty. Over the past months of Caroline's rehabilitation, Aunt Hannah had been there for her all the way, without a single murmur of complaint. And it was because of her aunt that she even had a teaching position here in Riverton at all. They'd both come from Ohio and had always been quite close.

But although Caroline laughed off her aunt's concerns, she had her own misgivings. She still couldn't walk very well and wondered how she could effectively teach the Amish children on her own. Back east, there were many children packed into each Amish parochial school, so they usually had at least two teachers. But that wasn't the case here in Colorado where the Amish community was quite small. They only had one teacher and Caroline was it. No wonder the bishop had told her the day before that he was going to assign an assistant to help her. But she wasn't happy at all when he informed her that her new assistant was going to be Ben Yoder.

"Don't worry so much. The *kinder* will be there to help me. And I'm gaining in strength every day." Caroline spoke with a confidence she didn't completely feel. She hated the thought of relying on a man like Ben to chop firewood and clear snow from the paths. But she really had no choice. Not unless she wanted to defy the bishop and school board, which she would never do.

"But what if you fall in the classroom?" Aunt Hannah asked.

"Then I'll pick myself up just like I do at home," Caroline replied, omitting the fact that at home, she could crawl over to a wall or table to brace herself against as she got to her knees and then stood. She'd have to do the same at school. But that could be a problem during recess, when she was outside with no walls to offer support.

"I saw everything!" Cliff Packer exclaimed. "Rand threatened to run her over. He and his friends cause trouble for everyone in town. They shoplift and vandalize our stores and hassle our customers. I can call the police, if you like. This should be reported."

"That won't be necessary. We're leaving town now. No harm was done." Sarah Yoder spoke briskly, taking Aunt Hannah's arm.

Caroline wasn't surprised the bishop's wife rejected Cliff's offer. Her people shunned contention of any kind. As pacifists, they would never fight back, nor would they sue anyone in a court of law. It wasn't their way. The last thing they wanted right now was to call the police.

"Rand and his friends zip around the county roads and terrorize the Amish in the area, too. The bishop should be told. Maybe he'll decide it's finally time to talk to the police about it." Aunt Hannah spoke in *Deitsch*, so Cliff couldn't understand her words.

"I don't know what the police can do. You know Amos has spoken to the boy's *vadder* before and he wouldn't listen," Sarah said.

"*Ach*, please don't tell the bishop. Please!" Caroline begged, knowing they would never make a vow of silence the way Ben had.

"But Caroline, we have to tell him," Sarah said.

"He doesn't need to know," she continued. "People fall all the time. And it certainly doesn't impact my ability to teach. As many times as I fall down, the *gut* Lord will give me the strength to get back up."

But even as she said the words, Caroline knew Sarah would run right home and tell her husband everything that had transpired. By tomorrow morning everyone in her community would know about it, both Amish and *Englisch*.

Hopefully, the bishop and the other two school board members wouldn't care. They knew what she'd been through this past year and how hard she'd worked to rehabilitate herself. She desperately wanted to keep her job. She needed to believe that she was worth something and could benefit her community. That she wasn't just a burden to everyone around her. After all, she could never marry now. Not after what had happened to her.

She turned away and blinked back tears of grief, resolved not to give in to the discouragement. Out of her peripheral vision, she caught Ben's steady gaze. He watched her quietly, as if he could see deep inside her heart. Surely, he had heard all the gossip about her, too. Including how she'd lost much more than just the use of her legs in that horrible accident. She'd also lost her ability to have children. And what Amish man would want her now? The Amish cherished large families. Children meant everything to them. Even if she could find a man to love her for who she was, she could never marry him. Not when she knew she could never give him the kids he would undoubtedly want.

Instead, she must be content with being a teacher. Over time, she would settle into a routine. She would work and live her entire life in this community, but she was determined to pay her own way. She'd almost lost her life and ability to walk. She couldn't lose her career, too. Her job gave her a reason to get up every morning. To keep trying. That was all she needed.

She was determined to return to the classroom and love the children she taught as if they were her own. It would be enough to ease the ache in her heart. It must be! Because the alternative was to become an invalid and spend the rest of her life with bitterness and loneliness as her constant companions. And she was not willing to accept that. No way, no how.

* * *

"Ben, will you carry Caroline to our buggy, please? I fear she's too worn out to walk there by herself now," Aunt Hannah said in a polite tone.

Ben looked up, startled by the request. "Of course."

Realizing Caroline was in no condition to walk on her own, he nodded and reached out to scoop her into his arms. As he did so, he caught the uncertain look in her wide eyes. The fear and dread.

Looking away, he carried her the short distance to the parking lot where an open-air cover and hitching posts had been erected by the town for the Amish to use. He tried to ignore the pounding in his heart. If their two aunts hadn't witnessed what had happened, he would have kept his promise to Caroline. He would have kept the incident a secret to his dying day. But now it appeared that everyone in the *Gmay* would soon hear all about it. No doubt the *Englischers* in their community would, too.

"I'm so sorry about this." Caroline spoke so softly that he almost didn't hear.

Her apology hit him hard. "You have nothing to be sorry about."

And he meant it. Through no fault of her own, she needed his help. And he was happy to be of service. The bishop, his uncle, had spoken to him about her situation last night, just after he'd returned from informing Caroline that the school board had assigned Ben to tend to her and the needs of the school this year. From her sour expression, Ben figured she wasn't happy to be saddled with him. But she had no choice.

Until she could walk and get along well on her own, Ben was to put aside his regular farm work with his uncle and focus entirely on Caroline and the school. The bishop and his sons would assume Ben's chores for the time being, but that wasn't the biggest problem here. Caroline was strong-willed and independent. No doubt she didn't want him hanging around her all the time. But more than that, Ben sensed she was afraid of him. He could see it in her eyes every time she looked at him. Surely, she'd heard the gossip surrounding his name and thought he was a dangerous man. And she was dead right.

"Everything's going to be okay." He spoke just as softly, wishing he could believe his own words. But he knew what she must think of him.

Killer. Murderer. It's what he thought of himself, too.

"I hope you're right," she said.

He looked away, not knowing what else to say. His parents had died when he was young. As an only child, he'd been taken in by one of his uncles in a small farming community in Iowa. By the time he was a teenager, he'd grown to a great height and had learned to work hard and love *Gott*. But more than anything else in the world, he wanted a *familye* of his own. A wife and children to shower his love upon. To the Amish, *familye* meant everything. But for Ben, it was even more personal. If he had a *familye* of his own, it would help make up for what he'd lost with his parents. Give him a sense of belonging. A woman and kids to spend the rest of his life with would be his dream come true. But in his heart, he knew it was futile.

He'd killed a man with his bare hands. No good Amish woman would ever marry him now.

He set Caroline in her buggy and stepped away. He saw the flutter of her lashes as she looked down. She made a pretense of tucking several strands of golden hair back inside her white prayer *kapp* before straightening her white apron and long, burgundy dress. She glanced up and he saw her true feelings emblazoned in her beautiful blue eyes. Distrust. Fear. Repulsion. They were all there, plain as the small, upturned nose on her face.

She didn't speak but looked away. He gazed at her pretty profile for several moments, feeling mesmerized. Since the day he'd first seen her in church, he'd thought she was the most amazing woman he'd ever met. She had a smooth, creamy complexion any woman would envy and delicate eyebrows that arched perfectly over her eyes. But jealousy wasn't part of the Amish faith. In fact, his people rejected *Hochmut*, the pride of men. And because of how demure she was, Ben doubted Caroline was even aware how lovely she was.

As she folded her hands in her lap, he got the feeling her movements were contrived so she could avoid speaking to him again. And he didn't blame her one bit. With his reputation, he wouldn't want to be friends with him, either.

"*Danke*, Ben. I'm so grateful you were here today." Hannah broke into his thoughts.

He nodded, stepping back several paces. "It was my pleasure. I'm glad I could help out."

Without a backward glance, Hannah hurried to the driver's seat and took the leather lead lines into her practiced grip. She didn't say another word as she slapped them against the horse's back.

"Haw!" she called and the buggy jerked forward.

"You take care and travel safely." Sarah waved as she called after her and Caroline.

Hannah gave a curt nod.

"*Komm* on. Let's go *heemet*." Sarah touched Ben's

elbow as she hurried toward their own horse and buggy
tethered a short distance away.

"*Ja*, I'll take you home." He nodded his assent and followed, ensuring that all her packages were stowed safely
in the back. Then he climbed into the driver's seat.

As he drove them home, he couldn't help thinking
about the past. The legal system had ruled the killing as
self-defense and he hadn't faced any jail time. But that
didn't matter to Ben. Even though it happened seven
years earlier, he still couldn't forget. Couldn't get the
awful scene out of his heart and mind. He'd taken another
human life, and it haunted him day and night.

"Just wait until your *onkel* Amos hears about this. I
don't know what he'll say. I'm sure he'll be upset. Rand
Henbury has made it so none of us dare venture into town
to do our shopping or even drive our *kinder* to school. We
never know when that *Englisch* boy might come upon us
and terrorize us with that awful truck of his." Sarah sat
beside him, staring out the windshield, shaking her head.

Yes, Uncle Amos would be mighty upset by the news.
Ben's uncle was the bishop of the Amish *Gmay* here in
Riverton and had a duty to protect his flock. He was also
a kind man who'd agreed to take Ben into his household.
He'd insisted that, if Ben relocated here to Colorado, he
could start anew. But Ben had learned differently. Gossip traveled far and wide, and it had followed him here.
Everyone in his *Gmay* knew what had happened to him
back in Iowa, and they didn't want anything to do with
him, either.

The quick clopping of the horse's hooves on the asphalt
built an urgency inside Ben. What if Rand Henbury was
still driving along the county road and came upon Car-

oline and her aunt as they made their way home? Rand might hassle them again and upset Caroline even worse.

"Haw!" Ben hurried his horse into a faster trot, hoping to catch up to them. He wanted to ensure they got home safely.

Within minutes he saw their black buggy just ahead. The fluorescent slow-moving-vehicle symbol on the back gleamed in the morning sunlight. It swayed back and forth as a reminder for automobiles to slow down, but many drivers ignored the caution. Some were busy texting or talking on their cell phones and ran right over the Amish. No wonder they had so many buggy accidents. Many drivers were too inattentive and in too big a hurry. The town had started putting up cautionary signs along the roads, but it didn't seem to help much.

The bishop's farm was only a mile past the turnoff to the Schwartz's place. When the buggy Caroline was traveling in turned off the county road and headed toward their home, Ben breathed a sigh of relief. They were on the stretch of dirt that led directly to their farm. Rand wouldn't bother them now. In just a few more minutes Ben would have his aunt Sarah home safe, too.

As they pulled off the main road, Sarah breathed a heavy sigh. "I'm not sure Caroline is really up to teaching right now. I think she needs another year to recover from her accident. I'm glad your *onkel* and the school board decided to assign you to drive her wherever she needs to go and to work at the school. They feared that making her wait another year to teach might break her morale. She's already lost so much. All she has left is that teaching job. Poor Caroline."

Yes, poor Caroline. Ben remembered what she was like before the accident. Confident, vivacious and happy.

The single Amish men from miles around had flocked to her side, vying for her hand in marriage. But not him. He had nothing to offer her except a tainted reputation. With her sweet nature and pretty face, she could marry anyone she wanted. As a proper Amish girl, she wouldn't be caught dead riding around with a savage man like him. In fact, he was surprised the bishop would assign him to accompany her wherever she needed to go. Being near him could sully her reputation. But with the bishop's sanction, no one would dare challenge him. Not even Caroline. So she was pretty much stuck with him, whether she liked it or not.

"Once the bad weather sets in, she'll need your help more than ever. And until she can walk better, you'll even have to drive her to and from school," Sarah continued.

Ben nodded but didn't speak. He wasn't surprised that Sarah knew about his new task. Last night the bishop had explained in great detail what he wanted him to do. Ben just hoped Caroline wasn't overly upset about the assignment.

"This might be just what the two of you need. You've both been hurt and seem like kindred spirits. With all the time you'll be spending together, maybe you can become *gut* friends," Sarah said, her voice filled with hope.

Ben forced himself not to laugh out loud. He doubted Caroline would ever consider him a friend. Not if he was the last person on earth.

They drove past the one-room schoolhouse, a red log building that inhabited one corner of the bishop's eastern hay field. All of the Amish fathers had built the house from a kit they'd ordered from a local manufacturer here in Colorado. The schoolyard included a spacious dirt area where the kids could play baseball outside. An outhouse stood in the back, along with a small barn for stabling ponies and horses until the children were ready to go home in the afternoon. And twining past the property, the sparkling waters of Grape Creek glimmered in the sunlight with clutches of wild purple iris and cattails growing along the grassy embankments.

It was a lovely place to go to school, though it definitely needed some playground equipment. They'd recently purchased a swing set, teeter-totter and tether ball equipment, and it would be one of Ben's jobs to put it all together and install it securely on the playground. At least he'd have something to do during the daytime while he waited to accompany Caroline home each afternoon.

Ben thought about how different Caroline had been since the accident that had interrupted her teaching career last year. Gone was the confident gleam in her eyes. Instead of walking with a bounce in her stride, she could barely shuffle across the street without getting run over. He was happy to help her. Though he'd come here to flee his shadowed past, he had deserved what he got. But not Caroline. She'd done nothing to deserve the angst and pain she'd been forced to suffer.

"Are you *allrecht*?" Sarah asked as they pulled into the graveled driveway of his uncle's farmyard.

"*Ja*, why do you ask?"

She laid a hand on his arm and met his gaze. "I know how hard life has been for you since you lost your parents, Ben. I'm sure what happened to Caroline today has upset you, too. But remember to turn the other cheek. It's what Jesus taught us to do. If you trust in *Gott*, everything will work out fine. You just need to have faith."

Hmm. If only it were that easy.

With one last pat on his hand, Sarah turned and

climbed out of the buggy. As she walked toward the house, Ben stared after her, feeling a bit shocked by her words. Did she think he might retaliate against Rand Henbury for what he'd done to Caroline today? Of course he wouldn't. He knew vengeance belonged to *Gott* alone. It would profit him nothing to retaliate against Rand. And yet, because of Ben's past, people still doubted him. One big mistake had almost ruined his entire life.

As he drove the horse to the barn and unhitched the animal from the buggy, Ben's mind was filled with turmoil. Both him and Caroline were victims of violence. She'd been treated brutally and now was struggling to recover from what someone else had done to her. And Ben had become that which his people detested more than anything else. A brute. A killer of the most heinous kind.

He'd been taught from his youth to turn the other cheek. But he'd failed. And now he silently yearned for redemption. If only God could forgive him for what he'd done.

If only he could forgive himself.

Chapter Two

The week before school started, Caroline coordinated a work project. Morning sunshine gleamed warm and bright as Aunt Hannah pulled the buggy into the graveled schoolyard. Sitting beside her with a broom and bucket of cleaning supplies, Caroline smiled with satisfaction. A number of the mothers were already there to meet them, including Sarah Yoder, Norma Albrecht, Linda Hostetler and Becca Graber, the young woman who had substituted at the school last year while Caroline was in the hospital. The temporary assignment had proven to be a blessing for Becca. She had met her future husband, Jesse King, when she had been tutoring his young son, Sam. The two had fallen in love and would soon wed in late November. Caroline wished something that amazing might happen to her but doubted she'd ever be so blessed.

"*Ach*, it looks like you've got a *gut* cleaning crew ready to work. This project shouldn't take us very long," Aunt Hannah said as she directed the horse and buggy around back where she parked.

Caroline was pleased by the turnout. They'd sweep and dust the school and be finished before lunchtime. She might even have time to hang the new alphabet symbols around the room, along with some Amish proverbs she'd written out on poster board.

Looking up, she saw Ben Yoder standing at the back woodpile, and a tense feeling blanketed her.

"I still don't know why he has to be here," Caroline said beneath her breath.

Aunt Hannah shrugged. "The bishop explained all of that to you. The school board wants him to assist you until you're back on your feet."

"I am on my feet," she grumbled, gesturing to her black practical shoes.

"Not very well. You fall easily and can't lift much yet. Give yourself time. And until then, Ben is here to help," Hannah said.

Her aunt's candor didn't make the situation any easier. Yes, Caroline knew the bishop's reasoning and understood what he wanted, but she still couldn't accept it. She didn't want Ben Yoder here—it was that simple.

She gestured to her elbow crutches. "I'm slow but I'm walking better every day. I won't need help for very long."

Aunt Hannah made a tsking sound. "Be patient and give yourself time, dear. It's a blessing the bishop and school board have been so considerate of you."

A blessing! Caroline felt it was anything but. Ben would be hanging around all the time, a cloying reminder of the violence that had brought her so much pain.

She pursed her lips to keep from making a derogatory comment, her gaze returning to Ben. He was busy with his chore and had no idea she was watching him. Because it was still summertime, he wore a plain straw hat, the long sleeves of his gray shirt rolled up to his elbows. He held an ax in his capable hands and brought the tool down on a small log, splintering it into several chunks of wood.

Whack!

Lodging the blade of the ax head into a large tree stump, he picked up the split pieces of kindling and stacked them tidily in the woodpile. Standing straight, he looked directly at Caroline as she struggled to get her elbow crutches beneath her so she could disembark from the buggy.

"Wait just a minute and I'll help you." Aunt Hannah scurried to get out of the buggy and come around to assist.

Before she knew what was happening, Caroline found two strong hands reaching out to lift her off her seat. Ben didn't linger before setting her on her feet and handing her the crutches. Startled by his speed and strength, Caroline looked up into his dark eyes.

"Guder mariye," Ben said.

"Good morning," she returned, her voice sounding anxious and strained to her ears.

She drew away, leaning on the crutches as she reached for her bookbag and a bucket of cleaning supplies. Ben whisked the bucket out of her hands.

"Here, let me. I can carry it for you," he said.

She pursed her lips together in irritation. "I'm perfectly capable of doing it by myself. These crutches are temporary and I'd like to do what I can without your help."

Okay, not a very charitable thing to say. Ben produced a rather wilted expression and handed the bucket back to her. Caroline took it but felt bad for her stinging remarks. After all, the guy was only trying to help.

"I'm sorry. I didn't mean to be so rude," she said, feeling confused by her own actions. This wasn't like her. She'd never lashed out at anyone like this before. What had gotten into her?

His gaze met hers and he showed a slight smile. It softened his face, making him look quite charming. But she must not forget who this man was and what he'd done. She was not going to become friends with him.

"It's all right. I'm used to it," he said.

Oh, no! That made her feel even worse. She hated to be counted among the people who pushed him away, but she just couldn't get over the fact that Bishop Yoder had forced her to accept this man's help. She didn't want Ben here. She wanted to be left alone. And it rankled her hard that she had no choice in the matter.

"*Ach*, come on, then. We've got work to do." Aunt Hannah headed toward the schoolhouse, carrying a mop and feather duster.

Caroline draped the handle of the bucket over one of her crutch grips and shuffled forward.

"*Hallo!*" the other women greeted them.

"Are you excited to start the new school year?" Becca asked, falling in step beside Caroline.

"I am. Are you excited to get married in a few months?"

Becca nodded, a soft smile curving her lips. "I am. But I'll miss teaching school, too."

"*Ja*, I missed it so much. It feels *gut* to get back to work. I really appreciate you filling in for me after the accident. They might have had to close the school if not for you." Caroline couldn't explain it, but she felt inordinately happy to be here today, even with Ben trailing behind her.

"You're *willkomm*. I was happy to help out. After all, it was this job that led me to my Jesse. I'll always be so grateful that I got to teach here," Becca said.

Caroline smiled. Oh, how she wished she could meet someone who already had children for her to raise, but she knew there would be no happy fairy-tale ending and no ready-made *familye* for her. At least Becca could have children, whereas Caroline could not.

"When are your cousins coming into town?" Sarah asked Hannah.

The group walked slowly toward the schoolhouse, letting Caroline set the pace. They all knew that Hannah's cousin from Ohio was relocating here with her young *familye*. Though she was Caroline's first cousin once removed, she'd known and loved her and her husband all her life. They were friends as well as *familye*.

Caroline absentmindedly listened to the conversation but focused on her steps, conscious of Ben staying close by her side. With so many other people offering to help, she didn't need him here today. She wished he would leave her alone.

"My cousin's name is Anna Bontrager. She and her husband, James, will be here in two weeks and I can hardly wait. They wanted to arrive this week, so their two *kinder* could start school with the other kids, but they just couldn't manage it. It's a lot of work to move all the way from Ohio. They'll be a week late for school, but since they'll be living with us until they can finalize escrow on their own place, Caroline said she could bring the kids up to speed on their schoolwork."

"*Ja*, that is *gut*. How old are the *kinder* again?" Linda asked.

"Mary is five and Seth is six," Hannah said. "Anna

is hoping to have another *boppli* next year. And James is planning to buy the old Harlin place. The paperwork is all in order. They just need to get here and sign the final documents."

Caroline made a mental note to include the two new scholars in her lesson plans. It had been several years since she'd seen the children and she doubted they would even remember her. But she knew and loved their parents dearly and looked forward to being with them again. She wanted to make the kids feel welcome and include them in the classroom setup.

"I heard old Mr. Harlin died a while back. And since he had no *kinder* of his own to leave his farm to, the county took it over in a property tax sale," Norma said.

"That's right." Hannah nodded. "Mr. Harlin was *Englisch* and he kept his place in immaculate condition when he was alive. But he's been dead for eleven months now, so his farm has gone to weed and the fields have laid fallow all summer long. James and Anna are getting the house, barn and fields for a very fair price. It includes forty acres of fertile land and it's right next to the bishop's farm."

"So close, isn't that nice? They'll be within walking distance. I'm sure they'll work hard and make a nice go of the place. Our *Gmay* is really growing. It'll be so *gut* to have them in our community. Amos says new members are the lifeblood of our *Gmay*," Sarah said.

Caroline silently agreed. Back east, the Amish communities were clustered close together and most farms were within walking distance of each other. But here in Colorado, the farms were spread far apart. Getting the children to school each day required extended buggy rides. She was glad her cousins would be living close to her.

They had arrived at the schoolhouse. Standing at the top of the front steps, the women parted the way so Caroline could step forward and unlock the door. As she pulled the shiny silver key out of her bookbag and slid it into the lock, she felt a poignant burst of energy. After the accident, she didn't think she'd ever get to do this again. And here she was, opening the schoolhouse as the teacher. It was a rite of passage for her. A silent signal that she could live and work as a vital member of her community again. If she couldn't marry and have a *familye* of her own, at least she could help raise the other children in her *Gmay.*

Turning the key, she opened the tall oak door and pushed it wide. She hobbled inside, followed by Norma. But Caroline was looking down at her feet when Norma screamed.

Caroline jerked and stumbled against Ben. He reached out to steady her and she felt his solid chest against her shoulder blades for several long moments. Sarah shrieked and hopped to the side as a black raccoon with a striped tail ran beneath their feet and darted through the open doorway. The animal made a little chittering sound as it scurried down the steps, raced across the graveled driveway and disappeared into the bishop's hayfield.

"*Ach!* What was that?" Sarah asked, breathing hard.

"I have no idea but that animal scared me half to death." Norma pressed a hand to her chest as she took several deep inhales.

The other women appeared startled, too, glancing around for more intruders.

Caroline gasped. "Oh, *ne*! *Guck emol datt!* I can't believe it."

In unison, they turned to look at the schoolroom. Caroline's mouth dropped open and she gripped the handles of her crutches hard. The place was an absolute mess. Chewed-up bits of wood, paper and pencils were strewn across the wooden floor along with animal excrement. Dirty paw marks covered the tan walls and window casings. The blinds had been torn off the windows. Several of the desks were scratched up and one of the wooden legs had even been gnawed off. From across the room, Caroline noticed the curtain that covered the supply closet was ripped to shreds, as if the animal had used it to climb up to the top shelves.

As one body, they stepped inside and Ben held out a protective hand to the women. "Wait here a few minutes while I check to see if there are any more animals inside. Coons can be pretty fierce, especially if they feel cornered, and I don't want any of you to get hurt."

Grateful for his offer, Caroline watched silently as he searched every corner of the room, under her desk and inside the supply closet. Finally, he returned, a deep frown curving his full lips downward.

"It seems there was only one raccoon today, but I can tell there have been more in here. They've raised babies inside the supply closet this summer. I found their nest," he said with a deep sigh.

"But how did they get in?" Caroline asked.

"Come with me."

They all followed as he walked over to the supply closet and pointed up at the ceiling. Crowding close, they tilted their heads to get a better look. A hole just large enough for a raccoon to squeeze through had been gnawed through the air vent above, with more dirty paw tracks covering the walls.

"I had no idea they could chew through such things or that they could climb walls so well," Caroline said.

"*Ja*, they have sharp teeth and little arms and claws that work just like hands. It makes them very nimble," Ben said.

"Do you think they came through the crawl space in the rafters?" Caroline asked.

He nodded. "And once they got inside, they had free rein to do whatever they liked with the place."

"But how did they get into the crawl space?" Caroline asked, trying to understand so she could do something to stop it from happening again.

"I suspect we'll find that answer outside." He headed toward the door and Caroline followed.

Ben was tall and strong and moved pretty fast. It wasn't easy for her to walk, but as the teacher, she felt it was important for her to know exactly what was going on with her school. When he realized she was following him, Ben slowed down, patiently giving her time to catch up.

"*Ach*, I guess we've got a bigger cleanup job than I thought. While you two check out how the little bandits got inside, we're gonna get to work tidying up this mess," Becca called after them.

She hurried to take the bucket of cleaning supplies from Caroline, and the other women rolled up their sleeves in preparation of a long, hard day of work.

As Caroline made her way toward the door, she was beyond grateful they were all here. If she had faced this situation alone, she honestly didn't know what she would have done. Mentally, she was prepared to do whatever was necessary to make this teaching assignment work.

But physically, she didn't have the strength or dexterity to do the chores by herself. Not yet, anyway.

Ben paused at the threshold, waiting for her. She still felt annoyed by his presence but was glad he was here right now. No doubt they would need some repairs to the ceiling, and she had no idea how she could climb up on a ladder without his aid. Maybe the bishop had been wise to assign Ben to help her after all.

Outside, they slowly made their way around the building. They perused the log sides for any holes and looked up at the roof for any openings that would give the animals access to the interior of the school.

"There it is!" Ben pointed up.

Caroline lifted her head and saw a piece of metal flashing that had been ripped away from the side of the rain gutter. She stared, feeling stunned by the ingenuity of the raccoons.

"But how can such a little creature climb up there and pull all that metal away from the building?" she asked.

"Remember they have sharp claws and teeth. They're persistent little buggers." He chuckled, placing his hands on his hips and shaking his head.

He looked strong and masculine, and Caroline forced herself to look away. On the surface, Ben would make an ideal Amish husband. Devout, hardworking and kind. But what she knew about his past made it impossible for her to like him.

"The school board told me we had enough paper and other supplies for the school year, but it's all been destroyed by the raccoons. It looks like I'll need to make another trip into town to buy some more," Caroline said.

Ben nodded. "I'll drive you there once we're finished with the cleanup. I can drop you off at the general store while I go to the feed and grain supply to get a live animal cage trap."

She glanced at him. "You're going to trap the animal if it comes back?"

He nodded. "The live trap is a humane way of catching the raccoon, and then I'll take it into the mountains and release it far away from the school so it won't return and do more harm."

She knew many of her Amish people would just get a pellet gun and kill the little varmint. She liked that Ben was trying to preserve the raccoon's life. Although the animal had created quite a mess, she didn't wish it any harm. But she also didn't want it to come back. And neither did she like the idea of traveling all the way into town alone with Ben.

"I… I can drive myself and pick up the cage, too. I'm sure the store owner will show me how to work the trap," she said.

Her words were false bravado and she knew it. Where wild raccoons were concerned, she was in way over her head. And what if Rand Henbury came upon her along the road?

Ben was shaking his head even before she could finish speaking. "*Ne*, I'll drive you there. I'll need to pick up some flashing, roofing supplies and nails, too, so I can repair the damage before bad weather sets in."

Yes, he was right. She definitely needed his help and didn't have the heart to argue with him right now.

He turned abruptly, cutting off any further reply, and waited for her to precede him back into the schoolhouse. As she lifted her elbow crutches and shuffled forward, she hated the thought of him walking behind her. She could feel him watching her, his eyes boring a hole in her back. The crutches were cumbersome and she was highly aware of how awkward and clumsy she must look. It made her even more determined to get rid of the crutches just as soon as possible. She couldn't stand the things!

With the other women's help, the floors were soon swept and mopped, the walls washed, the potbellied stove cleared of ashes, and the outhouse cleaned and readied for use. Ben tidied up the little horse barn and chopped more firewood in preparation for the colder mornings. They all worked cheerfully together, discussing the news of each *familye* in their *Gmay* and laughing often. Their happy chatter eased some of Caroline's tension and made her feel like she wasn't alone.

"Many hands make light work," Aunt Hannah commented as they stood back and perused their finished efforts.

"*Ja*, and now I've got to get home and prepare supper for my *familye*. Amos will be coming in from the fields soon," Sarah said.

Norma nodded in agreement. "Me, too."

Sarah looked at Hannah. "Ben has told me that he's going to drive Caroline into town in our buggy. Would you mind giving me a ride home on your way?"

"Of course not. Let's go," Hannah said.

Caroline stared at the women, wondering how to argue the point without sounding childish. After all, they all knew by now that the bishop had assigned Ben to work with her. In the end, she shut her mouth and accepted that he would be driving her into town and taking her home afterward.

They all stepped out into the afternoon sunshine. A dry, hot wind ruffled the ties on the women's white prayer *kapps*. They each rolled the long sleeves to their plain

Amish dresses down to their wrists. Soon, the weather would change, and Caroline dreaded the ice and snow. From past experience, she knew it would make every surface slick and treacherous. She vowed right then and there that she would be walking without the aid of crutches before the first snowfall. The sooner she could walk on her own, the sooner she could get rid of Ben Yoder.

While she locked the front door, the others waved and said their farewells. She turned and found Ben standing beside the bishop's black buggy, waiting for her to join him. As she stepped forward, he hurried to assist her. Without asking permission, he reached out and took hold of her arm, his hand gentle but firm against her skin. And once more, she wished she could walk without any help.

The rhythmic *clip-clop* of the horse's hooves striking the black asphalt helped soothe Ben's jangled nerves as he drove Caroline into town. She sat as far away from him on the other side of the bench seat as possible. Her slender spine was rigid and she stared straight ahead, as if he weren't even there.

"I still don't understand why you have to drive me into town. I'm not incapable, you know. I don't need to walk well in order to drive myself. I just need to be able to sit." She spoke so suddenly that he flinched. Her voice sounded tense and thick with resentment, and he couldn't really blame her.

"I know you're capable of driving yourself, but I have my orders," he said.

She whirled around and stared at him hard, her eyes narrowed. "*Ja*, my *onkel* Mervin and Bishop Yoder put you up to this. I know all about it."

He nodded, unwilling to deny it. After all, he hadn't asked for this task. But neither would he shirk his duty.

"The bishop has given me the explicit assignment of helping you with all the needs of the school. I'm to look out for your welfare in all things, including repairing damage caused by the raccoons. I have to go into town to get supplies to do that, so it makes sense that we ride together. I promise to get you *heemet* safe and sound," he said.

There. That was good. Perhaps she wouldn't fight him so hard if he reminded her that he was on orders from the bishop and the school board.

"*Ach*, so you're my bodyguard now?" she asked, her voice filled with incredulity.

"*Ne*, I'm just your assistant."

She gave a giant huff of indignation and faced forward again. He could tell from the stiff set of her shoulders and her tight expression that she wasn't happy about this. Not at all.

"I don't need a babysitter," she grumbled.

"I'm not your babysitter. I'm just here to work. I earned my school certificate and can do a lot to keep the kids in line during recess. I'm also very *gut* at reaching things on the top shelf." He suggested these ways he could be useful, wanting to soothe her tattered feelings. He didn't want her for an enemy.

She glanced at him and then a slight smile curved her lips, as if she couldn't stay angry at him any longer. "Hmm. So you're my teacher's assistant, huh? Do you always look for the good in things?"

Her smile lit up her face and made her eyes sparkle like blue cornflowers. He was utterly charmed and couldn't help returning her smile.

"*Ja*, I try to make the best of life. Sometimes it's not easy but I'd rather be happy than angry and sad," he quipped.

She frowned suddenly, as if remembering she didn't want to be friends with him.

"*Ach*, either way, it sounds like I'm your pet project now. No doubt the bishop is playing matchmaker again. He's done things like this before. Many times, in fact. Getting single people together so they'll fall in love and marry. But I should warn you right up front, I'm not interested," she said.

Wow! She sure was blunt. And he couldn't blame her. Why would a sweet young woman like Caroline Schwartz want anything to do with a big, gruff man like him? He was a killer. He wasn't in her league. She should find and marry any man but him.

It appeared the bishop's matchmaking efforts would be in vain.

"I understand. But the bishop didn't tell me he wanted me to court you. He just asked me to help you out with the school and keep you safe at all times," he said.

"Of course he wouldn't tell you that, but I've known your *onkel* for years now. As the bishop, he's eager to build our Amish community. And he does that by getting eligible couples together. He's said so in church on many occasions. No doubt he's hoping you and I will get together, too." She sounded rather grouchy and annoyed.

"*Onkel* Amos would never make us do anything we didn't want," he said. "Let's just make the best of the situation and think of the children we're serving, okay? I can assist you while you continue to heal, and I promise not to expect anything more. Once you're able to walk well enough on your own, I'll ask the bishop if I can stop coming to the school every day. Agreed?"

She peered at him suspiciously, as if she didn't believe him. He knew there was no way she could fight against the bishop and the other school board members. Not when it meant they could fire her from this job. But he'd rather not be the target of her resentment, either.

Finally, she nodded and raised her chin slightly higher. "Agreed. For the time being. But I don't have to like it."

Whew! He was beyond relieved. He didn't want to do anything to upset the bishop or Sarah and their *familye*. Right now Ben was just grateful to have a place to live. A place that included his relatives and people of his own faith. Even if members of the *Gmay* still looked at him with suspicion and doubt, it was better than living in the *Englisch* world where he had no one at all. But neither did Ben want to upset Caroline. Whether she admitted it or not, she truly did need his help at the school. But it'd be a long, miserable winter if she kept fighting him on this. He'd rather they got along.

He parked the buggy in front of the general store and helped Caroline down. Although it was almost suppertime, the summer days were longer and the sun was still high in the sky. Thinking only of her safety, Ben was determined to get her home before dark.

As he escorted her to the front door, she struggled with her elbow crutches. He reached out to help, but she jerked away and he let her do it on her own. Her cute button nose was elevated slightly, showing her spunk. She was trying so hard, and he couldn't help appreciating her persistence.

"Will you be all right if I leave you for a few minutes? I need to go to the feed and grain store now," he said.

"Of course. I can do my own shopping." Her voice sounded rather tart, and he admired her flashing eyes for just a moment.

"*Gut*. And will you also buy a couple cans of cat food?" he asked.

Leaning forward on her crutches, she tilted her head in confusion. "What on earth for?"

"Raccoons love cat food. I'll use it as bait so I can trap them in the cage before relocating them far away from the school," he said.

"Ah, I see. *Ja*, I'll buy some cat food."

She turned and shuffled away. When he knew she was safely inside, he got in the buggy and drove down the street. And for the first time in a long time, he felt joyful inside. They had an agreement between them. A truce of sorts. It was a good plan that should make everyone happy, including the bishop and the school board. Ben would assist Caroline in any way possible and try to stay out of her way in the process. As soon as she was able to function well enough on her own, he would leave her alone and never bother her again.

It was what they both wanted. Wasn't it? So why did the thought of not being near her anymore make him feel so sad and empty inside?

Chapter Three

The following Saturday, Uncle Mervin drove Caroline to the schoolhouse early in the morning. It was customary to hold an all-school singalong and picnic before the start of school. All the students' families would be attending, including the school board members. For such an important event, she wanted to ensure everything was in order before the parents started arriving.

Brilliant sunlight gleamed against the shiny new flashings Ben had hung along the edge of the roof to repair the damage caused by the raccoons. As Mervin helped her out of the buggy and reached for her elbow crutches, Caroline hoped the varmints stayed away permanently. Maybe Ben had already caught one of the animals in his live cage trap. She shuddered at the thought of handling the coons on her own and was grateful he was dealing with the problem for her.

"I'll be back in time for the picnic in a couple of hours. Are you sure you'll be *allrecht* by yourself until then?" Mervin asked.

Caroline hesitated. A brief moment of panic flashed through her mind. What if she fell down and couldn't get up? What if there was an emergency and she couldn't walk fast enough to get help?

Gathering her courage, she forced herself to show a bright smile. She must be positive. She must have faith!

"*Ja*, I'll be fine," she said.

With a nod, Mervin hopped back into the carriage and pulled away, leaving Caroline alone. As she watched the buggy fade from view, she took a deep breath and turned to face the schoolhouse. Walking toward it on her elbow crutches, she was startled to hear a tap-tapping sound coming from the side of the building. Now what?

Using caution, she rounded the log house, surprised to see Ben standing outside beneath the window nearest her teacher's desk. Holding a hammer, he pounded nails into a little white box he'd affixed just beneath the windowsill. She recognized it as a flower box.

"*Hallo*, Ben," she called without enthusiasm.

He jerked, startled, and hit his thumb with the hammer. She cringed, knowing it must have hurt.

"*Ach!*" he cried, dropping the tool to the ground. He turned to look at her and shook his hand, as if to ease the pain.

"Oh, I'm terribly sorry, Ben. I didn't mean to surprise you. Are you okay?" Realizing she'd distracted him, she hurried toward him as fast as she could move on the crutches.

Seeing her, he nodded and gave a half smile. "*Ja*, I'm fine. Nothing that won't heal in time."

Standing beside him, she looked up at his tall frame. She was completely alone with him and wasn't sure she liked that at all. They had a treaty between them, but she still felt uncomfortable in his presence.

"Why are you here so early?" she asked.

He squinted at the bright sunlight and his eyes crinkled. "I was going to ask you the same question."

She gestured toward the building. "I wanted to ensure everything was in order before the families start arriving. I also wanted to make sure no more raccoons have gotten inside the schoolroom."

He nodded, turning back to his work. "I've already checked inside and everything is in order. There are no raccoons in the trap I set up outside, either."

So. He had a key to the schoolhouse. Caroline knew without asking that the bishop must have given it to him.

She breathed a heavy sigh, grateful the raccoons were gone but feeling grumpy that Ben had a key to her inner sanctum. "*Gut.* I want everything nice and in order for the parents to see. I'd be mortified if they saw the classroom looking the way it did when we found it after the raccoons had been in there."

He chuckled. "I can't blame you for that."

He lifted his hammer and put some finishing touches on the flower box. It was pristine white, and she could see several more of the little boxes sitting nearby on the ground. Just enough for each window of the schoolhouse.

"What are you doing?" she asked.

Without meeting her gaze, he indicated the boxes. "Since you'll be cooped up inside teaching all day, I thought you might like to look out your window and see some pretty flowers during your workday. While you're occupied, you can look out the window anytime and hopefully, it will make you happy."

She stared, stunned by his consideration. Nearby on the ground were several bags of potting soil and flats of yellow and purple pansies. No doubt he intended to plant them inside the flower boxes.

"Let me guess. The bishop put you up to this, too," she said.

He stared with a blank expression. "*Ne*, I thought it up all by myself. If you don't like the flower boxes, I can take them away."

A flush of embarrassment heated her cheeks. She hadn't meant to offend him and searched her brain for something kind to say. "*Ne*, I love them, actually. It was very thoughtful of you, Ben. *Danke*. But how did you pay for the materials?"

He tapped the box he'd just hung beneath her window with one hand. "Consider them a gift from me to the school. The boxes look like wood but they're made of cellular PVC, so they won't rot like wooden boxes would. Each one comes with a self-watering reservoir, so you only have to fill the pipe once per week and then it wicks out from beneath the soil to water the roots of the plants underneath. Don't worry about lifting a heavy watering can to fill the reservoir. I'll take care of that chore for you."

She didn't know what to say. Seeing the white box affixed beneath her window, she could just envision a bunch of colorful pansies growing inside and loved what he had done. His gesture warmed her heart, and she couldn't help wondering if there was more to this big, gruff man than she'd first thought.

"You've been very kind. I can tell you put a lot of thought into this project. No doubt you're a *gut* carpenter," she said.

That wasn't surprising. Many of the men in her Amish community worked with wood and made all the furniture in their own homes. She was glad that Ben had this same talent. If not for his dark past, he would make some woman a fine husband.

He nodded. "I wanted the boxes to be beautiful but not require you to work too hard to keep them nice. Winter is coming, so the flowers won't last long. But pansies are hardy in the cold weather, and you should have a couple of months to enjoy their color before a killing frost arrives in our valley. Next summer I can plant other flowers for you. I was trying to get the project done in time for the back-to-school picnic but I don't think I'll quite make it."

Wow! He'd even put some thought into which plants to put in the boxes, to provide the longest growth possible before the cold set in. Yes, there was definitely more to this man than she'd first realized.

"It's *allrecht*. I think the parents will notice and like what you're doing anyway. They're beautiful, Ben. *Danke* so much," she said.

His features softened and he showed a slight smile. "You're not just saying that? You really like them?"

She nodded. "I really like them. A lot."

And it was the truth. She'd been cooped up so much in her convalescence and hadn't been able to get outside to plant and work in the garden like she used to. Being able to see flowers growing outside her desk window and around the rest of the schoolhouse as she worked each day would be more than pleasant. It would be cathartic.

He finally faced her. "Even though we didn't have a raccoon in the cage trap this morning, the bait was gone."

"What does that mean?" she asked, frowning as she shifted her weight to ease the ache at the small of her back.

"It means something was able to get inside the trap and steal the food away without getting caught."

"*Ach!* You don't think the animals will come back and destroy the classroom again, do you?" Caroline scanned the schoolyard, looking for any signs of the varmints. Right now her greatest desire was to keep things running smoothly so the school board realized she could do this job and do it well.

"Don't worry," he reassured her. "I've moved the cat food deeper inside the cage so the critters can't bypass the metal plate that closes the door. We'll catch one next time."

He sounded so sure of himself. So confident. And Caroline couldn't help feeling relieved. Right now she needed to focus on the students and lesson plans, not a pack of raccoons who could destroy the school.

"*Ach*, I better get inside now. The bishop should be coming soon with the tables to set up for the picnic." She gestured toward the red log building.

"I've already set up the tables and chairs down by the creek. I figured it would be pretty and offer more shade down there."

Setting his hammer aside, Ben took her arm without asking permission and led her toward the trees. The trickle of crystal-clear water met her ears. Sitting beneath the shade of several elm trees were a number of long tables and backless wooden benches—the same ones they used during their church services. The slight breeze rustled the leaves overhead and carried the light fragrance of honeysuckle. The spot was ideal for a picnic. So pleasant and lovely.

"My *aent* Sarah will be here soon with some plastic tablecloths to cover the tables for you," he said.

She blinked, beyond relieved by what he'd done. She had thought she would have to set the tables up by herself and wondered how she would manage. But she shouldn't be surprised. Her people were hard workers and took care of one another. She should have known they'd help her set this up, too. But more than that, she was finally starting to understand that Ben truly was going to be her constant companion for the time being.

"Wow! You're a good teacher's assistant. You've gone above and beyond the call of duty today. I appreciate it so much," she said.

He flashed a smile that lit up his brooding eyes and made her stare at his handsome face.

"You're *willkomm*," he said.

He turned and walked back to the flower boxes, continuing with his chore of hanging them beneath each window. Caroline watched him for a few moments, her mind churning. It seemed he'd truly taken to heart his assignment to look after the school. He was a dedicated and hardworking man. But she must never forget he had a foul temper and had killed another human being. That alone put up a wall between them that must never come down.

"Komm play with us, Ben!"

He turned and saw little Rachel Geingerich, Elijah Albrecht, Sam King and Andy Yoder gazing at him with hopeful expressions. He was surprised by their request, until he remembered they were no more than seven years old. Too young to know or care what he had done in his past.

Elijah held a red ball, which looked almost bigger than the child. Ben doubted they could bounce it well on the graveled playground, but they could sure play a game of keep-away.

Abandoning the flower boxes he'd been working on,

he reached for Rachel and lifted her high in his arms. She squealed with delight, resting her small hands on his shoulders. The girl was so trusting, and he wished Caroline could feel the same way toward him.

"You want to play, do you?" He spoke to them in a teasing voice filled with the promise of fun.

"*Ja*, we do!" the boys called.

"*Allrecht!* Let's play keep-away. It'll be Rachel and me on one team and you boys on the other," he said.

The kids laughed and spread out in preparation for the game. Ben glanced over at the gathering of parents as they milled around the tables of food. Some of the adults were watching him with skeptical expressions. He ignored them, his gaze automatically seeking out Caroline. It had become a habit for him to watch over her, see what she was doing, anticipate her needs and help her out if he thought it was warranted. She always looked a bit irritated by him doing this.

Most of the parents and other children were congregated around the long tables he'd set up down by the creek. An hour earlier Caroline had led the children in several songs they'd learned last school year, and the crowd had then enjoyed the picnic lunches each *familye* had brought to share. As far as Ben was concerned, the day had been a great success. Caroline must be pleased.

He saw her standing beneath an elm tree, speaking with several parents. He could tell from the scrunch of her shoulders and the way she constantly shifted her feet to redistribute her weight on her legs that she was tired and needed to sit down. No one else seemed to notice, but he'd become highly tuned in to her body language.

"We'll play, but first, I need to take care of one tiny thing," he told the kids, holding up a finger.

"Ah!" The children groaned in dismay.

Setting Rachel down, he hurried over to retrieve a folding chair and placed it beside Caroline. She blinked at him in surprise. The parents she'd been chatting with also looked surprised but he paid them no mind.

"You should sit down and rest for a while," he said quietly.

As usual, her lips pinched together but he turned away before she could scold him. He saw a flash of disapproval in her eyes and knew she wasn't pleased by his interruption. Her gaze mirrored that of the other adults standing nearby. They didn't approve of him, either. But his gesture awakened their common courtesy.

"*Ach*, of course you should sit, Caroline. I'm sorry I didn't think of it myself." Linda Hostetler reached to take Caroline's crutches.

Satisfied that he'd tended to Caroline's needs, Ben returned to the children. They clapped their hands and jumped up and down with excitement. In their sweet faces, he saw nothing but trust and anticipation. And before he knew what was happening, they were chasing him around the playground. When he let them catch him, they mobbed him, laughing, climbing all over him and having a great time.

Their fun drew the attention of some of the adults. Looking up, Ben saw a few frown and shake their heads before whispering together behind their hands. No doubt they were discussing him and whether he was a good influence on their young children. But he didn't care. Not today. Because the kids were the only ones who didn't judge him. They took him at face value. When he was with them, he didn't have to worry about what they knew about his past. He didn't feel inadequate, either. He just had fun.

The afternoon passed quickly, and it was soon time to clean up and go home. Ben had installed three of the six flower boxes. Next week he would finish the project. But as he helped the other men load the benches and folding tables into the horse-drawn buggy-wagon to put them away, his gaze sought out Caroline once more. She was carrying a wicker basket filled with extra paper plates and plastic utensils over to her uncle's buggy and didn't pay him any mind. He leaned an arm against the wagon, wishing she would notice him and look his way—wishing just once that she would trust him as freely as the young children did. He longed to see her look at him without fear and repulsion in her eyes.

But he realized that hope would probably never come to fruition. He and Caroline would never marry, as the bishop had hoped. They might not even become friends. And that thought made him feel even worse.

Chapter Four

Caroline slid her McGuffey Reader into her schoolbag, then reached for her red personal-size cooler that contained her lunch. Standing beside the kitchen sink in her uncle's home, she leaned her hip against the counter before opening the cooler and peering inside to see what Aunt Hannah had prepared for her: a ham sandwich and a wedge of *snitz* pie. Very nice.

"Where's Levi? He hasn't had his breakfast yet." Balancing her baby daughter on her hip, Aunt Hannah turned from the stove and scooped a wedge of scrapple onto the boy's plate before setting it on the table. Scrapple was like a wedge of meatloaf and was made of sausage, diced apple, sage and cornmeal. Very filling and delicious.

The other children crowded around the long table. The loud sounds of their conversations and the clatter of eating utensils permeated the room. Mervin had gone out to the barn over an hour earlier and would soon be coming inside for his own meal.

"I'll get him." Little five-year-old Benuel slid off his chair and ran to the foot of the stairs before hollering up. "Levi! *Komm* and eat."

"Benuel, stop yelling. Go to your brother's room to get him!" Aunt Hannah called in an equally loud voice.

Caroline cringed at the noisy racket. Though she was used to the daily chaos in this home, she was beyond distracted with her own thoughts today. Forcing herself to concentrate, she reached into the gas-powered fridge for an orange and a bag of raw carrots to round out her lunch. After placing them inside the cooler, she snapped the lid closed, then swiveled on her crutches and took a deep inhale. It was the first day of school and she was ready to go. Maybe she should return to her room, just to be alone and gather her thoughts for a few minutes.

The rattle of a horse and buggy coming from outside drew her attention and she glanced at the clock on the wall. Her uncle Mervin was early this morning. Surely, he wouldn't take her to school before eating his breakfast. Or maybe the driver was Alice, Caroline's fourteen-year-old cousin, who would accompany her to school along with her three younger siblings.

After hobbling over to the window, Caroline moved aside the plain brown curtains and peered outside. The sun had just peeked over the eastern mountains, spraying the sky with highlights of pink and gold. Chickens scratched in the yard and she caught the contented lowing of the milk cows out in the pasture.

A black buggy was parked in the backyard but the driver was nowhere to be seen. Caroline didn't recognize the roan horse and realized it wasn't her uncle after all. Who could be visiting the farm so early on a Monday morning?

A knock on the back door caused her to turn.

"I'll get it." Benuel raced past the long table and chairs

and gripped the knob with both hands as he tugged open the door.

Ben Yoder's wide shoulders filled the threshold. Dressed in his everyday work clothes, his straw hat shaded his expressive eyes.

"Ben! *Komm* in. Have you had your breakfast?" Aunt Hannah asked. She held a plate of sizzling sausages, hot off the stove.

He stepped into the room, his gaze resting on Caroline.

"*Ja*, I've eaten. I've *komm* to drive Caroline to school," he said, his voice low and matter-of-fact.

Caroline stared at him, shocked to her toes. "But…but I didn't ask you to do that. Alice is going to drive me."

"*Ne*, she'll drive the other *kinder* later on, after they've finished their morning chores," Aunt Hannah said. "Since you need to go so early and *komm* home later in the afternoon, Ben is here to drive you now. Alice will need to *komm* home right after school so she and the other *kinder* can finish their evening chores before supper. Ben will drive you home once you're finished with your work. He'll stay at the school until you're ready to leave."

Confusion fogged Caroline's brain. She hadn't expected this at all.

"But that wasn't the agreement. Ben is only helping me out at school. Right?" She couldn't believe this. Surely Ben Yoder wasn't going to be her constant companion every waking moment. Or was he?

"Until you're able to drive yourself, the bishop asked that I accompany you to and from school, as well. He doesn't want you out on the roads alone in case Rand Henbury should come upon you and spook your horse." Ben spoke in a quiet voice, as if sensing her discomposure.

Oh, no! This just kept getting worse.

"But he didn't tell me that. I thought you were just going to be hanging around the schoolyard, not coming into my home and driving me around all the time." A flush of heat suffused Caroline's face. Only now did she realize just how far the bishop's orders extended. But she hadn't planned on this. It was too much for her to accept.

"It's what the school board wants," Aunt Hannah said, as if that settled everything.

Great! Even Aunt Hannah was in on this. Dawning flooded Caroline's brain. Ben had truly been assigned to be her constant companion. He would stay with her throughout the day, morning to evening. Always there. Watching over her. Waiting upon her. Seeing to her every need. A relentless shadow.

A huge nuisance.

"But I don't need a chaperone on my way to school. Surely, you have better things to do with your day," she said, unable to keep a note of exasperation from her voice.

"I have plenty of other work that could occupy me, but the bishop and his sons have taken over those chores. He believes the work I will do with you is imperative right now. I agree with him that your well-being is of paramount importance," he said.

She was conscious of his silent gaze resting on her like a ten-ton sledge. And then it occurred to her. Maybe he didn't want to be with her, either. After all, what fun could it be to accompany a woman around all day long? Helping her in and out of the buggy. Holding her arm while she negotiated the stairs. Repairing messes made by the raccoons. Maybe this wasn't easy for him, either.

Aunt Hannah lifted Caroline's lunch box off the counter and handed it to Ben. She did have the good grace to look a bit sheepish, telling Caroline that she had known about this all along and had neglected to inform her about it.

"Of course you don't need a chaperone, dear," Aunt Hannah said. "You're quite capable. But right now Ben is your driver. And while you're at school, think of him as your handyman. I know a lot of previous teachers who would have loved to have a full-time assistant helping them out."

Like who? Becca Graber sure hadn't needed a full-time assistant last year. Caroline knew of no one who would have been happy with this arrangement. She stared at her lunch box as it swung easily from Ben's long fingertips. He stepped aside to give her access to the door, but she couldn't move. Couldn't breathe. It felt as if her feet were stapled to the floor.

"Are you ready?" he asked in that deep, calm voice of his.

She flinched. Unable to find an excuse to delay their departure, she nodded and scooted her elbow crutches forward before taking several steps. What choice did she have? It was either accept Ben's constant presence or face the bishop and school board. Neither option thrilled her.

At the threshold, he gripped her arm with his free hand and helped her over the bumps of the back porch and down the steps. She longed to throw him off. To snap at him to leave her alone. But that would mean giving in to the foul temper she'd accused him of having. She would sound like an old harpy and a hypocrite. And besides, she really did need his help.

For now.

Instead, she accepted his assistance as he helped her

climb into the buggy. Then he hurried around to the driver's seat.

Once she was settled in, he took up the lead lines and slapped them gently against the horse's back. The buggy lurched forward and they were off. What followed was a long, awkward silence. They'd pulled onto the county road before either of them spoke again.

"Your *onkel* must need your help with chores on his farm," she finally said.

"*Ne*, I have been assigned to take care of you and the school. Until you no longer need me, that's what I intend to do."

So. Caroline really was Ben's full-time job, including buggy time. It wasn't as if there weren't enough hands at the bishop's farm to help with all the chores there. Bishop Yoder and Sarah had a large *familye* of very capable children. But still. Caroline hated to pull Ben away from his other work like this. It reminded her that she was impaired, and it made her even more determined to get rid of the crutches as soon as possible.

They rode in silence most of the way to the school. When they arrived, she had to endure Ben's gentle touch as he helped her out of the buggy and escorted her up the front steps. When he swung the front door wide, she hesitated, dreading what she might find inside. If the raccoons had returned, she'd be forced to clean up the mess before she could begin teaching. But everything looked fine and she breathed a sigh of relief.

She hobbled over to her desk and set her bookbag on top. Looking out the window, she saw a spray of deep purple and yellow pansies in the window box Ben had installed there. They trembled in the mild breeze and looked lovely. A constant reminder of Ben's presence in her life.

"I'll get some drinking water and firewood." He picked up the clean water pitcher off the corner of her desk and turned toward the door.

"It's still hot outside. I doubt we'll need a fire today," she called.

He nodded. "Just in case."

She watched as he disappeared out the door. Through the window, she saw him pulling on the water pump to fill the pitcher, then he tucked several chunks of wood beneath his free arm. By the time he returned, she'd gathered her composure and stood in front of the chalkboard, writing out the day's lesson plans.

"We've caught a raccoon in the live cage trap." He set the pitcher of water on her desk with a little thud.

Caroline cringed, startled by this news. "*Ach*, he came back, then?"

"*Ja, she* has returned. But she won't cause you any trouble." Ben looped his thumbs through his black suspenders, looking rather solemn. "Some of the students have started arriving and will be coming inside now. If you're okay for the time being, I'll take the raccoon for a ride and release her several miles away from the school."

She caught his meaning. With students here, she wouldn't be alone and he could leave to take care of the chore. And even though he'd been more than kind, she couldn't help feeling like a little child who needed constant supervision. His mere presence raised the hairs on the back of her neck, and she couldn't help bristling.

"You can do whatever you like, Ben Yoder. It doesn't matter one single bit to me," she said.

He paused, his dark eyes unblinking. Then he tugged

on the brim of his straw hat and spoke most gently. "As you wish. When I return I'll be putting together some of the new playground equipment. You'll be teaching school by then. If you need me for anything at all, just send one of the kids outside to get me."

Before she could respond, he turned and walked away, his long arms moving rhythmically with his stride. She stared after him, stunned and feeling a bit unworthy. In spite of her tart words, he'd offered no biting comments or angry facial expressions. Instead, he'd extended a kind invitation.

As she watched him go, it occurred to her that she may have hurt his feelings. That she was being ungrateful and unkind. And yet, she felt as if he'd been foisted upon her. An unwanted burden she wished would go away.

His offer to help reminded her that he was here to stay. Short of mutiny and openly defying the school board, there was nothing she could do to get rid of Ben. Though she felt mightily uncomfortable around this man, she should at least try to get along and be polite. But she sure didn't have to like it.

She was watching him. Ben could feel Caroline's gaze drilling a hole in his back. Crouching over the new swing set he was putting together, he resisted the urge to turn and look up. But he knew she was there, sitting at her desk, gazing at him from the window in her classroom, watching him work.

He'd just returned from taking the raccoon and releasing it several miles away. The weather was still warm, so the animal should be able to find a new home without any trouble. He hoped they'd have no more varmints in the school but had reset the cage trap just in case there was more than one.

Now he was tightening a bolt on the new swing set he was putting together. When he finished, he stood straight to ease a cramp in his lower back. As he reached for another screw, he couldn't resist glancing at the schoolhouse. Sure enough, Caroline sat primly at her desk, gazing out her window at him. When she caught his eye, she jerked and looked away, as if embarrassed to be caught staring.

The white flower boxes with the purple and gold pansies offered a pretty frame for her, and he watched her for several moments. She wore a black dress with a white cape and apron. The colors suited her but made her delicate skin seem that much paler. But what he wasn't prepared for was the startled look on her face. She didn't want him here. She'd made that clear. But more than that, he thought she hated him. He'd been thrust upon her by the school board, and she could hardly abide his presence.

She ducked her head over her paperwork, her pencil moving fast as she jotted some notes. He could just imagine the pink stain of discomfiture on her cheeks.

Acting casual, he turned back to his task and tried to gather his own thoughts. At the end of the previous school year, they'd held a boxed social fund-raiser to earn enough money to pay for a variety of playground equipment. It was now Ben's job to put it all together. Over the next few days he'd dig holes and sink the stands of the swing set, teeter-totter and tether ball into cement so they wouldn't tip over on the kids. He enjoyed the work. It occupied his time while he waited for the school day to end. When Caroline was ready, he would drive her home. And right now he dreaded the long ride. Mostly because he knew it would be filled with resentful silence. But more than anything, he wished he could make her smile instead.

Kneeling on the ground, he kept working and had the frame of the swing set put together by the time Caroline rang the noon bell. In a burst of energy, the front door was thrown open and the children poured forth into the schoolyard, carrying their variety of lunch buckets with them. They all scurried his way, mostly to see what he was doing. The older children hung back, watching him with quiet curiosity. The younger children crowded closer.

"What are you doing?" six-year-old Elijah Albrecht asked, winding his free hand around his black suspenders.

"What does it look like I'm doing?" Ben returned in a pleasant voice as he reached for a Phillips screwdriver from his silver toolbox.

"Like you're building a swing set," Elijah said.

Ben chuckled and reached up to ruffle the boy's unruly hair. "*Ja*, that's exactly what I'm doing. You're a smart boy."

"Swing sets are for girls," Enos Albrecht said, scowling with disgust.

Ben continued to tighten another bolt as he spoke. "*Ach*, boys can enjoy a swing set just as well as girls."

"Not me. I wouldn't be caught dead on a swing," Caleb said. He was Ben's twelve-year-old cousin and a tad precocious.

"Why don't you build us a backstop for our baseball diamond instead?" one of the older boys asked.

Ben looked up, smiled and winked. "That's a *gut* idea. Maybe I will, in time. But you should always put your *weibsleit* first. And right now I'm building them a swing set."

Ben spoke from his heart. His uncles had taught him to put the womenfolk first. If he had a wife, he would treat her like a queen. And he realized he probably felt that way because a woman of his own was something he dearly wanted but would never have, so he appreciated the sentiment even more.

Enos tilted his head in confusion. "But you just said the swings were for the girls and the boys."

Ben nodded, trying not to chuckle. "*Ach*, they're mostly for the girls, though."

"Aha! I told you so," Enos exclaimed.

A deep laugh escaped Ben's throat. He couldn't help himself. "It's true, but I'm sure they'd be happy to share if you want to ride the swings, too. You can pretend you're flying."

"Not me!" Enos vowed.

"Or me, either," Caleb said.

Ben shook his head at the two children. "*Ach*, you boys have a lot to learn."

"Scholars! Leave Ben alone so he can do his work. Go on and eat your lunches now, then you can play for a while."

They all turned in unison and saw Caroline standing on the front steps to the school, holding a heavy desk bell in one hand. That wasn't an easy task since she was also trying to manage her elbow crutches at the same time. She leaned heavily on the crutches and Ben got the impression she was overly tired today. Not surprising, since it was the first day of school. She was spirited and determined, but he feared she was not as strong as she thought she was.

As the children raced over to the baseball diamond to gobble down their lunches before playing a quick game, Ben longed to ask Caroline if she was okay. Fearing her sharp response, he was slow to get the words out before she turned and shuffled back inside.

He worked for ten minutes more, then reached for his own lunch. Before he sat in the cool shade along Grape Creek to eat his food, he stepped over to the open doorway of the schoolhouse and peered inside. As usual, Caroline sat at her desk, grading papers. Her sandwich and an orange sat ignored beside her on the desk.

"Ahum!" He cleared his throat, not wanting to disturb her, yet he felt compelled to speak.

She lifted her head in weary acknowledgment. "*Ja*, Ben. What do you need?"

"Nothing at all, Caroline. I was just wondering if I could get you anything?" he returned.

"*Ne*, please just leave me alone."

He nodded without guile. "As you wish."

Turning, he walked outside. He didn't disturb her again until the last student had left the school at the end of the day. And still he kept working and waiting for some sign from her that she was ready to go home.

Finally, she stepped outside and turned to lock the front door. Without a word, he came to take her arm and helped her into the buggy. He could tell from the tilt of her head and the slump of her shoulders that she was too tired to object.

On the ride home, she was quiet as usual. He let her think, giving her the space she seemed to desire. When she finally spoke, he forced himself not to flinch in surprise.

"Did everything go *allrecht* with the raccoon this morning?" she asked.

He nodded, looking straight ahead. "*Ja*, the animal is fine."

"You…you didn't hurt it, did you?"

He caught the hesitancy in her voice and glanced her way.

"Of course not. I let her go, just as I said I would. The moment I lifted the cage door, she took off like a shot into the woods. I'm sure she'll be just fine."

She nodded, gazing at the trees and lush green fields flashing past the side of the road as the buggy hurried forward. "*Gut*. I wouldn't want the scholars to think we had killed the varmint, although I'm glad to have it gone."

He could understand her reasoning. He preferred not to have to clean up another mess, too. But some of the littler kids such as Rachel and Fannie were softhearted and might feel bad if they thought he'd hurt one of *Gott's* creatures needlessly.

"I reset the trap, just in case there are more," he said.

She whirled on him so fast that his gaze clashed then locked with hers. She pressed a hand to her chest and he gazed into her beautiful blue eyes, feeling helplessly lost there for several profound moments.

"You don't think there are more, do you?" she asked, an edge of urgency tainting her voice. No doubt she feared the school might get torn up again.

He smiled and turned away, trying to alleviate her qualms. "*Ne*, I think they're all gone now. But I want to make sure. I'll leave the trap where it is for the time being and check it each day. And I would suggest that someone check on the school regularly next summer when school is not in session. That way, the animals won't move in again. But don't worry about it. I'll take care of it if any more show up."

She exhaled a shallow sigh, her shoulders relaxing slightly as she rested her hands in her lap. "*Danke*, Ben. I'm grateful to you."

Ben's heart skipped a beat. Just a few simple words of gratitude, yet they meant everything to him. For the first time in years, he finally felt like someone really needed him. Not just for what he could do for them, but because they couldn't do it for themselves.

Even though Caroline didn't want him here, he thought perhaps she was beginning to appreciate his talents just a teensy bit. And right now he didn't dare ask for anything more.

Chapter Five

Caroline awoke with a start. She stared at the ceiling in her bedroom for several moments. Thick darkness gathered around her, though an eerie red light flared in steady rhythm just outside her open window. A brief squawk of static broke the stillness of the night. It sounded like a radio but she couldn't be sure. She peered through the shadows at the clock on the wall. Just past three in the morning. What on earth was going on?

Flipping the covers back, she sat up and clasped the handles of her elbow crutches before shuffling over to the window. As she did so, she noticed her legs weren't as stiff as they had been a week earlier and knew she was gaining in strength every day.

Peering down below, she saw a police car parked outside in the farmyard. The red emergency light on top of the car went out suddenly, and an officer got out of the car. He was accompanied by an *Englisch* woman dressed in blue jeans and a dark sweater, two Amish men and two young Amish children. Through the darkness, Caroline couldn't make out any of their faces, but she recognized the wide set of shoulders on one of the Amish men.

Ben Yoder.

She barely had time to consider what he was doing here at this time of night. A loud, hollow knock sounded on the front door. It echoed through the entire building, and she feared it might wake up the whole household.

As she drew away from the window, Caroline heard her uncle and aunt's voices coming from their room across the hall.

"What is it? Who could be coming to our house in the middle of the night?" Aunt Hannah asked in a hushed whisper.

"I don't know. I'll go and check. You stay here where it's warm," Uncle Mervin replied.

His consideration of her aunt touched Caroline's heart. How she wished there was a man somewhere in this world who might love her the way Uncle Mervin loved her aunt.

Within moments the stairs creaked as he went down to see what was amiss. But it wasn't long before Aunt Hannah went downstairs, too.

Curiosity got the better of Caroline. Turning, she pulled on her modest robe and secured the belt tightly around her waist. With several quick movements, she twisted her long hair into a bun at the nape of her neck and pulled her white prayer *kapp* over top to hide the golden strands.

The scrape of a chair and low voices came from just below. The visitors must be in the main living room. She recognized Uncle Mervin's voice but didn't know the strangers. Except for Ben, who didn't speak.

It took her a little time before she could hobble to the door and step out on the landing. Slowly, she made her way downstairs. As she stepped into the living room, she blinked at the bright gas light filling the area. Her gaze immediately took in the sight of Aunt Hannah fully dressed and sitting in a chair at the end of the sofa, her face buried in her hands. Her shoulders trembled as she wept softly. Uncle Mervin stood behind her, one of his gruff hands resting on her arm in silent comfort.

As Caroline came near, she didn't speak, waiting for the problem to be revealed. The police officer stood beside the front door, his dark blue uniform, badge and holstered gun a glaring contrast to the humble Amish home he'd invaded. The *Englisch* woman stood facing the sofa, her silvery eyes filled with sad compassion as she held a manila file folder in her arms.

Sitting on the couch were Bishop Yoder and Ben. Two young Amish children dressed in traveling clothes sat huddled between them, their eyes wide, faces pale and tear-stained. Caroline guessed the girl looked to be about five and the boy around six. The boy held a tattered straw hat in his lap that was flattened beyond repair. Ben had lifted one arm up along the back of the couch and wrapped it around the two children's shoulders, his big hand dwarfing them both. And without asking, Caroline knew the kids must belong to their cousins from Ohio. Uncle Mervin was planning to pick up the *familye* from the bus station in town first thing in the morning. But where were their parents? Anna and James should be here, too. And why were Bishop Yoder and Ben here?

"What's happened?" Caroline finally asked, shuffling farther into the room.

"*Ach*, Caroline! They're gone. James and Anna. They've been killed." Aunt Hannah spoke in *Deitsch* as she popped out of her seat and ran to her and hugged her tight, sobbing against her shoulder.

"What?"

A sick feeling of shock and pain enveloped Caroline. It couldn't be true. Dear Anna. She was Caroline's first cousin once removed. Anna's mother and Caroline's grandmother had been sisters. And though they weren't related, Caroline had known James all her life. They'd grown up together in the same Amish community in Ohio. The couple couldn't be gone. They just couldn't.

She did her best to comfort her aunt while still keeping hold of her crutches. Over Aunt Hannah's head, she met Mervin's gaze and saw the forlorn look in his eyes.

"Anna and James…were killed this evening," Mervin confirmed.

Caroline gasped. She couldn't stop herself. A sharp pain speared her heart and a rush of tears filled her eyes.

"I'm afraid there was a bad accident on I-70, just outside of Denver," the officer said. "We believe the driver of a semi-truck fell asleep at the wheel. When he lost control, he crossed the median and drove into oncoming traffic. Four people died, including the driver and the children's parents."

Caroline's heart gave a powerful squeeze. She could hardly absorb what she was hearing. It was too much. Too horrific. She understood the ramifications only too well. It didn't matter whose fault it was. The two children sitting before her were now orphans.

"My name is Sharon Wedge. I'm a social worker with CPS." The *Englisch* woman looked all businesslike as she stepped forward and extended her hand.

As if in a fog, Caroline wiped her eyes and shook the woman's hand. "CPS? What is that?"

"Child Protective Services. Since both the children's

parents were killed tonight, I was called in to help with their placement," Sharon said.

Placement? Like in a foster home?

"They brought the children to my house and I directed them here. I've explained that this was their final destination," Bishop Yoder said.

The policeman nodded. "That's right. The kids weren't exactly sure where they were supposed to go, but we knew Bishop Yoder would be able to help us figure it out since he's the leader of you Amish people living in the area."

Yes, this was true. There wasn't much that happened in the lives of the Amish people in Riverton that Bishop Yoder didn't know about.

Hearing this exchange, little Mary turned her face toward Ben and burrowed close against his side, her small hand clasping a fold of his blue shirt.

"There, there." Ben soothed her by patting her tiny arm with his free hand. Her muffled sobs sounded like a shout in the quiet room.

Watching Ben comfort the little girl did something to Caroline inside. She was crying, too, the tears running freely down her face.

"You should sit down, Caroline." Ben's gentle voice reached her as he inclined his head toward a hard-backed chair.

How dare he? Even in the middle of the night, when she was in her own home, he presumed to tell her what to do.

As if spurred into action, Mervin took her arm and led her to the chair. She sat for just a moment, her mind churning. She didn't want Mary and Seth to be placed in a foster home. She didn't want any of this. It wasn't right for them to lose their parents this way. It wasn't!

"Since you are their cousins and they were on their way to live here with you, I think we can let the children stay here for the time being," Sharon said.

Caroline shifted her weight, feeling nervous and upset. She'd heard horror stories of CPS getting involved in the lives of Amish children and didn't want to see Mary and Seth taken away and forced to live in an *Englisch* foster home.

"And what about the future? Mary and Seth are Amish. We are their family and I am their new schoolteacher. They should remain here with us," she said.

"That is true. We are their people." Bishop Yoder sat straighter, his expression stern.

Sharon smiled kindly. "I agree. Mr. Schwartz has given me some contact information and I'll make inquiries. But from what I've been told, you are the children's closest living relatives. I have no problem letting them stay here for now."

For now. But what about later on? Would CPS start meddling in the children's lives? Above all else, the Amish kept to themselves. They didn't want the *Englischers* to force their worldly ways upon them. Especially not on two young, impressionable children who had just lost their parents.

"We are their *familye*. They belong here with us," Uncle Mervin said.

Bravo! Caroline was pleased by her uncle's support.

Sharon didn't respond. She just looked at all the adults gathered in the room, seeming to assess each one of them in turn. On the one hand, Caroline was glad someone was looking out for them. But on the other, she didn't want this *Englisch* woman to start making decisions for these two Amish kids.

"I'm afraid the children's bags were lost in the accident," the police officer said. "It'll take some time to sort through the wreckage. We'll bring their luggage to you as soon as we can identify what is salvageable and what belongs to them."

Aunt Hannah didn't say a word. Her eyes were glazed and she stared with shock, so Caroline took charge.

"That's fine. We'll make sure they have everything they need in the meantime," she said.

The poor dears. The two kids looked frightened and exhausted. Right now they needed love and reassurance. And a good night's sleep, of course.

Caroline used one of her crutches to push herself up. As she stood, her gaze locked with Ben's. She saw something in his eyes, an emotion she didn't understand. Compassion, maybe? Or pity? She wasn't sure which. Maybe both.

She walked over to the children and extended one hand as she spoke in *Deitsch*. Amish children didn't learn to speak English until they started going to school at age five. These children were still young and might not know how to speak English very well, if at all. She would have knelt before them but couldn't manage that movement with her crutches.

"I'm your cousin Caroline," she said. "You probably don't remember me, but I remember you and your parents very well. I used to hold and feed both of you when you were very little *bopplin*."

Seth nodded and sat forward just a bit, seeming relieved to meet someone he could identify with. "*Ja,*

Mamm told us about you. She said you used to pick apples with her in our orchard."

Caroline smiled. "That's right. We bottled apples and applesauce and made cider together. Are you hungry? Why don't we get you both a cup of hot cocoa and a slice of *schnitz* apple pie? Then we'll tuck you right into bed."

She held her breath, hoping no one objected. Hoping the two children came along willingly.

"That's a *gut* idea. *Komm* on." Ben slid forward and got to his feet.

Without asking permission, he leaned down and pulled little Mary into his arms. The girl promptly laid her head on his shoulder, looking at them all with huge round eyes and a pink rosebud mouth. Ben reached out and took Seth by the hand. The little boy followed eagerly, as if desperate to escape the room. They went into the kitchen, leaving Bishop Yoder, Uncle Mervin, Aunt Hannah, the policeman and social worker alone to work out the details. Ben sat in a hard-backed chair with Mary on his knee. Seth sat beside him, turned toward Ben as if he were a lifeline and the boy might need to latch on to him at any moment.

After all that had happened, it seemed strange for the kids to gravitate toward Ben, given that they'd just met the man. Perhaps it was his broad shoulders that drew them to him, which Caroline thought must seem strong and comfortable for a child to rest against.

Tomorrow was a regular school day, and they'd all be up early for morning chores. Maybe it was best to leave Mary and Seth home for the day. They needed time to recover in a quiet, loving home, without any other pressures on them. Caroline made a mental note to suggest this to Aunt Hannah just as soon as the *Englischers* left their home.

As Caroline went about dishing up pieces of pie, she listened to Ben's soft voice. He spoke to the kids about inconsequential things, though they didn't respond even once. But they clung to him, especially Mary. They seemed to trust him completely. And knowing about Ben's past, that surprised Caroline most of all.

Ben sat at the kitchen table with the children, one on each side of him. Mary stared at her hands in her lap while Seth leaned back and stared at the wall. It was as if they'd both pulled into themselves, ignoring the rest of the world. And Ben couldn't blame them. He'd done the same thing when he'd lost both his parents at a young age.

He watched as Caroline poured fresh milk into a pan and slid it onto the stove. While it heated, she sliced several pieces of *schnitz* apple pie. Her steady, purposeful movements seemed so calm and soothing in this atmosphere of gloom. She moved methodically, and he thought she did it so she wouldn't fall with her crutches. She seemed to have her routine down quite well. He felt the urge to get up and help her but thought the kids needed him more right now.

Caroline set the plates of pie on the table. He noticed she'd given him some, too. As the kids picked up their forks and took a bite, the room was absolutely quiet. Only the low sounds of voices coming from the living room and the bubbling of milk on the stove could be heard.

"Is that *gut*?" Ben smiled at the children, keeping his tone light and positive.

Mary nodded and cast a shy glance at him, but Seth didn't respond. The boy just stared steadfastly at his plate as he chewed. It was obvious they were hungry, for they wolfed down the pie. Ben had no idea when they'd eaten last and thought Caroline had been wise to offer them food. Especially something sugary and sweet. They needed it right now to help alleviate the shock they were undoubtedly feeling.

"Here we are. Some nice hot cocoa will warm you right up on the inside and help you feel better. Be careful not to burn your mouth." Caroline poured the frothy brown liquid into three mugs before sliding them closer to the children.

"*Danke*, Caroline." Ben picked up his mug, blew on the steaming mixture, then took a shallow sip. "Um, it's very tasty but definitely hot."

The two kids just stared at their cups, their eyes wide and glazed with moisture. Ben remembered that look from his own life. Disbelief. Shock. Grief.

No doubt the kids were wondering what had happened to their world. And though each of their situations were completely different, he couldn't help thinking they were all alike in a way. Ben and Caroline had both lost so much, and so had the kids. Though Seth and Mary still had each other, they were alone in the world, just like Ben and Caroline. Yes, they had their *Gmay*, their Amish people, and even relatives who cared about them. But they were still alone in so many ways. In his heart, he said a silent prayer asking *Gott* to be with them and provide comfort right now.

Caroline slid into the chair next to Mary and lifted a hand to caress the little girl's cheek. "Try some cocoa, my *liebchen*. It'll help you feel better so you can sleep."

As she held the cup for the girl, Mary took a shallow drink. When she pulled the cup away, the girl had a little mustache on her upper lip. She licked it off and lifted her brown eyes to gaze at Caroline.

"My *mammi* is gone for *gut*, isn't she?" Mary said, her voice filled with tears. In the quiet room, her words seemed like a shout. The statement was so final. So real.

"Our *daed* is gone, too," Seth said, his voice sounding thick with resentment.

Yes, these two kids were just like Ben and Caroline. The hurt. The anger and bitterness he'd felt all these years.

"*Ja*, they are gone, but you're not alone. We're here and you'll always have us," Ben said.

Caroline glanced at him and blinked. Maybe he'd spoken out of turn. Maybe he shouldn't give them false hope. And yet, he couldn't stand to have them go through life feeling isolated or like they had no one who really loved them.

"That's right," Caroline said, showing that soft and sincere smile of hers. "You have many people who love and care for you right here in this home. You're a part of our *familye*. You have us forever. You'll never be alone. Not ever."

Ben blinked, thinking she must have read his thoughts exactly.

Leaning heavily on her crutches, she stood and stepped away from the table. "*Ach*, I think it's time for you two to be in bed now. *Komm* with me, please."

Ben noticed that she'd used her kind but authoritative teacher voice. When she beckoned to them, the children didn't argue. They each scooted back their chairs, and Ben almost flinched when little Mary took his hand. As he accompanied them upstairs, something went all soft and mellow inside his chest.

Caroline stumbled on the stairs and Ben reached out to clasp her arm. As she found her balance, she nodded her thanks. Since Mervin and Hannah's children were already sleeping, they didn't turn on a light. In the dark, Ben helped Seth as he got ready for bed and slid beneath the covers next to one of his little cousins.

"I think it would be best to put the two *kinder* near each other tonight. Mary can sleep over here with Alice," Caroline whispered for his ears alone.

Ben nodded, once again impressed by her insight.

While he stood beside the open door, she sat with the kids for several minutes. Mary closed her eyes and slept almost instantly, but Seth rolled on his side and faced the wall. From the vague moonlight gleaming through the dark window, Ben could see the boy's eyes were open, his body tense. He was a bit older than Mary and not so quick to forgive what had happened to them tonight.

"I'll be right across the hall if you need me. *Gutte nacht*," Caroline whispered as she stood and shuffled to the door.

Ben took her arm to help her but she shook him off.

"I'm fine, *danke*. I don't need any help," she said.

He let her go, feeling stung by her dismissal. She pulled the door closed but left it slightly ajar, in case the children called out in the night.

"Do you think they'll be *allrecht*?" Ben asked as they stood together on the landing. He caught her fragrance, a clean, fresh smell that he quite liked.

"*Ja*, I'll look in on them later, before I go back to bed," she whispered.

She looked up at him and, for just a few moments, he gazed into her brilliant blue eyes. They stood there, locked in silence. There was so much he longed to confide in Caroline. So much he wanted to say. But he feared her disapproval too much.

"They're just like you and me. They're all alone in the world," he said, then instantly regretted it.

She might take his statement the wrong way. He didn't know why this woman was so easy to talk to. Maybe because of what they'd both lost, he thought they had a lot in common.

"*Ne*, they're not alone. Nor are you and I. We each have this *Gmay* and we have our Savior. He is always with us, no matter what trials we must face in this life. We are never alone, because we have Him," she said.

With those gentle words, she turned and worked her way downstairs. Her solid faith amazed him, and he wished he could discuss it with her a bit longer. But now wasn't the time.

No doubt she was eager to talk to her uncle and find out more details about the night's events. So was Ben. Above all else, he didn't want the *Englischers* to interfere and try to take Mary and Seth away from their Amish *familye*.

As he followed Caroline into the living room, he thought about what she'd said. They were never alone. Yet, in his darkest moments after his parents died, Ben had not felt the Lord near him. Of course, he hadn't been looking for *Gott*, either. Maybe if he had, he wouldn't have gone through life filled with so much anger and bitterness. And he hated the thought that Seth and Mary might do the same thing now that they were orphans.

Maybe he could make a difference in the two children's lives. And though Caroline had her faith and a solid belief in *Gott*, maybe Ben could make a difference for her, too.

It was something to think about.

Chapter Six

Caroline picked up a plate from the drying rack and swiped both sides with a clean towel before setting the dish aside. It was late afternoon and it had been a long, tiring day. First, they'd prepared approximately three hundred sandwiches, cupcakes and noodles to feed the *familye* and friends attending the funeral. The service had lasted two and a half hours. Then there was the graveside service. As the nearest living relatives, Caroline and her *familye* had remained beside the graves until the pall-bearers had completely buried the two coffins. When they'd returned to the house, the long tables had been replenished with food by the other women in the *Gmay*. But Caroline wasn't very hungry. She reminded herself that death was a part of life and she must accept *Gott's* will, but it wasn't easy.

By three o'clock, the tables, benches and songbooks had been packed away inside the bench wagons and hauled away. Through it all, Ben Yoder was right there, helping the other men. Thank goodness for the members of their *Gmay*, who had pitched in willingly to help with the work.

Over the past week, there had been a nonstop flow of men and women coming in to assist with farm chores and clean the house and barn from floor to ceiling. The outpouring of love from her *Gmay* reminded Caroline how much she loved her faith and that she was never alone, no matter what trials she must face in this life.

Gazing out the kitchen window, she listened quietly to the muted voices around her as the women finished washing the dishes. Across the cow pasture, she saw a line of horse-drawn buggies marching along the county road in single file. The entire Amish community of Riverton and many members from the Westcliffe *Gmay* had come to the cemetery, even though they hadn't known the deceased. It didn't matter. Anna and James had been two of their own, and they wouldn't abandon them or their children in their time of need.

In tandem, the line of buggies had followed the two hearse wagons, which carried the earthly remains of James and Anna Bontrager. Each buggy was overly crowded with large families, but no one minded. This was a time for love and introspection as they all considered the living hope and salvation Christ provided each of them.

Caroline glanced over at the table. Little Mary sat alone, picking at a piece of shoofly pie. Even the rich molasses, cinnamon and brown sugar couldn't tempt her to take a full bite. The girl looked so small and defenseless, sitting there in her black dress, apron and shawl. The *familye* was in mourning and would wear nothing but black for the next year. Since they'd arrived at the house several days earlier, neither child had eaten much. But starting tomorrow, Caroline was determined to make that change. After all, she was their cousin as well as their teacher. She was obligated to look after them and intended to do just that.

Lifting her head, Caroline gazed out the window again. Seth stood leaning against the corral gate, staring off into space. As usual, he was all by himself. And though he seemed to have formed an attachment to Ben, the boy was overly quiet and sullen. Caroline figured that was to be expected but hoped it would change once the boy started attending school next week.

As she watched, Caroline saw Ben walk over to the boy and rest a hand on Seth's shoulder. The child didn't reject the silent comfort Ben offered. But maybe Ben wasn't the best person to be comforting Seth. With Ben's past, Caroline certainly didn't think he represented a good example for the child. Maybe she should intercede. Maybe she should…

"Those two sure are a pair. The poor dears."

Caroline glanced over and found Sarah Yoder standing beside her. The woman followed her gaze and nodded at Seth and Ben.

"What do you mean?" Caroline asked.

Sarah shrugged. "Ben wasn't much older than Seth when he lost both his parents. If anyone can relate to what Seth and Mary are going through, it's Ben," Sarah said.

Oh. Caroline had heard a few rumblings about Ben's parents but hadn't given it much thought. Had he been overly quiet and hostile following the deaths of his parents? No doubt he had felt lost and all alone, just like Seth. Caroline felt a stab of compassion for what he must have suffered in his life. But that was no excuse to kill a man later on.

"I think it's important to teach Mary and Seth to accept *Gott's* will and not to fight it. I hope they can learn to have a calm, peaceful heart. Even though their parents are gone, they must go on living," Caroline said.

"I hope so, too. But those are not easy lessons to learn at such a young age. Ben can attest to that. I have no doubt he can impart his wisdom to Seth, and the boy would be better off for it." With those words, Sarah reached for a large clean casserole dish and set it on the table beside her wicker basket. The dish must belong to her and she wanted to take it home when she departed.

Caroline thought about what the bishop's wife had told her. No doubt she cared a great deal for Ben. After all, the man lived in her house and was her nephew by marriage. But Caroline wasn't sure she approved of Ben's friendship with Seth. The boy was quiet and respectful, but he was also young and impressionable. She would prefer he had a better example to follow. Someone like Uncle Mervin or Bishop Yoder.

But then she reconsidered. Ben had been nothing but kind and respectful to her. And she couldn't fault his dedication to hard work. Over the past eighteen months since she'd first met him, he'd never done anything to indicate he had a foul temper. Not once.

But he'd still killed a man. Surely, his anger was there, buried deep inside him. She was certain of it.

"Caroline?"

She looked down and found Mary standing beside her, holding her plate and fork. As Caroline took the dish from the girl, she noticed she'd barely touched her food.

"*Ja*, sweetums?" Caroline longed to bend down and meet the girl's eyes but still couldn't manage that movement.

"Where is our *heemet*? Where will we live now?" Mary asked.

"You'll live here with us, of course." Aunt Hannah spoke from nearby, her voice a bit wobbly with emotion. This had been a difficult day for all of them, and she was trying hard to be upbeat for the children's benefit.

"This isn't our *heemet*!"

Caroline jerked toward the open doorway. Seth had spoken. He stood beside Ben. They must have just returned to the house. The boy's hands were clenched and his face was red with anger.

"We were gonna buy our own farm to live on. But our *mamm* and *daed* are dead. We don't belong anywhere now," Seth said. Before anyone could respond, he dashed outside toward the barn, rudely brushing past several people as he went.

Along with Aunt Hannah and Ben, Caroline stared after the boy in surprise. She'd never heard such a rude outburst, yet she couldn't be angry at him. He had every right to be distraught. But he needed to learn respect and that death was not the end, but rather the beginning.

"Oh, dear. He seems quite upset," Aunt Hannah said, looking red and flustered.

"Don't worry. I'll speak with him," Ben said.

Without waiting for their approval, he hurried after the child, his long stride so strong and confident. Caroline wondered again if he was the best person to talk with Seth about death and eternal salvation. Though Seth had lost so much, this was a teaching moment. The child needed to be taught acceptance and reverence. He needed to understand that *Gott's* will must supersede his own. That hope and faith must be exercised at all times, even during the darkest ones such as this. And he needed to learn that such outbursts of emotion were not acceptable in the Amish faith.

Could Ben translate these beliefs to Seth in a satisfactory, calm manner? Caroline had her doubts.

Ben wasn't sure what he was going to say to Seth. As he entered the dim interior of the barn, he blinked and glanced around, looking for the boy. He found him in one of the empty animal stalls, sitting on a bale of hay, facing the wall.

Looping his thumbs around his black suspenders, Ben paused and considered his words carefully. Memories washed over him of the day his mother had died, followed by his father less than a year later. And he knew there was nothing he could say to ease the hurt. But maybe he could provide a bit of comfort.

"Seth, we need to talk," he began in a gentle voice.

The boy hunched his shoulders, the only indication that he'd heard him. As Ben stepped nearer, he blocked the exit out of the stall. He hadn't planned it this way, but if Seth made a break for it, there was no way out except through him. The boy would have to listen to him. For now. And yet, Ben didn't want to be stern. After his parents died, he'd been treated harshly and it had done nothing but alienate him. It had made everything worse.

Deciding to be gentle, Ben stepped inside the stall and sat beside the boy on the bale of hay.

"First, I want you to know that none of this is your fault. And it's not Mary's fault, either. Things just happen sometimes," Ben said.

He paused, letting that sink in. He remembered how he'd thought he'd done something bad to cause his parents' deaths and knew it would have made a difference if someone had told him it wasn't his fault.

"Second, I know what it feels like to lose your *eldre*

when you are young. I lost my *mudder* when I was seven and my *vadder* just after I turned eight," he continued.

Seth looked up at him, his mouth dropping open in surprise. "Did they die in a bus crash like my folks?"

Ben shook his head. "*Ne*, my *mamm* died of cancer. And I think losing my *mudder* when she was so young was what killed my *daed*, even though the doctor said it was a heart attack. I believe my *vadder* died of a broken heart. But either way, I was left all alone in the world with no *familye* of my own."

The boy sat up straighter. Ben realized he had caught Seth's attention.

"You didn't even have a *schweschder* or *bruder*?"

"*Ne*, not even a brother or sister."

"What did you do?" Seth asked.

"I went on living. My *onkel* Grant took me in to his *heemet* to live with him and then, almost two years ago, I moved here to Colorado to live with my *onkel* Amos."

"But he's not your *daed*," Seth said.

"*Ne*, but he's been awfully *gut* to me and I love him dearly. It's always best to be with your *familye*. They share your same heritage and beliefs."

"Do you like living here in Colorado?" Seth asked.

Ben ducked his head, considering the question. Did he like it here?

"I'm not sure. It's as *gut* as any place, I suppose. I'm grateful to my extended *familye* for taking me in, but it's not the same. More than anything, I'd like to have a *familye* of my own. A place that I can really call home. But I know my *aent* and *onkel* love me. I'll always have a place to belong with them."

Wow! He'd just confessed more out loud to this little boy of six years than he'd been willing to admit even to himself. But he didn't want to give the impression that it was all bad. In that moment Caroline's words of faith entered his mind and he knew what he should say.

"I feel blessed to be a part of our faith and to be with people who care for me. You still have your sister and she's depending on you. No matter what, you still have a *familye*. You'll want to always take care of Mary. Your *mamm* and *daed* are depending on you. They would expect nothing less. And the Lord expects it, too. I don't presume to know all of His ways, but I do know He walks beside us no matter what hardships we might face. With *Gott*, you're never alone, Seth. I hope you really believe that," Ben said.

Seth bowed his head, as if thinking this over. "I don't know. It's not the same now."

"I know, you're right. But I've learned that love and service continue even after our *mamm* and *daed* are gone from our lives. It's a test of sorts. To see if we will learn how to serve and love others," Ben said.

"Is that what you did?" Seth asked.

"I try to serve others whenever I can. But I trust in *Gott* that I'll one day have a wife and *familye* of my own. And you'll hopefully have that, too." As he said the words, Ben prayed what he said would come true.

A small sound came from behind them, and Ben turned. Caroline stood in the open doorway of the barn. At first glance, her cheeks went bright pink and he knew she'd been eavesdropping. A blaze of mortification heated him from the neck up. How much had she overheard? What must she think of him now?

"I… I'm sorry. I didn't mean to interrupt. I just wanted to make sure Seth was okay," she said.

"I'm fine. You don't need to check on me all the time."

Seth stood and edged toward the door. The angry expression had returned and it was obvious he felt embarrassed, too. The boy had let down his guard for a few minutes with Ben and seemed angry that Caroline had witnessed it.

"It was kind of you to check on him. But Seth is *allrecht* now. And I think we're finished here if you need the barn," Ben said, trying to be polite and show by example how Seth should act.

Without a word or backward glance, Seth fled the barn. In the silent aftermath, Ben walked over to Caroline and gazed down at her face. Tears glimmered in her eyes and she brushed them away, obviously struggling not to lose her hold on her crutches. At the cemetery, she'd been walking with just one crutch, and he thought she was getting stronger every day. But now her face was drained of color, her eyes clouded with pain and grief. From the droop of her shoulders, he could tell she was exhausted. And little wonder. It had been a difficult week for her and her *familye*.

"*Danke* for speaking with Seth," she said.

"It was my pleasure. I just hope it helps. Were you very close to Anna and James?" he asked.

She nodded and licked her upper lip. "*Ja*, I've known them both all my life. Anna and I were very close when I lived in Ohio, and I'll miss her and James very much."

Her voice spiked and he could tell she was overcome by emotion. A fresh welling of moisture filled her eyes and ran down her cheeks. Before he could think to stop himself, Ben reached out and wiped one tear away. Caroline stared up at him, her lips slightly parted. How he hated to see her cry.

"I'm so sorry. I wish I could do something to change this outcome," he said.

"There's nothing anyone can do. We just need to exercise faith and keep on living. We have Mary and Seth to think about now." She turned away, breaking the special moment between them.

He followed as she made her way back to the house. She stumbled several times, attesting that she'd overexerted herself today. Each time, he was there to hold her arm until she could regain her footing. And once he had her inside the house, he whispered a few words to Hannah, who insisted Caroline should sit down for the rest of the evening.

Soon afterward Ben took his departure. Caroline was right. The funeral was over with and they had to go on living. School was back in session, and there was much work to be done there and also on his uncle's farm.

But Ben wished Caroline hadn't overheard what he'd said to Seth. It was too personal. Too painful. And he didn't want her to think any less of him than she already did.

Chapter Seven

Two weeks later Caroline and her *familye* had settled into a routine. Ben picked her up each morning and drove her to school. Her aunt and uncle had integrated Seth and Mary into their daily chores and conducted their affairs like nothing had disrupted their lives. Hannah was so busy raising her own seven children that she didn't have time to coddle two more kids who were grieving for their parents. Caroline had naturally stepped in, spending extra time reading and comforting the two orphans. But no matter what she or others did, Seth grew more sullen and distant, seeming to withdraw into himself. He didn't willingly participate at school and he only spoke when absolutely necessary. Even little Mary, who was having occasional nightmares, was worried about her big brother. He never played with her anymore and had even started pinching her and pulling her hair. Needless to say, Caroline was worried about the boy.

"He's disappeared again." Hannah came in the back door to the farmhouse, carrying the kitchen garbage can. The screen door clapped closed behind her as she set the can down with a loud thump.

Caroline sat at the table, tallying a list of numbers in her grade book. It was early morning and she had just finished her grading before Ben would pick her up for school. The table was set for breakfast, and she had cleared a little space to work. Caroline and her aunt had prepared several pans of food, which sat warming on the stove, waiting for the children to finish their farm chores before they came inside to eat. The air smelled of sausage and eggs, fresh-baked biscuits and homemade strawberry preserves. The *familye* had been up since four o'clock that morning.

"Who's disappeared?" Caroline asked, jotting a final number at the bottom of her notebook before she snapped the book closed and slid it into her schoolbag.

"Seth, that's who. I asked that boy to dump the garbage can over an hour ago and now I can't find him anywhere. Anytime I ask him to do something, he just ignores me and I end up doing it myself. I hate to say it, but I'm afraid that boy is downright lazy. I don't know what to do with him." Hannah raised her hands in exasperation and released a big huff of air.

Caroline understood her aunt's frustration. The Amish were extremely hard workers and couldn't abide idleness or disobedience of any kind. They relied on every member of the *familye*, including the little children, to help with the tasks. That was what it took for a large *familye* like this to earn a living and survive. Seth's defiance had become a huge problem for them.

"Maybe I can find him." Pushing back from the table, Caroline clasped her elbow crutch and stood with minimal effort. Walking was getting much easier, and she thought she'd soon be able to trade the crutch for a cane.

Hannah released a sarcastic laugh as she picked up a

dish towel. "I've already looked and looked. You won't be able to find him. Not unless he wants to be found. I've spent the last ten minutes calling for him. I'm ready to have your uncle take the rod to him."

Caroline cringed. The thought of Uncle Mervin beating Seth with a rod of hickory made her stomach churn. Seth had lost so much already. She couldn't stand the thought of striking him for disobedience and was determined to get to the bottom of this.

"I'll find him." She spoke with a confidence she didn't really feel.

Ignoring her aunt's pursed lips, she stepped outside on the back porch. Sunshine blazed across the yard. Levi, her ten-year-old cousin, stood in the pigpen, dumping slop into the feeding trough. Alice, his older sister, was helping secure the gate so the pigs didn't escape. Joseph and even five-year-old Benuel were in the chicken coop gathering eggs and feeding the chickens. Everyone was busy doing their chores, except Seth. So where was he? And why on earth was he hiding again?

Caroline's intuition told her something was very wrong here. She didn't think Seth was lazy. This was a bigger problem. She'd noticed Seth disappeared from time to time, but only when he was asked to dump the garbage. So what was amiss?

Standing beside the corrals, she scanned the open yard, trying to imagine where she might hide if she were a six-year-old boy. A quick scan of the tall elm tree branches in the yard told her he wasn't up there. The obvious choice was the barn, but surely, Aunt Hannah had checked there already. But maybe she'd missed a small nook or cranny where the little boy might go unnoticed.

Shuffling along on the crutch, Caroline walked through the barn, peering into every dark corner.

"Seth! Where are you?" she called over and over again as she walked along.

No response. Not a single sound.

She crossed to the back of the barn and peered outside. Uncle Mervin had already milked and fed the cows and draft horses before turning them out into the south pasture. He was now out back, burning their garbage in a tall canister. Red flames flickered above the metal rim, consuming a variety of paper refuse. What Uncle Mervin couldn't burn, he tossed into the compost pile to use as fertilizer on their fields. They wasted very little on this farm.

Still, Caroline caught no sign of Seth. But he must be here somewhere.

With the pungent scent of smoke filling her nostrils, she stepped back inside the barn. Standing in the shadows, she held perfectly still and listened intently. After a few minutes she heard the slightest rustling just overhead. Several strands of hay wafted through the air and fell to the ground.

Hmm. Someone was up there. She thought she'd finally found Seth's hiding place.

"Seth," she called in a quiet, gentle tone. "Can you please come down from the hayloft now? It's almost time to go to school and you haven't had your breakfast yet."

She waited, hoping he wouldn't make her climb up after him. Because frankly, she wasn't sure she could physically do it, and she didn't want to fetch Mary or one of the other children to come and get him down.

He finally obeyed, peering over the edge of the loft. He had the good grace to look sheepish as he climbed down the wooden ladder. When he stood directly in front of her, she reached out slowly and plucked several pieces of straw away from his hair and clothes, then rested her hand on his slender shoulder.

"Seth, I know this is tough and I know you're angry that your parents aren't here. But when you want to run away, can you draw me a picture instead?" she asked.

His eyebrows drew together in a frown of confusion and he glanced at her. "What for?"

"So I can see what you're feeling inside. I'll leave some paper and crayons for you in the living room. You can draw what you're feeling right on the piece of paper. But no more running away and hiding. Otherwise, we'll be worried that you're in danger. Okay?"

He gave a noncommittal shrug. "Okay."

She smiled. "*Gut*. Now, can you tell me why you didn't dump the garbage can again?"

No answer. He just stared at the ground, silent as a tomb.

"*Komm* with me and I'll show you what needs to be done next time Aunt Hannah asks," she said.

She turned and headed toward the back of the barn where Uncle Mervin was burning garbage. The wind carried the strong smell of smoke on the air. Seth followed for three steps but then stopped dead in his tracks. As he gazed at the burning barrel, his eyes widened and his face contorted in a look of absolute terror. And before Caroline could say or do anything to help the boy, he turned and ran screaming toward the house.

"Seth!" she cried, trying to follow him, but she just wasn't fast enough.

He disappeared inside the house, slamming the door

behind him so hard that the entire structure seemed to shake on its foundation.

By the time Caroline made it inside, Aunt Hannah was sitting at the kitchen table feeding the baby and looking completely bewildered.

The screaming continued as the boy pounded up the stairs to his bedroom. The slamming of the door told Caroline that he didn't want any intruders.

"What on earth is going on? Is Seth hurt?" Aunt Hannah asked, coming to her feet.

"*Ne*, not the way you think. I can't explain right now, but I think I've figured out what's wrong with him. I'll take care of it." Caroline shuffled through the room and made her way upstairs.

It took her a few moments to climb the stairs. She paused at the top of the landing, trying to catch her breath. Seth's screaming had stopped but she could hear his muffled crying on the other side of the door. Lifting her hand, she knocked gently, hoping the portal wasn't locked.

"Seth? May I *komm* in?" she called in a calm voice.

No response.

Turning the knob, she stepped inside. Seth had curled up on his bed, his head buried beneath a pillow.

Caroline sat next to him but was careful not to touch him.

"Seth, I think I know why you don't want to empty the garbage can. It's because of the fire, isn't it?" she said.

He didn't speak but his body went more rigid, telling her she was right.

"When your *mamm* and *daed* died, there was a fire, wasn't there?" she asked.

She waited, giving him plenty of time to think. As a

teacher, she'd discovered that it took her students several seconds to digest what she'd asked them and come back with a response. So she paused now, exercising lots of patience. Finally, he pulled his head out from beneath the pillow and sat up, but he didn't meet her gaze.

"There was a fire, wasn't there?" she asked again, just in case he'd forgotten the question.

He nodded and she almost breathed a sigh of relief. Finally, they were getting somewhere. She reminded herself that both Seth and Mary had been on the bus with their parents when the semi-truck had plowed into them. And she was ashamed of herself for not asking him about what had happened. The Amish were a stoic people who didn't mollycoddle their children. But neither did Caroline think it was good for Seth to keep the experience bottled up inside. Maybe talking about it would help make things easier.

She touched his hand, just to see if he might let her hug him. But he pulled away. She didn't push but she made him a promise.

"*Ach*, I can tell you this. You don't have to empty the garbage can ever again, nor do you have to go out by the burning barrel anymore. Okay?" she said.

He looked up at her, his eyes filled with giant crocodile tears that ran unheeded down his cheeks. He looked so sad and forlorn that she felt inspired to pull him into her arms. If he fought her, she'd release him immediately. But above all else, she didn't want to force this traumatized child into doing anything he didn't want to do.

He curled into her arms and held on tight, and she released a satisfied sigh.

"You know, whenever I'm upset about something, I have a little scripture from the Bible that I repeat in my mind and it helps me feel better every time. Maybe you'd like to try it out?" she suggested.

He didn't answer. Didn't move a muscle. But he didn't refuse her offer, either, and she took that as approval.

"Peace I leave with you, my peace I give unto you: not as the world giveth, give I unto you. Let not your heart be troubled, neither let it be afraid."

She paused, letting it sink in.

"Do you know who said those words?" she asked.

He shook his head, listening intently.

"It was Jesus Christ, our Savior. The passage is found in the Book of John." She reached over to the bedside table and retrieved a Bible. After flipping it open, she handed the book to him and pointed out the exact verse.

"Perhaps, whenever you're feeling upset, you might like to repeat that scripture in your mind and feel the Lord close to you, offering His support. Do you think you might like to do that?" she asked.

He nodded, taking the book onto his lap and tracing the verse with his fingertip.

Downstairs, she heard a knock on the back door and thought Ben must have arrived to take her to school. But still, she sat with Seth for several more minutes, until she knew he was calm again. Then she stood.

"You and Mary are going to be *allrecht*, Seth. I promise you. Just trust in the Lord. And I'm always here any time you need to talk."

He didn't acknowledge her words, but she knew he'd heard her.

"Now, hurry and get ready. I want you to have your breakfast so you can do *gut* work in school today. I'll expect you to do your best," she said.

She wasn't a psychologist or trained in dealing with

childhood trauma, but she sensed that both Seth and Mary needed lots of love and understanding right now. But they also needed to understand her expectations. And before she left for the day, she was going to make sure that both Aunt Hannah and Uncle Mervin knew that Seth was absolutely terrified of fire. Not because he might be burned, but because there had been a fire the night his parents had died in that horrible accident. And until he could cope with their deaths, she didn't want to push the boy beyond what he could stand.

As she slid her elbow crutch in front of her and stepped out of the room, she hoped and prayed she'd said and done the right things today. Because she knew that helping Seth recover from this trauma was going to take patience and time. And as soon as the school day was over, she was going to pay a short visit to Becca Graber. Becca had substitute-taught for Caroline last school year. And though neither woman was formally trained in dealing with an issue like this, Becca had studied quite a lot so she could help her soon-to-be stepson, Sam, when the boy stopped speaking following the deaths of his mother and two sisters. Maybe Becca could offer some insight into how Caroline could help Seth and Mary.

"Caroline?"

She looked down and saw Aunt Hannah standing at the bottom of the stairs. She held baby Susan in her arms. The little girl was teething and overly fussy and had kept Hannah up most of the night. Hannah looked tired and overwhelmed.

"Ben is here to take you to school," Hannah said.

Caroline nodded. "I'll be right there."

"Is everything *allrecht* with Seth? Is he hurt?" Hannah asked, looking worried.

"*Ne*, he's fine for now," Caroline said.

As quickly as possible, she negotiated the stairs and quietly explained to her aunt what had happened.

"Oh, dear. What can I do?" Hannah asked.

"Just give him a different chore. Maybe he could gather the eggs instead and Levi could dump the garbage for the time being," Caroline said.

"*Ach*, of course." Hannah nodded.

Caroline hugged her aunt, offering her some reassurance, too. Then she turned to gather up her bookbag and went outside to greet Ben. She didn't know why but this morning's events had made her want to talk to him. In spite of his reputation, he had a soothing way about him that always made her feel at ease. He was just a plain Amish man and didn't know how to handle a child suffering over the traumatic deaths of his parents, and yet Ben always seemed to know the right thing to say.

And that realization confused Caroline more than ever. Because she didn't want to be around Ben any more than necessary. But he might be able to help with Seth, too.

Ben sat on the porch swing and crossed his ankles as he waited for Caroline. Sitting in front of Becca Graber's house, he enjoyed the way the afternoon sunlight glimmered through the treetops. Instead of verdant green, the leaves had changed to a light, lemon color. Soon, the weather would get colder and the leaves would turn orange and brown and fall to the ground.

He'd been momentarily surprised when Caroline had sat next to him in the buggy that morning and explained Seth's problem. She'd asked him to drive her over to Becca Graber's house as soon as school was out, so she could speak with the woman about possible solutions. Eager to be of service, Ben had agreed.

Caroline wasn't inside very long. Ben straightened when the door to the little log farmhouse swung open and she stepped outside with Becca on her heels.

A rather thick book was tucked beneath one of Caroline's arms. Because she was struggling to walk with her elbow crutch, he quickly stepped forward and took the book before it could fall to the ground.

"*Hallo* Ben," Becca greeted him with a bright smile.

Tugging on the brim of his black felt hat, he nodded respectfully. "Ma'am."

"I think you're on the right track," Becca said to Caroline. "Giving Seth a scripture to memorize and repeat in his mind every time he gets upset and letting him draw his feelings on paper was a very smart move. I'm sure it'll help him a lot."

They'd reached the buggy, and Ben opened the door and set the book on the front seat.

"I hope so. I didn't know what else to do. *Danke* for all your great ideas. I'll be sure to read the book and then implement some techniques to help both Seth and Mary," Caroline said.

She turned and hugged Becca, then did something that completely took Ben offguard. She slid her arm brace onto the floor of the buggy, then reached for his hand to support her as she climbed inside.

"You're so kind to help Caroline like this. I'm really glad you're here for her. She told me how blessed she is to have you as her assistant," Becca told him.

The praise felt alien to Ben. The Amish weren't given to fawning over anyone except the Lord. But he admitted—only to himself—that her words pleased him enormously. Mostly because he thought everyone in his *Gmay* disliked him.

Becca stepped back and Ben closed the door.

"Goodbye!" Becca said before turning back toward the house.

Ben paused, his mouth dropping open in surprise. Caroline had told her she was blessed to have his help? Because the buggy door was closed, he didn't think Caroline had heard Becca's words, but they touched his heart like nothing else could.

"Danke. Mach's gut," he called to Becca.

From the windshield, Caroline waved to her friend as Ben hurried to climb into the driver's seat. Taking the leather lead lines into his hands, he released the brake and slapped the lines lightly against the horse's back. The animal jerked forward and off they went.

"Did Becca have some *gut* ideas for you?" he asked after they'd been driving for several moments.

"Ja, she's so knowledgeable. She makes me think that maybe I'm not the right person to be teaching the scholars of our school. They need Becca. She's older and so much more experienced than I am," Caroline said.

He snorted. "That's because she taught them last year. But I've watched you with the kids and you know just as much. You've simply come across an unusual issue that needs dealing with. But look at you! You're going the extra mile to find out how to help Seth and Mary. They're blessed to have such a caring teacher as you. And besides, Becca is marrying Jesse King in another month. She'll have her own *familye* to care for soon enough and can't teach anymore."

Caroline looked at him, her expression one of surprise. He hoped he hadn't said anything inappropriate.

His words had been chosen out of respect and support, not an attempt to upset or disappoint her.

"*Danke*, Ben. I appreciate your kind words, more than I can say. You've been more than generous and I appreciate it," she said.

He stared straight ahead, trying not to show a big, silly smile. But inside, he was grinning like a fool. He'd tried to say the right things and she'd turned it about and made him feel good.

As he drove her home, Caroline rattled off several ideas Becca had given her to help Seth and Mary. And it occurred to Ben that Caroline had never been this chatty around him before. Which told him she was starting to become more comfortable with him.

"The first thing I want to do is get Seth and Mary to start drawing pictures for me," she said, her voice filled with discovery. "Then we can discuss them. Mary hasn't been acting out but I'm wondering if we should nip some problems in the bud now, before it catches up to her. She has had a few nightmares and I don't want things to get worse. Don't you agree?"

He coughed, stunned that she would ask for his opinion.

"*Ja*, I think that would be wise," he said.

"Of course, *Aent* Hannah and *Onkel* Mervin should be included in everything I'm doing with the kids. They'll be raising Seth and Mary now and need to know how to handle certain situations."

She picked up the heavy book that Becca had given her and thumbed through some of the pages. "*Ach*, I suppose I'll be up late reading tonight."

She smiled, and Ben thought he hadn't seen her this happy since before her buggy accident. It was nice.

She continued to talk and bounce ideas off him. Her acumen surprised him, and he simply nodded and agreed with what she proposed. After all, what did a big, gruff Amish man like him know about helping a child overcome a traumatic experience? He hadn't yet gotten over his own bad childhood and felt completely inept.

"*Danke*, Ben," Caroline said when he parked in front of her home and helped her out of the buggy.

He assisted her inside and returned her wave, then got back in the buggy and pulled out of the yard. And during his ride home, he had plenty of time to puzzle over Caroline and her zest for life. She was like a hound with a bone now. Seth and Mary needed her help, and she was determined to do whatever was necessary to make them happy again.

Ben wasn't surprised. Since the moment he'd met Caroline, he'd known she was an amazing, wonderful woman. All others paled in comparison to her. And once more, he regretted his past and wished their situation could be so much different.

But the reality wouldn't budge, and dwelling on what could have been did neither of them any good at all.

Chapter Eight

"Teacher Caroline. Come quick! The *buwe* are fighting."

Caroline looked up from where she sat on the front steps of the school. Little Mary had run around the corner of the building, her eyes wide and her face creased with worry.

Coretta and Annie, two girls from the fourth-grade class, sat on either side of Caroline. She'd been teaching them how to do a double crochet stitch. A wicker basket of dark purple yarn sat beside her, and she held a crochet needle and a half-finished dishcloth in her lap. The girls were making hot pot holders, hanging dish towels and dishcloths as a surprise for their mothers.

The screams and yelling of recess permeated Caroline's consciousness. She'd been concentrating so hard on counting stitches that she hadn't noticed how frenzied and shrill the sounds had become.

Looking out at the playground, she realized some of the kids were playing at the side of the schoolhouse and she couldn't see them from her vantage point. But now that she listened, she realized she wasn't hearing the happy cries of children at play. No, these were angry sounds.

After setting the dishcloth and needle inside the basket, she clasped her elbow crutch and pushed herself up. The girls rushed to take her arms and help her stand. And once she found her footing, she shuffled forward as she followed Mary.

When she rounded the corner of the schoolhouse, the shrieks became louder and Caroline couldn't believe what she saw. Seth and Caleb Yoder grappled around in the dirt, hitting and punching one another in the face and torso. Several other children stood around them, looking horrified and fretful. Elmer Albrecht, who was the oldest boy in the school, was trying to pull the two boys apart and demanding they stop, to no avail. The two fighting boys were so angry, their expressions filled with such hate, that they didn't seem to hear or see anything but each other.

"Schtopp!" Caroline called as she hurried over to intercede.

The gawking children parted the way for her, but Seth and Caleb didn't quit punching each other. They didn't even acknowledge her presence. They continued to hit and kick as Caroline endeavored to push her way between them.

"Oww!" she cried when one fist connected firmly with her jaw.

Her face exploded with pain, and the impact knocked her backward. She felt herself falling. Before the ground slammed up to meet her, strong hands caught her and set her back on her feet.

"Are you *allrecht*?"

Ben! As usual, he'd come to her rescue.

He restored the crutch to her hands, and she stood there shaking and gripping the handle so hard that her knuckles turned white. She gasped for breath, trying to ignore the pulsing pain in her face. Her legs trembled like gelatin and she rubbed her aching jaw. She knew that Ben had been working in the back, putting the last of the playground equipment together. And she'd never been so happy to see him in all her life. What if he hadn't been here?

"*Ja*, I'm okay. But the boys!" she cried, desperate to stop the fight.

With a satisfied nod, he turned and she saw something she'd never seen before. As Ben faced the two recalcitrant boys, a horrible emotion flared across his face. It was dark and ferocious and turned his normally calm expression into one of absolute fury. His wide shoulders tensed and his eyes narrowed to dangerous black points as his jaw hardened like a block of granite. From the time they were in the cradle, Amish children were taught that fighting was unacceptable. It went against everything they believed in. It brought nothing but heartache. The Amish were pacifists and never used force. No, not ever. And after what had happened to Ben, Caroline figured he understood that principle better than any of them.

"That's enough!" Ben roared.

Caroline flinched. Several little girls clung to her in fear. They watched as Ben took each boy by the arm and pulled them apart. He didn't hurt them, but they couldn't escape his solid grip. Like ravening wolves, they wriggled and fought to get at each other again, and Caroline thought she had never seen such atrocious behavior in all her life.

"*Schtopp!*" Ben thundered once more at the two boys.

Finally, Seth and Caleb came to their senses and stopped struggling. As if realizing the trouble they were in, they cowered and hung their heads, their argument suddenly forgotten.

"What do you think you're doing?" Ben spoke in *Deitsch*, his voice low and dangerous.

Neither boy spoke. They just stared at him with absolute contrition. And yet, Caroline saw something in Seth that she'd never seen in one of her students before. A sullen resentment glimmered in his eyes. The boy was far from cowed. He wanted to hurt Caleb. To kick, hit and punch the other boy. And she realized helping him overcome the trauma of his parents' deaths wasn't going to be as easy as she thought.

Caroline watched Ben carefully, wondering what he might do. In those few short moments, she'd received an inkling of what he must have been like when he'd killed a man. Cruel and ferocious. And yet, he seemed completely in control of his actions. Just as she imagined Jesus must have been when he chased the money changers out of His father's temple.

Ben always seemed so gentle. So considerate and kind. But seeing him like this made her realize that everyone had a dark side. And it frightened Caroline more than she could say.

"Do you not know that fighting is forbidden? Jesus taught us to turn the other cheek. Do you think He would approve of what you've done here today?" he asked the boys.

They didn't respond, but Seth's face darkened. He didn't appear repentant at all. Not in the least.

"And you struck Teacher Caroline, too. How dare you

do such a thing? You owe her your respect. You should be protecting her, not hitting her," Ben said.

Both boys glanced at Caroline, their arms still firmly held in Ben's grasp.

"I'm sorry for fighting. I didn't mean to hit you, Teacher Caroline," Caleb said, his eyes filled with tears.

"I'm sorry for hitting you, too. I… I didn't mean for you to get hurt," Seth said.

But Seth hadn't apologized for fighting. A terrible, blinding energy emanated from the boy, telling her he was still filled with rage. He wanted to fight. He wanted to scream and kill something. She could hardly comprehend such a harsh emotion. And for the first time since she'd been back at her teaching job, she felt like she was in over her head. She hadn't been able to stop the fight. If Ben hadn't been here today, she didn't know what she would have done. The situation could have escalated and been so much worse. Someone could have gotten seriously hurt. And what would the parents and school board say when they found out?

Ben released the two boys and stood back, his expression completely calm but still stern. For Caroline, it was like watching the night turn to day. One moment Ben was like a brick wall, filled with such power and enmity that she was stunned by his energy. And the next moment he was perfectly still. All Caroline could wonder was, who was this man?

He came to stand beside her, as if waiting for her to take charge now that the situation was under control. Caroline coughed to clear her voice and tried to regain her composure. Ignoring the ache in her jaw, she stepped forward.

"Students, I would like all of you to return to the classroom now. Recess is over. I want you to study quietly in your workbooks. Caleb and Seth, you will remain here for the time being," she said, her voice vibrating slightly.

All of the other children returned to the schoolhouse. Once the other kids were inside, Caroline faced Seth and Caleb again. She was highly conscious of Ben remaining right where he was, like a silent bodyguard watching over her. And she wasn't sure if that was good or bad.

"I'm so disappointed in you boys today," she began, grateful that her voice sounded much calmer. "You both know better than to fight. Your parents will be told about this and there will be a punishment forthcoming, once I figure out what that should be."

"I don't have any parents!" Seth shouted, his eyes filled with angry tears.

Oh, dear. Caroline cringed, wishing she'd chosen a better word. She hadn't thought before she opened her mouth. Her heart ached for all that this child had lost. She wanted to go easy on him but knew the bishop and her aunt and uncle wouldn't approve if she didn't do something to impress upon the two boys' minds the importance of what she was trying to teach. No fighting. Period.

"I'm sorry, Seth. I misspoke. But you do have a *familye* here that loves you very much. And there are parents in your *heemet*. You have us. Remember you were going to draw a picture and recite a scripture whenever you were feeling angry or upset? Did you forget about that?" she asked.

Seth's face darkened, his hands clenched as he glared at Caroline and Ben. "I didn't forget. But you're not my *mudder* and *vadder*. They're dead!"

He turned and sprinted toward the school. A sense of

panic swept over Caroline. If the boy ran away, she didn't have the physical strength to chase after him. And she really didn't want to ask Ben to do it. She watched in relief as Seth pounded up the steps and entered the schoolhouse, slamming the door behind him. He was still very angry, but at least he'd stayed here. He was safe for now. But she needed time to think how to handle the situation. Once he calmed down, she'd ask him to draw a picture. She must be consistent and not deviate from her plans to help him. Otherwise, she'd lose him for sure.

"Please return to the classroom," she told Caleb in a very soft voice.

The boy ducked his head. "I'm so sorry, Teacher Caroline. We were just playing a game and he dropped a pocketknife. I picked it up and handed it back to him and he blew up at me. I… I'm sorry I fought back. I know I shouldn't have. And it won't happen ever again. I promise."

A pocketknife! It wasn't so odd to have such a thing at school. Many of the boys helped cut willows and liked to whittle on sticks. The Amish school didn't have a "no weapons policy" like the *Englisch* schools did, mostly because it had never been an issue before. Even though the Amish were pacifists, they all had guns and knives and hunted for food to feed their families. But why would Caleb's touching the knife be cause for Seth to attack him?

She heard the true remorse in Caleb's words and nodded. "*Gut*, I'm glad to hear that. But you should also apologize to Seth, once he's calmed down a little. And I'll expect you to never fight again."

Caleb nodded solemnly, then jogged back to the schoolhouse. Caroline breathed a heavy sigh and looked at Ben. She hated to go back inside the classroom and try to continue their lessons. There was such a feeling of contention in the air. Even the other children who hadn't been fighting must surely feel it. Everyone was highly upset.

"It'll be *allrecht*." Ben gave her a gentle smile of encouragement.

How did he always seem to know what she was thinking?

"I'll be nearby if you need me," he said before turning and walking away.

She watched as he disappeared around the back of the school and knew he'd be listening for any sounds of trouble inside. On the one hand, she was glad to have him here. She hated to admit it, but Bishop Yoder had been wise to send Ben here to help her out this year. Yet, on the other hand, she wondered if he was a good influence on the kids. After all, he'd fought back, and look what had come of it. A man had lost his life. Most of the children, including Caleb, who was Ben's cousin, had heard the gossip. They knew what Ben had done. But Seth didn't know about it yet. At least, she didn't think so. Maybe one of the other kids had told him. And how would that look once Seth found out? Ben had just told the boys not to fight, yet he was a hypocrite for killing a man.

And then a thought occurred to Caroline. It wasn't fair for her to hold a grudge against Ben because of his past. If she truly believed in the forgiveness of Jesus Christ, then who was she to keep remembering what he'd done? She understood that everyone could repent and all sins could be washed away and forgotten. The scriptures talked about sinful men casting stones at others, and she had her own failings to work on. And if that was the case, who better than Ben to help her soften Seth's anger?

Hmm. Maybe she should ask Ben what he thought.

* * *

Ben leaned against the buggy and folded his arms. Like many times before, he was waiting on a woman. Waiting for Caroline. But he didn't mind. After all, it was the task the bishop had assigned him. And he realized every time he was waiting on a woman, it was because she was serving someone else. How could he ever begrudge that?

An hour earlier he'd watched as she'd come outside to greet Sarah and Hannah when they'd picked up their kids from school. She'd spoken with both women about Caleb and Seth's fight today. Ben had kept his distance, busying himself with pouring cement to anchor the swing set into the ground. But he'd seen the surprise and then the revulsion on each woman's face when they found out their boys had been fighting at school. It was such a rare occurrence in an Amish school. But for one of the bishop's sons to be a participant must be a great embarrassment for Sarah. After all, the bishop's *familye* should set an example for everyone else in the *Gmay*. They should be above reproachful behavior. And Ben could just imagine the severe conversation he would hear later that evening at the supper table when his uncle addressed the issue with Caleb.

Now a soft scuffle caused him to turn. Caroline stood on the landing of the front steps, locking the door to the schoolhouse. Finally, she was ready to go home. But from the set of her shoulders and the way she inclined her head, he could tell she was still distraught.

He stepped near, just close enough to catch her should she stumble on the stairs. When he'd first been given this assignment, he'd learned really fast that she wanted to do things by herself, if she could. And he admired her spunk. In spite of great odds, she hadn't become clingy or whiney. She was as strong and independent as it was possible to be in her situation. But he wasn't sure he could help her with this new problem. It was way over his head.

"Danke," she said when he offered his arm for her to climb into the buggy.

It delighted him that she didn't push him away, and he realized she was coming to accept his presence at the school without objection.

With a nod, he hurried around to his side of the buggy and took the leather lead lines into his hands. They drove in silence for a short time, and he purposefully didn't intrude on her thoughts. He'd learned enough about this woman to know there were times when she needed to be left alone.

"Mary hasn't been sleeping very well since the funeral. Sometimes she has bad nightmares," she finally said.

Hmm. That was an interesting subject for her to bring up out of the blue.

"Ach, I'm not surprised. Losing their *eldre* can't have been easy on either her or Seth. Especially since they were there when the accident occurred. They may have witnessed some horrible things that haunt their memories," he said.

She glanced at him. "You're right. They were there and saw it all. *Ach,* the poor little lambs."

Her chin wobbled slightly and she lifted a hand to her face. Her fingers trembled and he thought she might cry. He hated to see her in distress and wanted to comfort her.

"Don't worry. As you and the rest of your *familye* show them a lot of love and support, they'll adjust soon enough. The entire *Gmay* will make those two *kinder* feel loved and wanted," he said, remembering exactly how it felt to lose his own parents. He'd adjusted to living without them but had never recovered from the loss. And he feared Mary and Seth might suffer the same fate.

One of the windows was open, and the ties to Caroline's white organdy prayer *kapp* waved in the breeze. He longed to reach out and tug on it and tease a smile from her lips.

"How long did it take for you to get over losing your *eldre*?" she asked.

Here it was. The one question he didn't want to face. He stared straight ahead, concentrating on the road. Losing his parents when he was so young had devastated him. Not a day went by that he didn't miss them terribly.

"I'll let you know if I ever do," he said.

She heaved a deep sigh. "I'm afraid both Mary and Seth have taken their *eldre's* deaths quite hard. But even with the sleeplessness, Mary is still talkative and affectionate. She's folded right into our *familye* gatherings at home."

"*Ja*, I've noticed she seems to gravitate to you quite a bit," he said.

She nodded. "We have become quite close already. She's so easy to love. But Seth is another matter. I'm worried about him. He's so quiet and surly all the time. I've tried to get him to open up and talk but he won't say a word. He's so withdrawn, even with *Aent* Hannah and *Onkel* Mervin. And now he's picking fights at school. I asked him to draw a picture of how he was feeling and he wadded up the paper and threw it across the room. I'm not sure how to get through to him."

A blaze of delight speared Ben's chest. He couldn't believe Caroline was confiding all of this in him. It was the first time she'd purposefully started a conversation with him, as if she were seeking his advice.

"*Ach*, that was how he was feeling, then," he said.

"What do you mean?" she asked.

"He wadded up the paper and threw it away. That was his drawing. He didn't need a pencil or crayon to show you what he felt inside, just his hands to wad up the paper."

A look of amazement covered her face, as if a light had clicked on inside her mind. "*Ach!* I see what you mean. I didn't think to look at it that way. I'll talk to him about it when I get *heemet* tonight. You're absolutely right. The wadded-up paper was his artwork. But I need to ask him about the pocketknife, too. If it's going to be a problem, I don't want him to bring it to school again."

"*Gut* idea. Seth is tall and husky for his age, so he's kind of a target for older boys, just like I was at his age," Ben said.

Caroline snorted. "Caleb is quite a bit older than Seth and has been known to cause mischief before, but I don't think he picked the fight today."

"I agree," Ben said. "I don't know all the details, but Seth has suffered a great loss recently. He's angry and hurting and doesn't know where he belongs in the world. That can make him want to lash out at others for no real reason."

"*Ach*, he belongs here with us, of course. I don't know why he doesn't get that," she said, not seeming to understand.

They pulled onto the county road and he took a moment to consider his words carefully before he responded. "Of course he belongs here but he doesn't quite know that yet. He's filled with a great deal of anger and doesn't know how to control it right now."

She glanced at him. "You seem to have some things in common with Seth. Maybe…maybe you could speak with him?"

It was a question, not a statement. He couldn't believe she was actually asking for his help.

"*Ja*, I'd be happy to talk to him. But I can't tell you how much I regret what happened to me. I don't want Seth to ever go through that. Not ever."

Another long pause.

"He'll probably hear about it sooner or later," she said.

"*Ja*, I should tell him first and explain that violence isn't the way to go. It brings nothing but pain and discouragement," he said.

"What did happen to you?" she asked.

He inhaled sharply. No one had ever asked him to talk about it, not even his two uncles. Only the police had asked for his side of the story, and he hadn't discussed it with anyone else since that terrible time many years earlier.

"I… I lost both my parents when I was young, and as I mentioned, I was large for my age, just like Seth." He spoke in an aching whisper, the memories washing over him in shattering waves. "I was always peaceful inside, but I became a target of some older *Englisch* boys who wanted to fight because I was so tall. They'd been dogging me around town for months, even coming out to my *onkel's* fields when I was there working alone. I was able to avoid trouble for quite some time. But one day they caught me alone in an alleyway in town."

His heart pounded in his chest and he gripped the

lead lines harder. He felt like it had just occurred, and he wasn't sure he wanted to talk about this anymore.

"What happened?" she pressed.

He took a deep inhale, trying to steady his nerves. "They knew the Amish didn't fight and they took delight in goading me. I... I was only seventeen at the time. Too young to know my own strength and too young to have the self-confidence I needed to resist them. There were nine of them. I took their beating without so much as a murmur, until one of them started calling my *mudder* foul names. Then I... I lost it."

Even now, after years of being without his mother, the pain still felt fresh. His dear, sweet mother. So gentle, kind and good. The one person in this world who had loved him unconditionally. He couldn't stand the thought of anyone besmirching her pure name. And something had happened inside him that day that he still didn't understand. A fury had washed over him like he'd never felt before. It had boiled up inside him like a raging inferno, completely out of control. But he didn't tell Caroline that.

"I didn't strike anyone with my fists. I never lashed out. But when one of the young men got in my face and called my *mudder* names, I pushed him away," he continued. "He fell back and hit his head on the edge of the cement gutter. I tried to help him but he died in my arms."

She gasped. "Oh, Ben! I'm so sorry for what you've been through, but you must know it was wrong for you to use any force whatsoever, even to push someone away. If you hadn't pushed that man, he wouldn't have fallen and struck his head. He wouldn't have died."

He nodded. "*Ja*, I know better than anyone how tragic it can be to fight back. And oh, how I wish I hadn't. I might have been the one to die that day, but that would have been preferable to being responsible for someone else's death."

Yes, he knew only too well how horrible it could be to use force. What had followed had been more than traumatic for him. Before the incident, he'd had many friends and numerous options for marrying a nice Amish girl. He'd had a bright future with his people. He was one of them and welcome in their homes.

But after what happened, they'd all turned away. Because he hadn't yet been baptized into the Amish faith, he hadn't been shunned, but he might as well have been. He'd killed a man and they wanted nothing to do with him. When he was in their homes, an uncomfortable silence prevailed. No one sought him out or spoke to him during church meetings, unless they needed him to help with a work project. He didn't belong with them anymore. He didn't belong anywhere.

"What happened after you...after you...?" She didn't finish her question but she didn't need to.

He took a deep breath, thinking maybe it was good to get the whole story out. To tell someone what really happened. But as he did so, he realized he was placing a lethal weapon in Caroline's hands. If she chose, she could use the information to hurt him even more. By confiding in her, he was placing a lot of trust in her.

"Since nine men had attacked me, the law ruled it as self-defense," he said. "But I couldn't go anywhere alone anymore. Because they blamed me for killing one of their friends, the gang of *Englisch* boys increased their attacks on me. And during the months that followed, I learned firsthand about the pains of ostracism, loneliness and guilt. People in the *Gmay* turned their backs whenever I was near. They may not have formally shunned me, but

I knew they wanted nothing to do with me. Finally, my *onkel* Amos invited me to come here to Riverton, to start afresh. He thought if he could get me out of that community, I could begin anew. But I don't think that's possible anymore. The gossip has followed me. Everyone in our *Gmay* knows what happened and no one wants me here, either."

She listened quietly but didn't say a word for a long time. She seemed to be digesting everything he'd told her and making her own judgments. Then she looked straight at him, unblinking.

"That's not true. The people in our *Gmay* want you, Ben. I think they're just getting to know you. But the people in your old community shouldn't have pushed you away. They should have shown you an increase of love and been more supportive," she said.

Her words shocked him. How kind and generous of her. And yet, he'd felt her disapproval, too. At first.

"I don't want Seth to go through what happened to you," she said. "I want him to grow up feeling loved and wanted. I want him to be happy. Will you help him, Ben? Please!"

Ben! He loved it when she said his name. It was an acknowledgment that he existed and was worthy of being part of her world.

"As you wish. I'll speak to him and try to make him understand that violence isn't how *Gott* wants us to live our lives. I'll talk with him about being passive and showing the same love for everyone that the Savior showed to us, even if it's someone who wants to harm us," he said.

"*Ach*, would you? I really think it might help. Especially since he looks up to you already. He really admires you," she said.

And that concerned him. Seth admired him, but once he found out what he had done, Ben feared the boy would be disappointed in him.

Caroline lifted a hand to touch Ben's, and he felt a surge of energy shoot up his arm. The gesture softened his heart. It made him feel confident. Like he would do anything for her. But then she jerked her hand away, as if she realized what she'd done and that she didn't want to touch him after all.

"Of course I'll do it. But I don't think he looks up to me. I think he's just a very lost little boy right now," he said, feeling pleased by her words but unable to really believe them.

"He does look up to you, Ben. Haven't you noticed how he watches you all the time when you're working in the schoolyard on the new playground equipment? And he stays close by you at church whenever you're around. *Aent* Hannah told him you'd lost your parents when you were young, and I think he feels a kinship with you because of it."

Ben blinked. "She did? He does?"

She laughed, the sound high and sweet and like honey to his heart.

"*Ja*, he does. You should pay more attention to him. Because he sure notices you," she said.

He smiled, too, and glanced her way. "I'll do just that. I'll shower him with attention."

"And maybe…maybe we could take both Mary and Seth on an outing together. Something that would make them feel *gut* and happy again," she said.

He hesitated. "Are you suggesting that we team up to help these two *kinder*?"

"I guess I am. We were both there when the police

brought them to my *onkel's* home the night their *eldre* died. They've known us since they arrived in town. I'm their teacher and you're…you're their special friend. I think we both could make a big difference in their lives."

He thought about that for a moment. Her insight into what might be good and helpful for the kids touched his heart. In many ways Caroline reminded him of his mother.

"Maybe we could take them fishing. Kids love to fish, and I know a little place where we could catch some trout for supper. If Seth doesn't already know how to fish, I can teach him," he said.

She nodded eagerly. "*Ja*, that would be great. I can prepare a picnic lunch for us to take along. We could go out next Saturday, before it gets too cold."

She smiled, sounding excited by their plans. Then she looked at him and frowned, as if she'd suddenly remembered who he was and what he'd done. She'd expressed sympathy for his situation, and he hoped she wasn't a hypocrite like many other Amish people he'd met throughout his life.

He turned away before she could retract her offer. He would enjoy teaching Seth to fish, but he'd like even more having Caroline and Mary along for the event.

"I like that idea," he said. "It'll be fun. Don't worry, Caroline. We won't lose these two kids. I promise we'll do everything we can to help them."

And he meant every word. He felt just like Caroline, desperate to help the two orphans in any way he could. But more than that, the fact that Caroline had sought his advice touched him like nothing else could. It made him feel like he could overcome the stigma of his past. He wanted to please her. Wanted her approval. And he was determined not to let her down.

Chapter Nine

This was a mistake. The moment Caroline suggested she make a picnic and go fishing with Ben and the two orphans, she regretted it. It had seemed like a good idea at the time, and she'd gotten caught up in making plans. But now she wasn't so sure. She had sympathy for Ben and the tragic events that had brought him here to Riverton, but she also wasn't sure she should spend extra time with him. What might people say? She didn't want them to think she and Ben were romantically involved. Because they weren't. They never would be. But now it was too late to back out.

As promised, Ben picked her and the children up on Saturday, just after they'd finished their morning chores. She'd spent a lot of extra time talking and reading to both Seth and Mary each evening. And when she'd asked Seth about the pocketknife he'd brought to school, she'd been shocked to find out it had belonged to his father. When he'd accidentally dropped it on the playground at school and Caleb Yoder had picked it up, Seth had gone ballistic and attacked the other boy. For some reason Seth had felt threatened, even though Caleb was trying to return the knife and meant no harm. Now Seth felt horrible for what he'd done.

Aunt Hannah was relieved that Caroline had taken such an active role in Seth and Mary's discipline. She was too busy with her own brood and didn't know how to handle a rebellious boy like Seth. The situation was foreign to her, and she was happy to abdicate her parenting role.

Though the farmers expected a killing frost any day now, even the late-October weather wouldn't cancel their fishing trip. The sun was shining bright, not a cloud in the sky. In fact, the warm day felt more like summer than fall.

"Is this all you're taking with you?" Ben asked.

Standing at the back door, he hefted the large wicker basket where Caroline had stowed their picnic lunch—ham and cheese sandwiches, deep-dish apple pie and ruffled potato chips bought yesterday from the grocery store in town. It would be an extra special treat the children should enjoy since they didn't get them very often.

"And that, too, please." Caroline pointed at a folded blanket she'd laid on the kitchen table.

"I wanna go fishing, too." Five-year-old Benuel sat at the table finishing his breakfast of eggs and toast.

Aunt Hannah turned from the stove. "Remember we talked about this? Ben and Caroline are taking just Mary and Seth this morning. Your *daed* will take you into town with him once his chores are done."

The boy scowled and stirred his fork around in his eggs. Eight-year-old Joseph and ten-year-old Levi frowned from their seats nearby, too. Caroline knew her aunt had explained the situation to her children, but they still weren't happy to be excluded. After all, most Amish children enjoyed fishing. It was a chance to escape the constant drudgery of work and do something fun. But Caroline feared that, if they took the other children along, Seth and Mary might get lost in the shuffle. Caroline's aunt and uncle had agreed that the orphans needed a special day all to themselves.

Besides, Hannah had been all smiles ever since Caroline informed her of Ben's idea to spend extra time with Mary and Seth. No doubt Hannah hoped the outing would draw Caroline and Ben closer, too. And while Caroline didn't disabuse her aunt of such notions, she had no intention of letting that happen.

It was becoming more and more difficult not to like Ben, especially after all that he'd told her. She understood how bad he felt for causing the death of that young man. And she thought Ben had repented of his actions. He deserved the right to move past it all. But that didn't mean they were anything more than friends. Because there were other barriers between them, such as the fact that she could never have a child of her own.

Ben gathered up the blanket, then turned with the basket and went outside to stow the items in the back of the buggy. The screen door clapped closed behind him. Mary and Seth were already outside. From the open doorway, Caroline could see Mary hopping around with excitement. But Seth just stood beside the horse, his head hanging as he kicked at a stone with the tip of his black boot.

"*Ach*, I guess I better get out there," Caroline said.

Hannah stepped over and hugged her tight. "Have fun, dear. And be sure to laugh at least twice today. This is such a *gut* idea. Seth and Mary aren't the only ones who need a nice outing. I think you and Ben need it, too."

Caroline froze. She wasn't sure that was true, but it

didn't matter anymore. Bracing her cane in front of her, she walked out into the brilliant sunshine.

"*Komm* on, Seth. It's time to go," Ben called to the boy as he helped first Mary and then Caroline into the buggy.

The boy did as he was told and sat in the back with his sister. Within minutes Ben directed the horse onto the county road, but they only traveled on it for a quarter of a mile before he turned off again.

"Where are we going?" Mary leaned forward and rested her chin on Ben's shoulder as she looked out the windshield.

"Over to Cherry Creek. I know a nice little spot where we can catch some fine trout," he said.

"I don't wanna go fishing," Seth grumbled from the backseat.

"*Ach*, then you can sit in the buggy while we go fishing. But I suspect that will get pretty boring after a while," Ben responded with a heavy dose of laughter in his voice.

Though he was teasing the boy, Caroline swiveled in her seat and saw that Seth was wearing a grumpy frown. The child wasn't amused, and she wished he would climb out of his doldrums.

They soon arrived at their destination, a sparkling pond of water along Cherry Creek where beams of golden sunlight shimmered against the pebbled shore.

Ben parked the horse and buggy beneath the shade of tall aspens. Before doing anything else, he helped everyone out of the buggy, then offered the horse a drink and let the animal nibble at the tall sedge grass.

Caroline helped retrieve the fishing box from the back of the buggy, then chose a grassy spot near the shore to spread out the blanket. Mary was off like a shot, racing down to the water's edge.

"Not too far, *liebchen*. Stay where I can see you at all times," Caroline called to the girl.

"I will," Mary responded in a happy voice. She picked up a stick and poked the ground, turning over rocks and studying bugs in the dirt.

Smiling with satisfaction, Caroline sat down, thinking this was a perfect vantage point for her to watch the children fish with Ben. Tall sedges and cattails grew along the embankment, the water crystal clear and rippling like liquid glass. It was absolutely lovely here.

"I didn't know the bishop had such a beautiful fishing hole on his property," she told Ben.

He shook his head and set the wicker basket beside her on the blanket. "This land doesn't belong to my *onkel*. It's part of my land."

She blinked. "Your land?"

"*Ja*, I own thirty acres bordering my *onkel's* property. I bought it from him a year ago but haven't had time to clear and plant the land yet."

Really! She'd had no idea Ben had bought farmland here in the Riverton area. She just assumed he would live out his entire life working on the bishop's farm.

"What will you grow here?" she asked.

He gazed at the open fields of land spreading out before them. And in her mind's eye, she could just imagine fences and furrows he would build one day.

"Mostly hay and a little barley and oats. I doubt I can grow much of anything else," he said.

She nodded. "*Ja*, it's too cold here in this valley. Before my accident, I always covered our tomato plants at night and got a nice harvest that way. My *aent* and I bottle a lot of produce from our garden. We Amish do okay here in Colorado. And it's a *wundervoll* place to raise a *familye.*"

The moment she said that, she regretted it. She didn't want to give him the wrong idea. They could never be more than friends and even that was iffy. But she realized the more time they spent together, the more friendly they had become.

"I plan to raise horses, too. This is a great place for our Amish people to live. We have wide open spaces for our farms and can practice our faith without anyone bothering us," he said.

"This is near the Harlin place, isn't it?" she asked, trying to change the subject.

He nodded. "*Ja*, the house is right over there."

He jutted his chin toward an open field that was overgrown by tall weeds and wild grass. Off in the distance, Caroline could just make out the shapes of a white farmhouse and tall, red barn. And all at once, the ramifications of her cousins' deaths washed over her like a cold dunk in the river. Anna and James weren't here to buy the place. They'd never get to live in the farmhouse or raise hay and livestock. Little Mary and Seth would never grow up here. All their dreams had been dashed to pieces.

Caroline looked away and blinked fast so Ben and the children wouldn't see the sudden tears that filled her eyes. She wondered what would happen to the Harlin farm now that James and Anna were gone. Already the place had been neglected. An outlying farm like this didn't sell fast here in Colorado. It was too remote from the town. Also, with the short growing season, colder weather and drought issues, it was hard work to make a go of such a place. No doubt the years would take their toll and the farm would fall into disrepair and ruin. It was so sad, really. A home like that was meant to be lived in. Caroline had always dreamt of occupying just such a farm with her husband one day. Instead, she must be happy staying with her aunt and uncle on their place.

Ben handed a fishing pole to Seth but the boy just stared at it. No doubt he understood their brief conversation and was missing his parents, too.

"Did you ever go fishing with your *vadder*?" Ben asked as he opened a container of night crawlers.

"*Ja*, of course I did," Seth said, his voice defensive.

"*Gut!* Then you know how to bait a hook."

Seth frowned with uncertainty.

"Yuck! I'm not gonna bait a hook," Mary said from nearby.

Ben chuckled. "Don't worry. You won't have to. Not as long as we men are here to do it for you." He turned and faced Seth again. "I'm glad you have some *gut* memories with your *vadder*, Seth. He'll always be your *daed* and no one can ever take those memories away from you."

The boy stared as Ben turned and headed toward the water. Not seeming to know what else to do, Seth followed. Caroline watched as the two sat together on a large boulder, their fishing poles lying beside them as they baited their hooks. From what she could tell, they didn't speak much. And in spite of his words, Seth didn't seem to know what to do. With utmost patience, Ben showed him how to bait the hook and then cast out his line.

Mary picked up some rocks and tried to skim them across the surface of the pond. Instead, they raised great geysers as the stones pounded the water. Caroline longed to join her, but the rocky shore was so uneven that she feared she might fall.

"*Schtopp* throwing rocks, Mary! You'll scare all the fish away," Seth snapped.

Mary frowned and came walking back to Caroline, her slender shoulders slumped in discouragement. The girl plopped down on the blanket beside her and released a giant huff.

"Fishing isn't so much fun for a girl," she said.

Oh, no! This outing had to be fun for both children. What could she do to make Mary happy today?

"You can fish, too, if you want to. Ben would let you hold his pole. Why don't you go and ask him?" Caroline suggested.

"But I don't want to catch the poor little fish. I'd only want to throw them back. I'm bored," Mary said.

Kneeling on the blanket, Caroline reached to clasp a tree trunk and pulled herself up. Though she still needed help, it was definitely getting easier. "*Ach*, we can't have that. How about if you and I go look for some pretty pinecones to take home with us? I promised *Aent* Hannah I'd make a wreath for Christmas this year. You can help me gather them up. Okay?"

Caroline held out her hand, and the girl immediately smiled and clasped her fingers as she hopped to her feet.

Though she had to move slowly, Caroline found the soft leaf litter and needles much easier to walk on than the pebbled beach. She moved through the surrounding trees, searching for some pine trees. Mary smiled happily and, when they found some particularly pretty cones, she eagerly gathered them into a brown paper bag Caroline supplied.

Soon, they both got hungry and headed back to shore. They returned at just the right time. Seth's fishing line gave a hard tug and his reel began to buzz. Taken off guard, the boy almost dropped the fishing pole into the pond. Ben grabbed the handle and pulled backward before he placed the rod in Seth's smaller hands.

"Don't let go, Seth. Reel him in," Ben encouraged, helping him.

Mary squealed with delight and ran over to cheer her brother on. "Pull him in, Seth. Pull him in."

Together, Ben and Seth alternatively tugged and reeled until the eight-inch trout was safely on the shore. Ben helped the boy snag the thrashing fish with the net. Once the catch was secure, Caroline saw something she never thought possible. Seth grinned wide and held the fish up high.

"Look, Mary! I caught one! I actually caught my first fish," the boy crowed.

He laughed out loud, and Caroline could only stare at him in wonder. It was the first time she'd heard such a happy sound come from the boy, and it surprised her. Then she remembered what Aunt Hannah had told her—to make sure she laughed at least twice today. And with that thought rippling through her mind, Caroline did just that.

Hearing her enjoyment, Ben glanced her way, looking both pleased and startled by the sound. He laughed, too, and Caroline realized she couldn't remember the last time she'd had so much fun.

Regaining her composure, she hugged Seth and congratulated him over and over again. Within minutes he had his hook baited and was perched on the boulder, ready to snag another one.

"I don't want to disappoint Hannah, so I better catch some more fish for supper tonight," Seth said, his expression intense and his voice filled with delight.

Mary sat beside her brother, chatting away about how beautiful his little trout was and how tasty she knew it would be once they ate it later that evening. The two children looked incredibly happy, and Caroline realized their outing had been a great success.

Ben turned and looked at Caroline from over his shoulder. His eyes twinkled with merriment as he pushed his black felt hat back on his head. Then he did something that both startled and delighted her. He winked and mouthed one single word to her.

Victory!

Caroline nodded and looked away, unable to contain a smile of satisfaction. Yes, she couldn't agree more. They'd had a great triumph today. Hearing Seth's laughter and seeing him so animated and excited had made this trip worth the effort. Both children were happy. So was Caroline. And for a short time, she'd been able to pretend that this was her *familye*. That the children belonged to her. But soon, they would go home. They would have to return to reality. Because these weren't her kids, and Ben would never be her husband. No, not in a million years.

"How come you don't fish, Teacher Caroline?" Mary asked sometime later when they were eating their lunch.

Ben listened, eager to hear Caroline's response. She had just taken a bite of sandwich and chewed, then swallowed before answering.

"I used to fish, when I was younger. In fact, I'd go with your *mamm* and *daed* and we'd have a nice picnic lunch just like we're eating today," she said.

"You did?" Seth's forehead furrowed in a disbelieving frown.

She nodded. "*Ja*, remember your *mudder* is my first

cousin once removed and I've known both your *eldre* all my life. Your *mamm* was five years older than I am but we grew up together back when I lived in Ohio. Because I was younger, she always looked after me like a big sister."

"Really?" Mary asked.

Caroline nodded and Ben liked the sweet way she spoke to the children.

"Really. My grandmother and your *mamm's* mother were sisters. So you see? We really are *familye*. And I have lots of memories of your *eldre*."

"What memories?" Seth asked.

Caroline smoothed her black skirt for a moment, as if she were thinking back to the days when she'd been young.

"I remember going to church with your *mamm*. She made the best apple strudel I've ever eaten. Because my *mudder* died when I was sixteen, Anna came to stay at my *vadder's* house for a few weeks, to cook and clean and help take care of my younger *bruder* and *schweschder*. She was so sweet and made me feel like everything was going to be all right. Now I hope I can repay the favor by helping you feel happy and realize that you're both going to be okay."

She hugged Mary, and the girl snuggled against her side, accepting her words without reservation. But Seth gazed at her, his expression one of deep thought.

"Can you tell us about our *vadder*?" Mary asked.

"Of course. I always looked up to James. He was seven years older than I am, and I thought he was so strong and handsome. All the girls in the *Gmay* were crazy about him, but he only had eyes for your *mudder*. He would pick wildflowers for Anna, and all the other boys would tease him about it. But he didn't care one bit," Caroline said.

"*Ja*, our *daed* loved our *mamm*," Mary said, nodding.

"He sure did, and your *mamm* adored your *vadder*. Your *mamm* taught me how to crochet," Caroline said.

"She did?" Mary asked with awe.

Caroline nodded. "She was much better at it than I am. Her stitches were so small and even. And your *vadder* was always the fastest boy on the playground. No one could beat him in a footrace. But he was kind, too. I remember once one of the other *kinder* came to school without their lunch, and he shared his with them without even being asked."

Ben listened as Caroline related story after story about the children's parents. The kids seemed enthralled as they absorbed every word. Likewise, Ben enjoyed hearing about Caroline's childhood. Finally, when it was time to go home, they packed up the wicker basket, the fishing poles and fish, and loaded them into the buggy. It was late afternoon and they'd had a marvelous day. Ben was sad to see it end.

As the horse trotted down the county road, the comfortable swaying of the buggy soon lulled the two children to sleep. With them in the back and Caroline sitting next to him in the front, Ben got a sense of peace he hadn't felt in a long time. It was as if this was how it should be. All of them together like one happy *familye*. But he had to remind himself that these weren't his kids and Caroline wasn't his wife. And from what she'd told him, she never would be.

"They had a *gut* day." Caroline spoke softly enough that she didn't awaken the kids.

"*Ja*, I did, too. *Danke* for this outing," he said, unable to remember enjoying a better time in his life.

"Do you think it will help with Seth's fighting at school?" she asked.

He shrugged. "Who knows? It couldn't hurt. But no matter what, we've created some happy memories for the two kids."

She smiled, her expression soft and easy. And once again, he thought he'd never seen a more beautiful woman in all his life.

"You seemed to know just what to say and how to help the kids today," she said.

"And you also. Telling the *kinder* so many stories about their *eldre* was just what they needed. I'm sure it helped them feel closer to their *mamm* and *daed*. And I'm sure it helped them feel closer to you, too."

She looked down at her hands, which were folded in her lap. "I hope so. Have you had the opportunity to speak with Seth about fighting yet?"

"*Ja*, I reminded him that his *vadder* is counting on him to be a *gut* boy and watch out for his little sister. That's what I talked to him about while we were fishing. I encouraged him not to let his *daed* down by fighting. I told him I knew firsthand how bad it could be, but I didn't lay it on too thick. I didn't want to spoil the day with such a heavy topic. But I'll address the issue again as time goes on," he said.

"You're wise. I doubt this problem will be fixed with just one outing. It'll take a bit of time," she said.

"*Ja*, it may take a lifetime of love and support. But we can provide it. As long as we don't give up on these two *kinder*, they'll know we're always here for them and they'll both come around soon enough."

"I agree. They need consistency and love. That's all any of us needs," she said.

He nodded, wishing they could be so much more than friends. But deep in his heart, he knew he must not expect anything else. Because he could never meet her expectations.

"What do you suppose will happen to the Harlin place now that James and Anna aren't here to buy it?" she asked.

He shrugged. "It'll sit empty, I suppose. And one day, years from now, some *familye* will buy the land and make a go of it."

He wished he could buy the place. It bordered the property he'd recently bought from his uncle, so it would be perfect for him. With the added acreage, he would have plenty of land to farm. He could raise hay and livestock to sell. And the house and barn were already built. All he would have to do was tidy up the house, move in and go to work. But what good would it do for him to live in a big old farmhouse by himself? A place like that needed a wife and children to make it complete. He couldn't stand the thought of moving in and becoming an old Amish bachelor there. That kind of loneliness would break his heart.

They didn't speak much after that. No doubt they were both lost in their own thoughts and regrets. And just like Seth, Ben was determined to hold on to his good memories. To be a credit to his mother and father. Because once Caroline no longer needed his help at the school, he would need his sweet memories of her to sustain him through the long, lonely days to come.

Chapter Ten

A week later Caroline stood outside in the schoolyard and gazed at the white flower boxes Ben had installed beneath each windowsill. It was the first of November, and the weather had caused a distinct chill in the air, even though the afternoon sun gleamed bright against the autumn leaves and the slight breeze made the flowers tremble slightly. Because the boxes were tucked close to the schoolhouse, the pansies had clung to the warmth and remained bright and colorful. But Caroline knew a killing frost would soon end that.

Turning, she gazed at the children as they played a game of baseball. Their happy chatter and laughter filled the air. Recess didn't last long, and they were eager to make the best of it. They'd gobbled down their lunches, then picked up where they'd left off the last time they played. They didn't pick sides but simply rotated positions and ensured everyone had a turn at batting. It was so pleasant to see Seth getting along well with Caleb Yoder. Maybe they were through the worst of it, and Seth was beginning to adjust to his new life.

Though they never kept score, the kids were highly

competitive and did their best. Just now, the bases were loaded as little Leron Albrecht came up to bat. Though the boy was merely five years old, his solid stance and intense expression told Caroline that he was determined to hit the ball and bring the runners home.

But where were Mary and Seth?

Leaning heavily on her cane, Caroline turned, her gaze scanning the schoolyard. Walking toward the baseball diamond, she noticed Ben was missing, too. Normally, he stood on the sidelines, yelling encouragement to the batter or correcting their stance. But he wasn't there today.

Several nights ago Aunt Hannah had presented her with a thin, wooden cane. Caroline had been more than happy to cast aside the elbow crutch. She'd been a bit wobbly at first. But now she could move more easily on her own and hadn't fallen in over a week. Soon she planned to get rid of the cane, too.

She turned and scanned the area for some sign of the missing man and children. She saw them, sitting near the embankment where Cherry Creek ran through the middle of Bishop Yoder's property. Ben sat on a tree stump with little Mary on his knee. She had her arm draped around the big man's shoulders. Seth stood beside them holding a stick and was scraping the pointed end against the ground.

She could tell Ben was speaking. Now and then, Seth would nod in acquiescence. Both children seemed to be listening intently, and Caroline wished she could overhear their conversation. It appeared that Ben was keeping his word and continuing to work with Seth. He was showing an increase of love for both kids and helping them realize they weren't alone. During school time and each night at home, Caroline tried to do the same.

Huddled together with their backs to Caroline, the three of them looked so lost and isolated from the other children. They each seemed adrift in a world they didn't know how to navigate. And a feeling of deep sorrow swept over Caroline. She understood all too well how they must feel. She wished she could make the children happy. How she longed to ease their loss—and more than anything to be their mom.

"Teacher Caroline! *Komm* and play with us."

Annie Beiler waved at her from the outfield. The kids had noticed she was getting around better, though she still didn't think she was up to hitting the ball and running the bases.

She smiled, waved and headed their way, but not before she saw that Ben and the two orphans had ended their discussion and were headed in her direction. Caroline waited for Ben to join her. Mary took up a position with Alice at third base while Seth went to replace Timmy Hostetler as catcher so Timmy could have a chance to bat.

"Are you going to play?" Ben asked.

Standing beside her, he slid his thumbs through his black suspenders. He'd removed his black felt hat when he'd been installing the rope to the new tether ball pole. Sunlight shimmered against his dark hair, and his eyes gleamed with merriment.

"*Ne*, I'm not up to it yet. But now that I'm using just this cane to walk, I feel more and more like my old self," she said.

He flashed a smile that crinkled his eyes. "*Ja*, you're getting around quite well. I've finished putting together all the new playground equipment. Soon, you won't need my help here at the school anymore."

She looked away, thinking how she'd become so used to his presence that she would miss him when he was gone. Of course, she wasn't going to admit that out loud. But over the past few weeks, her heart had softened toward Ben, and she realized he was a good friend and she'd come to like him very much. But knowing she could never give him children made her more resolved than ever to remain detached.

She took a step toward the schoolhouse, thinking it was almost time to ring the bell and call the children back to the classroom for lessons.

"I noticed you were talking to Mary and Seth," she said.

"*Ja*, they asked me if they'd ever see their *mudder* and *vadder* again."

She hesitated and glanced at his face. "And what did you tell them?"

"I told them *ja*, they would see their *eldre* again in heaven." He nodded with finality, as if that settled the matter.

"And what about Seth's fighting? Did that topic come up again?" More than anything, she hoped Seth's anger might dissipate and he'd be less confrontational with the other children.

"*Ja*, I told him of some calming techniques I use whenever I feel angry, sad or upset."

She continued to walk slowly toward the school. "And may I ask what those techniques are?"

He stopped and faced her. As she looked up into his eyes, she was surprised by his quiet expression. At that moment he showed no guile whatsoever. Just a kind thoughtfulness that touched her heart.

"I think of something that makes me happy. Something that brings me joy. I think about the future and all my hopes and dreams for what is yet to come, and it makes me feel better," he said.

She blinked, wondering what those happy things might be. Perhaps a wife and *familye* of his own? And working his farmland to build a future for them? She longed to ask but thought it was too personal to pry.

"And did Seth know of something that makes him happy?" she asked instead.

Ben inclined his head. "*Ja*, he thinks of fishing. His heart is still filled with hurt but I think he's getting better. I suggested a few other things, and both he and Mary realized they have a lot to be thankful for."

Hmm. Caroline had never thought about doing that before. Her mind scanned the myriad blessings in her life. People and things that brought her great joy. And she was startled to realize that Ben was one of those people who made her feel happy inside.

"*Danke* for speaking with Seth and Mary today. I'm sure it will make a difference for them," she said.

A loud cheer came from the baseball diamond. Leron had gotten a hit, and the shortstop made a pretense of dropping the ball so the little boy could make it to first base. Caroline laughed as everyone whooped and congratulated Leron. And she realized one of the things that made her happy was these children. Their goodness and kindness to one another.

"*Ach!* I better get inside and ring the school bell. I think we're way overdue to resume our lessons," she said.

Ben nodded. "You go ahead and take the *kinder* inside. Since you're short on time, I'll clean up the baseball equipment for them today."

"Danke," she called over her shoulder as she hurried toward the front steps.

As she picked up the heavy hand bell and rang it several times, she watched Ben's long stride as he hurried over to the home plate. The kids came running, and he waved some of them on when they tried to pick up the two bats and ball.

Once the last child hurried through the door, she stepped inside. It was Seth, his face flushed from running. He hung back from the other children, but she noticed his eyes didn't seem as sullen and angry today. In fact, his shoulders were no longer tensed, either. Maybe Ben's words to the boy were having an impact. She sure hoped so.

As she went inside and closed the door, she couldn't help thinking what a difference Ben had made in her own life. He'd become a confidant of sorts. Someone she could confide in and ask for advice. He'd taken a lot of physical burdens off her shoulders, too. His kindness and generosity had made it possible for her to teach the children this year. But soon, he'd be gone. Because he was part of her *Gmay*, she would see him regularly at church and other gatherings, but it wouldn't be the same. And she knew, when he stopped coming to the schoolhouse, she was definitely going to miss his presence and their daily chats.

On the ride home that afternoon, Ben waited for Caroline to speak. Other than to discuss Seth and Mary, she'd never talked much to him, but she was even more quiet than usual. He wondered what was on her mind. Perhaps she was thinking about Seth and Mary or another student who was having trouble with their studies. He knew she loved each of the scholars and fretted over how to help them. Each one was unique, with their individual strengths and weaknesses. Her care reminded Ben that *Gott* must feel the same about His children.

"I think Seth has made a lot of progress just over the past few weeks since he came to live here," he said.

Caroline jerked, as if his voice had startled her out of her musings.

"*Ja*, he's at least trying to do his schoolwork now. I was worried that first week after they arrived. All he would do was stare off into space. He wouldn't even make an effort," she said.

As they skirted the dirt road, Ben gazed at the thick stand of shrub oaks lining the bishop's outer field. Higher up in the Wet Mountains, he could see tall stands of aspen shimmering in the sunshine. The fall weather had brought cooler temperatures at night and the leaves had fallen, revealing the barren, jagged branches of tree limbs.

They rode in silence for a short time. A gust of chilly wind buffeted the buggy. Caroline shivered and he reached back for the blanket he kept on the backseat and handed it to her.

"*Danke,*" she said as she spread the warm folds over her legs.

He glanced at her cane. "That must give you a lot more freedom."

"It does. I'll soon be walking on my own."

"I'm glad," he said.

She smiled with satisfaction, and he was truly happy for her. It had been a long, grueling recovery. At one point no one believed she'd ever walk again. But with her determination and tenacity, she'd beaten the odds. And though *Hochmut*, the pride of men, was something his people shunned, Ben couldn't help feeling proud of her accomplishment. But he didn't tell Caroline that. Nor did he tell her that, when he was feeling down, he thought about her to make him happy again.

The blare of a horn startled him and he looked into his rearview mirror. A black pickup truck had pulled up right behind them, hugging their rear bumper way too close. Ben knew exactly who the driver was.

Rand Henbury.

Caroline gasped and pressed a hand against the wall of the buggy as she swiveled around in her seat to get a better look. When she saw who it was, she made a small sound of anguish in the back of her throat. Her face drained of color, her eyes opening wide.

"Oh, *ne!*" she cried.

Ben slowed the horse, pulling him over to the shoulder of the road to give Rand plenty of room to pass. But the truck stayed right on their tail. Rand blared his horn again and again. In confusion, the horse jerked sporadically, showing his distress.

"Can you pull all the way off and let him pass?" Caroline begged.

Ben did just that, pulling off onto a dirt road. To keep from appearing confrontational, he waited to get out of the buggy, hoping Rand would zip on by. Raising his arm in a crude gesture, that was exactly what Rand did. Ben got out and soothed the agitated horse. And when he got back inside, he had to do the same for Caroline. She didn't speak, but he could see from her frightened expression that she was absolutely terrified.

He touched her arm. "It's *allrecht*, Caroline. He's gone now. You don't need to be afraid."

She breathed in short, panicked gasps as she met his

gaze. "I… I guess now is a *gut* time for me to think of something that makes me happy."

He chuckled. "*Ja*, I suppose all of us can use that technique when we're upset."

She showed a tentative smile and he knew she was trying her best to regain control. He squeezed her arm to let her know he was here and that everything would be okay. She turned away and he removed his hand. Not knowing what else to do, he gave her a moment to calm herself.

Staring out the window, she spoke in an aching whisper, so soft that he almost didn't hear. "I wish Rand wouldn't do that. It…it reminds me of the day of the accident when…when that drunk driver hit my buggy from behind. It's like I'm reliving it all over again."

Ah, now he understood. And he should have realized how something like that could upset her. Seth and Mary weren't the only ones who had suffered a bad trauma in their lives.

"No matter what Rand does, I won't let him or anyone else hurt you. Not ever," Ben vowed.

She faced him, her gaze locked with his. "Would you fight with him, Ben? Would you push him away, too?"

Her words were so startling that all he could do was stare at her. He had no answer. In his heart, he told himself that he wouldn't fight back. Never again. But if Rand did something to hurt Caroline, what would he do? He couldn't stand to see her injured again. Would he use force to stop Rand or someone else from harming her? He wasn't sure.

"Caroline, I…"

Her lips were slightly parted and her breath had slowed. More than anything, he wanted to keep her safe. To win her trust. And before he knew what was happening, he leaned his head down and kissed her. Softly. Like the gentle caress of butterfly wings.

She didn't resist but pressed the palm of her hand lightly against his chest. In his arms, she felt warm and sweet, and her fragrance spiraled around him in a mist that he longed to become lost in. Then she pulled away and he let her go.

"I… I really need to go home," she said, her voice wobbling as she pressed her fingertips against her lips.

"Of course." He took the lead lines into his hands and urged the horse to turn around.

Why had he kissed her? What had he been thinking? And what would her aunt and uncle say if they found out? What would the bishop think? No doubt they'd all be pleased. But he knew that marrying this woman would mean he could never have the children he longed for. He could never have a *familye*. And he had to ask himself, if Caroline had no reservations about being his wife, would he still want her?

The answer was a resounding yes!

However, it didn't matter because Caroline had made it perfectly clear that she wasn't interested in him. And he had to accept that.

He glanced over at Caroline and noticed she sat stiffly in her seat, her spine straight, her shoulders set in a solid block that reminded him she wanted nothing to do with him. Caroline was so wonderful and good. She deserved so much more than a man like him.

They didn't speak the rest of the way to the turnoff leading to her aunt and uncle's farm. The buggy rattled as it moved along the dirt road. Ben's mind whirled with turmoil. He longed to say something that might ease his guilty conscience. Something to let her know he meant her no harm. To apologize for kissing her. But he realized he wasn't sorry. It might be the first and last time he ever got to hold her that close, and he wanted to cherish the moment, not regret it.

He pulled up in front of her house and hurried to climb out. Fearing she might go inside before he could apologize, he took her arm to help her down. She quickly pulled away, as if his fingers had burned her skin.

"Caroline, I'm sorry. I didn't mean to frighten you. I didn't mean to take advantage, either," he said.

Standing on her own feet, she gripped her cane and looked up into his eyes. "I know. I didn't mean anything by it, either. And there's no need to apologize. We're both grown adults. But I meant what I said when you were first assigned to help me at the school. There can never be anything between us, Ben. Not ever. And I don't want to mislead you into thinking that has changed. So how about if we just forget it ever happened. Okay?"

She gave him a wan smile before stepping away. He stood there and watched her limp up the cobbled walk path leading to her uncle's back porch. The click of her cane striking the stones filled his mind, and he longed to go after her. Longed to deny what she'd just said. He'd kissed her, but he was a man and she was a woman and they could make their own choices now. But how could he ever forget her? How could he return to normal life again?

She disappeared inside, closing the door firmly behind her. She didn't look back. She didn't even peer out the window at him. He knew because he stood there and watched to see if she would.

He walked around to the driver's seat of his buggy. The conveyance rocked slightly as he climbed inside. Urging the horse forward, he pulled out of the graveled driveway, his mind filled with thoughts of Caroline. He'd killed a man, and no good woman would ever want him now. But Caroline wasn't just anyone. She was the only woman he'd ever seriously considered making his own. No other woman could take her place. Not in his heart. Nothing had changed for him. He could never marry. Never know the joys of having a *familye* of his own. Never feel the confidence of holding a woman's undying devotion and love. And though he thought he had accepted it and gotten on with his life, he realized it still hurt more than he could stand.

Chapter Eleven

Caroline stepped up onto the wooden boardwalk and turned to face the general store. It had been a week since Ben had kissed her. Or she'd kissed him. Or both. She wasn't sure anymore. She only knew it should never have happened. Because now she was haunted by the memory.

"I shouldn't be very long. I just need a few school supplies, and my *aent* Hannah asked me to also pick up some sour cream and a couple other groceries," she said.

Ben stood beside her, having just driven her into town and accompanied her safely to the front door of the grocery store. She'd told her uncle that morning that she could drive herself into town, but he wouldn't hear of it. Not with Rand Henbury on the loose. And even though she was now walking without even the help of her cane, the bishop had told her he wouldn't release Ben from his assignment of assisting her and the school until after the Thanksgiving holiday in two more weeks.

"I'll just pop into the building supply store for a few minutes and be right back to pick you up," Ben said.

He turned and hopped off the boardwalk with athletic agility before climbing into the buggy. She watched as he pulled away, heading down Main Street. The drive into town had been rather wooden and formal. Even their discussions about Seth and Mary were a bit stilted. After the kiss they'd shared, she felt embarrassed and didn't know what to say to him anymore. For those few short moments, she'd forgotten herself. Forgotten that she'd lost her ability to have children and shouldn't encourage any man's attention. Especially a man like Ben Yoder, who longed for a *familye* of his own and had suffered enough pain to last a lifetime. He deserved more than she could ever give him.

Heaving a sigh of frustration, she turned and went inside the store. It would do no good to feel sorry for herself, and she was determined to get on with her life.

Within minutes she'd purchased two special slide rulers and a box of chalk, as well as the food items her aunt needed. Placing them inside the wicker basket she was carrying, she stepped outside. A chilling breeze whipped past and she shivered, pulling her black woolen cape tighter around her throat. The sky was filled with leaden clouds, and the first snow of the season was forecasted for tonight. But she'd be home safe long before then. The fall harvest was secure. Over the past couple of weeks, even Ben had been hurrying home after dropping her off from school to help his uncle with the heavy workload. Her uncle and the other men of the *Gmay* had gathered up their hay just in time. Winter was upon them.

She glanced up and down the street but caught no sign of Ben or his black buggy. Deciding that she could use the exercise, she headed along the sidewalks toward the building supply store. As she moved along, she took special delight that she walked without the aid of any devices whatsoever. Her legs and hips were strong again, and she felt so happy and free.

Turning the corner, she bumped into someone and immediately drew back.

"Excuse me," she murmured.

Conditioned to stay as far away from *Englischers* as possible, she ducked her head and moved aside. But she stole a quick glance at the young man. Within a matter of seconds, a hard lump formed in her throat and she went all cold and clammy inside.

"Well, lookie who we have here. Our little cripple Amish girl. Where are your crutches, Amish girl?" Rand Henbury stood in the middle of the sidewalk, a snide grin on his face.

She tried to brush past him but he blocked her path. A feeling of absolute panic swept over her with the force of a hurricane, but she fought it off. She was a mature woman and had no reason to cower before this man. Rand was just a big bully, and she mustn't let him intimidate her.

Drawing herself up straight, she looked him square in the eyes.

"Excuse me, please," she said, trying once more to get by him.

"What have you got in there?" he asked, tugging on her wicker basket.

She pulled it away from him. "I beg your pardon but that is none of your business."

He laughed. "Woo-hoo! You beg my pardon? It looks like you've got a little extra spice in you for an Amish girl."

He'd backed her up against the outside wall to the feed

and grain store and reached out to tug on the ties to her black traveling bonnet.

"Please, let me go," she begged.

"What's your hurry, little Amish girl?" He leaned close and planted an arm against the wall beside her head.

Feeling boxed in, she cringed and turned her face away. Tears of frustration and fear burned the backs of her eyes. A sensation of absolute helplessness caused her arms and legs to tremble. If he didn't let her go soon, she was going to lose it. And she didn't want to crumble at his feet or show any other weakness before this man. But neither would she use force to get away from him.

"Let her go."

A low voice came from behind Rand, like the rumbling of thunder off in the distance.

Rand turned and Caroline saw Ben standing there, his expression severe. He towered over the *Englisch* man like a great hulking giant. He looked strong and stern, like a man who knew how to handle himself.

"What's it to you, Amish man?" Rand sneered.

Without a word, Ben reached around and clasped Caroline's wrist before pulling her behind him in a protective gesture.

"The buggy is parked in the back. Go on," Ben ordered her.

A feeling of outrage bubbled up inside Caroline. Who did Ben think he was, bossing her around like she belonged to him? Yes, her religion taught her to obey the men in her life, but Ben wasn't her husband. He wasn't even a relative.

And for that matter, who did Rand Henbury think he was? Blocking her path and taunting her? She wanted to yell and scream at both men to leave her alone. But she sensed that now was not the time for such actions.

"Come with me. You must not fight," she spoke to Ben in *Deitsch*, knowing Rand wouldn't be able to understand her words.

"I'll be along shortly, once I know you're safe," Ben said, never once taking his eyes off Rand.

Rand tilted his head. "What's that silly gibberish you're using? What are you saying?"

Neither Caroline nor Ben answered him. She'd heard that Rand was about eighteen years old and had just graduated from high school last spring. She had hoped he would leave town to go to college, yet he'd stayed. But it didn't seem that he spent his time working on his rich father's ranch, either. She couldn't help thinking he was wasting his life.

Rand stepped forward, lifting his chin as he glared at Ben. "I heard you killed a man back east somewhere. Is that true, Amish man?"

Ben didn't respond, but Caroline saw his hands clench. His eyes narrowed and his expression looked so fierce that she feared he might strike Rand.

"Come on, Ben. Please! Leave him." She tugged on his arm, desperate to get him out of there—as desperate to protect him from using violence as he was to protect her from Rand's harassment.

He shook her off, pushing her toward the buggy. "I'll be along shortly. Go on, now."

Feeling completely exasperated by the situation, she heaved a sigh and hurried away. In the back parking lot behind the building supply store, there was a covered canopy and hitching post with a sign that read Buggy Parking Only. Ben's buggy was the only one there, and she climbed inside and closed the door. Huddling on the front seat, she gazed out the window and wished Ben would come soon.

She thought he'd changed. Since he'd been helping her at the school and she'd gotten to know him well, she thought he'd gotten over his anger issues and was passive in the face of oppression. But now she wasn't so sure. If he started fighting, he might get hurt. Or worse. He might hurt or even kill Rand Henbury. She'd thought Ben had been truly repentant and had a humble heart. Yet, she feared she was dead wrong about him. Because what she'd seen today told her that Ben still had a lot of anger simmering just below the surface.

Ben wasn't a young seventeen-year-old boy anymore. Now he was a fully grown man who had been baptized into their Amish faith. And Rand's father had a lot of wealth. If Ben used force against Rand, she feared the consequences. He'd be shunned by their people. Because it would be a second offense, he could even be turned out of the *Gmay* for good. He could end up in jail. She'd never get to see him again. Never be able to talk with him or enjoy his comforting presence in her life. And that frightened her most of all.

Ben waited until Caroline disappeared around the corner to the Amish buggy parking lot. He stood like a mountain, keeping Rand from following after her. He didn't know what he would do if Rand tried to get past him, and he prayed the *Englischer* used more common sense than to try to chase after her.

"Ah, what's the matter, Amish man? You're not scared of little old me, are you?" Rand heckled him.

Ben almost snorted. He knew what he was capable of.

If it was a matter of sheer strength, he could have picked Rand up and tossed him into the street with very little effort at all. But no matter what, he must not use force. He must remain passive. Because Caroline was counting on him and he couldn't let her down. But he felt a rage rising up inside him that made him want to pound Rand into a pulp.

That's not what Gott or Caroline would want me to do.

The thought entered his mind like a soft whisper. So quiet and gentle that he almost ignored it. And yet, he couldn't.

Ever since he'd kissed her, Caroline had been giving him the cold shoulder. She'd been kind and understanding when he'd told her about his past, but she didn't want to get tied up with a man like him. He couldn't let her down. Couldn't disappoint her by fighting. Nor did he want Seth to hear that he'd reverted to his old ways. He'd told the boy about his past, and Seth understood how badly he regretted it. What message would it send if Ben started fighting again? Not a good one, that was for sure.

And just like that, Ben let go of his anger. His clenched hands relaxed and his tensed shoulders eased. He didn't want to fight anymore. He wanted forgiveness. To go on with his life in joy and happiness.

As he gazed at Rand Henbury, a gentle peace enveloped him. Instead of seeing Rand as a threat, he saw him as a misguided boy who was insecure in himself and felt like he had to bully other people to boost his own self-esteem. With added insight, Ben thought maybe Rand's actions were a cry for attention from his own father. But Ben knew there was nothing he must face in this life that couldn't be reconciled through the forgiveness of Jesus Christ. He didn't have to fight. Not now, not ever again.

Two of Rand's friends stepped out of the café across the street. When they saw what was happening, they came running. Like wolves scenting blood, they surrounded Ben, their faces contorted in angry sneers.

"What's going on?" one of them asked Rand.

"Ah, this Amish man thinks he's a tough guy," Rand said mockingly. Then, emboldened by the presence of his friends, he shoved Ben back against the railing. "You're not so tough, are you, Amish man? You're big but you're a pacifist. You can't fight back, can you? You're a coward."

A coward. No, Ben wasn't a coward at all. Because in that moment he knew what was coming and he was prepared to take the beating no matter what. Even if it cost him his life, he was determined not to fight back in the slightest. And Caroline and Seth would both know that he'd kept his faith. Nothing else mattered right now.

"Hey! What do you boys think you're doing?"

Byron Stott, the owner of the building supply store, stepped out onto the sidewalk. Wearing a dingy carpenter's apron, he gripped a hammer in his hand.

"Don't you interfere, Byron. This has nothing to do with you," Rand said, pointing a warning finger at the older man.

"Ben's done nothing to you. You leave him alone." Byron lifted the hammer in warning as he stepped closer.

"That's right. I've already called the police and they're on their way." Berta Maupin, the owner of the general store, stepped around the corner carrying a long-handled broom. "You boys had better skedaddle before they get here or you're gonna wish you had. The Amish are peaceful and we're not letting you harass Ben."

Seeing the commotion, Cliff Packer came out of the post office and jogged over to them. Several other *En-*

glisch people Ben didn't know stopped as they walked by. He hated to draw a big crowd and was desperate to escape this situation.

"You go on, Ben. Get in your buggy and go on home. I know you can't fight, but we can. We'll hold Rand here until you can get a good head start," Byron said.

Ben stared at them all, feeling dumbstruck. The townsfolk were *Englisch*, but they were protecting him. He could hardly believe this was happening.

And then a thought struck him. *Gott* had provided him with an escape. He had sent some guardians here to protect him so he wouldn't suffer a beating or break the vows of his faith by using force.

Taking this unexpected gift at face value, Ben turned and sauntered away. He didn't need to be told twice.

When he reached the buggy and opened the door to the driver's seat, Caroline jerked and whirled on him, her eyes filled with fear and tears.

Ah, did she have to cry? He hated that more than anything.

"Are you…are you okay?" she asked, her voice trembling.

"I'm fine."

Taking the lead lines into his hands, he directed the horse onto the road and hurried the animal into a fast trot out of town. He figured he had only minutes before Rand got away from the townsfolk and came after them in his black pickup truck.

"Did you…did you fight with Rand?" Caroline asked.

"*Ne*, I did not."

He didn't look at her, intent on getting her home now while he had the chance. There was safety in numbers, and he'd be sure to bring another man with him next time he came into town. The abuse from Rand and his cronies was escalating, and he didn't dare come alone from now on. Not if it meant Caroline might be hurt.

"I could see the anger in you. You still haven't overcome your violent tendencies," she said, her voice filled with accusation.

What could he say to that?

"I didn't hit him," he said.

"But you wanted to."

"I did, I won't deny it. At first. But I know *Gott* wouldn't approve. And neither would you. Being obedient to *Gott's* will doesn't always mean that we want to obey, but that we hand our will over to Him."

She nodded. "True, but obedience also requires that *Gott's* will becomes our own. And I don't think that's how you feel when it comes to anger."

Hmm, maybe she was right. But maybe it wasn't that simple, either.

"I have let go of my anger," he said. "I don't want to fight anymore, Caroline. I'd rather die first. And I was prepared to do just that today, if it meant you could leave and be safe."

Her mouth dropped open in surprise. But he meant what he'd said. Every single word. And he realized that, whether she believed in him or not, he believed in himself. He trusted *Gott*. And with the Lord beside him, he was never alone. Not even in his darkest moments. And knowing that, he realized *Gott* had forgiven him for what he'd done. Ben hadn't meant to kill anyone all those years earlier. He'd just been trying to get away from a crowd of thugs who wanted to beat him up. And in so doing, he'd caused one of their deaths. But now he wanted to go on living. To be happy and useful to others.

He wanted Caroline.

They were quiet for some time after that, with each of them lost in their own thoughts. And finally, Ben got the courage to ask Caroline a question that had been troubling him for months now.

"My *onkel* Amos told me that, after your buggy accident, you can't have children anymore. Is that true?" he asked.

Her head snapped around and she blinked at him with absolute shock. Then she turned and stared straight ahead. Her spine was ramrod straight, her delicate hands folded tightly in her lap. Ah, maybe he shouldn't have asked. It wasn't his business and he knew it must be a painful topic for her to dwell upon. In that moment she looked so sad and vulnerable. So very alone. And a fierce emotion rose upward inside him. The desire to protect and keep her safe forevermore.

At first, he thought she wouldn't respond. Then she spoke in an aching whisper as she confirmed what he'd been told.

"*Ja*, it is true. I cannot have children," she said.

His heart gave a powerful squeeze. How he wished he could take away her pain. He wished he hadn't dredged it all up again. Yet, he felt compelled to ask.

"I know it must upset you terribly, but the Lord has a way of providing for all our needs. You must not give up hope," he said.

She snorted. "I don't see how the Lord can provide me with kids."

"I don't, either, but I do know *Gott* has never let me down. I thought He had, but I was wrong. I hope you'll give Him a chance to work wonders in your life," he said.

She frowned and glanced at him but didn't respond.

They were friends and had a sort of bond between them, but he'd pushed her too far today. Way too far.

"I'm sorry for frightening you. The last thing I wanted to do was cause you any distress," he said.

"Danke," she said, her voice sounding small.

"Caroline, I… I'd like us to be more than friends," he said.

"What do you mean?" she asked.

"I… I have romantic feelings for you," he said.

"Ne! Don't say that."

"I mean it, Caroline. I have deep feelings for you and I'd like to court you with the intention of marriage." There. He'd finally said what was in his heart. Now it was in her hands.

"That isn't possible. I don't want to marry you. Not ever," she said with such finality.

"I know you're afraid, but I think we could…"

She shook her head. "I said *ne*."

"May I ask why?"

"I… I don't want to be married without knowing I can have *kinder*. Maybe you can, but I can't," she said.

"But don't you think we could—"

She cut him off. "Please, let's drop it. Nothing is going to change, and I don't want to keep hashing it over."

Okay, he got it. Even though he'd made it clear her inability to have children didn't matter to him, it obviously still mattered to her and he had no idea how to convince her otherwise. He wished she could be happy with just him, but he couldn't blame her for wanting more.

They didn't speak the rest of the ride home. And when he helped her out of the buggy and watched her go inside her uncle's farmhouse, he breathed a sigh of relief. At least she was safe. For now. But what about tomorrow or next week? She'd have to drive back and forth to school every day and go into town on errands. How could he protect her from people like Rand Henbury? How could he ever ensure that she and the other people he loved were okay?

He couldn't! And though he'd been taught that whatever happened was *Gott's* will, he struggled to accept that. Because they each had freedom of choice. Even people like Rand could choose to do works of goodness or works of darkness. But it was Ben's job to have enough faith to accept whatever came his way. And that was easier said than done. But he now knew that, no matter what anger he might face in the future, he didn't need to fight back. He also knew that he longed for Caroline with all his heart, but she didn't feel the same. Now he prayed for the strength to accept that.

But he feared it might be the most difficult thing he'd ever had to do.

Chapter Twelve

Caroline shivered as she pulled her gray scarf tighter around her throat. Sitting in the buggy, she gripped the leather lead lines, her gloves doing very little to warm her frozen fingers. The early-morning air felt frigid, the sun barely peeking over the eastern hills. Ice crystals clung to spindly tree limbs lining the county road. The fields and mountains surrounding the valley were covered in pristine white for miles around. It had snowed in the night. Just two inches, but it was enough to make the roads slick with a sheet of ice, though not enough for her to cancel school.

It had been two days since she'd seen Ben and she missed him, she couldn't deny it. But it was for the best. Wasn't it?

She focused on the snowplow markers at the side of the road, keeping the horse even with the shoulder so he didn't pull them into the ditch. Though it had been dark and cold, she'd left the house early on purpose, before Ben had arrived to drive her to school. After his declaration of intent to court her, she'd decided it was time she became more independent. Time she drove the buggy and got herself around without help. But this was the first time she'd driven since her injury. On the one hand, it felt good to be by herself. The tug of the horse gave her a feeling of exhilaration and freedom. But on the other, it reminded her of how vulnerable she was and that bad things could happen when she least expected them.

Shaking off that morbid thought, she took a deep inhale and held it a moment before letting it go. She could see a puff of her breath on the chilly air. Her heavy woolen cloak was more than welcome today. She'd also folded a heavy quilt around her legs but still felt the cold emanating into the cab of the buggy.

She wondered what Ben and Bishop Yoder might say once they found out she'd driven herself today. And then, in spite of her desire not to, she marveled at how much she missed Ben's presence. She'd grown used to him always being by her side. He never talked much, but she realized with some surprise how comfortable she felt when she was around him. He made her feel safe and calm, which was just another reason for them to separate. She couldn't marry him. There was no use discussing it. And now that she could walk well on her own, it was time to let him go.

As she pulled into the schoolyard, the horse and wheels of the buggy dug deep trails in the unspoiled snow. She drove to the back before climbing out and stabling the animal in the small horse shed. Taking deep breaths, she slogged through the snow to the schoolhouse, grateful that she'd worn her black snow boots. She quickly swept off the front steps, then went inside and started a nice fire in the potbellied stove. She'd get the classroom toasty warm and everything ready for the children before she went outside to shovel the walk paths.

She'd just finished writing the day's lesson assignments on the blackboard when she heard the scrape of a shovel outside. Peering out the window, she saw Ben clearing the driveway. He was dressed in a heavy coat, the edge of a knit cap peeking out from beneath the rim of his black felt hat. Like her, he wore gloves and boots as he pushed the snow shovel easily to remove the layer of white from the stone walk paths.

Hmm. Even though she'd left without him this morning, he'd followed her here. She'd hoped he'd take the hint and leave her alone.

Still wearing her warm cloak, she stepped outside and wrapped her arms around herself. It was more a protective gesture than one of warmth. She wasn't sure what to say to him.

He paused in his work and leaned against the handle of the snow shovel. Looking up at her, he smiled, but it didn't quite reach his eyes. Without him saying one word, she knew he wasn't happy that she'd left without him that morning or that she'd rebuffed his offer of marriage.

"Guder mariye," she called, unable to infuse her voice with much cheer. After all, she didn't want to encourage him.

"Hallo, Caroline. You left without me this morning," he said.

She almost laughed, wondering how he always seemed to know exactly what she was thinking. His candor didn't surprise her at all. If she'd learned nothing else about this man during the weeks they'd been working together, it was that he was blunt and forthright and usually said what was on his mind.

"I really appreciate all that you've done for me, Ben," she said. "But I don't need your help anymore. I'm walking just fine on my own and can do these chores by myself. You should concentrate on your own work now."

There. That was good, wasn't it?

A flash of hurt filled his eyes and he looked away, gazing at the thin creek bed where crystals of ice coated every available surface. Maybe she'd been too direct and hurt his feelings, which wasn't what she wanted. Not after all he'd done for her.

"I'm afraid I can't do that, Caroline. The bishop hasn't released me from my assignment yet. And it'll make things much easier on you if I shovel the walkways. It'll give your legs time to really heal," he said, his voice soft and undemanding, yet holding a note of authority.

Everything he said was true. Although she was getting along nicely, all it would take was a little fall to undo weeks of improvement. And she realized she sounded ungrateful. After all, he'd made window boxes for her and put up all the new playground equipment and helped her with Seth and Mary. He'd definitely gone above and beyond the call of duty, and she appreciated it. She truly did. But they'd become too close. They'd confided things to each other that they'd told nobody else. And she'd come to realize that was dangerous to her heart. Because in spite of her will to remain aloof, she'd fallen for this man.

She hadn't realized it all at once, like a bolt of lightning. The knowledge had snuck up on her like a thief in the night. It had occurred to her last evening as she'd said her prayers and climbed into bed that she looked forward to seeing him today. And that was when she knew. She cared deeply for this big, gruff man, in spite of all that he'd done. But even if he truly had become a peace-loving pacifist, they could have no future together. Because she could never give him a child.

And even though he said that didn't matter, she knew in her heart that it did. Because she still wanted children. She wanted to be a mother and she wanted Ben to be a father. Becoming parents was ingrained in both of them since the day they were born. They had been raised to know they would someday be parents. And now that wasn't possible, she had no idea how to get past it or stop longing for it in her life. And even though Ben said he was okay with it, she feared he would come to resent her for it. Maybe not at first, but later in the future. He'd see other men's children and know what he was missing and she couldn't stand the thought that he might come to resent her. He deserved to find and marry another woman who could give him kids.

"You're right, of course," she said. "*Danke* for all your help. I appreciate you shoveling the snow. But once you're finished, you should go *heemet* and help the bishop with your chores there. I have no need for you to stay around here anymore."

A frown tugged at his forehead. "I will go after I've chopped some firewood, but I'll be back later this afternoon to ensure you get home safely."

She heaved a little huff of exasperation. He was being stubborn. Before she could argue the point, the rattle of another buggy coming into the yard drew their attention. In unison, they looked up.

Darrin Albrecht, the deacon of their congregation, waved as he pulled up in front of the schoolhouse. Six of his school-age children poured out of the buggy wearing a variety of boots, hats, scarves and gloves. The air was suddenly filled with laughter and the voices of children as they hurried inside the warm building. And Caroline was grateful for the distraction.

She focused her energy on the kids, ushering them inside and helping them doff their heavy winter clothing. She ignored Ben, forcing herself not to look back at him as she closed the door. She didn't want to talk to him anymore. Didn't want to feel close to him or depend on him or confide any more of her concerns and fears in him. It was time to pull back.

Because she cared for him, she must let him go. Because he deserved to marry a woman who could make him a father. And whether Ben and Bishop Yoder agreed with her or not, it was time for her to be on her own.

Ben watched as Caroline disappeared inside with the children. She didn't look back at him, though he couldn't help wishing she would. As he resumed his shoveling, it wasn't long before more children arrived. They all waved at him and he stopped to chat with each of their fathers. Funny how he'd become much better friends with all of them since Caroline had entered his life. Maybe it was because they saw him every day here at the school and were getting used to him. No doubt their children told them about his work here, too. Maybe they were finally starting to accept him.

Ben's uncle Amos and Mervin Schwartz pulled into the yard at the same time, followed by the Geingerich *familye*.

"*Guder mariye*, Ben," Mervin called.

Ben lifted a hand in greeting.

Normally, the older children drove their younger siblings or their mothers brought them to school. But today they all knew about Rand Henbury's escapades. Ben had reported everything to his uncle, and word had soon

spread. With the slick condition of the roads, the fathers
wanted to protect their children.

The kids hopped out of the conveyances and greeted
each other with eager waves. From his position near the
woodpile, Ben watched Seth and Mary with eagle eyes.
Mary wasn't much of an issue. She was sweet, young and
trusting, and the little girl was all smiles as she glommed
onto Rachel Geingerich. Their squealing laughter rang
through the air as they raced to the front door.

"Hi, Ben!" Seth waved at him.

"Hallo!" Ben returned. His heart lightened consid-
erably when Seth joined Sam King and Andrew Yoder.
Though the two other boys were a year older, Seth towered over them. They didn't seem to mind as he smiled
and went inside with them.

Whew! Just that small greeting meant everything to
Ben. It was such a vast improvement over Seth's previous actions that Ben realized they'd made great headway
in helping the boy overcome his anger and resentment
at the world.

Ben was surprised when his uncle Amos got out of
his buggy and walked over to him.

"I'm glad you're here to look after things at the
school," the bishop said.

Ben gazed at the path he'd created in the snow, noticing that the moisture was already starting to melt.

"Caroline doesn't want me here. She drove herself
today," Ben said.

The bishop's mouth tightened as he considered this.
"Ach, it doesn't matter. As long as you're here and she
and the *kinder* are safe, that's what's most important.
Because of that *Englisch* boy, the roads aren't safe anymore. Though I don't want to do it, I may need to pay a

visit to the sheriff in town. Maybe he can speak to the young man and his *vadder*."

Ben nodded, surprised that his uncle had confided in him. It was another sign of trust. The bishop had heard about the confrontation between Ben and Rand and knew that Ben had not fought back. And with a zap of delight, Ben couldn't help feeling for the first time like he truly belonged here.

"*Ach*, we'll be back to pick up the kids from school. You take care," Bishop Yoder said.

With a nod, he turned and walked away. Likewise, the other fathers pulled out of the yard to return home. Ben watched them go, feeling happy and sad at the same time. Happy because he really thought he could spend the rest of his life here in this *Gmay*. These were his people. But a feeling of despair overshadowed his joy because he had no one to share his life with. No home and *familye* of his own.

Caroline didn't want him.

If only she could accept him, they might have a chance at happiness together. No, she couldn't give him children, but marriage was more than that, wasn't it? Still, her actions that morning had spoken volumes. Even after all the time they'd spent together, she wanted nothing to do with him. When they'd been confronted with Rand Henbury in town the other day, she thought Ben was still prone to violence. That he was ready to fight. And knowing that he'd once killed a man, she wanted nothing to do with him. She wished he'd go away and leave her alone.

He had thought, with time, that Caroline would come to know and understand what was truly inside his heart. But now he could see that she didn't really need his help here at the school. At least, not all day long. He could go home and help his uncle with the many chores waiting for him there. He could even make plans and start to develop his own farmland. But he didn't know what he'd use it for. Why bother when he had no one to share it with and nothing to look forward to? He had friends in this *Gmay* now and knew he could marry one of their other young women. He owned land and could build a home and provide for a family. But he didn't want another woman. He wanted Caroline. No one else could ever satisfy his heart.

Lifting the ax, he took his frustration out on the woodpile by chopping enough kindling to last several days. Finally, he put the ax away in the shed so it wouldn't rust and made his way over to his horse and buggy. He'd leave and return later that afternoon, when it was time for Caroline to go home. Whether she wanted him here or not, he felt bound by the bishop's word and must ensure she arrived home safely that evening. He couldn't stand the thought that Rand Henbury might harm her and was determined to be here for her.

As he passed by the pretty window boxes he'd built for Caroline, he saw her inside. She stood in front of the chalkboard, holding an open book in her hands. She was speaking to the class, though he couldn't hear her words. She must have caught his movement because she turned her head and glanced at him. For several moments her eyes locked with his. Then she turned her back on him and walked to the other side of the classroom, where he couldn't see her anymore. She'd dismissed him like she would a recalcitrant scholar.

His heart gave a painful squeeze. After all these years, he'd begun to think he would never find someone he cared about enough to settle down with. But he'd been wrong. And he realized Caroline was special the moment he set eyes on her, long before the accident that nearly took her life. And because she was so special to him, he must let her go.

As soon as he got home, he'd talk to his uncle Amos about rescinding his assignment to accompany Caroline and tend to the needs of the school. Ben hated the thought of not seeing Caroline every day, but he also realized that seeing her all the time was making the pain even worse. It was like holding out a sumptuous banquet to a starving man and telling him he couldn't eat one single morsel.

Yes, it was time for Ben to go. He must leave her alone and let her live her own life, even if it was the hardest thing he'd ever faced.

Chapter Thirteen

That afternoon Caroline expected to harness her horse and buggy before driving herself home. But when she stepped outside after all the kids had left for the day, Ben had her buggy waiting and ready to go.

She shouldn't be surprised. If nothing else, she'd learned that Ben was quiet but strong-willed. He never forced his will on her, *per se*. She usually voiced her objection, he quietly listened and then he did whatever he wanted anyway.

Stepping out onto the top landing of the stairs, she glanced at him before making a pretense of tugging on her gloves and locking the front door. His own horse and buggy stood just behind hers, and she had no doubt he was going to follow her—all the way home.

The thought made her smile, and she realized how well she knew this man. But then she remembered her resolve to send him away and forced her lips into a stern frown.

"You don't need to wait for me anymore, Ben. I don't need you here. Please, go away," she said.

She ignored the flash of pain that filled his eyes and picked up her bookbag. She hated to hurt him but knew it was for the best. He must leave her alone. She was already mourning the thought of losing him and didn't want to make things worse.

Concentrating on her feet, she walked down the steps with little trouble. Though she could negotiate the stairs with ease, it was a habit to watch what she was doing. It felt so good to move freely. To feel steady and strong. Her heart delighted in how easy it was to walk without a cane, and she promised herself she would never take her legs and the ability to walk for granted again. *Gott* had been so good to her and yet, she wanted more. Much, much more. A loving husband and *familye* of her own. Children and a man to shower her love upon. But it was never to be, so she should accept it and move on. She must have faith that *Gott* had something else in store for her with the schoolchildren. It would be enough. It must be!

Ben didn't say a word as he opened the door and held out his arm to assist her in case she needed it. But she didn't touch him. Without another word, she moved past him and climbed inside before pulling the door closed with a final snap of the latch. Out of her peripheral vision, she saw Ben step back, looking a bit surprised. She ignored him, forcing herself to look straight ahead. Taking the lead lines in a practiced grip, she released the brake.

Just as school had let out for the day, it had started to snow again. Gigantic flakes of white floated through the air, turning the fields into a lovely, brisk winter wonderland. She figured she had just enough time to get home safely before it started coming down in earnest.

Without giving Ben time to get into his own buggy, she slapped the lines against the horse's back, and the buggy lurched forward. In her rearview mirror, she saw Ben scurrying to climb inside his own buggy and come after her. And she would have laughed out loud if it didn't make her so sad. In her heart of hearts, she wished he were sitting right beside her, listening as she chatted about the weather, the upcoming school Christmas program and how Mary and Seth were making so much great progress. Ben would undoubtedly give her that sidelong, mischievous look of his whenever she said something contrary or impertinent. How she wished she dared take his arm and hold on tight forever. But that couldn't be reality. Not for a woman like her.

As she pulled out of the schoolyard, she saw Ben's buggy following right behind. In spite of the questionable road conditions, he urged his horse into a fast trot to keep up. Knowing he was nearby provided her a bit of comfort, but her heart felt extra heavy today. She knew the bishop was planning to come over to her uncle's home later that evening to discuss using Mervin's little sawmill to cut timber for a new shed on his property. She was determined to confront both men and insist that she no longer needed a bodyguard. Somehow, she had to make them both understand. And yet, she did need Ben, if only to continue being her best friend in the whole wide world.

No! She mustn't think that way. It was time to plead her case and have Bishop Yoder rescind Ben's assignment to look after her and the school. Because, if she really acknowledged the truth, it was starting to break her heart. Having him near all the time and knowing they could never be more than friends was almost more than she could stand. It wasn't fair to Ben, either. After all, he had his own life to look forward to. His land needed clearing if he was going to start up his own farm. He'd need to build a house and barn and plant crops in the spring, which meant he might accompany the bishop to her home tonight to talk about using Uncle Mervin's saw-mill for his own needs.

The thought of seeing him again made her heart give a powerful leap. But she mustn't give in to the excitement. Nothing could ever come of it. There were a couple of pretty girls in their *Gmay* that Ben could ask out. At church this past Sunday, she had seen them eyeing him with interest. It seemed that, with the arrival of Mary and Seth, they'd heard about Ben's kindness to the kids and no longer feared him. He should marry one of them. But the thought of Ben paying court to someone else made Caroline jealous. She could hardly stand to think that she wouldn't be a part of his life anymore, but it was for the best. Because she loved him, she wanted him to be happy. She had to let him go.

The blaring of a horn startled her out of her thoughts. She jerked her head up and stared into the rearview mirror. Ben was right behind her. But as the road made a slight incline, she saw the outline of Rand Henbury's black pickup truck following too closely behind Ben's horse and buggy.

Oh, no! Not again! The guy was relentless.

That old feeling of absolute terror rose in her throat with the speed of a fist to the gut. Her hands trembled and she took a deep breath, trying to settle her nerves. But then something hardened inside her. What right did Rand Henbury, or any man, have to make her fearful? None whatsoever. Not if she didn't give them that power over her.

Caroline dug deep inside herself, determined not to be afraid anymore. The roads were damp and slick. The snow was no longer melting, but rather, sticking to the asphalt. With the shorter days of winter, the sun was quickly fading. Nightfall was coming on and the sky looked dark and foreboding. In the short time since she'd left the schoolhouse, the temperature had dropped and the roads were freezing with black ice. The horn blasted again and she fought to control her skittish horse.

Why wouldn't Rand just leave them alone? While he seemed to like hassling anyone he could, she feared she and Ben had become his main targets. No doubt Rand had noticed when and where they'd be traveling along the county roads each day, and he seemed to take particular delight in spooking her horse.

Looking up, Caroline saw that she was fast approaching the one-lane bridge that crossed over the Arkansas River. With the rainstorm they'd had over the past couple of days, the river was swollen and choppy. There was room enough on the narrow bridge for only one vehicle to cross at a time. The guardrails were rather thin, and it wasn't a place she wanted to be caught with Rand's speeding truck.

Deciding she'd rather be stuck all night in a snowdrift than risk being killed in another accident, she gripped the lead lines tighter and slowed her horse. Clicking her tongue, she pulled the animal over on the shoulder as far as she dared and hoped Rand would pass her by. She noticed Ben did the same, following her every movement as he pulled up close behind her. It seemed a protective gesture on his part, as if he were defending her. And though she was nervous and jittery right now, it gave her comfort to know he was there with her.

Rand didn't slow down. Not one bit. In fact, he speeded up, blasting his horn again as he veered into the other lane to pass them. As he zipped by, he rolled his window down about six inches and yelled obscenities at her. Caroline's ears burned with repulsion, and she realized he wasn't paying attention to his driving. Staring after him, she thought he must be insane. What was wrong with him? Driving like a lunatic on these dangerous roads. What had happened in his life to make him so careless?

Rand almost made the bridge, but his truck skidded on the black ice at the last moment. He lost control as his vehicle slid sideways and sideswiped the guardrail, sending his truck crashing into the icy river.

Caroline gasped and stared in horror as the truck quickly tipped upward and began to sink. It took only moments for it to go under, the water spinning around the truck like a whirlpool. The last thing Caroline saw before the vehicle was completely submerged was Rand's pale face frozen in shock and terror. And the awful truth of his predicament dawned on her. Rand couldn't crawl out the open window. It wasn't wide enough for him to fit through. Unless he could get the door open or kick out the glass, he was trapped inside his truck. He would drown!

She had to do something to help him. And fast!

She reached to get out of the buggy, but the door was suddenly yanked open and Ben stuck his head inside. She blinked in surprise and wonder. She'd never seen him looking so urgent before.

"Are you *allrecht*?" he asked, his eyes wide and anxious as they scanned her for injury.

"*Ja*, I'm okay but…" She didn't get to finish.

"*Gut!* Stay here where you'll be safe and warm." He slammed the door closed and raced toward the river.

She watched as he stood beside the embankment, as if considering his options. With swift movements, he shed his coat, hat and boots, tossing them carelessly aside in the snow. Then he dived headfirst into the icy water. The river closed over him, seeming to swallow him whole. A slight splash rose upward in the air in his wake.

"*Ne*, Ben!" she yelled, but too late.

He was gone. She hurried out of the buggy and raced over to the bridge, not caring in the least that he'd told her to stay put or that it was now snowing hard. Snowflakes landed on her cheeks and eyelashes but she didn't even feel the chill. Already, Ben had been under too long. He couldn't last. Not in this cold.

"Ben! Ben!" she screamed over and over again, scanning the surface of the water for some sign of him. But she saw nothing except choppy water.

Her thoughts scattered, though one pounded her mind. She'd lost him for good. The frigid temperatures would steal his strength. He wouldn't be able to survive. He would drown while trying to save Rand's life.

And that was when she knew the truth. Ben wasn't a violent man. He'd been young and frightened and pushed beyond his ability to cope. He'd fought back, not because he was vicious or mean but simply because he'd been scared and wanted to defend his dear mother.

She'd been working with him for weeks now. She'd witnessed his gentle ways and kind deeds over and over again. If he'd been a lesser man, he would have walked away from their faith and gone to live in the *Englisch* world. He could have escaped so much ridicule and hardship simply by leaving. But he'd stayed and faced it all with a quiet contrition that had impressed her beyond measure. She'd seen the truth in his eyes when he'd told her of his regrets. He was filled with the love of *Gott*, not the violence she so abhorred. Surely, he wouldn't have jumped in to save a bully like Rand if he wasn't good inside.

But even if she could give him children and they could be together always, the revelation had come too late. Because now he would die, and she'd never get to see him again.

She was vaguely aware of a car pulling off to the side of the road. An *Englisch* woman got out and ran over to her.

"What's happened?" the woman asked.

A man driving a truck joined them on the bridge. Caroline explained but had no idea what she said to them. She only knew one thing. She'd lost Ben. Lost him for good. And she was sick with the knowledge that she'd never get to say goodbye. Never get to tell him how much she truly loved him.

Yes, she loved him! She knew that now with absolute clarity. But it was too late because she'd never get to tell him how much.

The *Englisch* woman pulled out her cell phone and dialed for help while the man went to the water's edge to see what he could do. But Caroline didn't move. She stayed right where she was, her gaze scanning the murky water below for any sign of Ben. Nothing. Just a revolving vortex of freezing water.

And in her heart, she knew she had not only lost Ben Yoder that day. She had also lost the love of her life.

Ben grit his teeth the moment the freezing water enfolded him in its icy grip. Needles of pain dotted his flesh as he moved his arms and kicked his legs. He fought on, struggling to swim against the heavy current. Fighting for all he was worth. Because he had to save Rand. In that moment it didn't matter that the man was a bully. Nor did it matter that he was an *Englischer*. Rand was still one of *Gott's* children and Ben couldn't let him die. Not without trying to save him. Not this time.

Ben stared into the darkness, trying to see the truck as the water carried it down, down to the bottom of the river. The water rushed past Ben, trying to pull him with it. At first, he fought the undertow. But then he realized it could save his energy—or spell his doom.

He let it sweep him along. Then he swam fast and hard, trying to reach Rand. He grit his teeth and held his breath, until he thought his lungs would burst. The cold was sapping his energy. He was weakening! He had only moments before he'd be forced to give up the fight and rise to the surface. In the blackness, he lost sight of the truck. Where was it? Where was Rand?

There! A silvery shadow gleamed against the vehicle. It had thumped to the bottom of the river, sending up a cloud of mud that he couldn't see through. As he swam lower, the current didn't seem as strong and he was able to touch the front fender of the truck. Grabbing on to the grill and then the side mirror, Ben pulled himself over to the door of the driver's seat. He calmed himself, watching for another glimmer of light. Rand was inside the truck but looked unconscious. The cab had filled with water, which Ben thought was a blessing. It would equalize the pressure inside the cab and allow him to open the door.

He tugged on the handle but the door wouldn't open. Gripping the handle, he braced his bare feet against the side of the vehicle and pulled with all his might, vaguely aware that the current had pulled his socks off his feet.

Finally, the door gave and opened sluggishly, as if in slow motion. Letting it go, Ben clawed at Rand to pull him free of the vehicle. Although the Amish didn't own or drive any vehicles, they still rode in them occasionally when they had to travel great distances. Ben knew the layout and was grateful Rand wasn't wearing a seat belt that he would need to struggle to release.

As he pulled Rand out into the flow of the river and thrashed to get him to the surface, Ben's lungs burned for oxygen. His muscles cramped with cold and fatigue. He was weakening and feared he couldn't make it. Feared he'd never see his sweet Caroline again. Never hear her tinkling laughter or share another gentle kiss.

He kicked his legs, refusing to stop. Refusing to give in without a fight. He broke the surface and inhaled a deep breath. Waves of choppy water slapped him in the face and clogged his throat. He coughed, fighting to pull Rand to the shore. And suddenly, there were other hands there to take over for him. Men and women he didn't know took the weight of Rand's body from him—strangers who understood the situation was a matter of life and death.

Ben lay there gasping and coughing for breath, too exhausted to move, ignoring the pain as rocks dug into his skin. He was vaguely aware of a man rolling Rand onto his back before performing CPR. Rand looked pale as death, and Ben feared he'd been too late to save him. Too slow and weak to get him to the surface in time.

Rand jerked suddenly and gave a low gurgle as water ran from his mouth. Then he began to hack and spew water. He was alive! He wasn't dead at all. And then he was crying and coughing some more.

A cheer rang out among the small crowd of people. Ben lifted his head, wondering where they had all come from. They must have been driving along the road and saw the accident and stopped to help. But where was Caroline? Was she all right?

He tried to stand but slumped against the pebbled shore, lying among the rocks, snow and ice, too weak to move. He lost track of time, feeling as if he were living a nightmare. Someone laid a blanket over him but he couldn't get warm. He was shivering until he thought his teeth might rattle and break. He vaguely heard the shrill whine of a siren and knew the police and an ambulance had arrived. A paramedic and EMT started working on Rand.

Ben jerked in surprise when Eli Stoltzfus leaned over him. His foggy brain reminded him that Eli was an Amish paramedic who worked with the small hospital in town to help their people. It was so good to see a friendly face, but he couldn't tell Eli that. He mouthed the words but his voice was only a low croak.

"Ben, can you hear me?" Eli asked in English.

Ben nodded.

"*Gut!* We're gonna get you warm and take you for a ride in the ambulance. You stay with me, okay? Don't go to sleep. Don't you leave me," Eli repeated over and over again.

"Car... Caroline." Ben finally got her name out and struggled to sit up. He fell back. He couldn't understand what was wrong with him.

"She's fine, Ben. Just lie back and let me help you," Eli said.

And that was when Ben saw her. Looking up, he gazed at the darkened sky above, wondering if he would meet his Savior this very night. At first, he couldn't see anything except a swirl of snowflakes as they fell upon his face. He was aware of the moisture but he wasn't cold anymore. In fact, he couldn't feel anything now. Not his arms or legs. Not even his heart.

Caroline stood alone on the bridge above. From this distance, her face appeared gaunt and pale. He could just make out her features; she looked worried and near tears. How he hated to see her cry. He longed to stand and go to her, to hold and comfort her and get her to smile. To convince her that they should be together. He tried to lift his hand to beckon to her but his body felt too numb. His limbs wouldn't obey his will. He couldn't move at all.

And that was when Ben realized he was in danger, too. He wasn't shivering anymore. In fact, he felt pleasantly warm and lethargic. As if he were apart from his body, floating on air. No doubt hypothermia had set in. Even though he was out of the water, he still might die. But nothing mattered more than Caroline being okay. She meant so much to him. She meant everything. If only he could make her understand what was in his heart and mind. How much he loved and adored her. But she wanted a better man than him. She'd made that very clear over and over. It was what she deserved. And more than anything, he wished he could go back in time and change what he had done. Because his actions had pilfered his future happiness. They had stolen every chance he had of a joyous life with Caroline.

The shadows crowded closer, but he tried to fight them off. He wandered in and out of consciousness. Eli's insistent voice called him back each time he tried to sleep. And the only thought that kept him going was the knowledge that Caroline was safe.

He tried to lift his head, to see her on the bridge again. But she wasn't there. Good. She was out of the wet and cold. Oh, how he longed to see her again. To hear her voice and laughter. To see her face as she concentrated on a particularly difficult math problem on the chalkboard.

He could die happy if only he could feast his eyes upon her sweet face one last time.

But he knew even that would never satisfy him. No other woman had ever made him feel the way she did. Like he could do anything he set his mind to. He wanted none other. Even getting warm didn't matter now. Not when he couldn't have her.

Chapter Fourteen

"You're not coming inside to see Ben with us?"

Caroline shook her head. Little Mary's question took her off guard. She didn't want to meet the child's steady gaze. It was too bold. Too inquiring.

A variety of fears and failings whooshed around in Caroline's mind. She didn't want to face them. Not now, not ever. And yet, her faith taught her to trust in *Gott* and have a calm heart. But that was not how she felt. Not for a long time now.

They stood outside the small cinder-block hospital in town. It was early afternoon, the day after Ben had jumped into the river to save Rand Henbury. It had snowed in the night, laying down another two inches of white stuff. If not for that, they would have been here earlier. But now the sky was crystal clear, not a cloud in sight. The sun blazed from the sky, melting off the roads and sidewalks—a lull before a more serious storm was scheduled to hit their area in a couple more days.

Eli Stoltzfus, their Amish paramedic, had come to their farm earlier that morning to give them a report. Thankfully, Ben would be all right, but Caroline found she still couldn't stop worrying about him, much as she wished to. They'd also had a wonderful visit from Sharon Wedge, the *Englisch* woman from Child Protective Services. She'd informed them that Mary and Seth were theirs and could stay with them for good. As if they'd expected anything less.

"We have too many people to visit Ben all at once. You go on in and see him. I'll wait for you here," Caroline said.

Truth be known, Caroline was dying to see Ben. But knowing he was safe and would recover from his ordeal would have to be enough for now. Talking to him after all they'd been through would feel awkward now. And honestly, she feared she might relent and ask him to stay with her forever. What good would that do either of them? It would only lead to more misery and pain.

Aunt Hannah and Uncle Mervin stood on the front steps nearby. From their expressions, she knew they were concerned. For Ben and for her. But what did they expect? That she would fall into Ben's arms and they'd live happily ever after? Life didn't happen that way. Not for her.

"*Komm* on, Mary. Let's go in." Hannah beckoned to the child. Mary scowled but obediently took the woman's hand.

Caroline stared after the girl, her mind churning. When Mary and Seth had heard that Ben was in danger, they'd been inconsolable. Uncle Mervin had finally agreed to let them see the man and know for sure that he would be all right. Because the two orphans had already been through so much, no one wanted to add any more drama or uncertainty to their lives.

Forcing a smile on her face, Caroline walked over to her aunt and reached out to take baby Susan. Cradling the little girl close, Caroline smiled at Mary and Seth. "Besides, someone has to stay with Susan. A *boppli* can't go into the hospital because they're too young. There are too many germs for her to catch."

There. That was a good argument, wasn't it? Caroline was certain her logic was correct, even if they could have left Susan home with her fourteen-year-old sister.

At that moment Bishop Yoder walked outside the hospital. He was accompanied by an older *Englisch* man whose mouth was curled in a look of contrition. His legs were slightly bowlegged from riding a horse, and his face looked weathered by age and hard work. He wore a dusty, beat-up cowboy hat, blue jeans, a long Western coat and scuffed boots, along with a rather severe expression on his face. When he saw them, he paused. Then he brushed past them with a single nod of respect.

"*Hallo*, Bishop!" Mervin greeted the man.

"*Hallo*. Are you going in to see Ben?" the bishop asked.

"*Ja*. Wasn't that Garth Henbury with you?" Uncle Mervin asked.

Bishop Yoder nodded, his gaze following the man as he walked down the street.

"You mean that's Rand Henbury's father?" Hannah asked.

Both the bishop and Mervin nodded.

"I've just had a long chat with him. He knows Rand has been terrifying the Amish and that Ben saved his life last night. He's grateful and has promised that Rand will never cause any more trouble to our people from now on."

Caroline sighed with relief. "That's nice to know. I hope he means it."

Bishop Yoder nodded. "I do, too. But Rand will have

to decide that for himself. I hope he's grateful and realizes he has a second chance to make things right in his life."

Caroline hoped so, too. Nothing else needed to be said. They all knew Garth was the richest rancher in the area, but he sure didn't look the part. He was a stern, hardworking man who could buy almost anything he wanted. He had a reputation for demanding perfection from his workers, but when it came to his son, he made lots of exceptions. But this time, Rand's foolishness had almost gotten him killed.

"Rand is an only child," the bishop said. "Apparently, his *mudder* died when he was very young."

They each nodded, having heard this before. Whenever Rand got into trouble, which was quite often these days, Garth and his high-priced attorney from Denver got him off. It seemed that Garth refused to believe his son could do any wrong. Even if the Amish were prone to suing other people, Garth wasn't a man they wanted to tangle with. But this time was different. Apparently, Garth planned to rethink his actions on behalf of his son and do something about it. At least, that was what Caroline hoped would happen.

"I drew a picture of our farm for Ben." Mary broke into Caroline's thoughts as she held up a piece of paper.

With the innocence of her youth, the girl had no idea why she should be concerned by Garth Henbury's presence and barely paid the man any heed.

Mary's picture had been drawn with crayons and showed the rudimentary scribbles of a two-story red log house, barn and farmyard. Because the Amish did not believe in making graven images of themselves, no people were shown in the drawing. Just trees, flowers and farm animals.

Seth snorted. "Why did you draw flowers? It snowed and buried all of them yesterday. We don't got no flowers in our yard now."

"We don't have *any* flowers in our yard now." Caroline corrected his poor grammar. Then she leaned over to get a better look at the picture. "*Ach*, that's a lovely drawing. I'm sure Ben will like it just as it is. It'll remind him of spring."

"Come on, Mary. Let's go. I want to see Ben," Seth grumbled. He had joined Aunt Hannah on the steps, looking anxious to go inside.

"I'm coming." Smiling with satisfaction, the girl skipped up the steps, her picture waving in the breeze. The wide double doors swooshed open, and just before she went inside, Mary turned and waved goodbye.

Caroline smiled and waved back, then pulled her warm woolen cloak tighter at her throat. Oh, how she loved these two sweet children. How she loved life. *Gott* had been good to her and Ben yesterday. He'd kept them safe.

Her *familye* disappeared inside, leaving her alone with the bishop.

"You're not going in to see Ben?" the man asked.

She took a deep breath, trying to gather her courage as she met the bishop's unwavering eyes. "*Ne*. I think it's best if I wait here with the *boppli*."

Bishop Yoder's gaze held hers for several moments. "I see."

"How is he?" she couldn't help asking.

"*Gut*. He'll be able to *komm* home tomorrow. They treated him for hypothermia and frostbite, but he'll be all right," the bishop said.

Frostbite!

"Are you sure he's okay?" she asked.

"*Ja*, he wouldn't let the doctors amputate until they were absolutely certain they couldn't save all his fingers and toes. Eli supported him in that quest. And now it looks like they were wise. The circulation has returned and it appears all is well."

Caroline released a long exhale, only just realizing she'd been holding her breath. She hated the thought of Ben losing any of his digits. With a lifetime of farm chores ahead of him, he'd need strong hands and feet to do his work.

"I'm so glad," she said, meaning every word.

"Apparently, it was touch and go for Rand Henbury. Everyone feared he might die. But he is conscious now and was even able to speak to his *vadder* for a while. He's sorry for what he did. I have also offered Mr. Henbury our help in any way we can."

"Hmm. He didn't look too pleased to see us Amish here," she said.

A slight smile curved the bishop's lips. "He wasn't pleased. Especially not when he found out his son has been harassing the Amish people nonstop. Apparently, some of the townsfolk had complained to the police, and the sheriff spoke to Mr. Henbury. He refused to listen. But after what happened last night, I saw a different side to him today that wasn't there before."

She shifted the baby on her hip and tilted her head. "Oh?"

"*Ja*, this time he was afraid he might lose his son. I can't be sure, but I think Mr. Henbury will do as he said and put an end to the abuse. If Rand persists in his actions, we might not have as happy an ending the next time around."

"*Ja*, that's true," she said, relieved that both Rand and Ben would be okay.

"Although Rand is coherent and doesn't seem to have suffered any brain damage from his ordeal, he now has pneumonia. The doctor has put him on oxygen and it appears he will be in the hospital for a while longer," Bishop Yoder said.

"That's what Eli told us this morning," she said.

The bishop lifted his bushy eyebrows in question. "Eli paid you a visit?"

She nodded. "I'm sorry to hear that Rand isn't out of danger yet."

"The doctors are giving him the best care. You really should go inside and visit Ben."

His words shocked her. He was a kind, good man and their unconditional leader. She hated to defy him in anything.

"*Ach*, I can't, Bishop Yoder. Please don't ask it of me. And you should tell Ben that he doesn't need to look after me and the school. Truly, I can get along fine on my own. I don't need him anymore," she said.

Her words hung in the air like a gigantic, frosty cloud. It was true she didn't need Ben. But she supposed she didn't need anyone. Not to live and breathe air. But that wasn't what life was about. *Gott* expected more from His children. He expected them to love and serve one another. It was a commandment, after all. To love your neighbor as yourself. And she loved Ben, no matter how hard she tried not to.

His forehead crinkled. "I will admit when I gave Ben that assignment, I had hoped you two might do well together and decide to marry. Your *onkel* Mervin hoped so, too."

Uh-huh. She'd suspected as much. But it hadn't worked out. Not this time.

She looked away, her face heating up like a torch. "That isn't possible. You know I can't have *kinder*. And Ben wants a *familye* of his own more than anything else in the world. He deserves that. He deserves to be happy."

There, she'd laid it out for him. But surely, he already knew all of this.

"And you don't think he'd be happy with you and no kids?" he asked.

She stared at the baby in her arms. "Would you be happy if you and Sarah didn't have any *kinder*?"

The bishop didn't respond, but she could see him considering her words. Trying to imagine his life without all the sweet children living in his home. It just wasn't acceptable to an Amish man or woman to never have any kids.

"I think Ben would try, but we'd both feel a great emptiness in our hearts," she said. "He'd know it was me keeping him from being a *vadder*. And I don't think I could live with that, even if he could."

The bishop hesitated for several moments, as if thinking this over. Finally, he nodded. "*Allrecht*. I'll do as you ask. But I think you're wrong about Ben. His first love is his *Gott*. I know this, because he's told me so. But love and compassion between a man and woman can conquer a lot of pain we each must face in this life. And if the two of you truly love one another, and trust in the Lord, there isn't anything you can't conquer together."

She stared at him, not knowing how to respond. She longed to believe him but wasn't sure her faith was that strong.

"I'll say good day," he said, tugging on the brim of his black felt hat.

Without another word, he sauntered off. She watched him go, too stunned to speak. Her mind churned with thoughts and strong emotions she didn't understand. Was it possible he was right? Could the love she and Ben shared overcome their inability to have children? She wasn't sure. Not about anything.

It didn't matter now. Ben wouldn't be picking her up for school anymore or hanging around all the time. Bishop Yoder would see to that. And it was probably for the best.

Heaving a big sigh, she wrapped the baby more tightly in her blanket and told herself to stop worrying. As long as Ben was okay, nothing else mattered right now. She must be satisfied with knowing he was alive and recovering. It was enough for her. At least, that was what she told herself.

"Ben!"

He looked up just as Mary launched herself at him.

"Oof!" He exhaled suddenly as she wrapped her little arms tightly around his chest.

Sitting up in bed, Ben wore a hospital gown and had several thin blankets tucked around his waist and legs. He hugged the girl back but felt a bit awkward when he saw Hannah and Mervin Schwartz standing just inside the door. Seth stood beside them.

"*Hallo!* This is an unexpected surprise," Ben said, feeling a bit immodest without his long-sleeved shirt and other clothes.

"The *kinder* were pretty upset when they heard you

were injured. They wanted to come and see that you were all right," Hannah explained.

Seth stepped nearer but didn't speak. Ben had learned that he was a quiet boy who observed everything. It was a mistake to think that just because Seth didn't talk a lot meant he wasn't thinking and feeling emotions.

"Look what I brought for you." Mary held up a picture of a farmyard.

Ben took the paper between two fingers and admired it for a moment. "Did you color this?"

She nodded. "I made it for you, so you can look at it and not be lonely for us while you stay here in the hospital."

He smiled. "*Danke*. I love it. I'll keep it right here beside me until they let me go *heemet*."

He set the picture on the table next to him, then looked at Seth. "And how have you been? Taking care of your little sister?"

Seth nodded.

"How was school today?" Ben asked.

"We didn't have school. Everyone in the *Gmay* was worried about you so Teacher Caroline canceled today," Seth said.

Really? That was interesting. They only canceled school for serious emergencies. Maybe he wasn't without friends after all.

He looked up, his gaze searching the wide windows in his room that showed the vacant hallway near the nurses' station. Still wearing his heavy winter coat, Mervin hovered beside the door, holding his black felt hat in his hands.

"Where is Caroline? Is she not here?" Ben asked.

Hannah stood behind Seth and rested one hand on the

boy's shoulder. "*Ach*, she's waiting for us outside with the *boppli*. She wanted to be here, but we were told you can only have a few visitors at a time. She thought it would be better for her to let the *kinder* come see you instead."

Hmm. That was interesting, too. Was this Caroline's way of reminding him that she wanted nothing to do with him? Because if that was the case, he wasn't buying it. Not anymore. He'd almost died yesterday, and that experience had changed him somehow. It made him realize a lot of things that he'd been pushing aside for too long.

"You're really okay?" Seth asked quietly, his eyes filled with worry and a bit of suspicion.

Ben nodded. "I'm really okay. You know how doctors are. They like to fuss over you. They're just keeping me here one more night for observation. They want to make sure my lungs are working right and the frostbite is clearing up satisfactorily."

Seth's eyebrows lifted in a curious expression. "Frostbite?"

"*Ja*, they feared I might lose some of my fingers and toes." Ben laughed and waggled his fingers at the boy for emphasis.

"Really? You almost lost your fingers and toes?" the boy asked.

"Some of them. But they're fine now. The doctor just wants to make sure."

Seth smiled. "That's cool."

Ben laughed, thinking it was impossible to keep their Amish children from picking up some of the *Englischers'* language.

Ben hadn't lost any fingers and toes. And what a relief. The situation had been quite serious last night. Alone in his bed, in the quiet of the night, Ben had wept when he thought he was going to lose parts of his body. What would Caroline say if that were to happen? Already, she thought he was a monster because he'd killed a man. He didn't want her to be any more repulsed by him than she already was. But *Gott* had truly blessed him and he was more than grateful. And now he missed Caroline more than ever. Knowing she was all right was all that had kept him focused through the harrowing ordeal he'd suffered last night. But he longed to see her now.

Mervin touched Hannah's arm to signal they should leave. "*Ach*, we don't want to overstay our visit. We'll be going now. We'll check in with the bishop tomorrow to see how you're doing."

"But I don't wanna go yet," Mary whined.

"Me either," Seth said.

"We must, my dears. We need to buy some supplies and get *heemet* before dark. And Ben needs his rest now," Hannah said.

Ben nodded and hugged each child as he offered them a warm smile. "*Danke* for coming. I appreciate it. I'll see you in a few days."

His promise seemed to satisfy Mary and Seth, and they willingly preceded Hannah and Mervin out the door. Ben stared after them, thinking. He'd been told that Caroline was waiting outside.

Bracing a hand against the hospital bed for support, he stood carefully and peered out the window. Sure enough, Caroline stood on the shoveled sidewalk, bouncing baby Susan on her hip. She gazed lovingly at the child and spoke to her before laughing. The baby waved her tiny arms, completely enthralled by the beautiful woman.

Caroline lifted a hand to adjust the little girl's tiny black traveling bonnet. And though Ben couldn't hear her, he could just imagine Caroline's loving words as she tended the baby. In his heart of hearts, he knew Caroline would make the best mother, if only she could have children. How he longed to marry her and make her his own. But it was impossible. She couldn't seem to forgive his past faults.

And then a thought occurred to him. He'd never really asked Caroline if she could forgive him. What if her cool attitude toward him had nothing to do with him killing a man? What if her actions were simply protection for herself because she couldn't have babies? To keep them both from being disappointed?

Hmm. Maybe he'd been completely wrong about Caroline. It couldn't end like this. Could it? But what other choice did he have? Maybe it was time they had a long chat. And maybe he should be prepared to offer some possible solutions to her concerns.

A plan started to form in his mind—but it might not work at all. She might still rebuff him. However, with their future happiness at stake, he had to try one last time.

Chapter Fifteen

Caroline reached into the metal bucket she held, grasped a handful of grain and flung it low in the air. The chickens scurried forward, pecking at the ground to gobble up pieces of barley, wheat and corn. She skirted a couple of mud puddles, noticing the shadowed sky was clear of clouds today. The sun was just peeking over the eastern mountains. It was early and Aunt Hannah was inside the farmhouse, cooking breakfast. The smell of sausage wafted on the air.

Caroline had best hurry if she didn't want to be late for school. It had been ten days since the accident, and she hadn't seen Ben in all that time. She'd been told that he was home now and doing fine. Of course, they hadn't had church yet. But this weekend they'd have Church Sunday, and she had no doubt he'd be there.

It didn't matter. She'd keep her distance, focusing on the preaching and helping the women lay out the noon meal. She had no reason to even speak to Ben.

She told herself that was how it must be.

The rattle of a buggy coming into the yard drew her attention. She looked up and her heart immediately sank.

Ben Yoder!

What was he doing here? She thought Bishop Yoder had spoken to him to call him off. For the past week, she'd been driving herself to the schoolhouse with no problems. She'd heard that Rand Henbury had gotten out of the hospital and was home doing fine. Without his truck, he had no way of terrorizing the county roads anymore, even if his father hadn't told him to stop.

Surely, Ben had no business at their farm this early in the morning. She feared he was going to assert his will and try to drive her again. And she dreaded the inevitable confrontation. Because no matter how much she loved him, she must strongly insist he stay away and leave her alone. And that was that.

Uncle Mervin came out of the barn carrying two buckets of frothy white milk. Aunt Hannah came out of the house, wiping her hands on a dish towel.

Caroline almost groaned out loud. She really didn't want an audience right now. Not if she must be rude to Ben. Her entire *familye* adored him. Mary and Seth couldn't get enough of him. And she feared they'd all be upset when she had to tell him off.

To make matters worse, Alice and Levi came from the pigpen and chicken coop. She had no idea where Seth and Mary were. Probably in the barn helping with chores. No doubt they'd show up soon enough. No matter what, she must maintain her temper while firmly getting her point across.

"*Hallo*, Ben!" Uncle Mervin called as he set the buckets of milk on the back porch.

While Ben hopped out of the buggy, Mervin reached up and took hold of the horse's bridle to steady the animal.

"Guder mariye," Ben said, his gaze moving to rest on Caroline.

"It's so *gut* to see you up and about. Will you *komm* into the house for some breakfast with us? It's much too cold out here," Hannah said with a bright face.

Ben smiled, his gaze moving back to Caroline. "I'd like that, but I really need to speak with Caroline alone right now."

His words impacted Caroline like nothing else could. Her legs felt suddenly wobbly, and she wanted to fall to the ground and melt into a puddle right then and there. Anything to avoid a bad confrontation with him. Oh, how she loved him. And she didn't want to hurt his feelings any more than she already had.

"Ach, of course!" Hannah waved at Levi and Alice. *"Komm* inside, *kinder.* Let's leave Ben and Caroline alone."

The children did as asked. Caroline watched as her aunt held the screen door open for them to step inside the toasty kitchen.

"Why don't you go into the barn where it's warm and quiet? You can talk there," Uncle Mervin suggested.

Ben nodded and headed that way, waiting for Caroline to precede him through the wide double doors.

She hesitated, wishing she were anywhere but here. Wishing she didn't have to do this right now. Or ever, for that matter.

"Um, what did you want to talk to me about?" she asked when he'd pulled the doors closed but left them slightly ajar.

He immediately removed his black felt hat in a gesture of respect. Then he gazed at her, his lips slightly parted, his eyes filled with a moment of confusion and doubt.

He looked so endearing, shifting his feet nervously. She would have laughed if the moment hadn't been so serious.

"I don't know where to begin," he said.

"Then don't. Let's just part ways as friends, Ben. Really, we don't need to discuss anything at all. We'll forget this ever happened." She turned and took a step toward the doors but felt his hand on her arm tugging her back.

"Please don't go. There are things I must say. I have to get this out now."

She faced him and he released her arm, standing so close that she could see the golden highlights in his dark eyes. She clasped her hands together in front of her before lifting her chin high in the air. She was resigned to listening politely but being firm about what she would and would not do.

"*Allrecht*. Go ahead. What is it you want to say?" she asked.

He licked his upper lip, betraying his nervousness. "First, I love you, Caroline. I always have, from the very first moment I moved here and saw you sitting in church. Other than my *Gott*, I love you more than anything else in this world."

She closed her eyes, a feeling of weakness and euphoria sweeping over her entire body. Oh, how she'd longed to hear him say these words. And yet, this was the last thing she'd expected.

"Ben, I can't…"

"Wait! Let me finish, please." He spoke softly, insistently, as he held out a hand to stop her from speaking.

Biting down on her tongue, she forced herself to hear him out. She owed him that much.

"You're wrong about me, Caroline. I'm not a violent man. Not really. I have my faults like anyone. Sometimes

I lose my temper. But I didn't want to hit Rand Henbury. I don't want to strike anyone. But I'm not perfect. I need Christ's forgiveness every day of my life. And I'm trying to be a better man all the time. For you. But I would never hurt anyone. Never again. I hope you can believe that. I'd never lift a hand to you. Not ever!"

There was such passion in his voice. His eyes were filled with such beseeching that she truly believed him.

"I know that now, Ben. I really do. I'm not afraid of you. In fact, when I'm with you, I feel so calm and safe," she said.

He breathed an audible sigh of relief. "*Gut*. That's how it should be. Your example of faith has taught me to trust in the Lord and accept that I can finally forgive myself for the past. I can let it go and move forward. But I want you by my side. I'd like to buy the Harlin farm and add it to the acreage I already own. We'd have a nice home and barn and live a *gut* life there."

Oh, how grand that sounded. It would almost be the fulfillment of all her dreams.

"I… I can't, Ben. I know you are a *gut*, kind man. That's not the problem here. Not really," she said.

Oh, why did he have to say these things to her now? It made no difference. It couldn't change anything between them, except to make it worse.

"Then what is it? Why don't you want me? Is it because of what I did? Because I'm responsible for someone's death?" he asked, taking a step toward her.

She took a step back. Not want him? Nothing could be further from the truth. But she couldn't tell him that, or she would be lost forever.

"*Ne*, of course not. I know *Gott* has forgiven you for fighting back. You're so *wundervoll* and I respect you so much for all that you've overcome. But I can't have children, Ben. I can never give you a *familye*. You know that," she said.

He shook his head even before she finished speaking. "That doesn't matter to me. That night when Rand Henbury drove his truck into the river, I thought I might lose you for *gut*. I thought I would die. And when I awoke alive, it changed me forever. It made me realize how precious life is. And I knew then that I must not allow myself to have any more regrets. *Gott* wants us to be happy. We must take a leap of faith and trust in Him. We shouldn't waste any more time worrying that we aren't *gut* enough for each other. We must hold on tight and cherish the life we can have together. I love you, Caroline. I want you to marry me. Please say that you will."

She shook her head. "Oh, Ben. I can't. There would be no sons or daughters for us. We could never have a *familye* of our own. And you would resent me for it. Maybe not now, but later on down the road when we're older. You would come to resent me. And I couldn't live with that. I just couldn't."

A movement at the side of the barn caught Caroline's eye. She glanced over, startled to see that Seth had popped up from behind a bale of hay where he'd been hiding.

"I'll be your *sohn*. I'm an orphan and don't have parents now. I want to be part of your *familye* and live at the Harlin place with you," he said.

Caroline blinked in surprise. She had thought she was alone with Ben, but apparently not.

Ben jerked, startled, when little Mary stepped out from behind a milk barrel. Caroline was about to ask if there were any more children hiding in here but didn't get the chance.

"And I'll be your daughter. We need a *mudder* and a *vadder* and you need *kinder*. Why can't we be your *familye*?" the girl asked.

Before Caroline or Ben could respond, Hannah and Mervin slid one of the heavy doors aside and stepped inside the barn. It was obvious from their eager expressions that the two of them had been eavesdropping.

"I think that would be a *wundervoll* idea," Aunt Hannah exclaimed.

"I do, too," Uncle Mervin said.

Caroline almost laughed. So much for privacy.

"Our home always has room for more, but we are overflowing with *kinder* as it is," Hannah said. "If you and Ben decide to marry, I would agree to let you take Seth and Mary as your very own. And I know Anna and James would highly approve of you living at the Harlin place. It's what they would want you to do."

"And I have no doubt Bishop Yoder would support this idea, too, especially since the *Englisch* social worker has given us her approval to keep the *kinder*," Uncle Mervin added.

Caroline could only stare at all of them, stunned by this very generous offer for a ready-made *familye*. Ben eagerly looked at Caroline, and she saw an abundance of love gleaming in his eyes.

"I'm willing if you are," he said with a satisfied shrug. "I love you, Caroline. Say you'll be mine and make me the happiest man in the world."

She laughed, finally realizing that tears had flooded her eyes. "Do you all mean it? Is this what you really want?"

She looked back and forth between the two children, hardly able to believe this was happening. They each smiled and nodded, and Ben took her hands in his own. For once, she didn't have the willpower to fight him. Not when he offered her the very desire of her heart.

"Well? What do you say?" Ben asked her.

"*Ach*, yes. Yes!" Caroline cried and threw her arms around his neck. She hugged him tightly and found herself being picked up and spun around the room in his arms.

Her aunt and uncle and the two children joined them in a group hug. Excited laughter rang through the air as they made their plans.

"It's already late in the season, but I'm sure we could fit in another wedding before Thanksgiving. Becca Graber and Jesse King are getting married next Tuesday, and we could ask if they'd mind us combining your wedding day with theirs," Aunt Hannah said.

In a small Amish community like theirs, it would be best if they could have a double celebration. In fact, that was a frequent occurrence at Amish weddings.

"Do you think they'd agree?" Caroline asked.

Hannah waved a hand in the air. "Of course. We'll be helping with the feast anyway, and this way, we can share in the expense. Neither Becca nor Jesse has much money, so I'm guessing they'd be relieved to have us go in with them."

Caroline knew her aunt was right. Though a wedding day was extra special, it was always quite simple for the Amish. Their wedding attire was usually new but just a plain dress like what they wore every day. The biggest part of the event was the meal. Since their people weren't overly wealthy, sharing in the cost and work could benefit each of them. Caroline had no doubt Becca would agree. After all, they had become very close friends.

"Everyone in the *Gmay* is helping with the food. Oh, won't they all be so excited when they hear we're having a double wedding? We have so much to be thankful for this year. But we'll want to clear it with Becca and Jesse first. We'll go right over to Becca's house and propose the idea this very morning and see what she thinks," Aunt Hannah said.

"Yes, we should clear it with Becca first," Caroline agreed.

"And if she has any hesitation at all, we'll just hold your wedding the week after Thanksgiving. It won't be a problem at all. You just leave everything to me," Hannah said.

Caroline nodded, accepting her aunt's enthusiasm with a great deal of peace and joy. She gazed up into the face of the man she loved and found him looking at her with so much devotion she almost couldn't contain it all. And suddenly, the room became very quiet. Out of the corner of her eye, Caroline saw her aunt and uncle as they swept her children out of the barn, giving her and Ben a moment alone.

Her children! How wonderful that sounded to Caroline.

As she stared into Ben's eyes, he kissed her deeply, lovingly. And she let him. For the first time in her life, she cast aside all her reservations and held on tight. Because she realized this moment was all they were guaranteed. They should cling to one another for as long as they could.

A feeling of exquisite joy swept over her. "*Gott* has

been so *gut* to us. So kind and generous. He brought us together, such a perfect fit."

"*Ja*, it's true. I love you, sweetheart," Ben whispered against her lips.

"And I love you, my *Liebchen*. More than I can ever say," she returned.

"Do you really mean that?" he asked, his voice filled with disbelief.

"I do. I love you, and I'm not afraid anymore. I look forward to spending the rest of my life proving how much I love you," she said.

As he held her tight, no other words were necessary just now. Their love was all they needed to last a lifetime and beyond.

* * * * *

THE AMISH BAKER'S RIVAL

Marie E. Bast

My husband, Darrell; my son Brian and family, wife
Cynthia, Ezra, Ethan and Evan; my son Kevin and
family, wife Tammy, Cameron, Cory and Connor;
and my stepdaughter, Rebecca, and family,
Breann, Dannie, Autumn, Dawson and Michael.

Acknowledgments

Special thanks to Melissa Endlich
and the Love Inspired team and to Scribes202,
my critique partners.

With God all things are possible.
—*Matthew* 19:26

Chapter One

Was the rumor true?

Mary Brenneman hotfooted it to the front door, flipped the Amish Sweet Delights' bakery sign to Open and slid the dead bolt back. She peered out the window at the freshly painted storefront two doors up on the opposite side of the street, letting her gaze scour the words *Opening Soon* written in felt-tip marker on the brown paper still covering the windows.

If the rumor was true, and this was a fast-food franchise, it could hurt Sweet Delights' business. She raised her hand and blotted a tear at the corner of her eye. Just a year ago today, Seth Knepp broke their engagement so he could go live with the Englisch. Now it appeared she might lose the second love of her life. At twenty years old, she'd have nothing left.

Mary cranked her head to steal a better look.

The squeaking of cartwheels advancing into the bakery from the kitchen pulled Mary's attention from the window to her friend. "I wonder what's going in the new shop."

"Haven't heard," replied Amanda Stutzman, her friend and bakery assistant, as she pushed the cart toward the display case.

"Since bakeries started to pop up online and gas stations began selling fresh rolls and cappuccinos, Sweet Delight's business has tapered off. The bakery can't afford to lose more revenue." Mary huffed out the words. "We need to expand the menu."

Amanda started arranging the strawberry and chocolate cupcakes on the second shelf of the case. "What's the holdup? Your *stiefmutter* and *vater* have been saving a long time for remodeling the bakery."

"*Daed* wants to wait until after they've paid off my twin sisters' premature delivery cost and their long hospital stay. Most of the bakery's profits are earmarked for medical bills."

Mary missed her *stiefmutter*, Sarah, working next to her. But after the twins were born, Mary had assured Sarah she could manage the bakery on her own.

Mary gathered her notepad and pencil from the counter, checked the sales schedule, and updated the blackboard with this week's Monday specials: donuts half price with purchase of a beverage.

She brushed her hands together to remove the chalk dust and glanced at the Kalona Fall Apple Festival flyer tacked to the bulletin board. Her focus landed on the events section.

Bakers! Enter the baking contest for a chance to win a trophy and the grand prize of $10,000. The main rule—at least one of your three entries must contain apples, and the apple taste must shine through.

Her gaze trailed down to the next paragraph detailing the contest schedule.

Each contestant must submit a baked good for judging by 2:00 p.m Thursday, September 24, in one of three categories:
   1) breads, rolls, scones
   2) pies, strudels, cakes
   3) cookies, cupcakes, bars

Three winners from each category on Thursday will move on to make a different baked good on Friday. The judging panel will choose a winner from each group and those winners will receive $5,000. Those three will move on to compete on Saturday for the overall winner and the grand prize of $10,000.

Mary rubbed her fingertip across her entry confirmation letter clipped to her notebook. Ideas for a possible pie entry whirled through her head. But selecting the perfect, prize-winning apple dessert for one of the days wasn't easy.

After filling the cup dispenser, she glanced at Amanda. "If I won the baking contest, I'd remodel and buy the equipment needed to expand the menu. We'd serve breakfast croissants and biscuits in the morning, then switch to soups and sandwiches with homemade breads and buns for lunch. Maybe serve ice cream with pie. And we'd definitely add an espresso machine."

"You'll win." Amanda headed back to the kitchen with her cart bumping the doorway and the empty metal trays rattling. "You're the best baker I know."

"*Danki.* This year the prize money will bring bakers in from Des Moines, Chicago, St. Louis and all across the surrounding states. Many of them *gut* bakers from fancy pastry shops who have trained at culinary schools. I doubt a Plain girl with no formal training will stand a chance."

"You worry too much. Practice," Amanda called from the kitchen.

Mary sighed as she filled the cup dispenser. "I didn't win last year! Pastry chef Cynthia Návar carried home the prize."

The doorbell jingle jerked Mary around to the display counter. She laughed as Ethan Lapp pretended to stagger to the counter.

"Caffeine and sugar, quick!" He leaned into the counter as if he might faint without his morning breakfast. He removed his straw hat and put one hand under his suspenders as he slumped against the counter.

Mary laughed. "Your cinnamon roll is waiting." She handed him the bag and a cup of coffee.

Amanda appeared in the kitchen doorway and propped a shoulder against the door jam. "*Hallo*, Ethan." Mary caught the sparkle in her friend's eye and the special smile she reserved for Ethan. A frustrating sight, since Ethan never caught on to how Amanda felt about him.

"Hey, Amanda." He waved as he headed for the door.

Before the door closed, Frank Wallin strolled inside, letting a banging noise seep in from the street.

"*Gut Morgen*, Frank." Mary gestured toward the shop across the street. "Apparently, the carpenters are at it early today."

Frank removed his US Army veteran's hat and waved it in the air. "Morning, ladies," before pressing it back down over silvery-gray hair. "Mary, stopping here every morning is the best part of my day."

"Frank, it's *wunderbaar* customers like you that make me forget I had to get out of bed at 3:00 a.m."

Amanda pushed the pastry cart through the kitchen doorway. "*Gut Morgen*, Frank. It's always a great day when you stop by."

"Thank you, Amanda. Today, black coffee and an apple fritter, please."

"*Danki*." Mary handed Frank his coffee and paper bag as he laid the correct amount on the counter.

"My pleasure. When is the new farm-fresh grocery and deli opening?"

Mary jerked her gaze from the money to face Frank. "What grocery and deli?"

"The new store across the street. They're raising the sign into place now. Sorry, but I need to get to work. See for yourself." Frank hurried to the door and motioned across the street.

She darted from behind the counter and caught the door as it closed. "It can't be! Where did that sign come from?" Tears pressed against the corners of her eyes.

"What sign?" Amanda pushed a new tray of pastries into the display case.

"The empty shop across the street, they've hung a sign. It has cloth covering the name, but it's ripped." She paused and squinted through the dust hanging in the air from the hammering into the bricks on the old building. "I can see the words *Farm-fresh Grocery* and *Deli*."

Amanda ran around the cart and peered out the window. "*Daed* is going to be disappointed. He was hoping for a hardware store."

"If they carry breakfast biscuits and sandwiches, and have a microwave to warm them, they'll steal some of our morning customers." Mary slumped against the door. The news sliced another piece from her heart, like Seth when he dumped her on the eve of their wedding. "By the time I get the money to expand, our customers will be across the street and gone."

"*Nein*, not true, Mary. Everyone knows you're a fantastic baker. Your customers will stick by you. Besides they can go to the deli one day, and your shop the next."

"Even that will cut my revenue. I have to win that baking contest next month, or Sweet Delights will die an embarrassing death. That gives me six weeks to practice."

Amanda wandered back to the cart and finished unloading the pastries. "Don't worry. The bakery has loyal customers."

When the door opened again, Amanda tossed Mary an encouraging smile then pushed her cart to the kitchen.

A stream of morning customers rushed in and out, many making excited remarks to Mary about the new grocery. When the bakery was empty again, she stepped to the door and stole another look across the street. Old Bishop Ropp sauntered up and entered as Mary held the door open.

"*Gut Morgen*, Mary. Looks like some big excitement in town."

"I'm afraid so."

The bishop stopped short and faced her. "Nonsense. Your baking is *wunderbaar*. Don't be afraid of a little competition. Now if you would serve me a slice of that apple pie that Sarah's *vater* used to make, my day would be perfect. I would drive my buggy five miles in the rain for a piece of that pie."

"Sorry, I have a country apple, but it's my recipe. I'll have to ask *Mamm* about the one her *vater* made."

"Then I'll take an apple fritter and coffee." His smile stretched ear to ear.

Around midmorning, a young girl sailed toward the counter wearing jeans and a T-shirt and holding a five-dollar bill firmly in her fist.

"*Hallo*," Mary greeted her, "and what can I get you today?"

The little girl walked back and forth in front of the display case, smiling. "I don't know what to pick. It all looks good."

Mary nodded. "*Jah*, they are all *wunderbaar*. Take your time. I'm Mary, what's your name? I don't think I've seen you in here before."

"I'm Emily Miller. I'm eight years old. Most people ask since I'm small for my age." She pointed to the second shelf. "What kind of cupcake is the one with the pink frosting?"

"Strawberry, and I'll let you in on a secret. The inside has a strawberry surprise."

Emily's eyes scanned the pastries but a smile pulled at the corners of her mouth, then spread across her cheeks. "Okay, I'll have the pink one and a glass of milk."

"You can sit, and I'll bring it to the table." Mary pulled the treat from the case with her tongs and poured a cup of milk. She set them both in front of Emily and sat across from her. "Did you just move to town?"

"Uh-huh, my brother, Noah, moved my sister Jenny and me here from Iowa City. He's looking for a relative."

An *Englisch* person could just drive his car if he

wanted to see a relative. He didn't have to move to do that. But Emily probably misunderstood what her brother said. "Did your *mamm* and *daed* move, too?"

"No, they died a year ago in a car accident." Emily's voice quaked. "It's just my brother, Noah, Jenny and me."

"I'm so sorry to hear that about your parents."

"You talk funny." Emily laughed, then took a bite of cupcake. "Mmm, this is delicious." She took another bite, followed by a sip of milk.

The bakery door opened and a six-foot-tall man eyed Emily and her cupcake and gave a nod to Mary. "That looks good. I'll have the same as my sister if you please?"

"Good choice." Mary scooted back to the display case, her heart nearly buckling as she watched the cute man stroll through her shop. She tore her gaze away. After Seth canceled their wedding a year ago, she wasn't ready for another relationship. Not yet. And certainly not with an *Englischer*.

The tall stranger glanced at the chalkboard with the daily specials and then glanced at the bulletin board and the fall festival flyer, where he skimmed his finger down the listing of events. He turned and scanned the display case as he sauntered over to the table, pulled out a chair and sat next to Emily.

Mary pulled another strawberry cupcake from the case and poured a glass of milk. "Emily and I were just getting acquainted. I'm Mary Brenneman, and you must be Noah."

"Pleased to meet you, Mary."

His amber eyes caught her gaze and held it for a second before she jerked away. It sent a twinge straight to her heart. *Jah*, he was handsome, that was for sure and certain. His short, dark brown hair was the same color as his beard. It wasn't a long beard like that of Amish men but short and trimmed close, like what the *Englisch* called a five o'clock shadow. But it looked nice on him.

Emily held up what was left of her cupcake. "This was *wow-wee*, Noah," she mumbled, a couple of crumbs dropping from her chin.

Amanda hurried in from the kitchen and shoved a tray of sugar cookies into the display case. "Don't forget to introduce me," she said to Mary.

"*Jah*, Amanda Stutzman is my assistant and right hand. This is Noah and Emily Miller. They are new in town."

"Nice to meet you, Amanda," Noah said.

"And nice to meet you both." Amanda smiled and headed back to the kitchen.

Mary set Noah's order in front of him, trying to steady her hand. "Enjoy. They are on the *haus*, my way of saying *willkommen* to town. And tell Jenny to stop by for her cupcake. Emily said you moved here from Iowa City."

"Thanks, I will. It looks like I got here just in time, before Emily spilled the family secrets. Or did I?" He gave Emily an inquisitive look, but in a fun way.

"*Nein*," Mary protested, "I just asked where you moved from."

"I told Mary you're looking for a relative," Emily said.

Noah cut his glance from Emily to Mary. "Our parents' families were Amish, and I want to try and find our grandparents."

"What are their names? My *stiefmutter* has lived here all her life, she might know them. If she does, I'll introduce you."

"My father's name was Jeremiah Miller, and my mother was Naomi Knepp."

Mary's face heated, and her hands flew to her hips. "You're a relative of Seth Knepp?" The words snapped out a littler harsher than she'd intended.

Noah finished his cupcake, took Emily's hand and guided her to the door. "Apparently, you and he aren't good friends. But I don't know if he's a relative or not. He could be. Thanks for the cupcakes."

Her heart nearly stuttered to a stop. Had Seth sent them to get to know her and maybe to try and make peace between him and her? A likely story that Noah didn't know where his relatives lived. She might be on the verge of losing business to competition and now a possible relative of Seth visited her shop. Why? Was it just a friendly visit?

As the sting of guilt shimmied up his back, Noah pressed a hand on Emily's shoulder and hurried her across the street to his Farm-fresh Grocery, Delicatessen and Bakery. Mary hadn't mentioned his store, so apparently she hadn't realized who he really was, but she would soon enough.

He liked Mary, but the town was too small to support two bakeries. The pit of his stomach roiled at the thought of what was probably going to happen to her bakery. His store in Iowa City was very successful, and he had every reason to believe it would be equally so here in Kalona.

While he locked the door of his store behind them, Emily took off running toward the office. "I'm going to play games on the computer."

"Okay, but only for an hour, then you can sweep the floor." At the sound of shuffling feet and moving cartons, he turned and found Jenny stocking shelves. He scanned her handiwork. "Looks good."

Jenny finished placing serrated knives on a display stand. "I'm still wondering if this was the right move. This town is so small. What did the baker say when you went to get Emily?"

"I didn't tell her we owned the new store."

"Noah, you coward. You should have been honest."

He took a step back from the impact of her words. "She gave Emily and me a free cupcake and said for you to stop in for yours. I didn't have the heart to tell her right then. You can tell her."

"Thanks a lot." She rolled her eyes.

"Since you're going to attend nursing school in the fall, you won't be here if there's fussing."

She tossed him a disgusted look.

He took a step closer to Jenny. "Why don't you go over there and say hi? Her name is Mary. Since the Amish shunned our parents, we need to make friends in the Plain community before they find out who we are."

Jenny huffed as she set a few baking timers on the shelf. "We don't know that our parents were shunned. We know nothing about what happened after they left their Order. The only thing that's clear is that they left during their *rumspringa*, had a civil wedding and never went back to the faith. They said they didn't want to live by the *Ordnung* and the church rules. They wanted to live like the *Englisch*."

Naoh shrugged. "But you know as well as I do that we didn't live like the *Englisch*. Mom homeschooled us, and we weren't allowed to play or associate with *Englisch* kids at the park. We couldn't go to the movies or hang out with the neighbor kids our age. Our parents might not have wanted to be Amish, but our upbringing was strict and definitely not *Englisch*. And if our parents didn't join the Amish church, they weren't shunned."

Jenny set the last timer on the shelf. "If the community did shun them, maybe we shouldn't have opened a store here." She took a step closer. "And what makes you think that our relatives want to meet us?" She raised a brow, turned and headed toward the office.

He heaved a long sigh. *Sisters*. Jenny would thank him later when she had a grandma to wrap her in a hug and attend her wedding someday… But Jenny was right. He needed to visit them and put the question of what had happened to rest.

Emily slipped out the office door and sprinted to Noah. "I want to help stock shelves."

"Did Jenny chase you off the computer and tell you to help me?" He didn't have time to show an eight-year-old a task and then clean up the mess she made.

Emily tugged at a box and tried to get it open. "Can you help me?"

"Right now we're just unpacking a few things we brought from the other store. The trucks will be here tomorrow with our fresh vegetables. When I get it unpacked, you can help stock the shelves and bins." Noah could see the disappointment in her eyes. He pulled a stack of flyers from behind the counter and handed them to Emily. "Why don't you tape one of these on the shelf by the item they advertise? Then post some of the others around the store so the shoppers can see them."

"I'll do a great job."

He watched Emily hang one on the wall by the entrance. She walked to the first aisle and posted another by the fruit table.

When Noah finished stocking shelves, he checked

on Emily and every aisle that had a sale item had a flyer over the correct area. "Good job, Emily."

He headed to the deli area as his mind wandered back to what Jenny said about the Amish. If this was such a strong, Amish-supporting town, it might not be the Amish Sweet Delights driven out of business, but his store.

He shoved his hand into his pocket and pulled out an entry form. The fall festival had scheduled a baking contest with a $10,000 prize. What better advertisement for his bakery than winning a baking contest? His cupcakes were every bit as good as Mary's, if not better.

Mary would probably enter the competition. But if either one of them won, they could capture a lot of the town and tourist business. As a result, it could possibly drive the other out of business. And if that happened, he'd never see those cornflower-blue eyes or her silky blond hair again. He liked her, and he would truly hate never seeing her again.

Chapter Two

Grabbing potholders, Mary opened the oven door letting a steamy whiff of pecan-caramel rolls fill the kitchen. She pulled the pans out, set them on the cooling rack next to the cinnamon rolls and let their aromas mingle.

"Those smell *gut*." Amanda glanced up from rolling dough.

"*Danki*. It has been a busy morning, glad it's slowing down." Mary scooted from the kitchen to the front of the bakery, pulled out the medium roast and decaf bags, and started fresh coffee. She puttered around cleaning the counter, wiping off tables and straightening chairs.

When the front door opened, the aroma of fresh-brewed coffee wafted around the bakery on a cool breeze. Mary noticed a tall, slender young woman enter who looked remarkably like Emily.

Mary eased her way around a table and met the visitor at the counter. "Hallo. Are you Jenny?"

"Yes, I'm Emily and Noah's sister. I wanted to introduce myself." Her gaze roamed around the bakeshop and over the display case full of chocolate cupcakes, sugar cookies, cherry tarts, and a vanilla bean cake with deep swirls of buttercream frosting.

"It's very nice to meet you, Jenny. I'm Mary Brenneman. Pick out anything you like, and it's on the house. My way of saying *willkommen*."

"Thank you, and it's nice to meet you, too." Jenny took a step back and drew in a deep breath. "The strawberry pie smells divine, but I'll take a chocolate chunk cookie to go, please. I'm a cookie freak and choc-o-holic. I like washing down a warm, gooey cookie with a cold glass of milk."

"*Gut* choice. They're my favorite cookie."

"It sounds like there is a cookie break." Amanda walked to the front holding two small ice cream cones. "We are experimenting with serving ice cream with our desserts. It's old fashioned vanilla bean and on the haus." Amanda held out a cone to Jenny and handed the other to Mary.

"Thank you." Jenny licked a drip on the side of the cone. "Mmm, that's very good." She motioned toward the door. "Shall we step outside and eat these? It's a lovely day."

"*Jah*, a breath of fresh air might be nice." Mary opened the door and held it for Jenny. "Are you coming, Amanda?"

"*Nein*. I'll stay and box up the cookies and cupcakes for the fireman's bake sale tomorrow."

Mary leaned against a lamppost and took a lick of her cone. "Emily's a sweet little girl. She told me about your move here from Iowa City. How are you adjusting to small-town life? It's a lot different than the city, *jah*?"

Jenny laughed. "Yes, it's different. Noah wanted to expand the business to Kalona because of the large amount of Amish tourism. The leather-and-wood craft shops, the sewing shops and consignment stores are a big draw for the tourists."

The jingling of harness rings and the clomping of horses' hooves pulled Mary's attention up the street. She straightened her back and gasped. "Is that Noah standing in front of the Farm-fresh Grocery and Deli?"

Jenny followed Mary's gaze. "Yes, but I don't know who the other man is helping him move in that shelving. He's cute."

"That's Ethan Lapp. The new grocery and deli belongs to Noah?" The words exploded from Mary's mouth like a geyser.

"Yes. I'm sorry he forgot to mention it earlier that we own the store. I'm helping Noah set up the computer and bookkeeping system, but I'm only here until I start nursing school next month. He hired a manager to run the store in Iowa City while he dedicated his time here."

"Your *bruder* never mentioned that." Mary gritted her teeth and the words tumbled out a little stiffer than she'd intended. He visited her bakery and never said a word about owning the new store.

Noah and Ethan crossed the street toward Amish Sweet Delights. Noah took his hat off and wiped his brow. "Ethan, this is my sister Jenny." He stood silent a minute as those two seemed to take to each other right away. Noah took a step closer to Mary. "I owe you an apology for not telling you that I owned the new store."

She fumed as agitation streaked through her veins. "Did you visit my bakery to snoop and see how long it would take you to put me out of business?"

"No, of course not. I hope there is plenty of business for both of us."

"You do know it's a small town of less than five thousand, right? I don't understand how you could think there wouldn't be a problem here." Mary raised her chin, turned abruptly as a strand of hair bounced around her face and headed back into the bakery.

Now she had to win the contest and show Noah that she wasn't going to let him steal her business. Tonight, she'd pull out the recipe book Sarah had given her and look for the perfect apple recipe.

A twinge settled in her stomach. She liked Noah, but this was business. This time she was fighting for what she loved.

The next morning, Mary hitched her buggy and coaxed King into a gentle trot down Fifth Street toward the fire station. She slowed the buggy as it passed Carson's flower shop to gawk at the pots of gorgeous yellow and gold chrysanthemums sitting in the display window. She parked the buggy by the curb between Knit 'n' Sew and the fire station, stepped down and carefully lifted out the box of cookies and cupcakes to donate to the firefighters' annual bake sale. The proceeds would go to help needy families who had lost everything after a fire or natural disaster.

Mary set the box down, pulled out her individual containers of baked goods and neatly arranged them on the sale table. She glanced around at the other donations until her scan stopped at some delicious-looking pastries with Noah's store logo on the boxes: Miller's Farm-fresh Grocery, Delicatessen and Bakery.

Bakery, too! Heat rose from her neck and burned on her cheeks. Her pulse accelerated. So that's why he hadn't wanted to introduce himself. His store was also a bakery…and situated right across the street from Sweet Delights. How had she not noticed that?

Out of the corner of her eye, a firefighter dressed in yellow Nomex gear and clomping boots headed her way. Noah Miller. She turned and watched him hand out deli sandwiches to the other firefighters as he approached.

"Thanks for the donations, Mary." His overly friendly voice rang in her ear.

Mary stepped back and motioned to his gear. "So, there is no end to your talents?"

"I volunteered in Iowa City before we moved here."

"And your grocery and deli is also a bakery?"

He nodded toward his donations on the table and smiled. "Yeah. I'm a good baker, learned the trade from my dad."

The more she saw Noah, the more he annoyed her. "The community is fortunate to have you." She turned, walked back to her buggy, climbed in, snapped the reins and braced herself. King jerked the buggy into motion and skedaddled down the street toward the corral and her bakery.

A few minutes later, Mary slammed Sweet Delights' back door. Amanda jerked away from the sink and nearly lost her balance.

"Sorry, I didn't mean to scare you."

"What's going on? You look upset." This time Amanda braced her back on the sink.

"Go take a look out the front window at the uncovered sign on top of Miller's store."

Amanda hurried to the front and returned. "A bakery, too."

"*Jah.* He donated baked goods to the firefighters' bake sale. When I looked around, he was handing out a stack of sandwiches, apparently samples from his deli for the firefighters. Oh, and he's a volunteer firefighter."

Mary huffed to the sink, washed her hands and whirled around. "Put thick frosting on all the cupcakes today and decorate them extra special. Tomorrow is Noah's grand opening. We are fighting fire with fire! No, make that cupcake with cupcake!"

At 8:00 Friday morning, Mary stomped to the chalkboard and drew a delicious-looking cupcake, piled high with frosting swirls and topped with a fresh strawberry. She added another line with the special for the day— Free cupcake with the purchase of a coffee—then turned the board so the writing was visible from the sidewalk.

She dusted the chalk off her hands then poured a cup of medium roast. Usually, she was so busy in the morning that she didn't get a coffee break until ten o'clock.

"You're generous today," Amanda said, glancing up from sliding the cupcake tray into the display case and nodding toward the chalkboard.

"I'm trying to entice a few people to stop in." Mary walked over to the window and gazed up the street at the long line of customers waiting to get into Miller's Farm-fresh Grocery, Delicatessen and Bakery.

"Mary, you knew business would be slow with Noah's grand opening today."

"Yes, I did expect slow. I just wasn't prepared for no one, and tomorrow all our baked goods will be on sale as day-old."

Amanda picked up the empty tray and started for the kitchen, then stopped. "Why don't you go over to Noah's shop and put in a friendly appearance for his open house?"

"What? I couldn't do that." Mary took a step toward the counter. Her palms turned cold and clammy.

"Yes, you can. Go. He came to your bakery."

"He was spying."

"*Nein.* Go. Right now."

Mary sighed. Why did her friend have to be right?

She drew in a ragged breath, crossed the street and opened the door to the Millers' store and stepped inside, letting her long, navy dress swirl around her legs as she turned abruptly to head down an aisle. The mixed aromas of cinnamon rolls, brewed hazelnut coffee and caramel cappuccino hung in the air. Everyone was busy looking around and no one seemed to notice her.

She strolled through the bakery and glanced at his chocolate eclairs, cakes and cookies that smelled of rich European chocolate. The cherry turnovers and pies oozed with ripe-red juice and looked mouthwatering. She rounded the corner to the hot deli bar and the steamy aroma of minestrone soup was luscious. A cheese pizza warmed under a heater next to hot dogs and brats, and a cheeseburger sizzled on the grill. The cold deli bar had fresh melons and green, crisp lettuce and spinach.

Lastly, she walked between two rows of vibrantly colored carrots, cucumbers, beans, potatoes, cilantro and parsley that looked moist and fresh. It all looked *wunderbaar* and inviting. She caught a glimpse of Noah carrying a bowl of cut melon to the deli bar and ducked around the corner as she headed back to the door.

Now what was she going to do? The bad thing about his store was even she wanted to shop here. But she had better leave before Noah caught sight of her and the last thing she wanted was to talk to him about his wunderbaar store.

Mary hurried back across the street. Since Sweet Delights' business was slow, she sent Amanda home early, but she waited and locked up at three o'clock. Dread tugged at her feet as she forced one foot in front of the other all the way to the corral. She hitched King and set him at a leisurely pace as tears stung her eyes. With one hand on the reins, she pulled a hanky from her quilted bag, blotted her eyes and blew her nose.

She watched field after field and yard after yard pass by. The rain yesterday had brightened the countryside to a dark green. The sweet peas and petunias in the Wallins' yard were brilliant pink, purple and white. Her predicament with the bakery eased back into her mind. Noah's store would no doubt be a favorite in town.

Twenty minutes later, while she fought the tears drenching her cheeks, King turned into their barnyard, headed up the driveway and back to the barn. *Daed* met her at the barn door with a warm smile.

"You're home early today. I'll unhitch King and rub him down." He glanced at her face as she stepped down. "What happened, Mary?"

She swallowed a sob. "The new store had a very successful grand opening today. On the other hand, Sweet Delights didn't have any customers."

Daed sauntered forward and bent his six-foot-frame over her, a swatch of his graying hair poked out from beneath his hat. He wrapped his strong arms around her and hugged as his straggly beard brushed her chin. She could smell his sweat and feel the moisture clinging to his shirt.

"I'm sorry, Mary, but it's only one day. I'm sure your customers will be back tomorrow. You work too much and needed a rest." His words comforted her, but when she took a step back, she caught the lines creasing his forehead that signaled he was worried too. They couldn't afford to lose the business.

Mary nodded then turned toward the *haus*. Each foot hit the path as if it had a weight tied to it. She opened the kitchen screen door and set her bag on a chair.

Her *stiefmutter*, Sarah, turned her tall frame from the sink, a strand of cinnamon-brown hair bobbing by her temple. "You're home early."

"The Millers' new store had their grand-opening today. Everyone was there."

"Oh, I'm sorry." Mamm opened the gas-powered refrigerator door, poured a glass of lemonade and handed it to Mary. "Sit and rest." She resumed peeling apples at the sink.

Mary took the glass and sipped. "I'm worried the bakery won't survive."

Mamm glanced over her shoulder. "Why?"

"I strolled through Noah Miller's store. His baked goods looked *wunderbaar* and the deli had hotdogs, soups, salad bar and pizzas. Everyone will go there for their morning coffee and lunch."

"*Nein*. It's just new. You'll see."

"I need to win the bakery contest next month at the fall festival so we can expand our menu. We have to start serving breakfast sandwiches and lunch in order to compete with Noah's shop. We need that trophy to show we are the best." Mary's voice quivered.

Sarah paused her apple peeling. "So practice and win. I know you can do it. But I don't think the bishop will let you display a trophy, symbolizing you think you are better than someone else."

"If I win, I'll tell them I don't want the trophy. *Mamm*, will you help me pick out the perfect apple recipe? And give me some pointers on how to heighten the flavors and make them shine through for the judges? In the words of Noah's little sister, so it will taste *wow-wee*?"

"Of course. And if you get too busy at the bakery, your *Aent* Lillia said Cousin Nettie would like to come and work with you."

Mary wrapped her arms around *Mamm* and hugged. Her real *mamm* may have died, but her *stiefmutter* was always there for her. Sarah was sweet and always offered her love and support…but sometimes love couldn't fix everything. It certainly hadn't with Seth.

Saturday morning, Mary hitched King to her buggy. His big brown eyes danced with excitement at the chance to stretch his legs. She straightened her dress and settled back on the black seat of her open buggy. She shook the reins, nudging the steed down the drive, out onto the road and past the white picket fence. King set his own pace and fell into a steady trot.

The scent of wildflowers saturated the breeze and enticed her to draw a deep breath. The fresh fragrance cleared her mind and invigorated her senses.

Sarah was right. Of course, Mary could bake better than Noah. She'd baked all her life. Why hadn't she purchased something from his bakery so she could have sampled his talent? Now it would be awkward if she went back and bought a cupcake. It would look suspicious.

Where the road paralleled the English River, she pulled back on the reins. "Whoa, King, slow down, big guy." She wanted to enjoy the bright blue sky and the birds singing. The sun danced off the river like a thousand jewels just sitting there ready for plucking. Mary didn't often see the sunrise. Usually she was already at work before now, but since the shop had so many baked goods leftover from yesterday, today they wouldn't need to bake as much.

Pulling back on the reins, she steered King to a bare spot and stopped the buggy. Stepping down, she surveyed the riverbank until she spotted what she was looking for, a big rock positioned under a tree. She'd passed this spot hundreds of times and had always wanted to stop. It looked like the perfect place to sit, sort things out and organize her world into order once again.

She eased onto the rock, leaned back against the tree and watched the river flow and babble over rocks. The birds chirping, frogs jumping in the river and the relaxing sounds of nature soothed her mind. Her gaze landed on a leaf caught in the current, barreling down the river. It was the first fall leaf she'd seen, and it reminded her that change was coming—and she'd better get ready. She could no longer sit and do nothing.

The sound of tires crunching over sticks and rocks pulled her attention toward the road as an SUV stopped on the shoulder and parked. Noah Miller climbed out and headed in her direction. What did he want?

Mary scooted to the edge of the rock as she watched him approach. After her breakup with Seth, her life was just starting to return to some kind of normal, until Noah showed up in town.

His purposeful stride carried him to her side in seconds. Just as he stopped next to her, an annoying breeze kicked up, ruffled her apron, tugged a few strands of hair from her prayer *kapp* and tapped it against her cheek. And her day was only starting.

After choosing the shortest route over tall weeds to Mary's rock, Noah slowed his pace when he reached the clearing. The glimpse of her perched beside the river framed by shrubs and trees filled him with a smile. "Are you okay, Mary? Did your buggy break down?"

She jerked her head around at his remark. "I'm fine. The river just looked so peaceful this morning it beckoned me to stop. I enjoy a quiet spot." Her gaze swept over him before she turned toward the river. "Thanks for stopping."

"I saw you at the grand opening, what did you think?" He wasn't going to let her off that easily. He wanted to talk to her whether she liked it or not.

"I was merely putting in an appearance to pay my respects to a new shop opening. I wasn't there long, but it looked like you had a nice turnout."

"Okay, but what did you think?"

She kept her back to him. "It's nice, but I'm a better baker, Noah." She said teasingly."

"Is that right?" He took a step back.

"That's right" came a smug goading reply.

"Well, Miss Brenneman, I'm entering the fall festival baking contest. Are you?"

She jumped to her feet, whirled around to face him and lifted her chin. "Yes."

"Good. Game on. Let the best baker win." He laughed. She was sassy, but he wanted to pull her and that cute attitude into his arms. But the fear of looking like a complete and utter fool kept him away.

"You make it sound like a kid's game." She said the last word with a pout before she flattened her full lips into a straight line.

Noah started to leave, then stopped. "We both know there's much more at stake here than merely winning a contest. At this point, it's not even the money, is it? It's the title, the trophy and the prestige that goes along with the achievement."

"As usual, Noah, you've thought of it all." Her eyes challenged his.

He took a step closer. "I'm surprised your bishop would actually allow you to enter. It's such an open display of pride that you think your baking is so good you could actually win a contest."

The surprise that covered her face told him she hadn't thought about asking the bishop or the church for approval to enter the contest. It would be interesting to see how she maneuvered around that obstacle.

Without another word, he turned and tromped back to his car. A chuckle shook his body as he opened the door and sat. Yeah, this was not only going to be a game of skill, but one of wit.

He'd tasted Mary's cupcakes. They were delicious, but his parents had trained him well in how to run their store and how to bake. He was a better baker than Jenny. That was the reason she took care of the books, and he baked and ran the store. He had a knack for figuring out what flavors complemented each other. And he might even be a better baker than Mary Brenneman.

At twenty years old, Noah didn't have much experience with women. He'd never taken a girl out to the movies or ball games like most *Englisch* boys had. But he'd met a few women at the store, and they'd gone to lunch together. Most of them wore heavy makeup, short dresses or tight jeans. They flirted and pouted with red lips when he didn't ask them out for more than lunch. Many of them had been attractive, yet none had interested him. Mary was different. She was natural and beautiful.

Noah glanced back at the river and at her sitting on

the rock again. He'd asked her about his opening only because he'd wanted to stay and talk to her. The notion to tease her about the contest had just popped out, and it had gone a little further than he had planned. Now, in hindsight, he saw her point of view. His new business was taking some of her customers. To her, it wasn't a tease.

One thing was for sure and certain, as his *mamm* would have said, he might have just made her angry enough to search for days to find that perfect recipe to beat him.

Chapter Three

Mary jumped to her feet as Noah drove away from the river. Tears sprang to her eyes. Surely the bishop and the Gmay, the church members, wouldn't deny her this opportunity. Would they? Could they?

Nein, she hadn't considered that. She participated last year, but they only paid the winner $200 then. This year, they were trying to attract more festivalgoers so they increased the prize money.

She raced to her buggy. Her hands shaking as she picked up the reins and set King to a smart pace. The buggy rocked as he lengthened his gait. A mile down the road, Mary turned into Bishop Yoder's drive, parked and hurried to his front porch.

She hesitated at the door. It was early, maybe too early to pay the bishop a visit. She drew in a deep breath, blew it out and knocked.

After a few seconds, the door opened and Mrs. Yoder stared at her with a surprised look on her face. "*Gut Morgen,* Mary." Rebecca waved her in. "You're an early bird this morning."

"Mornin', Rebecca. Would it be possible to see the bishop? It's important."

"Of course. Wait right here." The stout woman gave her a peculiar survey before hurrying down the hallway off the vestibule.

Mary inhaled a deep whiff of fresh-brewed coffee as she pressed her right hand to her heart to slow its runaway drumming. The last time she'd visited the bishop's farm was a year ago when she had to inform him that Seth had canceled their wedding.

Bishop Yoder appeared at his office door. He nodded at his *frau* and headed toward Mary, his hair a bit mussed, as if he hadn't planned on a visitor this early.

"*Gut Morgen*, Mary. It must be important for you to interrupt my prayer time." His words were to the point but softly spoken.

"I'm so sorry. I didn't think about the time. I was on my way to work, but I can come back." Heat rose to her cheeks as she turned toward the door.

"*Nein, nein.* I'm up. We can talk. Come." He led the way down the hall to his office, motioned for her to go in, then stuck his head into the kitchen across the hall. "Rebecca, would you please bring us two cups of coffee?"

The room was small, cool and sparsely decorated with only a desk and three chairs, counting his. She sat in a hard wooden chair in front of his desk and waited for the bishop to give her a sign to start talking. He talked about the weather and asked about her family.

Rebecca knocked. After his reply, she set the tray on his desk and closed the door. He motioned for Mary to grab a cup. "Now, what is this all about?"

She took a sip and set the cup back on the tray. "I want to enter the fall festival baking contest and compete for the $10,000 prize." She blurted out as a nudge of excitement loosened her tongue.

The bishop's eyes widened. "Mary, our belief is that we live in community and give up personal expression. The *Ordnung* calls us to live in submission to God's will. We live in harmony with the others in our community. We do not *compete* for who is best."

His words speared her heart. Mary straightened her back as her old rebellious nature clutched her. "Bishop, the bakery is our livelihood. *Daed* and *Mamm* have medical bills from the twins' birth that we do not burden the community with. We pay from Sweet Delights' revenue."

"*Jah*, I understand. But we do not seek acclaim for what we do. We strive for a godly life to attain eternal salvation."

Mary sat forward on the chair and squared her shoulders. "I am not doing it to brag or boast. In fact, I have very little chance of even winning. Many who enter the contest will have gone to culinary school, like the winner of the contest last year. With the new grocery opening across the street, our bakery has already lost business. This is no different from offering a loaf of bread for sale. I make it, and if they like it, they purchase it. I need to compete with other businesses, and to do that, I need to expand our menu. In order to do that, I need the prize money."

The bishop rubbed his hand down his beard as he directed his gaze toward the ceiling.

Leaning back, Mary gripped the arms of the hard, wooden chair. The longer he took, the more her pulse increased and the further her heart sank.

Bishop Yoder lowered his gaze to her. "*Jah*, it would appear that you have the same right to offer your product, but this is highly unusual. Accepting the money for a recipe is one thing, but you must not accept a trophy. And the other ministers may want to discuss it, but we will see. I'll let you know. Now, Rebecca will have my breakfast ready." He stood, motioned toward the door and followed her down the hall to the entrance.

Heading out of the *haus*, Mary blew out a deep sigh. She climbed in the buggy and relaxed back against the seat for her ride to Sweet Delights. She unhitched King, led him to the corral and hurried to the back door.

As she approached, a light shining out a high window caught her attention. Had she left the light on yesterday when she went home? *Nein*, she always walked through her routine. Her keys jangled as she unlocked Sweet Delights' back door. She drew in a deep breath of humid Iowa August air. She pushed the door slowly open and peeked in.

She laughed at the sight of her assistant and then stepped into an atmosphere scented with medium-roast hazelnut brewing. "You're in early, Amanda."

"Couldn't sleep." Amanda yawned and clasped an elbow over her mouth for a second. "Coffee is almost ready."

"*Danki*, I could use some. I had to stop by Bishop Yoder's *haus* and ask if I could enter the baking contest. He's going to let me know." Mary stowed her quilted bag in the closet and grabbed the ingredients for a batch of sugar cookies.

Within a few minutes, she was popping them in the oven and starting on the chocolate chip batch. Amanda's yeast bread and rolls cooling on the counter sent warm, steamy whiffs of honey and cinnamon into the air.

"You're in early, too. Couldn't sleep? Thinking about Noah's bakery or Noah?" Amanda teased.

"Neither." That man infuriated her. "After Seth ran off to go live with the *Englisch*, I just want to avoid men, especially if they are *Englisch*. They can't be trusted. I thought I knew Seth, knew what he wanted. I thought he wanted me. I was blind." *Jah*, he talked about the *Englisch* world and wanting to be able to do whatever he wanted with no rules to restrict him. But she'd thought it was just talk. When Seth asked her to go with him and she said *nein*, he'd strolled out of her *haus* and out of her life…forever.

Amanda pulled a pan of tea biscuits from the oven and set them to cool. "We both are *gut* bakers, but we have terrible taste in men. I've always liked Ethan Lapp, but he doesn't know I exist, at least not anymore. When Ethan and I were younger, we were neighbors, grew up together, went fishing and palled around together every chance we got. I guess my feelings grew and his didn't. Now whenever he's in the bakery, he just asks me about Jenny. He asked me if I knew if she had a boyfriend. I've seen him talking to her."

"I'm sorry, Amanda. Do you want me to casually let it drop to Ethan that you like him?"

"*Nein*, but *danki* for the offer.

"You, my friend, are a lovely slim redhead, and a great baker. You'll find your Mr. *Wunderbaar*. He'll come along when you least expect it and sweep you away from my bakery."

"*Danki*. You are sweet to say that."

Mary tucked her broken engagement in the attic of her mind and slammed the door closed. "I have news. There is no chance Noah and I will become friends. He told me this *morgen* that he's entering the fall baking contest. He's planning on winning, taking the prize and getting all the benefits, meaning customers. He is now a rival."

Amanda gasped. "Don't worry, you'll win."

"*Jah*, I'll try to find the perfect recipes." Mary pulled her cookies from the oven while her mind wandered back to Noah at the river. She hated to admit it, but it was nice of him to stop and see if she had a problem.

Amanda pushed the cart up to the counter. "Ready to load?"

"Yes, *danki*, time got away from me." Mary helped Amanda pile the cart with rolls, bread and cookies, laughing like two young girls as they filled the display case.

At 7:00 a.m., Mary pulled the dead bolt back and flipped the sign to Open. Before she reached the counter, Carolyn Ropp pushed the door open, bumping her Miller's Farm-fresh Grocery bag against the doorjamb.

"*Morgen*, Mary." She sighed. "I'll sure be glad when canning season is over so I can get some rest. A loaf of wheat bread, please."

Mary picked up a loaf and turned to Carolyn. "Did you say one or two loaves?"

"Just one."

"Last week you got two." Mary bagged the loaf and set it on the counter.

Carolyn's face turned a bright red as she fished the money out of her purse. "I stopped at the grocery across the street. His bread looked so *gut* that I just had to try one."

"Of course, I understand." Heat engulfed Mary's chest. She pushed her mouth into a smile as Carolyn whirled around and headed toward the door.

Frank Wallin held the door open as Carolyn hustled

out. He raised his brow at her abrupt exit but nodded a greeting and headed for the counter. "Good morning, Mary. I'll take my usual."

She nodded and prepared his order. "I haven't seen you for a couple of days, Frank, been running late?"

"Ah, yeah…running late." Taking his breakfast, he laid down his money. "No change." He hastily turned and headed for the door.

Amanda poked her head out of the kitchen. "See, your customers are loyal. They just visited Noah's store because it was his grand opening."

Mary walked across the bakery, glanced out the window and noticed some of her other customers walking on the sidewalk, carrying paper bags with Noah's logo.

"Maybe, we'll see." The pit of her stomach flipped like a rubbery pancake. She returned to the counter just as Emily heaved the door open and jumped aside as it swept back closed.

"Good morning, Emily. What can I get you today?"

"I don't have any money. I just wanted to say hi. I was bored watching Noah stock shelves."

"You're not helping?"

"He says it takes too long to tell me what to do when he can have it done in the time it takes to show me." A lingering hint of hurt feelings pushed out the last few words.

"Well, I'm sure he's trying to get the store restocked quickly. Tell you what, wash your hands, and you can help Amanda and me make cookies."

"Okay!" Emily turned toward the washroom then stopped. "I heard Noah tell Jenny this morning that if nothing else, you're a good baker."

Mary jerked her head around. "Is that so?"

"Yeah. He also said you're heavy-handed, and he said

that meant you made your cookies and cupcakes really big so you can charge more."

Mary watched Emily disappear behind the washroom door. Was that right? If nothing else...she was a *gut* baker but heavy-handed. He had his nerve saying that.

The Lord nudged her heart at her uncharitable thoughts toward Noah.

Emily held her hands up as she entered the kitchen. "All clean."

"Very nice." Mary handed Emily a cookie scooper. "Please drop walnut-size peanut butter cookies onto the baking sheet. After you're finished, I'll show you how to sugar and flatten them."

Emily measured the dough out to precisely the size of a walnut and dropped it on the cookie sheet. "I like making cookies."

"You do a very *gut* job, little one," Amanda cooed.

Mary buttered the bottom of another pan. "When do you start school?"

"My first full day is the twenty-sixth. I'm scared though. Mom homeschooled me, but Jenny and Noah said they don't have time this year."

"You'll like it. You'll meet all the other kids in town, and you'll find some nice friends."

When the doorbell jingled, Mary hurried to the front of the bakery. "*Morgen*, Cyrus."

"*Gut Morgen.* Nice to see you, Mary. My frau is still canning and would like two loaves of whole wheat bread."

She bagged the bread and handed the sack across the counter to Cyrus, but he was staring off toward the kitchen with his jaw dropped open. Mary followed his gaze.

Emily stood in the kitchen doorway quiet as a rabbit. "Mary, I got all the dough dropped onto the cookie sheet."

"*Danki*, sweetie. Why don't you wash the dishes you used? I'll be there in a minute."

Cyrus waited until Emily disappeared into the kitchen and then whispered, "Who is that?"

"Emily Miller."

"She looks familiar, but I can't place her. Whose *tochter*?"

"Her parents are dead. She's the sister of the new owner of Miller's Farm-fresh Grocery, Delicatessen and Bakery across the street. He's *Englisch* but his parents left the community during their *rumspringa*."

"*Englisch*, you say."

"*Jah*. Is something wrong?"

"*Nein*. She just looked familiar."

After Cyrus left, Mary placed a glass and bowl of sugar in front of Emily and demonstrated how to press and sugar the cookies. "Okay, your turn."

Emily picked up the glass, dipped the bottom in sugar, then pressed it gently against the cookie dough.

Mary patted her on the shoulder. "That looks great. They are the perfect size cookies. Honey, did you know that man that was just in the bakery?"

"No. Should I know him? He could have seen me at the store."

"*Jah*, he just thought you looked familiar."

"Maybe he could be the relative Noah is looking for?"

When Emily had the cookie sheet filled, Mary slid it in the oven. "I don't know, but don't worry about it. Noah will find who he is looking for." Only Cyrus Miller and his family were very strict Old Order Amish, and she knew they didn't mix with the *Englisch*. If they were the relatives Noah was looking for, it would be interesting to see how they accepted Noah and his family.

* * *

The heavy aroma of buttered breads and rolls, frosted cakes and rhubarb pies hit Noah the second he opened the door to Sweet Delights. When he moved closer to the counter, he smelled cinnamon-spiced coffee—the flavor of the day according to Saturday's chalkboard.

Mary swiped her hands across her apron as she headed to the front of the bakery. Her step slowed when she saw Noah. *"Hallo."*

"Would Emily happen to be here?" His voice wavered as he approached the counter. He wasn't quite sure how she'd greet him after their confrontation at the river, but he wanted to make sure there wasn't rift between them.

"Jah, she's helping Amanda and me bake cookies. Can she stay a while longer so she can finish?"

"Sure, I just don't want her to be a burden."

Mary winced. *"Nein*, we *liebe* having her help and enjoy teaching her to bake. She is a *gut* student."

"I know, it's just that sometimes she's overly help-ful. She doesn't have any playmates, so she gets bored." He pushed his hands in his jean pockets and hooked his thumbs over the top.

"I understand." Mary nodded. "But she's doing a *gut* job helping us with baking."

"Thanks for showing her how to bake. I really appre-ciate it." Noah glanced at the pastry display case, then back at Mary. "Emily wanted to help me earlier when I stocked shelves, and I think I hurt her feelings. I tried to explain how to arrange the inventory, but she pushed ev-erything together on a shelf at her level." Guilt pricked at his heart as he forced the words from his mouth.

Mary nodded knowingly.

He pulled a hand from his pocket and gestured toward

Mary. "I know what you're thinking, that she's small and that's what makes sense to her, but I can't have the store shelves looking like that. And it takes me twice as long to straighten out what she did as opposed to just doing it myself. But I have a job lined up for her this afternoon."

Mary flashed him a reassuring smile. "She'll like that. She wants to be helpful. But send her over any time. We like having her company. There's always something she can do here in the bakery, and she's very entertaining." She raised a brow.

He wasn't quite sure now exactly what she meant by *entertaining*. Sometimes Emily repeated things that you hadn't even realized she had overheard. He tried to read Mary's face but her expression covered any other tell-tale hints.

Noah glanced around. "How long have you had this shop?"

"The bakery belonged to my *stiefmutter*. She had it for several years. Her *vater* started it, and when he died, she took over. A few years ago, she married my *daed*, and now she has three small *kinner*, so I've been managing it for the last three years."

"It looks like you're doing a great job."

"Danki. Cyrus Miller was in the bakery today and saw Emily. He asked her name and thought she look familiar. Do you know Cyrus?"

"No. Do you think he might be a relative of ours?"

"I'll ask *Mamm* if she knew your parents. Cyrus may be a relative, but there are a lot of Millers in the area."

"Oh, I get it now. Are you trying to shake me up, Mary? Are you saying I'm Amish and you want me to have to ask the bishop's permission to enter the baking contest, too?" He chuckled. "By the way, did he give his approval?"

"Ha! You'll have to wait until the contest to find out." The doorbell jingled and Mary turned to the counter. "Have a *gut* day, Noah."

Emily drifted through the kitchen doorway like a butterfly riding the breeze. She fluttered to Noah's side and stopped. "Mary and Amanda let me help make cookies." She held up a clear plastic baggie. "I got to keep these."

He could see how proud she was of herself. "They look good. I heard you were a big help. I have bins assembled at the store, and I'd sure appreciate it if you could fill them with kitchen supplies."

"Okay, but I want to come back again and help Mary sometime."

"If she doesn't mind, it's fine with me." He caught Mary's nod as he started for the door.

At least he and Mary were still on speaking terms. Well, for the present anyway. In a few weeks when the baking competition started, that might all change.

Chapter Four

The next Monday, Noah drove to Iowa City to help Sidney, his assistant, make the baked goods and supervise the seven kitchen staff at the preparation of food for both stores. For the time being, each day one of them would bring the food to Kalona and oversee the deli from 11:00 until 1:00. Right now, it was easier to carry the baked goods and deli food to Kalona until he could determine how much business and additional help he would need.

He jumped out of his SUV and grabbed the cartons from the backseat that he'd use to transport the baked goods back to Kalona. "Morning, Sidney."

"Morning boss. How are things going at the other store? Summer festivals are keeping me busy here."

Noah glanced at his assistant and nodded. He really liked Sidney, but the man could talk you to death if you let him. "It's going good. Each day, more locals stop in, so I think it's going to work out and the branching-out was a good investment. But time will tell."

Pulling flour and yeast from the pantry, Noah started the family-secret bread and roll recipes. It wasn't that he didn't trust Sidney, but the old family recipes were mostly kept in his head. There was a recipe book. His great-grandfather handed it down to his father, and he inherited it. But he kept it locked in the safe.

Noah mixed the ingredients, added the yeast and milk mixture, turned the dough onto a floured board and began to knead. He turned the soft mass and kneaded again. He plopped the dough in a bowl and pushed it to the corner to rise.

He reached into his memory and pulled out one of the old pie recipes from the book to try for the baking contest. He opened a bag of apples, cored and peeled them and made a piecrust. He mixed the cinnamon topping and sprinkled it on the pie. When he pulled it out of the oven, it looked perfect. He cut a piece and handed it to Sidney.

"Boss, this pie is a winner." He then proceeded to tell Noah about the breakup with his girlfriend, a festival he'd attended, baking and decorating cupcakes for his church's bake sale, all before Noah had finished baking and boxing his products to take back to Kalona.

The quiet trip back to the other store was a welcome change to a morning of listening to Sidney's chatter. The tall green corn waved in the breeze as Noah passed by field after field. Some farmers were combining oats and hauling it to silos. Bits and pieces of chaff blew across the road and lightly dusted his windshield. Now he'd need to add an auto wash to his list of things to do. He parked behind his Kalona store, carried in three cartons of baked goods, unpacked them and arranged the pastries in the display case.

When he finished, he glanced at the closed office door where Jenny was still working on the books and setting up the new computer system.

It was risky opening a new store in such a small town.

Especially since he'd heard that Sweet Delights was a tourist favorite. Could this town generate enough business to justify two bakeries?

But one good thing about the move to Kalona, he got to meet Mary Brenneman. An image of her fought its way into his mind. He squeezed his eyes shut and tried to block it out.

He couldn't do it. He didn't really want to do it.

But haunting thoughts of how he was complicating her life shrouded his view.

"Noah."

He jerked around and faced Jenny.

"Would you please take this stack of store flyers to the post office?" He frowned at her orders as she plowed on. "And on your way back, stop at Sweet Delights and bring Emily home. Supper is going to be early tonight because I have a church meeting. By the way, how long do you think it'll be before you can handle the store on your own?"

He drew a steadying breath. "I'll never be able to do all the work by myself. I can run the store, but I'll still need you to manage the office and do the bookkeeping. We should continue to run the business like Mom and Dad did."

One glance at her face told him that wasn't a good enough answer.

He paced the floor in front of Jenny. "I don't have the cash to hire someone to replace you right now. The move to expand the business was expensive."

"I've received a student loan, and I've signed up for nursing classes that start in September. You can have my share of the profits from the store in Iowa City to pay for your help. Remember, this move to expand was your idea. You were the one who wanted to chase down family members, who, by the way, have never seen us and probably don't want anything to do with us. This is your dream, and mine is nursing. I love you, Noah, but I want to live my own life, and that life is not here in Kalona."

He held up his hands. "You're right. I know I've been fighting you on this, but I want you to follow your dream."

She blew out a loud sigh. "Is Emily spending too much time at Sweet Delights? They're probably getting sick of her hanging around. I don't want her to be a bother to Mary and Amanda."

"Mary assured me Emily isn't a bother." He huffed through gritted teeth. "She's a little girl who lives above a store in the middle of town. She's new here and has no friends. And we don't have much time to spend with her since the folks died."

"Do you still want to send her to public school this fall? You could hire more help that would free up some time so you could help her with studies." Jenny's voice softened.

He saw where this was going. "She needs friends. And neither of us has the time to homeschool her, especially if you're attending school."

She nodded. "I need to get supper in the oven. After you stop at the post office, don't forget Emily. Supper will be ready in thirty minutes."

Noah grabbed his brimmed hat, screwed it down on his head and stepped out the door into a gust of wind. He glanced at the wall of dark clouds rolling in from the west, ran the one block up Fifth Street to the post office, mailed the flyers, crossed the street and hurried back down Fifth Street to Sweet Delights.

Windblown and slightly wet, he ducked into the bakery and met Mary's gaze as she looked up from wiping the counter. "Good afternoon. I'm here to get Emily." His heart jumped at the sight of that lovely face.

"*Jah*, she has been a great help this afternoon." He watched her eyes twinkle and wondered if it was all for Emily, or maybe just a little bit was for him.

Emily poked her head around the kitchen doorway. "Hi, Noah. I'll be done helping Amanda in a minute."

"Hurry, Jenny has supper ready."

"Just one minute." She held up her index finger.

His attention flicked back to Mary as his thundering heart began to quiet. "How's the entry for the contest coming along?"

"That's off-limits, Noah, I'm not saying a word about my entry."

He laughed. "I'm just making small talk." He turned toward the kitchen door. "Emily, come on we need to get going."

His sister appeared holding a box with a cellophane top showing three chocolate cupcakes inside. She held them up. "I made these all by myself. There were six but we ate three. Amanda said they were delicious." Emily's face beamed with pride.

He glanced at Mary, who smiled and nodded. "They look really good, sis. Tell Mary thanks, we need to go."

"Thanks, Mary." Emily raised her voice. "Thanks, Amanda."

"*Jah*, any time," came the voice from the kitchen.

As Noah headed for the door, a clap of thunder rumbled across the sky. "We better hurry."

He caught Emily's hand, pulled her under Sweet Delights' awning and watched the traffic for a good time to run. When the coast was clear, he rushed her across the street.

As they jumped the curb, sizzling streaks of lightning pierced the sky followed by a long haunting blast from the storm siren. When drops of rain pelted his face, Noah yanked the door open, pushed Emily into the store and jumped in right behind her. A strange tingle twisted in his gut. Whenever he heard a siren, it seemed disaster wasn't far behind. He'd heard that same sound shortly after his folks had left the house the night they'd been killed in a car accident.

He mouthed a silent prayer no one would be hurt this time.

While Amanda waited for her daed to pick her up at Sweet Delights, Mary scanned the ominous sky as she hurried to the corral and hitched King. He shook his head, snorted and pawed the ground. She patted his nose. "*Jah*, I can see you're nervous. Quit acting like that. You're scaring me."

She climbed in the buggy and tapped the reins against King's back. He bolted down the street as if sensing danger. The horse lengthened his gait to a full gallop. "Whoa, King." She pulled back on the reins. He didn't obey. Lightning streaked over their heads and hit the ground close by, causing sparks to fly. She could smell something burning. Wood? Maybe hay. She wasn't quite sure. A boom of thunder sent King galloping even faster.

Mary gripped the reins and pushed back firmly against the seat for whatever was going to happen. She had no control over King. He sensed danger, and so did she. They needed to get off the road but home was three miles away. Surely, they could make it.

Her heart banged against her ribs so hard she thought it would explode. Rain pounded the buggy roof and slashed against the side. When the wheels hit a rut, they slid this way and that. But nothing was slowing King down. Mary bit her bottom lip. If she screamed, the horse would panic.

Stay calm...stay calm...stay calm.

They neared the turnoff to the gravel road, but King was still at full gallop. "Whoa, King, whoa." Panic raced through every fiber of her being. "King, whoa!"

King knew the road and every blade of grass from here to the farm. He knew where his home was, and he wanted to be in his barn eating his oats. King ignored Mary's tugging on the reins. He turned off the asphalt onto the country road at nearly a full gallop. When he turned left, the buggy slid right, jerking King from his footing and pulling him down into the ditch.

The buggy swayed, the door flopped open and a cracking noise filled Mary's ears before something very, very hard hit her...

Noah trudged up the stairs wiping rain from his face and following Emily to their living quarters. As usual, Jenny was prompt. The table was set, a chicken vegetable casserole and Dutch slaw sat waiting in the middle while she poured lemonade.

"Sit—" Jenny gestured toward the chairs "—before the bread dries out." She placed the lemonade on the table and sat before Noah said the blessing.

He watched Jenny dish casserole onto Emily's plate and reach for his. "Oh, no! Don't fill my plate yet." He jumped from his chair.

"What's wrong?" Jenny's hand clutched her throat.

"I forgot to tell Mary to ask her *mamm* if she knew

our grandparents, and if so, where they lived. I'll just run over there and be right back."

He ran down the stairs, snatched his hat on the way out the door, dashed across the street and shoved the bakery door open.

Amanda jumped back from the counter. "*Ach,* you scared me."

"Sorry. Can I talk to Mary?"

"It looked bad out, so she hitched King and headed home."

"She didn't wait it out here?"

"*Nein.* She thought the rain looked like it was in for all night, so she wanted to try to get home before it started. I told her I'd lock up since daed is picking me up, and we only live on the edge of town."

The storm sirens roared to life again. Noah looked at Amanda. "That's the second time tonight they've gone off."

She nodded. "Now you have me worried about Mary, but she only lives three miles away. Maybe she made it home. It would only take a few minutes."

"Can you tell me where she lives? I want to make sure she got home."

"Well…" she glanced toward the window "…okay."

Amanda rattled off the directions. He nodded, tore out of the bakery and headed to the alley where he parked his SUV.

Noah's hand was shaking as he put the vehicle in gear. If she wasn't stranded along the side of the road, should he pull in her driveway and knock on the door to make sure she'd made it home? But if her dad answered the door, would he wonder why an Englischer was there to see Mary? He wouldn't want to get her into any trouble.

Yet he had to make sure she was safe. And maybe he could meet her *mamm* and ask if she knew his family.

He turned off the asphalt onto the gravel road. A triangle reflector, the kind on the backs of Amish buggies, caught his eye, and then he saw the buggy lying in the ditch. Nearby, a horse was trying to get up from the ground.

Noah parked just off the road, grabbed his flashlight out of the glove box, said a prayer and hurried to the accident. He swept the light back and forth. "Mary?"

The knot in his throat made it hard to swallow, and his stomach wanted to heave. The buggy's axle looked like it was broken and a wheel had slid off. "Mary, are you here?" The buggy door was open.

He listened. The horse raised his head and whinnied.

He had to find Mary. He flashed the beam all around on the ground. Carefully, he lifted the wheel and the beam danced across her white apron. He quickly set the wheel off to the side, clear of Mary.

She moved her head slowly and moaned. Water dripped off her cheek as Noah knelt next to her. "Are you hurt?"

"No," she said softly. "Nothing is broken. When the buggy veered into the ditch, the door unlatched. I fell out. I guess I got the wind knocked out of me when I hit the ground or when the wheel hit me."

"If you can walk, I'll put you in my SUV and take you to your farm."

She huffed out an exasperated breath. "*Nein*, I'll wait here. I'm sure *Daed* will be along shortly looking for me."

"I'm not leaving you out here in the storm. I'll take you home." He grasped her by the shoulders and pulled her up. "How do you feel?"

"A little dizzy, but I can walk."

Slipping an arm around her waist, he helped her onto the seat as her long, wet dress snagged on the door handle. He untangled the material and ran around to the driver's side. "Long dresses are a nuisance, why do you wear them?"

"It's a mile down this road," she said, "first place on the right."

He started the vehicle. "I'll have you home in a few minutes."

"Why are you out here in the country?"

He glanced her way. "I was concerned about you driving in this weather."

She nodded. "You asked why I wear a long dress. To be Amish means to practice the Amish ways at all times. We live our lives according to the *Ordnung*, which is the application of scriptural principles. It's the rules we live by, dress by and carry out *Gott*'s will for our lives. Some *Englisch* have tried to join our church, but many have trouble living according to what Scripture instructs."

Noah raised a brow. "I'm not sure I could do it either." He turned into the driveway and parked by the house. "I'll help you out."

She opened the door but waited until he got there. He slid his arm around her waist and steadied her as she walked to the house. Her *mamm* and *daed* flew out the door onto the porch and helped Mary into the kitchen.

"What happened, where is your buggy and King?" her *daed* asked, moving his attention from Mary to scan Noah with a scrutinizing gaze.

Mary sat on the chair that her *bruder* had pulled away from the table. "King was spooked by the lightning and thunder, and I couldn't get him to slow down. He took the turn onto the gravel road too fast, the buggy slid in the ditch, the axle broke and the wheel fell off. King wasn't hurt. Noah came along in his SUV, found me and brought me home. This is Noah Miller." She nodded in his direction. "This is my *stiefmutter* Sarah, my *daed* Caleb, my *bruder* Jacob, and this is my munchkin four-year-old *bruder* Michael Paul. And my *boppli* one-year-old twin sisters are probably in bed."

"I'm not a munchkin, sis," Michael protested. "I'm big. I help *Daed* with chores and milking." He wrapped his hands through his suspenders and stretched them.

"*Mamm*, Noah is the new store owner, well, him and his two sisters Jenny and Emily." She paused and rubbed her shoulder. "He's trying to find their grandparents. His *daed* was Jeremiah Miller and his *mamm* was Naomi Knepp."

Sarah glanced at Noah. "*Jah*, I knew your *mamm* and *daed*. I was sorry to see them leave. Jeremiah's parents are Anna and Thomas Miller. Your father's *bruders* are Cyrus and Jonah, and he has a *schwester*, Judith. Your *mamm*'s parents were Enos and Susan Knepp, but they have passed on. They had two other children, Carl and Lydia."

Caleb motioned to his son. "Jacob, we better go see to King and the buggy. We need to at least get him home."

"I can help you, Caleb." Noah started toward the door.

"*Danki*, but Jacob and I can manage the horse. If the axle is broken, we'll wait until the *morgen* to fix that."

Sarah nodded. "*Danki* for bringing Mary home." Her voice held a cool air as if it was a strange thing to say to an *Englischer*.

"*Danki* for helping me home, Noah." Mary slumped back in the chair, her eyelids almost closed.

They were polite, but it was a cool welcome. *Jah*, he got the hint. They were as uncomfortable with an *Englischer* in their *haus* as he was to be there. It was unlikely he'd be asked back. He touched the brim of his hat and nodded to Mary and her mother. He opened the screen door, stepped onto the porch, but the stiff spring banged the door close. Yeah, he got it. They closed the door between him and Mary.

Chapter Five

Mary stared out the kitchen window into the rainy evening until Noah drove out of sight. A smile tugged at the corners of her mouth at the thought of his warm amber eyes. He had a charming way about him. But he was chasing the same prize she was, and there could only be one winner.

"How did he happen along in the rain to help you home? Doesn't he live in town?" Her stiefmutter startled Mary out of her muse.

"Amanda told him I had headed home. We talk occasionally. Since it was storming, he thought he'd better make sure I'd arrived safely."

Sarah raised a brow. "Noah's *grossdaddi* Thomas is a quiet man, and it hurt him deeply when Jeremiah and Naomi left and never came back. I've been told Thomas is strict and doesn't mingle with the *Englisch*, so I'm not sure how he'll accept Noah and his sisters."

Mary moved her sore shoulder and winced. "If he doesn't want to be part of their lives, that'll hurt Noah's feelings. I don't know Thomas well, but his *frau*, Anna, is very nice." Mary cast a long look at the door Noah had gone through. She was almost sorry they were in competition for the same prize. But the fact remained… they were.

"*Mamm*, I need a recipe that'll charm the judges' taste buds. Old Bishop Ropp was in the bakery the other day and talked about an apple pie recipe that your *daed* made. He said he'd drive five miles for a piece. Do you remember the recipe?"

"*Nein*, but after supper, I'll dig in the boxes of stuff in storage and see if I can find his recipe book."

When the last clean dish sat in the cupboard, Mary followed Sarah to the attic. She dug in one box while *Mamm* unloaded another old carton but nothing turned up resembling a recipe book.

"I'm going back to the bakery tomorrow. I'll search through the recipe books there again. One of them has to be it."

"*Nein*, Mary, you should rest at least a couple of days after your accident."

"*Mamm*, I'm fine. I can't leave Amanda alone to do all the baking."

The truth was…she also wanted to see Noah.

Wednesday morning, Mary hurried around Sweet Delights packing three cartons with pastries, breads and cookies. She carted them to her buggy, or rather Mamm's buggy since hers wasn't fixed yet. She and Amanda had worked hard getting the food ready to contribute to today's barn raising. News had quickly spread that Noah's *grossdaddi*'s barn had burned to the ground after a lightning strike. But the Plain folk would have a new one built in no time.

From barn-raising flyers posted everywhere, Noah

would probably be there too. And she liked the idea of seeing him again. His tall, broad-shouldered frame and amber eyes flashed through her brain. *Jah*, he was sure cute.

After the four-mile trip, Mary turned King up Thomas Miller's drive and parked at the end of the long row of buggies. Glancing around the barnyard, there must have been a hundred men working who had already raised the outer four walls. Some men were sawing lumber, others nailing while the young climbed to the top of the structure. Ladders, hammers and saws were all busy.

Jah, she'd better hurry, the men would be hungry and thirsty after all that hard work.

The women were gathering in the yard at the long tables they used for the Sunday common meal and were setting out food. Mary carried her cartons across the yard to the tables and set them at one end. She laid out her pastries, breads and desserts, then noticed a group of women gathering at the other end of the table. Friends and women she hadn't seen in a while were talking and no doubt sharing their news and gossip.

Anna Miller, Thomas's *frau*, walked out onto the porch, glanced Mary's way and gave her a wave. She handed a tablecloth to a woman on the porch then disappeared back into the *haus*. Mary quickened her pace, caught up with Anna in her kitchen and smothered her in a hug. "Slow down, Anna, and don't work so hard. We are all here to help you."

Anna stepped back and drew a deep breath. "*Danki* for bringing all the rolls and bread, but there is a lot to do. Would you mind taking this tub out to the table for the dirty dishes?"

"Of course." Mary set it at one end of the table where

they had the plates, glasses and beverages. She wandered toward the other end where the women were gathering and noticed that something had their attention.

Mary weaved around a few women and gasped. Noah! He had brought breakfast and lunch sandwiches from his store, along with delicious-looking coffee cake, rolls, fresh salads and jugs of beverages with his logo. And he was handing out plates of deli food and telling everyone to visit his store. He had his nerve. Heat rose up Mary's neck and burned on her cheeks.

Mamm set a pie on the table, wrapped her arm around Mary and drew her close. "Your pastries look *wunderbaar.*"

Daed approached wearing a supportive smile. "Your red face is noticeable." His gaze bounced from Noah back to her. "This is the first time that many of the Plain folks have probably tried his food. They only want to try something new. Your baking is *gut.* Quit worrying, *honig.*"

She glanced skyward, counted to three. "He's going to steal all of Sweet Delights' business."

"*Nein,* sweetie." *Mamm* shook her head. "You'll win the baking contest then your bakery will be filled with customers."

Mary swallowed her next words. *Lord, forgive me for my jealousy.*

Daed patted her arm. "I've got to get back to work." He grabbed a breakfast biscuit and a fruit jar filled with water and headed toward the barn.

As the morning slowly crawled on, Mary's baked goods disappeared. *Jah,* the Lord answered her prayer and gave her a *gut* lesson. She would have to learn to get along with Noah. Kalona was a small town, and her family's bakery would have to survive on a smaller income, or she'd have to figure out how to expand, that was for sure and for certain.

After lunch, while she cleaned the table, she noticed Anna and Thomas Miller and their family walking around thanking the workers. They stopped next to her and Thomas cleared a tear-choked throat. "*Danki* for bringing all the *wunderbaar* food, Mary. We appreciate all the time you and Amanda donated to making it all."

"We were glad to do it." Mary glanced at the other end of the table. "Have you all met Noah Miller?" They shook their heads, but no one had a surprised look on their face. "I'll introduce you."

Noah looked up from unpacking a box as she led the small parade to his side. He gave a nod in greeting.

Mary gestured. "This is Noah Miller. Noah—" she motioned as she introduced each one "—these are your *grosseldre*, Thomas and Anna Miller, your *Onkel* Cyrus and his *frau*, Lois, and their son John, and your *Aent* Judith."

She stepped back while Noah told his family about his business and his sisters. But Mary could see the uneasiness in Thomas and Cyrus as they fidgeted with their straw hats and suspenders and looked around at the crowd that was still milling around the tables glancing over at them. Their Plain community was no doubt wondering if they were going to accept their long-lost son's family. This was big news! But she could tell by their stiff posture and stoic faces, it would be a slow process for Thomas and his family to accept Noah, if they ever did.

Cyrus abruptly nodded. "*Danki* for coming." His eyes darted to the men working on the barn, then back. "But we must get back to work." He turned and walked away, his frau following.

Thomas attempted a weak smile at Mary. "Your food was *gut*. *Danki* for coming." He turned to Noah. "*Danki* for all the gut breakfast sandwiches and food you brought." Thomas moseyed across the yard in the direction of the new barn.

Anna patted Noah's arm and smiled before heading toward the *haus*.

Mary watched Noah's brow furrow and a sad puppy dog expression cover his eyes. Her heart sank to the bottom of her feet. His whole family as much as rejected him, and earlier she begrudged him the right to bring his food and hand it out.

Aent Judith stepped closer to Noah as her family dispersed. "They'll come around, give them time. You look like your *daed*." She smiled. "Jeremiah was handsome, too."

Noah shrugged with a heightened color in his cheeks. "I knew when I drove out here to granddad's farm that my parents had left the community during their *rumspringa*, got married and never went home again. There are bound to be hard feelings."

"Is that all your *vater* told you? They left during *rumspringa*?" Judith sounded surprised.

"Pretty much. Dad said they didn't want to follow the strict church rules and have the community run their lives."

"Really, that was what he said?" Judith huffed as if exasperated.

Noah nodded.

"Did your *daed* tell you that he was helping our *vater* shingle the roof of the barn? When they ran short of shingles, Jeremiah rode to town to get another bundle. While he was gone, *Daed* fell off the roof and lay on the ground for hours before anyone found him. Cyrus believes that *Daed* limps because he didn't get medical attention soon enough."

Noah gasped. "*Nein*, he never said anything like that."

"When my husband was alive," Judith continued, "we went to see Jeremiah. I asked him to come back to the community, but he refused. He said he didn't feel worthy to be Amish and live in community."

Mary gasped as the hidden pieces rolled out of Judith's mouth. Had Sarah known all this and hadn't told her? Embarrassment rose to her face as she glanced at Noah. He probably didn't appreciate her eavesdropping. His face had paled. She took a step back then another but noticed several sets of eyes and ears trained their way. There were others interested, too.

Noah's shoulders sagged as he heaved a sigh. "I always wondered if something happened to cause them to leave."

Someone tapped Mary on the shoulder. She turned and drew in a sharp breath.

Seth.

She grabbed his arm and pulled him away from Noah and Judith. Her gaze drifted from Seth's blue chambray shirt to his broadcloth trousers held by suspenders.

"So you left the *Englisch* ways and have returned?" her voice strained as she fought for control. "How did the bishop let you back in our community when they shunned you? Has it been a year already?" She took a couple steps back from him.

"I went to Davenport and worked a few months in a small factory. But those *Englischers* did a lot of drinking after work so I didn't have any real friends. It wasn't quite what I expected. I had a small apartment in an old house, but I had to share a bathroom." He paused and kicked at a stick on the ground. "It was lonely. I wanted to go back home, but my bruder said *Daed* was still angry. I ran into a cousin. He said his daed needed help and asked me to come and live with them. They farm in a small Plain community by Des Moines. They knew I was shunned, but their bishop reduced my punishment time from twelve to nine months and took me in. I repented, and he performed the rite of restoration. It's been a year, so Bishop Yoder accepted me back into our community."

"So why did you come back here?" She held back the real question she wanted to ask. Was it worth giving up our love?

"I missed *Mamm* and *Daed* and my *bruders*. I'm back in the furniture business with my family. It's a fine living." He nodded toward Noah. "You introduced him to his family. Are you *gut* friends with him?"

"I know him. His store is right across the street from Sweet Delights." She could hear a defensive sound in her voice.

"He's *Englisch*, Mary. Stay away from him."

She snorted. "*Jah*, this advice comes from the man who left me standing at the altar so he could run after the *Englisch* ways."

He shrugged. "He's *Englisch* and you don't want to leave your faith. I know, it's not worth it."

She stared at him. "I don't need you telling me what I should do. You gave up that right. Remember?"

Seth nodded. "You're right. I did, but Noah's *mamm* and my *daed* were *bruder* and *schwester*. So your friend and I are cousins, and I'm not going to let him hurt you."

Mary turned on her heel, stomped to the table, grabbed her bag, the box of pans and headed to her buggy. Seth had his nerve talking to her like that. She tossed the box on the seat, flopped down and shook the reins. Did he think he still had the right to tell her what to do? Maybe he thought they'd just pick up where they'd left off?

She urged King into a fast trot and braced herself when the buggy swayed with the increased speed. The horse no doubt felt her tension in the reins.

Gritting her teeth, Mary tossed her ex-fiancé out of her head as her thoughts fluttered back to Noah and the confusion on his face as he learned about his family. He looked hurt, and her heart went out to him.

After she turned onto the highway, a cool breeze blew across her face and pulled her attention to the fields of corn swaying and rustling as their green stalks poked and pushed each other. She relaxed against the seat. She could never leave her Amish faith like Seth had. It was clear, too, that he never said he missed her.

Back in town, she unhitched King, carried her clanking pans into Sweet Delights and set them on the sink.

Amanda hurried through the kitchen doorway. "*Gut*, you're back. We're busy. How was your day?"

"Not as *gut* as Noah Miller's day. His food was a success. Everyone loved it and gathered around his table. He brought fresh salads and sandwiches made with his homemade breads."

"*Jah*, but our customers still stop in here for what they like best from Sweet Delights, right?" Amanda reasoned.

"You're not helping me feel better. I'm going to practice my apple pie and forget about Noah Miller."

Amanda stammered, "That reminds me, the bishop stopped by while you were gone."

Mary's feet froze to the spot. "What did he say?"

Her friend kept her chin down as she loaded a tray with cupcakes and cookies. "He said he'd talk to you later." She hesitated. "But his demeanor seemed serious." She gave Mary a quick glance before she scooped up more cookies and placed them on the tray. "On the other hand," she chuckled, "he always has a serious demeanor."

Mary blotted her forehead with her sleeve then pulled a bag of apples from the refrigerator. "He'll stop back if he has something to tell me." She peeled a couple of apples. "Amanda, did you know that Seth is back in town?"

The kitchen went silent as Amanda stood still. "How did you find out Seth is back?"

"So you did know."

"I'm sorry. I wasn't sure if he would stay or not, and I didn't want you to be hurt more by gossip if he wasn't back for *gut*."

"It would have been nice to know instead of getting blindsided."

Amanda turned toward Mary. "Did you talk to him?"

"He came up to me and warned me about being friendly with the *Englischer* Noah Miller. Of all people, him, the one who left me at the altar for the *Englisch* life. Now he has left that life and come back."

"Are you still in *liebe* with Seth?"

"Nein." The truth was she and Seth had always been friends. But she could never trust him again with her heart. She could never trust an *Englischer* or any man ever again with her heart.

After his family returned to the barn raising, Noah helped clean tables then hurried and placed his empty pans in a carton and set them in his vehicle. He needed to get back to town. He'd seen the way Mary eyed his deli food when he handed it out, the same way she had at the fire station bake sale. He could see the hurt in her eyes, and he wanted to explain to her. She probably thought he was trying to steal her customers.

And after meeting his family and his conversation with *Aent* Judith, he felt empty, like the last swallow of coffee had been sipped from the cup. He headed to the kitchen to find grandma. He stepped inside the house, glanced around the room of women and found her at the sink. "Grandma, I'm leaving now."

She whirled around, charged toward him and laid her damp hands on his shoulders. "*Danki* for coming and be sure to come back. And bring your sisters." Tears glistened in her eyes and rolled down her cheeks. She gave his shoulders a shake, then released him.

He nodded. "Sure." He cleared the frog from his throat and hurried to his SUV.

The four miles back to town went slowly at first, with several horses and buggies in front of him on the gravel road making their way home. After turning onto the highway, he made better time. Noah parked behind the store, dropped off his pans in the kitchen and stuck his head in the office to tell Jenny he was back.

"Noah, before you leave, I want to introduce you to your new assistant manager, Jean Dwyer." Jenny gestured to a woman sitting with her in the office. "She'll start on Monday."

"It's nice to meet you," Noah said with a quick nod. "I just have to run across the street to Sweet Delights for a minute, then I'll be back. If you have time, I'd like to show you around?"

"Yes, thanks, that would be great," she responded. "That way I'll know the ropes when I come in on Monday."

Noah jogged across the street to Sweet Delights, his

pulse racing; he thumped the door open with sweaty palms, giving the bell a hard shaking.

Mary startled from filling the coffee maker, turned, and met his gaze. "Hallo, Noah."

"Mary, I wanted to explain about taking all the food out to my grandpa's farm."

She waved a hand. "You don't owe me an explanation. They are your *grosseldre* and you had every right to do so. I'm sure they appreciated it."

"You're not just saying that?"

A grin plucked at the corners of her mouth before it stretched into a full grin. "As you *Englisch* say, you knocked it out of the park."

At first, her words startled Noah, and he wasn't sure how to take it. He blew out a long breath. "Thanks for understanding." He nodded. "See you later." As the door closed behind him, his heart rate began to slow to normal.

As he crossed the street and thought about his grandparents, a weird notion pulled Noah in two different directions: one toward his Amish family and one toward the *Englisch* world.

He'd grown up in the *Englisch* world whether firmly planted in it or not, but that's where he was comfortable. Yet his family was Amish.

So which one was he? Amish or *Englisch*?

Chapter Six

Mary gazed out the bakery window into a fiery-red sun rising over the horizon. The breeze pushed the clouds into a race across the sky and set her feet in motion to get to work. She grabbed a set of tongs and helped Amanda unload the pastry cart into the display case. "I can't believe we're running so late this morning."

Amanda cackled. "That's what we get for sipping coffee and eating our own rolls."

Mary watched two women stroll by the window carrying cups and bags from Noah's store, followed by three men who were usually her morning customers. She stomped back to the kitchen and grabbed a stack of empty pans off the cart, banging them as she set them on the sink.

Amanda jumped at the noise. "Is something wrong?"

"If I leave early today, can you close the bakery?"

"Of course. What's going on?"

"I'm tired of seeing Noah's deli cups go by the windows. I'm going to order a cappuccino and latte machine. Sweet Delights has to serve those fancy coffee beverages that women *liebe*. We are losing too much business."

She had to hand it to Noah, though. He knew what the public liked. *Nein*, it wasn't jealousy. It was a matter of learning how to compete with an *Englisch* store right across the street. But she'd learn.

After the rush of Thursday's lunch crowd, Mary retreated to the office and pulled out brochures of cappuccino and latte makers. She read each one and noticed the different features that each offered. Since she'd only had one cappuccino, it was hard to pick.

At 2:00 p.m., Mary hitched King to the buggy, but first there was one stop to make before the supply store.

She needed $1,000 to pay for the cappuccino and latte maker. It was expensive, but surely her *stiefmutter* would see the need. If Sarah didn't have the money, Mary could sell something, but what? The only thing she had of value was the quilt in her cedar chest that her *mamm* had made her before she died of cancer.

Tears clouded her eyes. Mary grabbed a handkerchief from her bag, blotted her tears and blew her nose. *Nein*, she couldn't sell the quilt *Mamm* had hand stitched it, each day growing paler as the quilt grew lovelier. She had very few things left that *Mamm* had made.

The quilt would easily bring $800.

Nein, Mary would ask Sarah for the money. She'd understand.

When they reached the farm, King slowed, turned into the driveway without coaxing and headed for the barn. *Jah*, this horse never missed a feeding. She didn't unhitch him but hung a bucket of oats on the barn door and hurried to the *haus*.

When she entered the kitchen, Sarah stood at the table making pastry.

"You're home early dear."

Mary slung her bag on a chair. "*Mamm*, we have to buy an espresso machine for the bakery. We can't compete with Noah's store unless we expand the menu, and those fancy drinks are favorites of everyone."

Sarah gave the dough two more passes with the rolling pin and placed the piecrust in a pan. She scrubbed her hands together over the wastebasket to remove the flour and bits of dough, then rinsed them under the faucet and dried.

Mary watched her *stiefmutter* and knew she was taking her time thinking about the answer.

"Mary, a *gut* commercial espresso machine would cost more than a thousand dollars. I'm sorry, but we just don't have that kind of money. Your *daed* wants to get the twins' hospital bill paid before we buy anything else."

A child's scream rose from the corner of the kitchen and drew Mary's attention to the chaos. Michael Paul had his wooden barn set up and the twins, Lena and Liza, were doing their best to aggravate him by hitting his animals.

"*Mamm*," Michael Paul pouted, "tell the twins to quit knocking my cows over."

"In a minute, Michael, I will put them down for a nap."

"*Mamm,*" Mary pressed, "if we don't expand the menu, the bakery will be driven out of business."

Sarah stepped beside Mary and patted her shoulder. "You need to work on the recipe that'll win the contest next month. Are you even sure Sweet Delights needs an expanded menu?"

Mary scowled. "What do you mean?"

"Our bakery has faithful, local customers and we have a lot of tourist business. Yes, revenue may drop, has dropped, but maybe we need to create new recipes and try that first. Many of Iowa City's bakeries have fancy cupcakes in the windows, pies with lattice work or braiding around the edges and flavored drizzles over the tops."

Mary placed a hand on the back of a chair to steady herself. "So you think that my baking is causing us to lose customers?"

"*Nein*, I didn't say that. I noticed a cooking magazine in the doctor's office the other day, and I've been meaning to talk to you about it. I also went into Noah's store yesterday."

"You did what?" Mary gasped.

"Sweetheart, if we want to compete, our product has to be better." Sarah walked to the counter and took the metal lid off a cake plate. There sat a dozen mini cupcakes with paper holders stamped with Noah's store logo. Each cupcake was a different flavor and piled high with swirled frosting and some with syrupy drizzle.

"Did you and *Daed* try Noah's cupcakes?" Mary's voice cracked, disbelief choking her words.

"Mary, his baking is delicious. Now he has started to make Amish spoonbread, friendship bread, and whoopee pies in all kinds of flavors. He uses glazes and flavored drizzles over cakes and cookies. They are attractive desserts."

Pulling a chair away from the kitchen table, Mary plopped down. "*Mamm*, we are Amish. We have never made our desserts look fancy. What will the bishop think?"

"It's only different colored frosting. What can he say?" Sarah sat across from Mary. "While I was looking at Noah's pastries and candy, I overheard two women talking. They said his hazelnut toffee and truffles won a contest in Iowa City."

Sarah's words dug sharply under Mary's skin. "I—I didn't know he was that *gut*." Her stomach did a flip. "I thought, or maybe I was hoping, it was his cheap prices that were bringing in the customers."

Sarah raised a brow. "He has sandwich cookies with faces made out of chocolate chips and candy acorn noses. Some *kinner* were squealing and saying how much they loved them." She grabbed a cookie from the jar and some chocolate chips, sat back at the table and showed Mary a simple design. "The customers don't want a plain sugar cookie or a plain gingerbread man."

"*Mamm*, the way you're talking, we need to rethink our whole baking strategy, too."

"We'll work on the decorations. We'll get together with Hannah, my former assistant. She is very clever and a *wunderbaar* baker." Sarah patted Mary's arm, then went back to her pie and dumped the bowl of cherries she had pitted into the shell.

After pouring a cup of coffee, Mary sipped the hot brew, thoughts spinning in all directions. Hard to believe Noah had that kind of talent. Funny, she hadn't noticed that on her one whirlwind tour through his store on opening day. He clearly kept changing his sale items to keep his customers interested, inquisitive and coming back. *So, Mr. Englischer, you think you can outsmart and outbake us…me.*

Mary's heart fluttered when an image of the handsome Noah Miller breezed through her mind. He was sure a cute cookie, but she was going to crumble that big ego of his.

She pushed her chair back, grabbed her bag and headed for the stairs. Mary closed her bedroom door and opened her cedar chest. She picked up the double-wedding-ring quilt that her real *mamm* had made. Caressing a hand across the quilting and over her favorite pastel colors, she hugged it to her chest. Tears blurred her vision.

Rolling the folded quilt tightly, she tied it with a ribbon and stuffed it in her bag. Mary hurried downstairs and out the kitchen door while Sarah's back was turned. She jumped in the buggy and headed to the consignment shop in Kalona.

Early Monday morning, Noah walked into the office and watched Jenny stare intently at the computer screen. "Hope there's not a problem."

She glanced his way before returning her gaze to the monitor. "No, just trying to catch up. I'm going to start interviewing applicants in a little while for my replacement, but Emily needs to get registered for school today. She's at Sweet Delights. Would you mind taking her to sign up? It'll be a good test for your new assistant Jean to see how she manages without your watchful eye."

Noah quirked an eyebrow at his sister, "I've trained her well, she'll do fine."

He ran across the street and opened the bakery door to the mingling aromas of cinnamon coffee and caramel topping of some kind. His eyes roamed aver the full tables and chairs to Emily sitting at a table with an older couple.

As he walked to the counter, his gaze swept across the new espresso machine. He stopped short when he saw the display case and the expanded assortment of sweets, whoopee pies, red velvet cookies and fruit-filled cookie snaps. He could barely resist trying one.

Mary looked up as he approached. "Mornin', Noah."

"Good morning, Mary. I see you decided to add cappuccino and lattes to your menu."

She smiled. "Afraid of the competition?"

"No, not from you." He held eye contract for a second before she looked away. If she would have stared at him a second longer with those blue eyes, he would have bought all her cookies. Feud or not, she was sure cute.

The doorbell jingled and Mary glanced at the customer. Her shoulders squared and the smile vanished from her face. Noah turned to see who had created such a reaction in her. A twinge of jealousy stung his heart. Seth.

His cousin entered the shop and stopped. He shot Mary a warm smile then yanked his gaze over to Noah. "*Hallo,* cousin."

Noah nodded at Seth. He had wanted to meet his family. But it had been a shock to find out that Seth, his mother's nephew, was the man who had broken Mary's heart.

Seth took a step toward Noah and held out his hand. Noah grabbed a hold and shook, but Seth didn't let go.

Noah jerked his hand away and stepped back.

"Since the dust of shame has settled after your parents' desertion, you've come sneaking back to claim your inheritance, right?"

"Sneaking?" Noah straightened his back. "I opened a store. That's not really sneaking."

"Your *daed* was the youngest son and the one to inherit the Miller farm. So now you're back to step into that role. Your *Onkel* Cyrus and his son, John Miller, aren't happy to see you snooping around their farm."

"Like I said, I own a store here in Kalona, and I own another in Iowa City. I didn't come here to work on a farm or to steal one from anyone." Noah glanced at Emily still sitting with the elderly couple at the table. He motioned for her to head to the door.

Emily hurried out in front of Noah. "Was he the man you were looking for?" she asked.

"What?" He strode across the street. "Well, not the one I had in mind, but he is a cousin of ours. He is the son of Mom's brother."

"He acted sort of angry." Emily glanced back toward the bakery.

Noah grunted. "He's jealous of Mary. He likes her and doesn't like that I talk to her. Do you understand jealousy?"

"Yes. Mom gave me a lecture once when I was jealous of a girl because she had a pretty dress on and mine was a plain one that Mom had made. I wanted one like the other girl wore. Mom said it's what God sees on your inside that makes Him smile, not what's on the outside. You have a good inside, Noah."

Noah reached over and squeezed Emily's hand. As young as she was, she could apply the lesson to this situation. It was the will of God that they should try to please, and then all else would fall into place. But how did anyone decipher the will of God? Noah was still trying to figure that out.

Chapter Seven

Mary slung her hands on her hips, traipsed around the counter and lowered her voice. "Please leave, Seth. I don't appreciate you coming into my bakery and making a scene in front of my customers."

Seth puffed his chest. "He needs to know how things are. He can't expect to move into our community and weasel his way into our *gut* graces."

Mary shook her head. "Farming is the last thing on Noah's mind, and who gets the Miller farm is none of your business, even if you are friends with John Miller." She nodded toward the door. "*Good*bye, Seth." He turned on his heels and marched out.

She returned to the counter, feeling her customer's eyes boring into her back. Business was bad enough without Seth coming in and making a scene.

She grabbed a cloth, cleaned the counter and tidied up around the coffeepots. When the bakery was empty, she hustled to the kitchen, trying to shake off his outburst. She pulled a bowl from the cupboard, scooped up a bag of apples, and peeled.

"Going to practice your apple pie again?" Amanda

pulled two loaves of cinnamon bread from the oven and set them on a cooling rack.

She tossed a peeling in the sink. "There is something about the crust that just isn't right. It's dense instead of flaky, and the apple filling is tart. It will never win a contest."

"Add more butter." Amanda pulled a package from the refrigerator and handed it to Mary.

"Danki." She dumped three cups of flour in the bowl, added the baking powder, salt and sugar. She worked in the butter, poured in the milk and added the spiced apples.

Mary glanced at the recipe for caramel sauce. She added sugar to an iron skillet and stirred continuously until it turned into light brown syrup. Gradually, she added the boiling water and let it simmer.

The trick to a delicious tasting sauce was getting the sugar to the perfect color before adding the water. Sarah had shown her how to create depth of taste. But it wasn't easy and sometimes it took her more than one try. On contest day, she'd have to make it perfect the first time. This recipe was spectacular...when it turned out right.

Mary washed her hands and took her floured apron off. "Amanda, can you watch the bakery for a little while? I have an order to pick up at Hochstetler's Cheese and Ice Cream shop."

"Of course. Tell, Fredda *hallo*. Ice cream will help you forget your fussing with Seth."

"You saw his little outburst?"

"Nein. I heard it all the way in the kitchen, along with everyone else in the bakery."

Mary gritted her teeth. "Seth better never set foot in this bakery again. People will be talking, especially since the gossip has just calmed down after he dumped me at the altar. We have enough trouble keeping customers without him acting like a hooligan."

Amanda's eyes widened, and she shook her head. "Seth did that because he still cares for you. He knows what he lost, and he doesn't want you mixed up with another sweet-talking, *gut*-looking *Englischer*."

"Amanda, you are a hopeless romantic." Mary collected her bag from the closet and opened the door to a thick, humid breath of August air. The blazing Midwest heat pressed in on her, propelling her quickly down the two blocks to Hochstetler's Cheese and Ice Cream.

Mary entered the shop, weaved around the cheese-tasting tables, the coolers and headed to the counter.

When Fredda saw her, she ran around the counter and crushed her in a hug. "I'm so glad to see you, Mary. We have your order all ready. Come and look at our new cheeses, and I'll pour two glasses of tea."

Mary browsed the cooler. There was goat cheese, cheddar, Swiss, Colby, shredded, sliced…and dozens more. Mary took a sample of Swiss on a cracker and turned toward Fredda as she approached. "This is delicious."

"*Danki*. How did your customers like the ice cream? Would you like to try some different flavors?" Fredda held up a tiny sugar cone.

Mary laughed. "*Danki*, but *nein*. They love the last order, but I'd never get out of here if I started sampling. You have really expanded since the last time I was here. You've done a *wunderbaar* job fixing this shop to display your cheeses."

"*Danki*, would you like to try some different cheeses?"

Fredda turned the plate of samples around and pushed it closer to Mary.

"Not right now. I'm going to expand the bakery's menu and start having biscuits and croissants for breakfast and sandwiches for lunch. When we've updated the bakery, I'll start out with the ones I ordered for today, then maybe add Swiss and provolone."

"*Jah*, whatever you want. I can give you some samples to try."

Mary finished her tea and caught up on all Fredda's news. "Danki, but I need to get back to the bakery." She bumped the door open with her hip, maneuvered her bags through the opening, and stepped down to the sidewalk and smack-dab into the path of a man.

Her bag of cheese dropped to the sidewalk. She wobbled back and forth then lost her balance. The man reached around her and pulled her up to a standing position. Cars passing by honked, and a buggy slowed down to nearly a crawl. *Ach.* She glanced at the street, people were watching.

"*Danki*, but please take your hands off me." Heat burned from her cheeks to the top of her ears.

"I'm so sorry. I didn't see you." His voice sounded all too familiar.

She jerked her head up to see his face.

"Noah Miller. I might have known it would be you." She started to reach down.

"I'll get the bag." He picked it up. "Sorry, I was looking across the street and didn't notice you coming out of the shop. It's my fault. I'll carry your bags back to the bakery."

"Please don't. I can manage." Mary glanced around

and noticed cars still slowing to watch them, trying to figure out what had happened.

"I insist after nearly knocking you out."

"Noah, I don't want you anywhere near me. You and Seth made a public display in my shop. Some of those customers will probably never come back. You humiliated me, then and now."

Mary brushed her hands down her dress to smooth her skirt and noticed red smudges. She glanced at her palms, scraped, bleeding and covered with dirt. She snatched the bags from his hands. "You are bound to destroy me one way or another."

Her gaze landed on his face and caught the grin he tried to conceal with his hand.

"So this is funny to you?" She tried to make her voice sound serious when she was stifling a laugh.

He pushed the smile away and gulped. "No, of course not, but what a coincidence."

"You are impossible." She turned, the bags crinkling in her hands, and hurried down the sidewalk.

Amanda was right. Noah was certainly handsome, but he was dangerous territory. He had an invisible off-limits sign posted to his forehead. Mary had made a mistake trusting Seth. She wouldn't make that same error again with another *Englischer*...and certainly not this one.

Tuesday morning, Noah climbed into his SUV and headed for his grandparents' farm. He turned onto the gravel road and just before their driveway, he saw his grandpa standing along the side of the road, pliers in hand, mending fence.

Noah pulled onto the shoulder and parked. He blotted moist hands on his trousers and forced himself out of the vehicle. With each step over the road bank, dry grass and weeds snapped and rustled under his feet, but his grandpa stayed focused on his work. Thomas Miller's abrupt manner had made it clear at their last meeting that he didn't care to mingle with *Englisch* folks. And that was what Noah was. *Englisch.*

Noah stepped to the side of his grandpa and cleared his throat, but the old man didn't acknowledge his presence. "It's a hot day to mend fence."

Grandpa grasped the pliers around the wire fencing with one hand, pulled it up tight to the wooden post, grabbed a staple from his pouch and nailed it in place with the other hand. The old man had a system, but it looked awkward to do with only one set of hands.

When he finished with that post, he silently walked around Noah and headed down the fence line watching for weak spots. He came to another piece of wiring that had pulled loose. Before his grandfather could grab his hammer from his tool belt, Noah pulled it out, snatched a staple from his pouch, placed it over the wire, and hammered it into the post.

In silence, they walked down to the next spot that needed fixing. Grandpa pulled the sagging fence up tight against the post. Noah stuck his hand in the staple pouch, pricked his finger on a sharp edge but pulled a staple out and hammered it into the post. When he finished, a drop of blood had smeared onto the staple and post.

"Your hands will be riddled with blisters and cuts if you keep on working without gloves." The old man pulled a pair of gloves from his waistband and handed them to Noah.

He slid them on as they walked farther down the fence.

In silence, they mended post after post. Not what Noah had expected, but he enjoyed helping his grandfather.

They worked another two hours. At noon, grandpa glanced up at the sun, turned and headed back toward his driveway.

Noah followed. When he came to the spot where he'd parked, he headed for his vehicle.

"Anna will have lunch ready, and I always feed my help before I send them home," Grandpa said as he kept on walking.

Stunned at the invitation, the words hit Noah like a steel bat. To reject would no doubt insult him, and he knew this situation was as hard on his grandparents as it was on him.

Noah pivoted and followed his grandpa to the house. When the old man hung his straw hat on a peg by the door, Noah hung his hat on the peg next to it.

"Anna, set another place." Grandpa motioned to the sink. "Wash up in the metal basin."

Grandma handed Noah a towel. He wiped his hands and handed it to his grandpa then sat at the new place setting. When his grandparents sat, he bowed his head for silent prayer and took his food when they passed the bowls and platter.

The silence was unnerving. But unfamiliar with Amish customs, Noah didn't want to talk if they weren't allowed to speak at the dinner table.

"Why are you here?" His grandpa's gruff voice shook the silence.

"I stopped by to…just say hello."

"*Nein*, I mean why did you move to Kalona if you have a store in Iowa City?" Grandpa kept his head down and continued to eat.

"I wanted to expand the business. The store in Iowa City is doing well, but Kalona is a huge tourist attraction because of the Amish community."

"So you thought you'd tell them you were Amish and get more business?"

Noah dropped his fork. It clanked against the plate then settled in his smashed potatoes. "No, nein. that's not what I'm doing. I'm just opening a store like anyone else. I've told a few people that my parents were Amish, but I don't advertise it." His back stiffened, and his appetite waned. He pushed his chair away from the table.

Grandpa motioned toward Noah's plate. "Finish eating."

Noah hesitated, but pulled his chair back to the table and took a bite of food. Maybe this wasn't a good idea. But if he didn't try, how was he ever going to get to know them?

Tension hung in the air like the dust from the gravel road, and silence clung to the steam rising from the food.

Noah finished eating. "You're a good cook, Grandma. Thank you for inviting me to dinner. It was a pleasure getting a chance to help you and share a meal with you two." The words pushed out on their own, surprising even Noah.

He shoved his chair back, gave a nod to his grandpa and retrieved his hat from the peg. "Goodbye."

He headed back to his SUV. His stomach was full, but his heart felt half-empty. He wasn't sure why he wanted a relationship with his grandparents, but he did. He missed his parents, and he missed not knowing his family.

He opened his vehicle door and looked back at his grandparents' house. He understood their reserved feelings, especially about the *Englisch*. His parents had said the Amish lived apart because they separated themselves from the fallen world. From nonbelievers.

He was a believer. Was it possible for him to have a relationship with them? And to have one with Mary?

Chapter Eight

After completing the Wednesday morning baking, Mary flipped open her recipe book. Was she wasting her time looking for that special recipe? The bishop hadn't given her his final approval to enter the contest yet, and it was in five weeks.

She pulled a pencil from a holder and added notes to her recipe card: more nutmeg and a dash of cinnamon. Maybe she'd add licorice or anise for a little different taste to the apples and try a cookie dough for the pie crust.

Mary mixed, rolled the dough, laid the butter crust in the pan, arranged the spiced apples, and then wove strips of pastry over the top. She slipped it in the oven just as the bell jingled over the front door. Blotting her hands on her apron, she speed-walked toward the display counter. When she saw the customer, her feet almost stuttered to a stop. Bishop Yoder. And he wore a solemn face.

She eased herself forward like a child en route to her father for punishment. Reaching the counter, she jerked her chin up. "*Gut Morgen*, Bishop Yoder. Do you have a sweet tooth this morning?"

"Just a cup of coffee, and could you take a minute to sit with me?"

"*Jah*, I'll bring it over." Her hands jittered as she poured the coffee.

He took the table by the window and placed his hat on the chair next to him.

Oh, Lord, please let this be gut *news.* She carried two cups to the table and sat opposite the bishop. She blew on her coffee while he poured sugar and cream into his brew and stirred.

He took a sip, pushed his cup to the side and clasped his hands on the table. "Mary, I was riding past Hochstetlers' Cheese shop on Monday, and I noticed you with Noah Miller. He had his arms around you. I'm sure I don't need to remind you of the problems with seeing an *Englischer.* You're a baptized member of the church. You will be shunned if you marry him, and the church could discipline you if continue to make such a public display."

Mary jerked her cup as she raised it to take a sip. Nearly spilling it, she set it back down. "I'm not seeing Noah."

"I know that he and his sisters spend significant time at your bakery."

"Emily likes to come over and talk to Amanda, and she enjoys helping us bake. She's new in town and lonely. It's harmless." Her words flurried out, uncontrolled.

"I also saw you with Noah at the barn raising introducing him to his relatives. Be careful, Mary." He emphasized the last three words. "What looks like something innocent today can turn into something serious when you least suspect it." The bishop took another sip of his coffee, grabbed his hat and pushed his chair back. "You have permission to compete in the contest." He stood and walked out.

At the sound of footfalls behind her, Mary sprang up from her chair. "Amanda, you gave me a start. I didn't hear you come in."

"*Jah*, I see that. You're as white as flour. Are you all right?"

"The bishop was just here and warned me about getting too friendly with Noah. But I got permission to compete in the contest."

"*Gut* news and bad. He's trying to keep his flock together. You can't blame him for that. And he knows that kind of relationship can end in heartbreak." Amanda wrapped her friend in a hug. "But you don't have feelings for Noah, do you?" Her voice sounded more probing than sure.

"Of course not." At least, Mary hoped she didn't. Although her back still tingled from Noah's touch after he lifted her from the ground. Her heart fluttered each time she thought about the encounter. But *nein*, she would be sure to protect her heart when Noah was around. She followed Amanda back to the kitchen.

"*Ach*, my pie smells done." Mary grabbed potholders and pulled the hot tin from the oven. A loud thump at the front door startled her. Her hands jerked, but she managed to get the pie to the counter before it slipped to the floor. "What is that commotion?"

"I have no idea." Amanda dropped her rolling pin and raced ahead of Mary to the front of the bakery.

Daed and Jacob carried a table into the bakery and set it by the window. Mary laughed and blew out a sigh. "Sorry, Amanda, I forgot to tell you that we are going to start serving breakfast biscuits and croissants in the mornings."

"What?" Amanda stared at the two new tables and chairs they were carrying inside and squeezing in next to the other five. "Mary, that's going to be a lot of work for just the two of us."

"The business has to expand in order to compete with Noah's store. We are just going to offer the biscuit and croissant from six to nine a.m. It shouldn't take much more effort to fry a few eggs, bacon and ham. My cousin Nettie is going to come in and help us.

Daed wrapped his arm around Mary. "I pray your business will improve. Now, Jacob and I must get back to the farm."

Mary ran her hand across one of the wooden tables *Daed* had made. He loved to work with his hands, and it showed. She picked up a piece of chalk and wrote on the chalkboard. Starting Friday, breakfast biscuits and croissants being served with egg, ham or bacon.

On Thursday, Mary and Amanda arrived early to make sure the kitchen was organized and there was space ready for additional biscuits and croissants. Later in the morning, the Country Fresh truck delivered the extra eggs, ham and bacon.

"I sure hope my idea works." Mary braced herself with a hand on the edge of the counter. Her brain spinning at the thought of the extra money she had spent.

"It will." Amanda patted her friend on the back. "You'll see."

Mary drew a deep, cleansing breath. "Well, at least Noah's store isn't in the Kalona tourist guide yet, so the tourists will probably stop at Sweet Delights first. But I'm sure he'll have it listed for next year's printing."

She put that out of her head as she started her long day of baking and preparing the bakery for serving a hot breakfast.

After Amanda set the croissant dough in the refrigerator and went home, Mary took one last survey of the kitchen's layout, turned the lights out, locked up and hurried, feet aching, to the buggy. She hitched King, and as she stepped in the buggy, a thought tickled her brain. Tomorrow, Noah would be in for a surprise when Sweet Delights started selling fresh breakfast biscuits and croissants.

Friday morning Mary's cousin, Nettie Brenneman, met her at the bakery and followed her in to the kitchen. "Danki, Nettie, for helping us out.

"I'm glad to do it. What do you want me to do?"

"Why don't you get the skillets ready for bacon, ham and eggs? Place your supplies where it's comfortable for you. I'll take the croissant dough from the refrigerator and finish making the first batch."

"*Danki*, Mary, I'm excited about helping, and maybe I can show you some of my baking."

She watched Nettie tear around the kitchen, accustomed to cooking for her parents and ten siblings. Mary had tasted Nettie's breakfast rolls, and they were delicious. *Jah*, maybe Nettie would bring some new flavor to the bakery.

Ten minutes later, Amanda rushed into the kitchen, letting in a cool gust of morning air. She glanced around. "Wow, you two have been working hard. The stations look ready to go."

Mary glanced at her friend. "*Gut Morgen. Jah*, Nettie will fry the eggs and meat. I'm finishing the croissants."

"I'll start the biscuits." Amanda poured a cup of coffee, took a sip and got started.

Mary rolled out the croissant dough, shaped the triangles and brushed with egg wash. She set them aside to proof. When they were puffed up and spongy to the touch, she spritzed a preheated oven, placed the croissants in the oven and spritzed again. At the end of the process, they were a golden brown.

Fifteen minutes later, Mary glanced at the clock. "Almost time to start." She darted to the front of the bakery, set out condiments, and filled the napkins holders.

At 6:00 a.m., she unlocked the door. Before she had time to walk back to the counter, Frank Wallin pushed the door open.

He stuck his nose in the air and made a loud sniffing sound. "It smells like bacon in here. I'll try a ham, egg and cheese biscuit, and my usual roll and coffee."

"Frank," Mary chuckled, "did you order a roll because you're not sure if you'll like the biscuit?" A smile pulled at her mouth, but she tried to push it away.

He laughed. "It was a hard decision. I want to try the biscuit, but it's hard giving up the roll."

Amanda scooted in from the kitchen with the biscuit. "You're feeling daring today, Frank."

Mary bagged the biscuit and handed it to Frank along with his coffee. "Let us know how you like it?"

"I will, but I have no doubt that it's delicious."

After Frank, Mary served one customer after another. When the steady stream let up, she glanced at the clock. 9:00. "*Ach.* It was a success."

Amanda ran to the front. "Wunderbaar."

Nettie stuck her head around the kitchen door. "Congratulations!"

Mary laughed and twirled around. "I can't believe the difference that a few eggs and ham can make."

The doorbell jingling, pulled her attention to the next customer. She straightened and threw on a smile. Noah Miller.

Noah stepped forward. "So, you're making breakfast sandwiches now. You're sort of a copycat," he clowned.

"The bakery has to compete with other businesses, Noah, or was it your plan just to run me out of town without a fight?" Her cheeks reddened.

He laughed. "Take it easy. I'm just teasing you. I don't blame you one bit for serving breakfast. I'd do the same thing. I stopped to thank you for introducing me to my family out at the barn raising."

Her cheeks lightened to a pink. "Glad it worked out for you." Her tone was warm.

"I'm not sure how it *worked out* just yet, but at least we know each other now. I stopped by my grandpa's farm the other day. He was mending fence, I helped him, and he asked me to stay to dinner."

"That's *wunderbaar*. He is strict in his belief, but maybe he will soften."

"I don't know about that. I helped him, and I think he felt obligated."

"You should see it for what it is. The feet walk the road, but *Gott* works in the heart to change the direction."

"Maybe someday I'll know God well enough that I'll understand what you just said."

Mary poured a cup of coffee and handed it to Noah. "I think your *grossdaddi* wants to get to know you, but you are *Englisch*. Your *daed*, his *sohn*, broke his heart when he left and never came home to visit or try to patch up whatever happened between them. That had to be hard on Thomas."

"You're right. I'm expecting too much." Noah braced a hip against the counter.

Mary's eyes locked with his then she pulled away. "Just keep seeing him. Maybe you can melt the ice that has formed around his heart. Eventually, you may chip it away. Where's Emily? I haven't seen her the last few days."

"She started school and has met some friends, so you may not see her quite as much now." He tried to hide the smile that wanted to break free. Mary had actually dropped her guard and let them have a gentle moment.

"*Gut*, she needs friends."

He glanced at the display case. "So how is your recipe for the contest coming along?"

"So that's your real reason for stopping by. Now I understand. For your information, Mr. Miller, it is out-of-this-world wow-wee."

Noah laughed. "I have no doubt. You're a terrific baker. I haven't decided what I'm going to make yet. But I'm sure I'll find the perfect one that'll stand up to yours."

"Noah," she huffed, "you are so conceited."

"I can see I have overstayed my welcome. See you around, Chef Brenneman." He stole another quick look at Mary before heading to the door. She was sure feisty.

But then why shouldn't she be? She was fighting for her bakery and the welfare of her family. He understood, but he'd invested a lot of money in opening this store, and he couldn't afford to throw it away. The contest would help decide which one of them would survive.

Either way, he would lose. If he won the contest, it would probably drive her out of business, since a town with a population of five thousand probably couldn't sustain two bakeries year round. If she won, he'd be driven out of town.

He crossed the street and looked back at Sweet Delights. Either way, he would lose a friend, one that sure could irritate him but also kept him on his toes.

Chapter Nine

Mary sorted through Saturday's mail and opened the box of new tourist brochures that had just arrived and glanced through the top one. She browsed the column under restaurants and bakeries. Lazy Susan's headed the list, followed by Miller's Farm-fresh Grocery, Delicatessen and Bakery, then Sweet Delights.

She stared at the paper until the words began to blur. She threw the brochure back in the box and snapped the lid closed.

Amanda looked up from filling the display case. "Something wrong?"

"Noah's shop is listed."

"Oh! Well, at least yours is listed first, *jah*?"

"*Nein*, they didn't just add it at the end, they put the shops in alphabetical order. His is listed before Sweet Delights because they forgot the Amish in front."

She lifted the box cover, picked up a brochure and handed it to Amanda. Her friend glanced over it, groaned and handed it back. Mary set the box in the cupboard, pulled the remaining old brochures out and set a stack on the edge of the counter.

"So you are going to use up the old ones first?"

"Please don't judge me." Uneasiness stalked up Mary's back.

"I'm not judging you. I know your situation. That feeling you have is coming from you judging yourself. You paid for the old brochures and have a right to use them."

The doorbell jingled, and old Bishop Ropp entered, tapping a cane along the tile flooring. *"Gut Morgen."*

Mary hurried around the counter to his side. "Bishop, can I help you? What happened?"

"I can manage. A cup of coffee and a piece of apple pie, please. And how about a sample of your contest entry dessert? I'll sit, rest and enjoy the pie…if someone gets it for me."

"Jah, jah. I'll hurry, but what happened? Are you feeling all right?"

"Old age is what happened. I think I can do anything I did when I was young, but my body lets my mind know who is really in charge. I twisted my knee trying to climb on my *sohn* Albert's hayrack. So like the old horses, I'm put out to pasture. If I keep coming in here for pie, I'll look like an old horse, too."

Mary hurried to the kitchen, returned and set two plates in front of the bishop. "Here is your pie. And this other one on your right—" she slid the plate closer "—is my contest entry. I'd like you to try it and tell me what you think?"

He took a bite of the pie in front of him, chewed and glanced toward the ceiling. He took a bite of the second one. "Both *gut* but not as *wunderbaar* as Sarah's papa's pie. I thought you were going to try to find his recipe?"

"Sarah found his old recipe book, but it wasn't there, or he didn't write the recipe down that you're talking about. We'll probably never find it. But are you sure this isn't close?"

"*Jah*, I'm sure."

She sighed. "Looks like I'll be staying late again to practice."

Just before closing, Mary made a pie but the result was the same as before. She cleaned the kitchen, locked the back door, hitched King and set him to a brisk pace. When he turned into the driveway, Mary glanced across the barnyard and noticed Hannah Smith's, Sarah's former assistant, buggy parked in the drive by the house.

She'd better hurry and say hi to Hannah before she left. She unhitched and fed King, then dashed into the kitchen.

"*Ach*, Hannah, it's *gut* to see you."

"*Danki,*" Hannah pulled out the chair next to her at the table and pointed to it. "I was hoping I'd get to see you. Sarah was just telling me that you're going to enter the fall festival baking competition. How *wunderbaar*. That should give you a lot of publicity."

Mary sat next to Hannah. "I was hoping we could put our heads together and come up with a fantastic apple recipe. Bishop Ropp was in the bakery today and insists Sarah's *daed* had an apple pie recipe that he'd drive five miles just to eat a piece."

Hannah turned to Mary's *stiefmutter*. "What recipe is that, Sarah? Did we make it?"

"*Nein*, I don't think so. I did find an old recipe book in the attic that belonged to Daed. It had an apple pie recipe."

Mary nodded "I made it. Bishop Ropp tried a piece and said that wasn't it."

"While you two talk," Sarah stood, "I'll go back upstairs and look again."

Hannah shook her head at Sarah. "I've seen that mess up in the attic before. We'll all go. Remember, safety in numbers."

Sarah raised a brow. "It's not that bad."

Mary climbed up the narrow attic steps first and pushed the small door open. She ducked her head and entered, but the ceiling was so low she had to stay bent over. She held the lantern as her *stiefmutter* and Hannah entered. "I'll hold the light while you two search these boxes."

Sarah pointed to a cardboard box. "Check that one, Hannah. I'm going to dig through this big one."

Mary held the lantern high to shed light on both the boxes. Piece by piece, Sarah and Hannah picked through years of collecting.

"Here are some recipes," Sarah shouted. "They're loose ones in the very bottom of the box." She pulled them out and carefully shuffled through the yellow, brittle pages.

Mary inched the lantern closer so Sarah could get a *gut* look at the writing. "What are they, *Mamm*?"

Sarah held up one of the pages, a smile playing across her face. "This one is an apple pie recipe. All of these loose recipes must have fallen out of the book when I grabbed it the other day."

"You found it?" Mary stepped closer.

"Well, I found an apple pie recipe. You'll have to make it, let Bishop Ropp try it and see if it's the one."

"Let's get this stuff back in the boxes and get out of here." Hannah wiped her brow. "It's hot up here."

As Mary led the parade back into the kitchen, her

daed entered from the porch. She held the recipe up for him to see. "We think we found the recipe that was lost."

"*Gut*. Have you told her yet, Sarah?"

"*Nein*, Caleb, I waited for you."

Mary glanced from Sarah to her *daed*. "What's going on?"

Her *daed* smiled. "Summer crops were *gut*. I have enough money to install additional kitchen electrical outlets and get it ready for the food-service expansion. That way, when you win the contest, you can install griddles, a panini press or whatever else you need. A carpenter will install a bar across the front of the bakery. We'll buy a few high stools and create more customer space.

Mary charged across the kitchen and threw her arms around her *daed*. "*Danki*." She turned back toward Sarah. "Both of you."

Danki, Lord Jesus, for touching Daed's heart so he could find a little money to spare. Mary glanced at the recipe and crushed it to her heart. Change was coming, and Mr. Noah Miller would soon discover that.

On Monday morning after getting his assistant squared away with her duties, Noah headed out the front door. A banging noise pulled his attention to the other side of the street. Was that racket coming from Sweet Delights?

Mary stepped out of her bakery, crossed the street and walked past his store, giving him the silent treatment.

"Nice morning for a stroll, Mary. Business must be good."

She waved a hand in the air.

"What's all that noise? Workmen at your bakery?"

She stopped and turned. "Smucker's Electric is adding more outlets, and Bender Building and Supply is adding a luncheon counter."

He hadn't figured she'd remodel. "That's good. You must be planning on winning the contest next month?"

"Worried, Miller?"

"Nope. Actually, I was going to pay my grandparents a visit and try to get to know them better. I wasn't going to stay long, but I thought since you're Amish, your presence might serve as a buffer between us. If you wouldn't mind riding along, and I'm sure grandma would like your company."

Mary glanced back at Sweet Delights. "I can get my mail later. Let me run and tell Amanda, but I can't be gone more than an hour or so."

"That's fine."

When she returned, Noah held the door for Mary while she slid in then ran around to his side. He started the engine and headed out of town. "How's the recipe for the festival coming along?"

"So that's why you asked me along?"

"Of course not. I thought if my grandparents see you, they might be nicer to me." That wasn't exactly the whole reason, but he couldn't tell her that.

"Noah, what did you expect?" She softened her tone. "It was your parents' decision to stay away." She reached across the console and laid a gentle hand on his arm. "Please try to understand it from their point of view."

"Yes, I realize that."

The next mile was quiet as Mary stared out her side window. She glanced his way, and he turned slightly to steal a look at her blond hair. Her cornflower-blue eyes set his heart ticking so hard he was afraid she'd hear it.

He'd fibbed to her. He didn't need her as a buffer between him and his grandparents, he just wanted to enjoy sitting beside her. She was lovely.

"This is the place." Mary's voice brought him out of his musing.

"Thanks, I wasn't paying attention." He pulled in the drive and parked by the house.

She leaned in. "Are you nervous about seeing your *grosseldre* again?"

Slowly, he turned toward her. "In a way, my family is such a mystery to me. They're kin, yet they're strangers. But I want to know them, see them and feel like I'm part of their family."

She smiled. "So you're thinking about converting to Amish?"

"No, I don't really see me driving around in a buggy, going without electricity and dressing like everyone else in the community."

She eyed his plaid shirt then dropped her gaze to his tan trousers. "*Jah*, I imagine Plain clothes wouldn't really be your style."

The barn door opened, and Thomas Miller walked in their direction.

Noah stepped out of his vehicle and opened the back door. "Mary, I brought a box of fresh green vegetables and some baked goods. Would you mind carrying it in the haus?"

"Sure." She glanced at Thomas approaching and turned to Noah. "Be honest with him. Don't pretend to be a grandson then disappear from his life."

Mary's words weighed on his heart as he walked to meet his grandpa. Mixed feelings pulled at his resolve.

He had a dream for his future and expanding his brand into Des Moines. Yet he had a yearning to know his family, and in some small way, be part of their lives.

As the old man approached, Noah held out his hand. "Good morning."

"*Morgen*. Did you come to help mend fence or learn to milk a cow?" Grandpa's frown deepened, but he shook Noah's hand.

Noah wasn't sure, but it almost sounded like his grandpa had made a joke. "I stopped by to bring Grandma some vegetables and baked goods from the store, but if you need help, I'll gladly do what I can."

"Farming is hard work."

"I know that, but I'd like to work with you, learn about farming and understand why you love it."

Grandpa harrumphed. A deep line creased his forehead.

The old man's expression tore at Noah's heart. The frown lines in his grandpa's face pointed to uncertainty, and it clawed at Noah's innermost man to think he wasn't trusted. He didn't want to disappoint his grandpa. He wanted to be able to talk to him and love him freely. But was that even possible? Would the old man let him? "Would you show me around your farm?"

Grandpa's face turned to one of puzzlement and then relaxed. "*Jah*, I can do that. Come, we'll start with the milking floor." He showed Noah all around the milking room and went through the procedures.

Noah walked beside Grandpa in silence, Mary's words circling around in his head. *Be honest with him.* That was the question. Was he being honest with the old man or was he being selfish?

* * *

Mary knocked on the door, and Anna opened it with a surprised look.

"*Gut Morgen*, Anna." Mary stepped in and set the box on the table. "Noah packed some fresh vegetables and breads for you."

"So our grandson has paid us another visit, and you came along. *Danki,* it's *gut* to have company. Would you like a cup of tea?"

"That would be nice."

"Is our grandson thinking about joining our community?"

Mary caught her breath. "Anna, you'll need to ask Noah that question. I can't answer for him."

Anna's eyes sparkled. "I thought maybe you were courting, and that would bring our family back together."

Her words startled Mary. "*Nein.* We are not courting."

Anna nodded with disappointment crossing her face.

Mary's chest ached for Anna. When Seth left, it ripped her heart in two and packed it with distrust. When he returned, it filled her with conflict. So she well imagined Anna's distress. Mary hadn't known that Anna and Thomas had a son Jeremiah. That's the way it was with the Amish. If a child left the community, he was out of their lives. Now, this elderly couple had to deal with the conflict again.

"Would you like to see my current quilt project, Mary?" Anna asked. "It's turning out lovely."

"Sure."

Anna led the way to the room with her stretching rack. "It's called a Prairie Star patchwork quilt."

"The fall colors are beautiful." Mary examined the stitching. "You do *gut* work, Anna."

"And how is your bakery business? I enjoy stopping there when I'm in town."

A door banged closed, and Anna headed for the kitchen with Mary falling into step behind her. Thomas was in the kitchen, pouring a cup of coffee.

He nodded at Mary. "Noah is waiting for you by his vehicle."

"*Danki*. It was nice seeing you both." She hurried outside and down the walk. Noah held open the door, and she slid onto the seat. "What happened?"

Noah started the engine, drove down the drive and turned onto the gravel road. "He showed me around, starting with the milking floor and explained the procedure. Then he told me I should be learning this from my father. He reminded me that he was Amish, and I'm *Englisch*."

Mary stared straight ahead. Thomas had politely drawn the line for Noah. It was a warning for him...that each should stay in their rightful community.

A twinge plucked at her heart. *Jah*, she too needed to take care and not spend too much time with Noah. He was *Englisch* and nothing could become of their friendship. She glanced his way as a hollow spot notched in her heart.

Chapter Ten

Tuesday at 9:00 a.m., Mary held open the front door of the bakery as Glenn and his *sohn* from Bender Building and Supply carried in the Formica countertop she wanted installed as a bar for stools.

"*Morgen*, Mary. We should be done by the end of the day. Pete's coming to do the electrical work, jah?"

"He promised he would be here today." A knock sounded on the back door. "Excuse me, Glenn."

She hurried to the kitchen and opened the back door. "*Morgen*, Pete. Glenn just asked if you were going to make it."

Pete set his Smuckers Electrical toolbox on the kitchen floor. "Sorry, I'm a little late, forgot something and had to run back to the shop and fetch it. But don't worry, the additional outlets should all be installed by the end of the day."

"*Danki*, I really appreciate it." Mary moved from the kitchen to the front of the bakery, checking on the progress of the countertop.

When convinced the men could handle things without her, Mary poured a cup of coffee and retreated to the office. She pulled out the bookkeeping ledger and journal and started catching up on bookwork. After three hours of nonstop work, she closed the books. The bottom line showed an increase in revenue. She was glad of that, but income still needed to be higher.

Mary wandered from her office into the front of the bakery and set her cup down. As her gaze swept the room, her jaw dropped open. The mounted counter fit perfectly under the windows. It was lovely and functional. The brown Formica matched the wooden stools. Hopefully, it would attract young customers to stop in for a cappuccino or latte.

Glenn pushed the front door open, set a box on the floor and began to fill it with scraps of wood and countertop. "It'll look better when I have the sawdust cleaned up and the stools unboxed and pushed under the counter."

"It looks *wunderbaar.*" She walked around to get a better look. "Don't worry about the sawdust. Jacob is going to help me clean and paint tomorrow. I'm just pleased you could work us into your schedule so fast."

"Glad to do it."

"Do I write a check now?"

"*Nein.* I have to add it all up and send you an invoice. We'll finish up and be out of your hair."

Pete poked his head around the kitchen doorjamb into the bakery. "I'm done. I'll total and send an invoice."

"*Danki*, Pete." Mary followed him to the kitchen and ran her gaze around. "The extra outlets look *gut*. It's going to be great having them. And the generator that powers the bakery's electricity will be large enough to handle the extra outlets?"

"No problem, it's big enough."

After Pete gathered his toolbox and left, Mary headed

back to the front of the bakery for one last walk through. She flicked the light switch, hitched King and steered him for home.

The peaceful clip-clop of horse's hooves on the road was soothing. Mary leaned back in the seat and let King set his gait to an easy trot. A new sensation bloomed in her chest. The old bakery was her *stiefmutter* Sarah's, but the newly decorated bakery was her idea. And even though the changes were minor, it made the shop feel like hers.

She clutched the string of her prayer *kapp* and twirled it around her finger. *Jah*, she would definitely have to confess that outburst of self-satisfaction and pride at what she'd done for the bakery. But who could blame her? It was finally happening! Her bakery was getting a new face.

King turned into the drive and headed for the barn. She unhitched the buggy, wiped King down and filled his oat and water pails. His brown eyes widened with anticipation. She patted his mane and closed the barn door behind her. She carried her quilted bag to the *haus* and hung it on a peg by the door.

Her *stiefmutter* turned from the sink. "You're home. How did it go today?"

"*Wunderbaar.* It looks great. I can't wait until Jacob and I get it painted tomorrow."

Jacob banged the screen door closed. "What am I going to get out of all this work?"

Mary ran over to him and mussed his hair. "I'll make you my contest apple pie and you can eat the whole thing."

He chuckled. "I'm going to hold you to that."

The screen door squeaked open and *Daed* wiped his shoes on the rag rug. "What's going on in here?"

"I was telling them the additional outlets and the new counter were installed today and it all looks *wunderbaar*." Mary gave *Daed* a kiss on the cheek. *"Danki."*

"Gut, I'm glad to hear it. Do you think it will help keep the bakery open?" His tone laced with skepticism.

Mary took a step back. *"Daed,* it sounds like you don't believe I can do it?"

"Nein. I didn't mean that. You are a terrific baker, and you can do whatever you set your mind to do. I'm only saying that Noah's store also has fresh vegetables, a nice deli and delicious baked goods."

"And how do you know how his food tastes?" she huffed.

Silence loomed across the kitchen.

Jacob shoved his hands in his pocket. "If *Daed* and I are hungry when we're in town, Noah's deli is a convenient place to grab a quick sandwich or a slice of pizza. His tuna sandwiches are super, and I don't care much for tuna fish."

"So you go behind my back and sneak off to the competition." Her voice strained. "And what do you think of his breads and pastries, are they *gut*?"

Jacob glanced at *Daed*. *"Jah,* his pastries are *gut*. His pecan pie is better than yours."

Mary gasped. "You're just saying that."

"Sorry, sis, but I'm telling the truth." Jacob reached up and pulled a string on her prayer *kapp*. "You better practice for that baking contest, because you're going to need all the practice you can get. Have you tried his baking? His croissants are the best I've ever had."

Mary turned toward *Daed*. "Is that what you think, too?"

Daed nodded.

Mary pulled a chair away from the table and sat. "*Mamm*, I had no idea."

Sarah wrapped her arms around Mary. "We'll work on some recipes. You'll see. We'll come up with some delicious new ones."

Horses' hooves tromped up the drive, and buggy wheels skidded to a stop. *Daed* stepped to the door and walked out on the porch.

A minute later, he burst back into the kitchen. "The bakery is on fire. Let's get to town."

"I'll stay here with the *kinner*," *Mamm* yelled. "Mary, you and Jacob go. Hurry!"

"Mary, get your things. Jacob and I'll hitch the buggy," *Daed* shouted on his way out the door.

Mary paced the ground until the buggy pulled up to the *haus* with both Tidbit and King hitched. She jumped in the back seat.

Daed shook the reins. "Hee-yah!" The horses jerked the buggy and tore off down the driveway. *Daed* slowed them to turn onto the road then headed to town. He tapped the reins again. "Hee-yah."

Mary twisted her hands on her quilted bag handles so hard her fingers hurt. "Go faster, *Daed*."

"*Jah*, I'm trying to do that, but others use the road too. The firemen are there taking care of it."

"I know, but I want to see what's happening." The three miles to town seemed endless to Mary.

Arriving at the edge of town, the air reeked of burnt wood. When the buggy drew closer, toxic fumes from the fire stung Mary's eyes. As the building came into view, she scooted to the end of the seat, threw her hands to her mouth and gasped. *Daed* stopped outside the barricades. Firetrucks, police cars and red lights filled the street in front of the bakery.

Mary sniffled as tears filled her eyes and drenched her cheek. *"Nein, nein."* Flames still engulfed the inside of the building as hoses spayed water from all sides. *"Nein."* She threw herself back against the seat. "Oh, *nein, Mamm* is going to be devastated."

She slipped her hand in her bag, scratched around and pulled out a handkerchief. She wiped the tears off her cheeks and blew her nose.

Daed turned King and Tidbit around. "I'm going to get the horses away from here. We'll walk back and get closer." He parked in a lot a block away.

Jacob opened the door, Mary jumped out, and they walked toward the destruction. Her body was numb, her legs almost unwilling to take another step. She stopped in front of Noah's store and watched the smoldering building from the other side of the street outside the police barricades.

Thirty minutes later, firefighters still shouted to each other and aimed hoses at the dying flames. Noah stood in his yellow Nomex gear beside something they'd taken from the burning building. Black char clung to the sides, so Mary couldn't make out the object.

Daed stepped closer and wrapped his arm around her shoulders. "Are you okay?"

"Jah, but even seeing it, I'm still in disbelief."

He squeezed her to his side.

Mary drew a deep breath with sobs catching in her throat. "Can we rebuild right away?"

Her vater patted her arm. "We'll have to talk to Sarah and see what she wants to do."

Mayor Conrad walked up behind *Daed* and patted him on the back. "Sorry about the bakery, Caleb. We need your business in town, so I hope you decide to rebuild."

"*Danki*, Mr. Conrad. It's just such a shock. Something we never expected to happen."

"We're all praying for your family. I'm going to go over and talk to the fire chief. Take care, Caleb." Mayor Conrad turned and faced Mary. "It's a real shame, but rebuild." He nodded, then headed across the street.

Jacob shuffled his feet around on the sidewalk, trying to get a better look. "*Daed*, I'm going to go over and talk with Noah Miller and see if the firemen know where the fire started."

Daed nodded. "They might not know yet, but I'll walk with you."

They crossed the street, staying out of the firefighters' way. When Noah had his hands free, Jacob approached him and they talked for a minute. After a few more moments, Jacob and Daed walked closer to the building where the chief was, but Noah turned and headed toward Mary.

He stopped beside her and turned back to look at the charred building. "How ya doing, Mary? Sorry about Sweet Delights." He stumbled over each word in a soft voice.

Tears blurred her eye. "Now you're the only bakery in town." Her voice quaked and tears streamed down her face. "I'll never get my business back."

His amber gaze of concern met and held hers. "You'll rebuild." He stepped closer, as if trying to lend her his strength should she need it.

"Amish don't have insurance. By the time we find the

money, which I doubt *Daed* could do, everyone would be used to shopping at your store."

"Don't underestimate your loyal customers. Sure, they might like something I sell, pizza, a favorite sandwich, but they still love Sweet Delights."

Her chest ached, her eyes felt puffy, and her face was wet with a continuous stream of tears. "The mainstay of my life has been ripped from me. Even if we can rebuild, it won't be the same place that Sarah's *daed* started. His soul filled those four walls. Customers remember all the *gut* times they had there, his recipes, his joking with them. He helped the community, and they loved him. Most of his recipes were just destroyed."

"Did you have his recipe book locked in a safe? The fire burned at 1,100 degrees Fahrenheit." He softened his voice. "There won't be much, if anything salvageable. The book would have burned."

She gulped a breath as her life was tearing into pieces at his news. "*Jah*, I locked the recipe book in the safe, along with the ledger and journal." She sobbed. "Now everything is gone."

Why, Gott...why? I have nothing to my name. I loved Sarah's bakery, and You took that. I don't even have my quilt anymore.

Noah wrapped an arm around her shoulders and pulled her close, so close she could feel his breath on her cheek. "Shh, Mary. Sometimes God takes away so He can give us something better." His words wrapped around her like a prayer. "It might not be much, but the safe survived the fire. It's smoldering now, but we had the hot fire put out in forty-five minutes. I'll have it moved to my store for safekeeping, if you want."

Mary sniffled and swallowed hard. "*Jah*, that would be fine."

* * *

A protective twinge tightened Noah's throat as he glanced down at Mary, snuggling close to his chest. "Do you want to come inside my store to sit and rest?"

"*Danki*, but I want to go home." She blotted a tear running down her cheek. "*Mamm* will be a wreck wanting to know what's going on. It was her vater's bakery, and it meant a lot to her. It will just devastate her. And I need to stop and tell Amanda."

"Mary, I can't tell you how sorry I am."

"Don't talk, Noah. My heart was just ripped out, and I don't want to discuss it. Not right this minute, I can't."

He drew in a ragged breath and nodded. He released his arm. "Listen, we aren't enemies. I never meant to hurt you or drive you out of business. I'm truly sorry I put my store across from Sweet Delights. When I rented the building, I knew there was a drug store on one side and an antique store on the other, but I didn't check the whole street. I'll give you space in my store, and you can keep your bakery going. You can use my ovens and whatever else you need until your shop is rebuilt."

Mary's eyes widened. "What? I couldn't possibly do that. Have you lost your senses?"

Noah smiled and shook his head. "Of course not, but thanks for asking. Everyone in town knows we're competing, and I don't want them to think I'd take advantage of you after your bakery burned. Someone might even say I started it."

Mary jerked her head up and locked eyes with him. "No one in this town would ever accuse you of that."

"It could start as a joke and get around. That would ruin my reputation, and it would be your fault for not working with me and squashing any loose gossip."

"Mr. Miller, you have a way of exaggerating the problem." She shook her head with a smirk.

"Yeah, but what do you say? I'd sure feel better about everything if you would let me help you."

Mary drew a deep breath of smelly, smoky, toxic air, coughed and stepped back. She glanced across the street at the smoldering building. "I don't know how long it will take to rebuild, or if *Daed* and *Mamm* will want to." Tears filled her eyes and clung to her lashes. She batted them away.

"We don't have to talk about length of time now. Moving a small part of your baking to my store is only a temporary situation. Unless you would rather come and work for me?"

"Not even as a joke. Then people probably would think you did it on purpose to get me to bake for you since your baking tastes terrible." A smile pulled at the corners of her mouth.

"I know it's a big decision, Mary. Take your time."

As she stared at her bakery, or what was left of it, he watched the change of emotions cross her face. What would it be like working side by side with her every day?

She turned and opened her mouth as if she was going to say something but then hesitated…

His heart drummed up into his throat, so hard he couldn't speak. He wanted her to say yes, but would she?

Chapter Eleven

Heat worked its way up Mary's neck and burned her ears. She couldn't move her bakery to Noah's store. It was an outrageous suggestion.

It was a solution, but one she abhorred. She couldn't sell her baked goods out of Noah's store, and she certainly didn't want to see him on a daily basis.

She couldn't work with an *Englischer*. What would her community think? Her *Gmay* frowned on a member having a partnership with an *Englischer*. Of course, it wouldn't be a real partnership, but others might not see it that way. And the bishop had warned her more than once about getting too close to Noah.

Not to mention, working that close to Noah would make it impossible for her to stay clear of him. All the reasons why she shouldn't agree.

Noah cleared his throat. "Do you want to think it over?"

She shook her head and faced him. "*Nein*. I don't think it would work." She glanced across the street at the charred remains of Sweet Delights and already regretted her decision.

"You know it could take a year to get your bakery rebuilt."

She straightened her back. "Why are you trying to talk me into it? Do you want me to show you how to bake really *gut* pastries? Is that it?"

"Oh, so you think I need your recipes?" He laughed. "I'm just trying to be nice."

"All right, Noah. I'll move my bakery to a small corner of your store and try to keep my customers that have a standing order. But this is only temporary, just for a few weeks. Could I put a small sign in your window?"

He hesitated but nodded. "I have a storage room that's large enough for a small office to fit a desk and your safe. I'll clear a corner of the store tomorrow."

"*Danki.* That's very nice of you and it gives me time to visit a kitchen supply shop in Iowa City to pick up a few of my favorite utensils and bowls."

"I'd be glad to take you. The SUV's got plenty of room for hauling whatever you need."

Mary shook her head. "I couldn't ask you to take time away from your work. You're already doing enough for me."

"I need to pick up a few things. You can ride along."

She eyed him curiously. "You act like you feel guilty that my bakery burned."

He paused and looked across the street. "No, it's not guilt. It's empathy." Emotion caught in his throat. "When both of my parents died at once in the car accident, the store was all I had for security, and my sisters looked up to me to take care of them. I don't know what I would have done if I'd lost the store, too. It would have been like losing my parents all over again."

Mary touched his arm, large tears blocking her vision.

He shuffled his booted feet. "I want to do this. I know how much it hurts, and I want to help."

"You make me feel like I can't turn down your offer. And I wouldn't know what to do with myself if I didn't get up in the *morgen* and bake." She raised her chin. "I'm sure we can work together…at least for a little while until I figure things out."

She turned toward the street as *Daed's* buggy pulled up next to the curb. "Ready to go, Mary? Your *mamm* will be waiting to hear the news, and there is nothing more we can do here."

Noah raised a hand and squeezed her shoulder. "I'll pick you up at 9:00 a.m., and we'll go to the supply store in Iowa City. We can come back and get you settled in your office. After that, we can clear a spot in the bakery and set up a table or two for your baked goods. It'll be a snug fit, but I think we can manage. While you're here, I'll do my baking over at the other store. I mostly do that anyway."

"That sounds great. *Danki*, Noah."

Mary climbed in the buggy and sat on the back seat behind Jacob. She took one last glance at Sweet Delights and pain knifed its way through her heart. She had a lot to think about. Could she work next to Noah when he was the competition?

She leaned back in the seat. *Jah*, it was nice that Noah had invited her to use a corner of his store. It would allow her to keep some of her customers. On the other hand, now her customers would get used to shopping at Noah's store.

She needed to win the baking contest now more than ever, and she needed to keep her distance from Noah. But were either of those even possible?

* * *

Wednesday morning, the bright sunlight poured into Mary's bedroom, startling her awake. She jerked upright in bed and glanced out the window at a few fluffy clouds racing across the blue sky. Her heart thumped as her memory rekindled last night's disaster. She forced herself to take a deep breath.

Yawning, she sat and stretched. *Mamm* had let her sleep after a long night of talking and crying.

She glanced at the clock. *Ach*, Noah would arrive soon to take her to the kitchen supply store. She jumped out of bed, dressed and hurried downstairs. When she stepped into the kitchen, *Mamm* was flipping pancakes. "Morgen."

"*Morgen*, sweetheart."

"*Danki* for fixing my favorite breakfast. I feel like you are trying to comfort me, but you lost a bakery, too."

"*Nein*, I felt bad because it belonged to *Daed*, but I hardly spend any time there now. My life won't change much that it's gone."

"What do you think of me having a corner of my bakery in Noah's store? You never really answered me last night."

Sarah turned from the stove and faced Mary. "It was nice of him to make that offer. It probably wouldn't hurt for a little while."

After breakfast, Mary hurried and washed dishes, and was just finishing when Noah pulled into the driveway. She grabbed her bag and ran for the door. "I'm leaving, *Mamm*."

She climbed into the SUV, closed the door and buckled up. "*Morgen*, Noah."

"Good morning." He drove down the gravel road,

turned onto Route 218 and headed for Iowa City. "You should have taken a couple of days off, even the rest of the week."

"*Danki* for the suggestion, but I think it's better if I fight my fear and keep going. If I give in to it, fear wins. This is a test, and I will persevere."

"Your faith seems to be lifting you up."

She faced Noah. "I think if I keep my hands busy, it will keep my mind off the horror of my situation."

Noah could smell the subtle fragrance of lavender from Mary's soap. Intoxicating. The profile of her delicate features, her blond hair and creamy complexion sent his heart into overdrive. He took a deep breath and tried to clear his head.

He kept his eyes on the road, and she seemed content to watch the scenery. The sky had cleared to a robin's-egg blue, and it was a beautiful day for a ride.

At the supply store in Iowa City, Noah parked his vehicle and escorted her inside. He watched her eyes light up with curiosity when they walked by all the electrical appliances. She stopped and read an ad for an air fryer, then turned to Noah. "Do you have one of these?"

"Yes, I like it. No grease and it reduces calories by seventy-five percent. It's very healthy cooking."

She moved around until she came to the fancy espresso machines. "I'd like to have one of these for my shop one day."

While he followed, Mary moved on to the glassware section and placed a three-piece bowl set in her shopping cart.

Continuing on to the bakeware area, she looked at the easy-release nonstick pans. "Sweet Delights had pans that were fifty years old, maybe older. Now, I'll need to buy all new." Her voice hitched.

Noah patted her shoulder. "Look at it this way, your new pans will give you inspiration to develop new recipes."

She gave a weak smile. "Maybe."

He gave her back a pat. "You okay?"

She nodded.

"If you want to wander around by yourself, I can meet you at the small appliance in thirty minutes? Or we can stay together?"

"Jah, I'd like to walk around by myself and just look."

He picked up what he needed then met Mary at the small appliances. She was looking at a panini grill and a triple slow cooker.

"I have one of those," he commented. "The three cookers come in handy."

She glanced around. "I could stay in here all day. I never knew some of these contraptions existed."

Noah laughed. "This store is a cook's dream come true."

When they reached the checkout line, he motioned for her to push her cart ahead of him. She placed her bakeware, bowls, set of cutlery and a large iron skillet on the counter and paid with a check.

Noah paid for his filters, bread pans and bakeware, then set his plastic sacks in Mary's cart. He pushed the cart out to his SUV and loaded their supplies in the back.

She settled into the passenger seat and buckled the seat belt. "We never really got into specifics last night. Exactly what did you have in mind? Do I bake for you in addition to baking for my own business, or am I renting the space and the use of your ovens? And how much would that cost?"

Noah jerked as he buckled into his own seat. "Whoa, slow down. That's too many questions."

"*Nein*, I want to settle it now." She raised her chin.

"I thought we could work it out. I'm not charging any rent. You can bake for your regular weekly orders, and I'll set up a display case for you to sell a few extras, whatever you want. But it won't be a big area. I don't have a lot of extra space."

She rubbed her hand across the edge of the dash then laid it back in her lap. "I was thinking I could rent the space and pay whatever amount you thought fair for using your ovens. I'll put a small pantry in my office if you want me to keep my supplies separate. If you're going to bake in the kitchen, I'll need a schedule of when I can use the ovens." She glanced toward Noah.

He met her gaze for a second then started his vehicle.

"I don't want charity, Noah."

He ran his knuckles across his jaw. "I'll need to think about what to charge you. I'll figure out the square footage and charge accordingly. Let me run some numbers, and I can let you know tomorrow." He hadn't really thought about all the particulars. This could get complicated, and he didn't just mean with the baking arrangement. He liked her, really liked her.

"I want to bake for my regulars in your store, but I ache inside like a piece of me has been cut out. Do you know what I mean?" Her voice wobbled.

"Yes, I know all too well."

She sat in silence. He glanced at her and saw tears pooled in her eyes. Her cheeks were pale. She was no doubt worried sick and in no shape to work, but he understood the need to keep hands busy. It had worked for him when his parents died.

When they reached his store in Kalona, he gave her a tour of the layout and the kitchen. He cleared spots in his cupboards and in the pantry for her supplies.

Mary nodded. "My heart feels as empty as those shelves you cleared for me."

She asked questions in a voice fighting for control. He could see this was the last place she wanted to be. It probably irked her that her competition was going to be right under her nose watching every move she made.

Noah gulped. This might be the worst decision he'd ever made.

When Jenny called Noah into the office to discuss an urgent matter, Mary took the opportunity to walk through his store by herself. She looked at every item in his bakery. Her eyes widened at her discovery. She offered similar products at her bakery, except his portions were smaller and cheaper than a serving at Sweet Delights. She hadn't noticed that when she toured his store on opening day. Now she got it when Emily had told her that Noah called her heavy-handed when she cut portions.

She glanced at the office door, still closed. She headed for the kitchen to give it a better examination than what Noah's whirlwind tour offered. A woman was there baking.

"*Hallo*, I'm Mary. I might be working here for a while."

She nodded. "I'm Jean Dwyer. Noah told me you'd be working here. It's nice to meet you. Sorry to hear about your bakery." Jean was lovely and very petite. Maybe thirty.

"*Danki*, it's nice to meet you, too."

When Jean left the room to take a tray of cupcakes to the front, Mary snatched a mini cupcake and popped it in her mouth. She shook her head in disbelief. "Mmm." It was maybe one of the best cupcakes she'd ever eaten.

Shame prickled her skin with goose bumps at sneaking the treat. She'd given Noah and his sisters a free treat. Therefore, she could reciprocate. She wasn't quite sure Bishop Yoder would see it that way. But if she was going to work here, no doubt she and Noah would be trying each other's products. Except for their contest entries of course.

She bit into a chocolate cookie and stopped chewing to savor the taste. It was delicious.

Now more than ever, she knew she needed that prize money.

Chapter Twelve

On Monday, while Mary used his kitchen, Noah loaded his SUV with a box of vegetables, breads and pastries. He stopped and picked up Emily at her friend, Kate's, house, and they headed to his grandparents' farm.

"Noah, I don't know them. What do I say to grandma?" Emily worried her bottom lip.

"You can talk about the store and what you do to help. Ask Grandma about her life on the farm." For the rest of the ride, he could tell by her fidgeting and kicking legs that Emily was concerned about meeting her grandparents.

Pulling into the driveway, Noah glanced around the barnyard, his grandpa wasn't anywhere in sight. He parked by the house, gave the lighter box with bread and rolls to Emily and carried the other two boxes to the house.

Just as they reached the steps, Uncle Cyrus drove a horse and hayrack up the drive and stopped by the SUV. Cyrus stepped down and shot Noah a stern look.

Noah entered the house and set his boxes in the

kitchen. "Grandma," he called, "I brought you veggies and bread. Emily came with me to keep you company."

Grandma hurried into the kitchen from the other room. "*Danki*, Noah. Come in, Emily. I'm glad you came. Your cousins will be here later, and you can meet them." She glanced at Noah. "We'll be fine."

Noah stepped off the porch and met Cyrus halfway.

"My *daed* is in the north forty bailing straw. You should have gotten here earlier so you could have helped him."

Noah straightened his back. "I'm here now."

"Why? Your father never cared. Why do you?"

"Cyrus, I can't remedy what my father did. I'm sorry he didn't like the farm. Nothing will change that now. But I'd like to help whenever I can."

Cyrus squared his shoulders. "Your *daed*, my *bruder*, was helping *Daed* shingle the barn roof. Jeremiah went into town for more shingles and was gone too long. *Daed* fell off the roof and lay on the ground a long time before anyone found him. It's Jeremiah's fault *Daed* walks with a cane. It would be better if you didn't hang around too much and get the old man's hopes up. You aren't part of our community. Why are you here?"

"Because I want to help my grandparents and to get to know them."

"You have a store to take care of, and farming is a full-time job."

"He's an old man, and he needs all the help he can get, even if it's just temporary. Instead of talking, let's go to the field and give him a hand."

Cyrus nodded and motioned for Noah to climb onto the hayrack. When they reached the field where his grandpa was baling, his uncle showed Noah how to grab the bales and stack them.

As the afternoon wore on, Noah stacked hundred-pound bales one after the other until blisters formed on his palms even with gloves. Dust filled the air and clung to his sweaty face and clothing. He coughed and swiped his mouth with his shirtsleeve.

Cyrus pulled the bandana from his neck and handed it to Noah. Noah wrapped it over his nose and mouth and tied it behind his head. The chaff irritated his neck, and worked its way down inside his shirt. He gritted his teeth but kept on stacking until they finished the baling.

When they reached the barnyard, Noah jumped off the hayrack. His feet were tired and wobbled.

Grandpa smiled and slapped him on the back. "After we eat, you better go home and take care of those hands. *Danki* for the help."

Noah nodded. He could see by the tears shining in his grandpa's eyes that he appreciated the help a whole lot more than he expressed.

After dinner, Noah helped Emily in the car. "Did you enjoy meeting your cousins?"

"Yes, we had a great time. They showed me how to knit." For the next three miles to town, Emily told him all about her cousins and what she'd learned.

Noah parked behind his store and slowly stepped out. After sitting for a while, his body was so stiff he could hardly move. He was tired, but his heart was full.

Tuesday morning, Mary headed to Amanda's *haus* in Kalona. The front door opened, and Amanda hurried to the buggy. She stepped in and slid onto the seat.

"Danki for stopping by yesterday and asking me to

come and help. *Mamm* finished canning, and I was getting bored. Saturday, I helped my friend at the newspaper get out some flyers. So spill, Mary, how is it working with Noah?"

"It's been a week since Sweet Delights burned, and so far, it's working. He goes out to his grandpa's farm sometimes, and he helps bake at the other store so we're not in the kitchen at the same time. But today, I want to practice my contest entry and thought you could make a dozen loaves of bread and six dozen rolls for our regular customers while I do that. I don't want to lose them to Noah."

"I'm glad to help."

Mary parked the buggy, unhitched King, then gave Amanda the tour of the kitchen layout. Having her friend by her side once again made her decision to bake at Noah's store seem normal. "I'll show you Sweet Delight's corner of the store. I'm so grateful he gave me the space."

She showed Amanda her pantry and settled her at her station in the kitchen.

Mary scooted to the pantry for her ingredients, mixed the practice dough, and set the rolls to rise.

Jean Dwyer flew through the swinging door like an unruly child. "Hello everyone I was almost late."

"And, Amanda, this is Jean Dwyer, Noah's assistant. Jean, this is Amanda Stutzman. She's going to be helping me with the baking while I spend time practicing my recipes for the contest."

"Welcome, Amanda," Jean responded with a smile. "I bake a few things here for Noah and watch the store."

"It's nice to meet you, Jean."

Later in the morning, Noah bumped the kitchen door open, carrying in a box of baked goods, but stopped when he saw Amanda. "Good morning, ladies. Smells like you two have been busy."

"We wanted to have most of our baking done before you and Jean get busy," Mary motioned to her full bakery rack.

"What is that apple dessert you're making? It looks good. Can I have a sample?" he said, teasingly.

"Not from this one. It's my practice for the contest."

He walked to the counter, leaned over and took a long sniff. "Your pie smells like it might be hard to beat." His tone was serious. "Your cupcakes look good, too. Can I have one of those?"

She nodded. "Be my guest."

He took a bite. "They're good." He let a smirk play on his lips. "But mine are better."

Amanda laughed. "Mary's chocolate cupcakes are delicious."

He countered, "Try one of mine. Let's go out to the bakery. You can each have one."

Mary followed Noah and Amanda to the store's bakery section. The three of them weaved their way around Mrs. Wallin browsing the cakes.

Amanda selected a chocolate cupcake, pulled the paper back and took a bite. "Mmm." She held it out to Mary. "This is really *gut*."

Mary took a bite. "I don't know. I think mine are better." A wry smile pulled at her mouth.

Mrs. Wallin moved closer. "Why don't you have a contest on Saturday? You can both bake those mini cupcakes and let the customers do a blind taste test."

Noah whistled. "Oh, I like that idea. That will bring customers into the store." He raised a brow. "What do you think, Mary?"

She hadn't expected this. It was sort of a pre-contest test to see what others think. "Amanda, could you have your friend put a write-up in the newspaper? Maybe say from opening until closing on Saturday, you're invited to Miller's Farm-fresh Grocery, Delicatessen and Bakery for a free mini cupcake taste-testing between Miller's bakery and the Amish Sweet Delight's bakery and voting for the best one."

"If Noah agrees to it," Amanda said, "I'll write it up and take it over to the newspaper right now."

Mary stammered, "I think we should also make the same kind of cupcake—chocolate, vanilla or whatever we decide."

Noah rubbed his hand across his chin. "Agreed. How about strawberry?"

"I'll agree to that." Mary tried to hide the smile pulling at her mouth. Strawberry cupcakes were one of her specialties.

Saturday just before 7:00 a.m., Mary set the last of her cupcakes on a bakery cart. Noah rolled both his cart and hers, each loaded with strawberry cupcakes, to the front of the store. One cart labeled A, the other B.

Mary followed him to the front and set paper and pencils next to a locked drum with a slit in the top. She opened a package of napkins and laid them on the counter next to the carts.

After Noah unlocked the front doors and headed off to stock the fresh lettuce, Mary watched the supply of cupcakes closely as she worked around the Sweet Delights area.

She swept the floor often to clean up the littered cupcake papers and crumbs. There was laughing and whispering, but Mary kept far enough away so she wouldn't overhear the customers' discussions.

She grabbed an empty tray from the cart and stopped by checkout where Jean was working. "There's a good turnout for voting."

Jean smiled. "Yes, did you see the write-up in the newspaper about the contest?" She pulled it from below the counter and handed it to Mary, already open to the article.

Mary scanned the headline and gasped.

Cupcake Bake-off Between Dueling Bakeries

Setting the baking pan on the counter, she snapped the newspaper closed and hustled across the store to the produce section where Noah was restocking. She shook the paper. "Did you see the article about our little contest?"

He paused and faced her. "No, I've been too busy."

"The newspaper is calling it *dueling bakeries*."

He shrugged. "That's sort of what it is, don't you think?"

She huffed, then trotted back across the store and handed the newspaper back to Jean. She grabbed the empty pan, took it to the kitchen, and brought another tray to the front. It seemed the whole town had turned out for their little contest.

In the late afternoon, Emily dashed across the bakery and hugged Mary.

Mary squeezed her tightly. "Where have you been? I haven't seen you in days."

"I have a girlfriend, her name is Kate. We're in third grade together, and I go over to her house to play."

"That's *gut*. How do you like your classes?"

"They're great." Emily eyed the contest sign then

turned toward the cupcakes. "Can I have a cupcake and vote?"

"Of course."

Emily ate cupcake A first, then B. "Mmm. They're both good." She took a slip of paper and a pencil, voted and stuffed it in the drum. She turned back to Mary. "Can I help you count the votes when it's all over?"

"Sorry, sweetie. Milton Accounting is going to count the votes, and they'll put the results in the morning's newspaper."

The store's door opened, and a local news team filed into the bakery with a camera and microphone.

Emily squealed, "Are we going to be on TV?"

Mary froze as her heart dropped to her stomach. "I don't know why they're here."

The reporter with the Channel 4 logo on his blue blazer weaved his way around the lines of people testing cupcakes and voting. He stepped forward. "Are you Mary Brenneman?"

She pulled her frame up to full stature. "Can I help you?"

"You're the owner of Sweet Delights bakery?"

Mary clenched her moist palms. "*Jah*, what's this all about?" Her gaze bounced from the reporter to the cameraperson filming the people in line.

"I'm Carl Thompson, Channel 4 News. Someone called in on the tip line. We also saw the article about the dueling bakeries and contest to determine the best cupcake."

Annoyance inched its way up Mary's back. If she lost the contest, they would report it in the newspaper and on Channel 4 News for everyone to hear and gossip about.

She hadn't thought about that when she agreed to this contest. She took a step back.

Noah's heavy footfalls approached from the kitchen. "What's going on here?"

Mary swung around. "Someone called Channel 4 and told them we were dueling bakeries."

"Is that what they said?"

"Someone called them on the tip line."

Carl butted in, "We also heard that you've both entered the Kalona Fall Apple Festival baking contest. They said you decided to have a cupcake contest first to raise the stakes between the two of you and put pressure on the loser."

Mary gasped. "I can't believe you would stoop so low to call a news channel, Noah."

"Roll camera," Carl told his videographer.

"Mary, I didn't do that." Noah turned to the reporter. "Who called you?"

"I'm sorry, it's an anonymous tip line. We don't know who called in. Apparently, everyone in this town knows what's going on between you two. We also heard you offered her a corner of your store after her bakery burned down. That's generous of you, Mr. Miller, one business owner helping another. Is that just until her bakery re-opens?"

Mary plopped her hands on her hips as heat rushed to her cheeks.

"Mary, I'm not the one who called," Noah insisted. "Apparently, someone in town has a sense of humor."

"Or you thought it would make for great publicity when you won," she snarled.

Mayor Conrad pushed his way through the gathering

crowd. "I called Channel 4. I thought this would make great publicity for our fall festival."

Mary blew out a heavy sigh and glanced at the clock. "Just a reminder, everyone," she raised her voice, "the doors close in two minutes." She moved to the counter and began cleaning.

Noah held the front door open while the last of the voters streamed out, along with the mayor who was talking to the news crew about the festival. The last person to leave was from Milton Accounting, taking the locked drum of votes for counting in a secure room.

Noah locked the door and turned to Mary. "I'm sorry. This was probably a bad idea."

She stopped cleaning. "No, I apologize. I shouldn't have jumped on you. The only thing that ran through my mind was how embarrassed I'll be if I lose. I made a spectacle of myself, and now they have it on film. If the bishop hears about me being on TV, he'll discipline me."

"Mary, I'm so sorry. I didn't think about that. I'll contact the channel and tell them they can't put your image on TV." He darted back to the office.

In a few minutes, Noah returned to the front of the store, plugged in a small TV and got it ready for watching the ten o'clock news. He glanced her way. "I can drive you home tonight and pick you up in the morning so you don't have to drive King all the way home after dark."

"*Danki*, but I'm going to spend the night with Amanda and her folks." Mary gathered her cleaning supplies and wiped down her Sweet Delights area while Noah went back to his office.

At ten, Noah carried out two folding chairs and placed them in front of the TV. Mary sat on the edge of her seat, her back straight, praying. *Dear Lord, please don't let my image appear on the television for all to see.*

When the cupcake contest segment began, the news anchor brought out the representative from the accounting firm. They cut to a short clip showing the front of Noah's store, the locked drum and the people waiting in lines to eat cupcakes and vote. But neither Mary nor Noah were shown.

The accountant presented the envelope to the news anchor. A drum roll blasted through the TV speakers, and the anchor opened the envelope and gasped.

"Well, viewers, it seems there is a tie, and the duel will continue until the Kalona Fall Apple Festival baking contest on September 27. Will the winner be Mary Brenneman from the Amish Sweet Delights bakery, Noah Miller from Miller's Farm-fresh Grocery, Delicatessen and Bakery, or someone else entirely? May the best baker win."

One last film clip caught the reporter, Carl Thompson, eating a cupcake. Then they cut to the next segment.

Noah flipped the TV off.

"*Danki*, Noah." Her throat tightened around a lump that tried to block her words. "For asking them not to put my image on TV."

She enjoyed the way he looked after her…almost like they were a couple, and he really cared. She could trust him.

"I'll see you tomorrow." Mary walked out the back door, shutting it tightly, as if that could stop the brewing of happiness deep inside from overflowing. She liked Noah, maybe too much. She was Amish, and he was *Englisch*. Where could the relationship go?

Chapter Thirteen

Thursday dawned warm for a September morning. Mary arrived at Noah's store, tried the door, then pulled out her key and unlocked it. She wondered where everyone was. Noah was usually here by now.

She hung her bag and found a note from Noah stuck to the door.

In the kitchen, she grabbed a bag of apples from the cooler and peeled enough for two desserts. Humming a song from the *Ausbund*, she prepared a dumpling pastry, set it in a pie pan, spiced the apples with cinnamon, ginger and a little nutmeg, then poured them in the dish. She covered the top with woven strips and set it in the oven.

Sliding the new attic recipe in front of her, she prepared a pie shell, arranged the spiced apples in the pan, topped it with a crust and set it in the oven to bake. The secret to this pie was simmering the spices in apple juice and thickening the sauce before pouring it over the apples. Her contest entry would have to come from one of these two pies.

Amanda pushed the back door open. "I don't think

I'll ever get used to coming to Noah's fancy kitchen in the morning."

Mary smiled. "I know what you mean."

"No one else is in yet?" Amanda bumped the bowls as she took them from the cupboard.

Mary grabbed the potholders, pulled her pies from the oven and set them on a rack to cool. "Jean will come in soon, but Noah left a note saying he went to Iowa City to bake. I think he wanted to practice his entry without me watching."

"That's *gut*." Amanda snorted as she scooted to the pantry "Then he can't see our secrets either. Have you heard when or if your parents are going to rebuild Sweet Delights?" She mixed a batch of chocolate cupcakes and sugar cookies.

"*Nein*, *Daed* has to wait on crops to see if he has enough money. But even if he does, the bakery will have only the basics." Her voice dipped, "I still have to win the contest. My pies should be cool enough to eat. Let's try them before Noah returns."

While Amanda poured two glasses of water and pulled out forks, Mary cut two slices from each pie. She handed Amanda her plate.

Her friend took a bite of the dumpling pie first. "Mmm," she hummed and raised an eyebrow. She sipped water and tried the other piece. "Oh, Mary—" she pointed to the pie with her fork "—this second one is *wunderbaar*. What do you think?"

Mary tasted her revamped recipe of the dumpling pie with the cinnamon and nutmeg and caramel drizzle. The crust was delicious and flaky. It was going to be hard to beat. Her hand tightened around the fork. She glanced at Amanda then cut into the pie made from the attic recipe. She put it in her mouth and slowly chewed. "Bishop Ropp was right. I, too, would drive five miles for a piece of this pie. I've found my entry."

After finishing her pie, Mary cleaned the mess while Amanda carried her frosted cupcakes to the front of the bakery. When the sugar cookies Amanda had made were cool, Mary carted the tray to the front. She set it down and started to arrange the sweets in the display case.

Amanda stayed quiet, too quiet. Mary glanced at her friend working on the display case. "Is something wrong?"

"My *mamm* just stopped by for a moment." Amanda hesitated. "Did you know everyone in town is talking about your alleged feud, the cupcake-duel and the tie? She said people are saying it went *viral*."

Mary jerked her head toward Amanda. "What does that mean?"

"It means that people are sending notes out online for the world to see. *Mamm* said it's all over and everyone is talking about your feud with Noah and the upcoming festival."

The door pushed open, and Frank Wallin strolled to the counter. "Good morning, ladies."

"*Morgen*, Frank," Amanda chirped as she headed for the kitchen.

"Mornin', Frank, it's *gut* to see you." Mary dished out a smile.

He chuckled. "Never thought I'd see the Sweet Delights ladies over here in enemy territory."

Mary huffed. "Noah and I are not enemies, Frank."

"Not the way it sounds on Twitter. Sounds like a big feud. Someone took a video of you and Noah having a few heated words and posted it."

"Frank," Mary gasped. "That was just a misunderstanding."

"The newspaper has an article in it that claims it's a feud and that's gone viral. Since there's so much commotion, the town is offering $20,000 in contest prize money instead of the $10,000. They said hundreds of bakers have already signed up for the contest."

"That's crazy. There must be some mistake." Mary propped a hip against the counter to keep her steady.

"Read the article. Over at Lazy Susan's this morning, Abigail Riggs said that you two have caused such a stir it's turned into big business for the town and the fall festival. Susan claims tourists have come to town and asked her to point you two out."

"What? Tell her not to do that."

He laughed. "If they want to pay me, I'm going to make a buck and point you out."

"You wouldn't!"

"Nah, I'm just kidding."

"Frank, are you sure about the prize money being raised to $20,000?"

"Yep. Just black coffee and a cinnamon roll, please."

Mary handed it to Frank. "On the *haus* for updating me on the news."

"Thank you. Have a good day, Mary."

She blew out a deep sigh. *Not likely now.*

The wheels on the cart squeaked as Amanda rolled it to the bakery shelves. "Did I hear Frank correctly? Did they raise the festival prize money to $20,000?"

Mary pressed her lips together then released them. "Jah, but I'm surprised we didn't hear about it."

Noah opened the back door to the kitchen and tromped in and out, carrying in his pastries.

Mary rushed from the bakery to the kitchen. "Noah, did you hear about the festival committee raising the baking prize to $20,000?"

"Yes." He pulled a newspaper out of his back pocket and handed it to Mary.

She unfolded the paper and read a few lines. "I can't believe they did this." She shook the article as she spoke.

Noah nodded. "The rumor is they expect maybe twenty to thirty thousand to attend the festival."

She looked up from reading. "Just because they think we're feuding?"

"Finish reading the article." He stood with his back propped against the counter, feet crossed, waiting.

"What!" Mary shrieked. "MyBaking Channel contacted the festival committee. They want to send a celebrity chef as a judge. The committee has agreed," she mumbled as she read. "MyBaking Channel is sending Simone André. She is offering the winner a chance to come to her show to make the winning dessert." She stopped reading and glanced at Noah.

He nodded. "The stakes just got higher, Mary. Winner takes all."

Jenny slipped into the kitchen, poured a cup of coffee and sat at the table. "So MyBaking Channel is going to judge? That will really bring in the contestants. You two better have great recipes."

Noah shot his sister a frown. "Nice to see you have confidence in me, sis. Sorry, I have to finish unloading." He banged the door on his way outside.

Jenny turned to Mary. "You know I didn't mean that. You both are great bakers and either of you could win."

"I know." Mary poured a cup of coffee, sat on the stool

by Jenny and sipped the brew. "This is unbelievable, all because we had a fight on TV."

"It's crazy but wonderful." Jenny stood. "Stop by my office before you go home, I want to show you a web page I made for Sweet Delights. It's my way of saying thanks for all the sweets you feed me." She added as she headed out the swinging door. "Practice hard, Mary."

Amanda caught the door and carried in empty pastry pans from the bakery. "I heard Jenny's comment, but Noah is one terrific baker."

"*Jah*, he's *gut*. Now with the prize money so high, and MyBaking Channel sending Simone André as a judge, and she's offering the winner a chance to bake their winning dish on her show, the bakers will come from all over the country to enter the contest." Mary squeezed her eyes closed. *Dear Lord, You've taken away my bakery, now with the stakes so high, culinary-trained bakers will enter the contest, and I won't have a chance to win. Lord, please strengthen my ability.*

After lunch, Mary stopped in to Jenny's office just as Ethan was leaving. "Sorry, I didn't mean to disturb you." Ethan gave them a wave as he walked out.

"It's fine. He was just leaving. We're just friends, but I told him I was going to nursing school. I wasn't sure if he was getting serious or not, but he was okay with it. He knew I wasn't going to join the Order." She touched a key on her computer. "So here is your web page."

Mary gasped. "It's *wunderbaar. Danki*, that is lovely." She gave Jenny a hug. "I see you have boxed up your things. I'm going to miss you when you go."

"I'll miss you, too, but I'll be home for visits."

Mary dried a tear as she headed back to the kitchen.

She started the bread dough for the next day and set it in the refrigerator to rise.

At 4:00 p.m., Noah rushed into the kitchen with worry lining his forehead. He glanced at the clock, then at Mary. "Emily is late coming home from school. Have you seen her?"

"*Nein*, not today, but the other day she told me she was spending a lot of time with a new friend. Maybe she's at her *haus*."

"She's supposed to tell me when she's going to Kate's."

The back door swung open, and Emily ran into the kitchen.

"Where have you been, young lady?" Noah hunched down to look in her face. "You're to tell me when you go to your friend's house."

"I know, but I wasn't at Kate's house. I was petting King. He was neighing and prancing around the corral. He wants to go for a walk."

"Please don't go into the corral without Mary's or my permission," Noah warned.

"Can Mary take me for a ride?" Emily wiggled around. "Please, Noah?"

"Mary is busy."

Emily ran to Mary, threw her arms around her waist and gave her a hug. "Please, Mary?"

Mary laughed and patted Emily's back. "Tell you what, when I'm ready to go home at five, I'll give you a ride."

"Great!" Emily giggled. "I'll take my stuff to my room and be back."

When Mary finished her prep work for the next day, Emily timed it just right and breezed through the swinging door. She grabbed her bag. "Are you ready for the ride?"

"Mary, would it be all right if Noah came with us?" Emily asked.

Noah entered the kitchen. "Where are we going?"

"For a buggy ride. I want you to come with us, Noah. Please?"

Noah glanced at Mary.

"Sure, if he wants to tag along, that would be fine."

Noah nodded toward the door. "Why don't you two go ahead? I'll finish here and lock up."

Mary led Emily outside to the corral and demonstrated how to hitch King to the buggy, letting her help at times. The procedure took twice as long as normal, but it was worth it. "Well done, Emily,"

Her little face glowed with the accomplishment. Emily ran around, jumped in the buggy and grabbed the reins. "Can I drive King?"

"I'll let you drive up to the door so we can pick up Noah, and we'll see how you do."

Noah was waiting. He raised his brow at Mary as he stepped in and sat on the seat next to her.

She gulped as he settled back. Her heart beat so hard she was scared he could hear the racket. She drew a steadying breath. "Emily wanted to drive, so I said we'd give it a try." She leaned back, but her arm touched his, sending a tidal wave of emotions through her. *Jah*, this might not have been such a *gut* idea.

Mary tugged the reins to the right. "Let's turn down Fifth Street, go past the fire station and turn right onto J Avenue."

Emily pushed Mary's hand away. "I can do it by myself."

King jerked the buggy into motion and picked up speed. Mary raised her hand and leaned toward Emily. "Slow King down, Emily"

"I don't know how to do that. He's going so fast."

"*Jah*, I will help you. When he's been corralled all day, he gets antsy and wants to stretch his legs." Mary laid her hand over Emily's and gently showed her how to pull back on the reins. "Do you feel what I'm doing? Tugging back tells him to go slower. When you want to turn right, tug the reins right, and he knows to turn right. The same with left."

Emily heaved a long sigh. "Oh, that's easy."

Mary could feel Emily relax back into the seat. If only she could do the same, but with Noah so close, that was impossible. His nearness was suffocating her. Moisture dampened her palms. "How do you like the buggy ride, Noah?"

"The seat is much more comfortable than I thought it would be, and the ride is fun."

As King turned onto J Avenue, the buggy wheel hit a rut in the road and bounced. Noah swayed and brushed against Mary. He recovered quickly and straightened. He was so close she could hear him breathing. Pressing a hand over her heart, she tried to calm it. She had to quit thinking about him. "So Noah, do you have your recipes picked for the contest?"

"I do, but I'll practice them a few more times to make sure they're perfect. How about you?"

"*Jah*, I was debating between two apple pie recipes, but I've made the selection. Having to bake three days in a row for the three-day contest is stressful." Mary leaned toward Emily. "Turn right onto Fourteenth Street."

Emily pulled back on the reins as they approached the

turn then tugged the reins right. King turned the corner smoothly. Emily laughed. "I did it."

Mary reached an arm around her and squeezed. "You are really getting the hang of it. You're a natural."

The clip-clopping of King's hooves were soothing and Mary even started to enjoy Noah sitting beside her. "Slow King down, Emily, and turn onto A Avenue."

"He won't slow down." Emily worried her bottom lip.

"Do you want me to help you? Sometimes King has a mind of his own."

"Yes, I'm scared."

Mary put her hand on the reins and firmly pulled back. "King, settle down." Her voice had a sharp ring. The horse wanted to get out on the road and go, but he'd just have to wait a while longer.

Settling back in the seat, she brushed against Noah and the touch sent her heart racing again. What was wrong with her? She was acting like a silly schoolgirl. "Turn onto Fifth Street when you come to it."

"Okay."

Another buggy approached them from the opposite direction. Mary poised her hand midair in case Emily got nervous, and she needed to grab the reins. The buggy neared, and Mary's heart dropped. "Oh, no."

"Something wrong?" Noah sounded concerned.

"I'm fine. I didn't mean to say that." She could sense Noah staring at her. "Sometimes King can get a little skittish when another horse is near."

But that wasn't it. As the other buggy drew alongside, she turned and saw Bishop Yoder's warning stare aimed in her direction. The bishop had counseled her about Noah once before. No doubt he would be paying her a visit after seeing her snuggled up next to Noah Miller in a buggy.

Now, she'd be confessing her sin for sure and for certain.

Chapter Fourteen

When Noah stopped his vehicle and parked in his grandpa's drive, Cyrus hurried out of the toolshed and headed his way wearing a scowl.

He stopped six-feet away. "Look, Noah, it's great that you come out to visit *Daed* and help him on the farm, but it's sending mixed signals. My parents have hopes that you're going to join our community." Cyrus's tone changed from impatient to one of concern. "I think we both know you're not going to do that. *Daed* is in the milking room, disinfecting the floor and stanchions. But it would be best if you left and didn't come out again."

The words bombarded Noah one after the other. He silently nodded and climbed back in the SUV, a knot twisting in his stomach. His hands gripped the steering wheel while his heart plummeted to his feet. He understood his uncle's concern, but that didn't make the situation easier.

Where the gravel road met the highway, Noah turned toward Iowa City. He couldn't face Mary just yet. She'd ask him how it went at his grandpa's farm, and he didn't want to talk about it.

He parked behind his store and tried to muster up a

friendly smile. His keys jangled as he unlocked the back door and stepped into a warm kitchen smelling of cinnamon and yeast rolls.

Sidney looked up. "Hi, boss. Since it's Friday morning, I didn't expect to see you today."

"How about some help? I need to do some thinking, and the kitchen is where I do it best."

"Always glad for the help." Sidney gave him a curious glance but went back to his work.

When he left later that day, Noah called Jenny and let her know he was heading to their grandparents' farm for a short bit before heading home. He parked in their drive, hoping Cyrus had gone home. He climbed the porch and knocked on the kitchen door.

Soft footfalls approached just before Grandma pushed the screen open. "Come in."

When Noah entered, his grandpa was sitting at the oak kitchen, eating supper. His grandma took her chair.

"Sorry to bother you," Noah said.

"Sit," Grandpa invited. "Are you hungry?"

"No, thanks. I'm only going to stay a minute." Noah rubbed his palms across the pockets of his trousers. For as long as he could remember, he had wanted to meet his grandparents and get to know them. But he had to do what was fair for everyone.

His grandmother was quiet, and he could see her uneasy gaze dart from his grandpa to Noah. His plan before he left Iowa City sounded good. Now, he wasn't so sure.

"Grandpa, Cyrus said he thinks it's best if I don't hang around here. I was wondering if that's the way you feel, too?"

The old man stopped eating and laid his fork on his plate. "Most times, Cyrus and I don't see eye to eye, but this time, he's right. The bishop doesn't like a lot of frat-ernizing with the *Englisch*. It can give the youngies the wrong idea."

Grandma sat with her head down, slowly eating. She didn't acknowledge the conversation.

"Okay. I'm sorry it has to be this way, but I under-stand. I enjoyed getting to know you both." The words caught in Noah's throat and stumbled out.

Silence stretched across the room.

Noah turned and walked out of the house, quietly clos-ing the door between him and his grandparents.

The goodbye cut deep into his heart. He wanted to be part of their family. But he couldn't give up his SUV for a horse and buggy, he needed his vehicle. He owned an expanding business, and he had responsibilities. But that didn't make the knot in his stomach go away.

The way he was shut out of his grandparents' world, he would probably soon be shut out of Mary's life, too.

Lord, God, I don't know where You're leading me, but I pray it's for the betterment of my family. Because it's tearing my heart in two.

When she heard the grocery door open, Mary had a feeling it was Bishop Yoder. She slowly lifted her gaze from her work at the bakery counter to the visitor, and blew out a long breath. "*Gut Morgen*, Ethan. I'm glad it's you."

"That's the best thing I've heard all day. It's nice to see you, too." Ethan livened his step to the counter. "Why are you glad to see me?" He removed his straw hat and rubbed it across his blue chambray shirt and suspenders.

"When I heard the door, I thought it was the bishop. Emily wanted to go for a buggy ride yesterday. I let her have the reins, and I sat next to Noah. The bishop saw us and gave me a warning look."

"Ah, the *warning look*. I know it well from my early *rumspringa* days. Tell the bishop you were bringing Noah out to see me."

"Shame on you, I couldn't lie. Besides, it was a harmless buggy ride. So what would you like today?"

"A double-chocolate donut and a black coffee."

She set his order on the counter. Ethan handed her the money, picked up his purchase, and turned to go but stopped.

Mary's eyes followed his stare.

Bishop Yoder held the door while Bishop Ropp entered.

Mary cringed. How long had they been standing there?

Ethan hurried out the door while Bishop Ropp walked around the bakery section, trying to decide what he wanted.

Bishop Yoder's stare was icy as he approached the counter. "Mary," he whispered, "you are making a mistake running around with that *Englischer*."

She clenched her fist. "I'm not involved with Noah. He generously offered me space in his store so I can keep customers with standing orders."

"It's time you thought about getting married, *jah*?"

She cringed. "Did you forget that just a year ago Seth dumped me to go live with the *Englisch*? And after we both had been baptized and joined the church."

"I haven't forgotten, but our faith tells us to forgive. Seth was immature. He was not ready to settle down when he decided to get married. He has repented and went through and the rite of restoration. He's back now and willing to pick up where you two left off."

Mary straightened her back and sucked in a deep breath. "I can't believe you're encouraging me to marry him."

"He cares for you in spite of his careless actions. Think about it rationally, you will see he's a *gut* fit for you."

"Mary," Bishop Ropp interrupted. "Do you have any Bismarcks with the lemon filling like Sarah's papa's partner often made?"

"No… Sarah never mentioned her *vater* had a partner. Who was he?"

"That's too many years ago, I can't remember his name." He waved a hand in the air as if to bat the question away.

Mary stared at the old bishop, hoping he wasn't getting senile. "Do either of you wish to make a purchase?"

They each shook their heads.

The old bishop shuffled out the door as Bishop Yoder held it open. As he turned to leave, he tossed Mary a stern look. "Go for a buggy ride, Mary, and give Seth a chance to explain. You know as well as I do that Noah will never give up his *Englisch* ways. If you leave our church, you will be shunned." When the bishop let go, the door banged shut.

She'd never marry Seth Knepp, no matter what the bishop said. But he was right about one thing, Noah would never give up the *Englisch* ways.

The swinging door from the kitchen creaked and Noah's footfalls grew louder with each approaching step.

She turned as he reached the counter. His brow was creased, and lines pulled at his eyes. "You look tired. Did you do a lot of work helping your *grossdaddi*?"

Noah stood silent a moment. "I drove out to help grandpa. Cyrus met me in the drive and said he thought it would be better if I didn't come out there anymore. He claimed my grandparents were getting their hopes up that I'd join the community, which I have no intention of doing. I drove back out to see them when Cyrus was gone, and my grandpa said the same thing."

Mary flinched at his admission that he wasn't going to join their community. "Noah, I'm so sorry they feel that way. But our bishop doesn't encourage friendships with the *Englisch*."

"I understand, but I was still hoping for some kind of relationship." He turned and headed back to the kitchen. "Have a good evening, Mary."

Jah, she knew that wasn't what Noah wanted to hear. The bishop paying her a visit today was a not-so-subtle hint to her, too, about the same thing.

Mary grabbed a wet cloth and started to tidy up the bakery counter before she left for home. She turned at the sound of shoes tapping the flooring toward the counter. "Jenny, I haven't seen you all day. You must be really busy."

"I'm glad you haven't left yet, Mary. I'm in the process of packing, and I'll leave for school this weekend. I wanted to make sure I said goodbye."

After blotting tears from her eyes, Mary crushed Jenny in a hug. Over her days here at the store, she and Jenny spent many coffee breaks together each day talking about their girlhood, growing up and their dreams. "I'll miss you and will pray for your success on the journey that *Gott* has set your feet upon."

"Thank you. I appreciate that." Jenny stepped back with tears escaping down her cheek. She dug in her pocket, pulled out a tissue and wiped them away.

Mary swallowed hard. Her life had changed so much in just a few short weeks. She loved her *Englisch* friends and didn't want to say goodbye to Jenny…or to Noah.

Chapter Fifteen

Saturday, Mary laid a dozen strips of bacon in the iron skillet and fried a dozen eggs in another. She pulled the hot biscuits from the oven and scooped them into a waiting breadbasket with a small towel laid in the bottom.

She flipped the bacon then turned the eggs. Hurrying to the gas refrigerator, Mary pulled out the milk, orange juice, and butter and set them in the middle of the table.

The kitchen screen door squeaked as *Daed* stepped in from the porch, crossed the kitchen and set a bucket of milk on the counter next to her. "Morgen, Mary."

"Gut Morgen, Daed."

"Are you running late getting to the store?"

"Nein, Amanda is starting our bread and rolls this morning. I wanted to help *Mamm* since the twins have a cold."

*Dae*d cleared his throat. "I ran into Bishop Yoder yesterday in town."

Mary recognized that tone from when she'd misbehaved as a young girl. She squared her shoulders for the lecture that no doubt would follow.

"He said you were out riding in the buggy with Noah

Miller." His words held an edge. "You know he's not the kind of man you should be seeing. His values are different than yours."

"We're not involved in a personal relationship. I work in his store. Emily badgered me for a buggy ride, and she wanted Noah to ride along. I couldn't very well say no. I'm not going to treat him rudely."

"I wouldn't expect you to, but he is a nice-looking lad, and I wouldn't want you to get your expectations up and your feelings hurt. From what I've heard, he's not planning on joining our community."

"*Daed*, the bishop insinuated that since Seth is back, I should consider allowing him to court me again. Did he mention that to you?"

"It would be understandable for the bishop to think that. At one time, you had your heart set on marrying him."

She drew a deep breath, simmered down and blew it out. "I'm not leaving my faith, and I'm not going to marry Seth. That's over and done with."

"Listen, *tochter*, I do worry, as every Amish *vater* does that one day his *kinner* might want to try the world of the *Englisch*. I've seen the hurt on many parents' faces."

She nodded. "I know. I felt it when Seth left, and that's why I could never trust him again. And it's why I could never trust Noah Miller."

Daed patted her shoulder. "*Jah, liebe* hurts sometimes. I have a surprise for you. The Plain community plans to start rebuilding Sweet Delights next Monday, so it should be ready in no time. Of course, it will only have the basics inside. Since the fire started in the old wiring, there might have been an overload so I asked for more electrical outlets and an additional circuit breaker. That will make it safer."

"That's *wunderbaar*." Mary lunged at her *daed* and threw her arms around him. *"Danki."*

Jacob and Michael Paul tore through the door from the porch, washed up and raced to the table for breakfast.

"I beat you." The four-year-old beamed.

"You are the best at running, munchkin." Jacob nodded.

Mary dished up breakfast and walked to the doorway. *"Mamm*, breakfast is ready."

Sarah slid onto the chair next to Mary and gave her a hug. *"Danki*, sweetheart."

After cleaning the kitchen, Mary headed her buggy to town.

As she entered the kitchen, Noah glanced her way. "Morning."

"Jah, you're back from the other store already?"

"I didn't go to Iowa City this morning. I wanted to practice my entries. I heard the festival committee has received a thousand entries. They're going to eliminate most in the first round with three rounds of judging. That means our entries will need to be perfect."

"Where did you hear that?"

"They sent out letters. Your mail is lying on the counter over there." He gestured toward the end of the counter.

"Danki. With that many entries, I'll never win."

"Don't sell yourself short, Mary. You're a wonderful baker."

After reading her mail, she pulled out her ingredients, stirred up chocolate chip cookies and began dropping them on a cookie sheet with two spoons.

Noah grabbed two spoons, stood beside Mary, and began to help.

"Danki."

"Don't mention it." His hand bumped hers as they both went for the same spot of dough. His touch sent a tingle up her arm. She inhaled a controlling breath and blew it out slowly, trying to hide the thumping in her chest. "Hey, Noah, I'm planning on winning the contest, just so you know."

He laughed. "That's funny, because I plan on winning it."

"Jah, and so does every one of those bakers that entered."

He dropped several cookies on the sheet. "Mary, tell me about your faith."

"We live by Romans 12:12, 'be not conformed to this world.' We seek to lose the idea of self and live instead for the community and putting others first. We believe happiness comes from putting Jesus first, others next and ourselves last."

Noah stopped his hands a second and glanced her way. "Would it be possible for me to visit your church sometime?"

Her heart skipped a beat. She finished dropping the last cookie, set her spoons down and popped the sheet in the oven. "Church Sunday is tomorrow, and it's your grandparents' turn to host. That might be a *gut* time for you to visit. It's a three-hour service, then a common meal at noon." A few minutes later, she pulled the cookies from the oven.

She glanced at Noah and tried to read his face. Was he thinking about joining the Old Order or just curious? But she wouldn't allow this to give her false hope.

* * *

Noah gathered the baking pans and set them in the sink. "How about we practice our entries again? I could help you if you need an extra pair of hands."

Mary tossed him a wry smile. "Oh no, you don't, you're not tasting it."

Laughing, he scooped a big bag of apples from the cooler. "You don't trust me?"

She pulled a bowl and colander from a cupboard and faced him. "Based on my experience with Seth, trust is more fragile than *liebe*."

"Someday, Mary, I hope you find someone you can love and trust." When he reached for an apple, her hand was already there, and his slipped over her soft skin. His heart galloped at her nearness as his fingers fumbled to grasp an apple. He wanted to reach over and pull her into his embrace, press a kiss to her lips and never let her go. He wanted to be that someone she could love and trust... but it wasn't going to happen.

She grabbed an apple and pulled her hand away quickly. He stepped to the side to calm his racing pulse, pretending to give her more room.

It was nice having Mary in his kitchen every day. He was going to miss her, miss her smile, and miss her sweetness when she went back to her bakery.

He opened the oven door, and they both set their pies on a hot rack. "How about a muffin and a glass of tea?" His gaze caught hers and held it for a second.

"*Jah*, a break sounds *gut* right about now." She followed him to the baked goods in the front of the store.

He handed her a poppy seed muffin. "Try this and tell me what you think." He poured two glasses of tea while she ate. "Has your dad decided yet whether to rebuild Sweet Delights?"

"*Jah*, just this *morgen* he said our community is going to raise it a week from Monday. But the new structure will only have the bare minimum in it. I still need to win in order to buy the extra things I need to expand the menu. So next Monday, I'll stay busy baking for the workers."

"That's not a problem. I can watch Sweet Delights while you and Amanda bake for the workers."

"Noah, why the interest in our church?" She took another bite of muffin. "Mmm."

He shrugged. "I just want more information about the Amish faith so I can understand my grandparents and their ways better." He bit into his muffin.

Mary licked a crumb from her lip. "Where did you get this poppy seed recipe? It's divine."

"From Mom's collection. My recipes are from either Mom or Dad. My great-grandfather owned a bakery until he died, and my father helped him. That's how Dad got interested in starting his own bakery which he then expanded into the farm-fresh grocery and delicatessen."

Mary turned quiet. Noah glanced at her, and followed her gaze until he saw Bishop Yoder's frowning face and Seth standing next to him.

"So here you are, Mary." Seth said as if he had a right to know her whereabouts.

Noah flinched as if he'd been caught smoking behind the barn.

"What do you want, Seth?" Mary's voice whipped across the aisle at her ex-fiancé.

"Just to talk."

"*Nein.* I don't want to talk to you, and quit telling people you want to pick up where we ended. Because as the word says, it's ended."

Noah felt the tension. This conversation was none of his concern. He took a step back, turned and slipped quietly away. He heard Mary's footfalls close behind as he pushed the swinging door open and held it for her. As soon as she entered, he closed it. "Are you okay?"

"*Jah.* Seth's been telling the bishop and *Daed*, I think, that he wants to court me again, hoping the bishop will talk me into it. But I can't trust him, and I'm not going back with him. Ever. Seth doesn't know if he wants to live as *Englisch* or Amish. He's an Englischer, and that's what we call an *Auswendiger*—an outsider. He can't be trusted!"

Noah took a step back. Mary's words stabbed at his gut. She didn't trust *Englischers*.

Chapter Sixteen

On Sunday morning, Noah parked in his grandparents' barnyard at the end of a long line of buggies. He glanced at the cloudy sky, hoping the rain would hold off, then ran his hands over his suit coat to smooth any wrinkles and prayed his attire was appropriate.

He walked to the barn and stopped inside the doorway. The women sat on one side and men on the other. His gaze scanned the benches until it caught Mary's eye. She tilted her head toward the men. He skirted around the benches and found a spot on the last one…next to Mary's ex-fiancé, his cousin. Seth nodded, and Noah sat.

The bench was hard, and Noah sensed the tension filling the space between him and Seth. In a few minutes, a man announced a hymn number and started the singing, which they all joined in, except the preachers, who left the area. When they returned, the singing stopped. The preachers sat, but one remained standing and spoke a few opening words.

He began, "Blessed be the God…"

He concluded with a reminder to the congregation to prepare their hearts and listen to the Word of God and to trust God. He spoke in a mixture of Pennsylvania-Dutch, German and English, which put Noah at ease for a few minutes.

After prayer, a preacher began the main sermon. "May grace and mercy be with you and the peace of *Gott*." Words Noah had often heard his mom speak in German.

Mary had prepared him, but the service seemed never ending. He tried not to squirm, but it was hard. Since his parents had spoken German, he understood a few words and phrases. The minister said a few words in English, Noah thought for his benefit: "Be ye not unequally yoked together with unbelievers."

The rest of the sermon was a blur. When it was over, Seth stood and disappeared with a crowd of men without saying a word. Noah jabbed his hands in his pockets and mulled around. It was tempting to leave, but he'd wait until after the meal. The men congregated in their own groups, so he strayed away from them. He looked around, but his grandpa was busy.

"*Hallo*, Noah. I didn't expect to see you here."

He jerked around and let out a soft sigh. "Hello, Aunt Judith. Well, I was curious."

"Are you thinking about joining our Order? That would be *wunderbaar*."

"After meeting the family, I wanted to understand your religion and what you believe." Guilt squeezed his chest. Truth was, his parents' death had torn his heart in two, and he was tired of hurting and feeling alone. He was angry at God for the accident that killed them, and it was time he got right with Him. He wanted to find God, have it out with Him, and make Him say why He had to take them. And he figured he'd find God at their church.

"*Danki* for coming, Noah," Judith said. "Whether our *daed* says it or not, I know he enjoyed seeing you here."

"I haven't talked to him. I'm not sure he knows I'm here."

"He knows you're here. I saw him watching you. Maybe I'll see you later. But now I must help serve the meal."

Noah turned and almost ran into Mary. "I was wondering if I'd see you."

"I'm helping the women, but I thought I'd better tell you that the men all eat together at that long table." She pointed, and he nodded.

The men didn't ask his name. But he was sure they recognized him as Thomas Miller's grandson, from his *Englisch* son Jeremiah. But no one acted like they were curious enough to ask what he was doing here. Or they were just polite.

Noah ate his meal with the men on either side of him asking him casual questions. It helped ease the butterflies churning in his gut.

When he saw Mary cleaning up after the meal, he excused himself and headed in her direction.

He sprinted the last few yards. "Hello, Mary."

She turned toward him. "What did you think?"

"It was nice, different. Sometimes I thought the preachers were talking directly to me."

She smiled. "They were talking to all of us."

"Emily stayed with a friend, and I said I'd pick her up on the way home. So I need to get going, but I'll see you tomorrow at work." He glanced past her, and noticed that her dad had a bead on him. She'd been hurt once before, and judging by Caleb's face, he wasn't going to let his daughter get hurt again. "Is my grandma in the house?" Noah asked. "I want to say goodbye to her."

"*Jah*, I'm sure she'd be upset if you didn't."

He stepped inside the kitchen and spotted his grandmother at the sink. "I need to get going," he said, "but I wanted to say goodbye."

She walked out onto the porch with him. "*Danki* for coming, and I'm sure Thomas is glad, too. No matter what Cyrus said to you, I want you to come back and visit."

Noah enveloped her in a hug and then kissed her cheek. "I'll be back to visit sometime."

Her smiled reached all the way to her eyes. She turned and headed back to the kitchen.

Noah swallowed hard and wandered across the yard to his vehicle, blinking a tear from his eye. He rubbed a hand across the aching in his chest. He loved them already…and he was going to miss them.

For a week, Mary baked for the tourists and practiced her three entries required for the three days of baking for the contest.

Monday morning, she grabbed the potholders, pulled two loaves of bread out of the oven and set them on the cooling racks. Standing back, she watched Amanda fill a jellyroll pan with cinnamon rolls and pop them in the oven.

"Amanda, I'm going to take this cart of honey-wheat and white bread to the front so it'll be ready to run across the street later for the men working at Sweet Delights."

"I'm right behind carrying cupcakes and sugar cookies." Amanda exchanged the potholders for a tray and fell into step behind her.

Mary parked the cart in the front of the store, the door opened and Jean whirled in and quickly closed the door before a gust of wind could blow a pile of rustling leaves inside. "Good morning, ladies. It's nippy out today."

"Mornin', Jean. Fall is just around the corner." Mary backed the cart farther away from the entrance.

The door flew open again, and Ethan Lapp scrambled in. "*Morgen*, Mary. Amanda."

"You, too." Amanda said as she started to arrange the sugar cookies and cupcakes on a shelf. Mary looked up. "Morgen, Ethan. You're not working at the bakery raising?"

"*Jah*, I just stopped in to say hi."

His eyes strayed from her. "How are you, Amanda?"

"*Jah*, I'm *gut*." She kept on working.

Mary had the feeling that maybe Ethan and Amanda wanted to talk. "Ethan, when you go back, will you roll this cart of bread and rolls over to *Mamm* so she can set them out for lunch for the workers?" Without waiting for his reply, she picked up the empty pans and carried them back to the kitchen.

She tidied up the counter and washed the sink full of dishes. Twenty minutes later, Amanda walked in.

"So what was that all about with Ethan?" Curiosity pulled the words out of Mary.

Amanda pulled a bowl from the cupboard, clunked it on the counter and started to make a cake. "Nothing really. Ethan's just started coming around and talking."

"Are you two a couple?" Mary whispered.

"*Nein*." Amanda paused. "I'm not sure what we're doing. It seems we're just talking." A little smile tugged at the corners of her mouth. "He might have said more, but he needed to get back to work. Where's Noah?"

"He left a note saying he was taking jugs of tea and coffee to Sweet Delights for the workers. Are you purposely trying to get off the subject of Ethan?"

"Okay, the other day he stopped by, and we just started talking about the festival and things."

"So has he asked you to go on a buggy ride?"

"*Nein*, we're just friends."

Why was it that neither she nor Amanda had snagged their perfect love? Why was it that both of them wanted what they couldn't have?

Mary sighed. It was harder each day seeing Noah knowing he was *Englisch* and that nothing was going to happen between them.

He would glance at her when he thought she wasn't watching, and she'd felt the spark when their hands accidently touched. She'd frozen in place and couldn't breathe. Now, she could still feel the tingle on her hand… and in her heart. But that was as far as it could go.

Opening the back door of the store, Noah dashed through and laid Mary's mail beside her. "We have our schedule from the festival contest director."

Mary whirled around to face him. "Have you read yours?"

He nodded. "We have to take our first entry to the judge next Thursday for the first-round judging. They will eliminate all but three in each of the three categories. On Friday, those nine will bake, and they'll pick a winner in each of the three categories. The winners will receive $5,000. On Saturday, those three winners compete for the trophy and grand prize of $20,000."

"You're a world of news." Mary tore open her contest letter and read.

"I hope you're ready, Mary."

She smiled and her eyes locked with his. "Game on, Noah."

Her voice was soft and melted into him like butter. "Ready to get busy and practice?"

She jerked her gaze from his. "Jah, let's get busy."

Noah pulled out the canister of flour, and they each practiced their entry one more time. He watched Mary slide hers in the oven on the bottom rack, and he set his on the top rack and closed the door.

Emily burst in through the back door and ran to Noah. "Can I compete in the children's baking contest at the festival?" she begged. "They're still taking entries. One of the prizes is a pink backpack."

He shrugged. "Sure. You're a good baker. Mary saw to that." He glanced at Mary and detected a hint of a smile cross her face before it discretely disappeared. "Do you know what you want to make?"

"Yes, peanut butter bars. I can win, Noah, my recipe is really, really good. My friend Kate is going to enter, too."

Mary handed a measuring cup to Emily. "Do you want to make a practice one now, and I'll watch?"

"Sure." Emily gathered her ingredients and carefully measured each one out.

Noah took a step back and leaned against the sink. Emily liked Mary, and for that matter, so did he. Maybe too much.

Mary lifted her cornflower-blue eyes and locked them with his. His chest thumped like he was a schoolboy with a crush.

He grabbed a tray of bread and headed to the front of

the store. What was he doing? Where could this relation-ship go? He was *Englisch*, she was Amish, and neither was willing to change.

Chapter Seventeen

On Wednesday, Mary pulled out a tablet and pencil and sat at the table in the store's kitchen. She wrote a schedule for herself and a baking schedule for Amanda. The next week would be hectic with extra baking for the tourists and festivalgoers, and creating perfect entries for the contest.

Noah rushed into the kitchen from the back door and threw open the pantry doors. He pulled out his pocket notebook and pen and jotted down things as he mumbled to himself. "We're running low on baking powder and flour. I'm going to run to Iowa City and get extra supplies. I spoke to Susan on the street and told her I'd pick up some supplies for her restaurant, too. Is there anything you can think of that we need?"

"More sugar," Mary answered without looking up from her list. She tried to ignore the tingling in her stomach whenever he was around. She kept her gaze down and made another note.

"Would you like to ride over to my store in Iowa City while I pick up a few things? You've never seen it, and it's only eighteen miles. Shouldn't take too long."

She raised her head. "*Jah*, I'd like to see your other store."

Thirty minutes later, Noah pulled up to the front of his store in Iowa City. "I'll let you out here. You can walk through, and I'll meet you at the back door."

She stepped out of his vehicle, shocked to see that this store was twice the size of the one in Kalona. She gravitated to the bakery section first. He had a few desserts and pastries here that weren't at the other one. They looked delicious. Now she was curious about how the rest of this store would be different.

He had an elegant coffee stand with a beautiful cappuccino and latte maker. A full salad bar was in the middle of the deli section with fresh vegetables and fruits. There were not only cold sandwiches, but a woman behind a counter was making grilled cheese, hamburgers, paninis and pizzas.

In Kalona, she had thought of Noah as a shop owner, but his talents spanned much more than just a small shop. She walked through the large produce area. He had all this to take care of and he still helped his grandparents. And he was giving her a hand, as well.

She weaved her way through the kitchen to the service door at the back and found Noah loading his SUV.

"What do you think?" A hint of pride was visible in his expression.

"It's bigger than I imagined. Your bakery here has a larger selection of pastries. It appears you learned the trade of your *vater* very well."

His smiled stretched all the way to his amber eyes, and his five o'clock stubble gave him a rugged but handsome look. He motioned to his vehicle parked at the open door. "Ready to go back to Kalona?"

"*Jah*, I need to get my baking done. I don't have a fancy store like this to support me." She teased as she climbed in and fastened the seatbelt.

He buckled up and started the engine. "I'm saving every dime I get out of this store to pay for Emily's college, and Jenny's, if she'll let me pay. But Jenny said she didn't want to work in the store, so she didn't want to take money from the business. But it's hers, too."

"Jenny owns a portion of the business? In the Plain community, it would have gone to the son."

"When our parents died, I put everything they owned in all three of our names. So if anything happens to me, they'd have a means to pay for their schooling or a way to support themselves. But as you probably know, the Amish in Kalona weren't coming to my store until after I gave out samples at the barn raising. Most of them patronize your bakery, Mary, and they grow their own vegetables. And as you say, Kalona is a small town, so I'm not sure I can keep that store open unless I win the contest." He glanced across the console. "You do realize whoever wins will be written up in the newspaper and in the tourist brochure. That should boost sales."

Mary's back straightened against the seat. "I'm sorry. I didn't realize that about your business. I suppose more of the Plain come to my bakery, but you have a *gut* deli business, and your pastries taste *wunderbaar*."

"Mary, my parents had said they left their community during their *rumspringa*, but I was shocked when Cyrus said my grandpa lay on the ground for hours while my dad fiddled around in town buying a bundle of shingles, which should have only taken a few minutes. That must have been why Dad pushed Jenny and me so hard."

Mary turned her head so fast her *kapp* strings swung

back and forth. "*Nein*, don't blame your *daed*. He was young and didn't know your *grossdaddi* had fallen. The older man shouldn't have been on the roof by himself."

"I know, but I can't get that out of my head." Noah's voice choked on the words.

Mary cleared the lump clogging her throat. She'd blamed Noah for trying to ruin her business. Now she knew that wasn't true.

The remainder of the trip was quiet as she watched the farmers in the field. Back in Kalona, Noah parked behind his store and picked up the heavy box from the SUV while Mary lifted the lighter one. She followed him in and set her carton on a shelf in the pantry.

Noah plunked his box on the floor in the back. "I have to take a couple of boxes down to Susan. Want to come along and carry one for me?"

"Sure. It shouldn't take but a few minutes to walk to Susan's restaurant."

Noah held Lazy Susan's front door open as Mary carried her box inside. She slowed her pace, and waited for Noah when Susan waved them over to the checkout counter.

As Noah's six-foot, bigger-than-life presence strolled next to her, Mary tried to keep some space between them. She looked around to see if anyone had paid attention to them walking in together. *Nein*, it didn't appear so. Everyone seemed to be talking or eating.

Was she leading Noah on by riding with him to Iowa City? There was an attraction between them, that was for sure and certain. But she could never leave her community. And Noah had made it clear he didn't intend to join their Order.

Was this just two friends working together or something else entirely? Something that shouldn't be...nein, that couldn't be.

But her heart said *something* she didn't want to hear.

Noah glanced at Mary, but she seemed deep in thought. Maybe she was worried about the contest. He stepped up to the checkout counter with his box of supplies. "Hi, Susan, where would you like these boxes?"

"Thank you, Noah, Mary," Susan greeted them with a smile. "Just set them here on the counter, and I'll have someone from the kitchen come and get them."

Noah handed her the bill. Susan took it and waved her hand toward a table. "Why don't you two take a seat? Order a sandwich and a piece of pie on the house while I write you a check." She hurried from behind the counter and headed toward the office.

Noah gestured at a booth. "How about lunch?"

Mary glanced at the front door then back at him. "I'll just have a piece of pie. I have things to do and need to get back to the store." She slid into the closest booth, and Noah sat opposite her.

After the server set their water down and scooted away with their order, Noah leaned back and blew out a sigh. "It's nice to sit and relax. You're quiet, Mary."

She ran her hand along the edge of the placemat. "Just have a lot on my mind. Making a recipe that'll beat yours for the contest, and Sweet Delights is almost ready to open." She kept her gaze lowered as she picked up her water glass and wiped the condensation off the bottom.

The server set their pie down and hurried away.

Somehow, he got the feeling Mary wasn't telling him something. Was it just her baking she needed to get back to? He took a sip of water, but tension hung in the air between them like smoke rising off a bonfire.

"Noah, I need to be honest with you. I'm baptized and have joined our church. That means that my actions, if deemed inappropriate by the *Gmay*, could be disciplined. The bishop has warned me about spending too much time with you."

He jerked and sloshed water from the glass he was holding. He set it on the coaster and flopped back against the seat. "Mary, I'm sorry. I didn't realize it was such a problem, but we work together. This is only a temporary situation."

He never should have asked her to come to such a public place with him. It wasn't fair to put her in an awkward situation. What was he thinking? They were from different worlds. It was an impossible situation for both of them.

You're a fool, Miller. Let her go.

Mary took a bite of pie, looked up and into the stare of Bishop Yoder approaching her table. Her fork dropped to her plate, and a piece of crust flopped onto the table.

The bishop approached and stood by her side. "Mary, could I have a few words with you?" His voice was low, but others at tables nearby looked their way.

Noah glanced at Mary. "I need to get back to the store. I'll excuse myself, and you can sit in my place, Bishop." He slid off the seat and headed toward Susan at checkout.

Bishop Yoder sat opposite Mary, taking Noah's seat. He pushed Noah's dishes off to the side and laid his clasped hands on the table in front of him. His face was solemn. "Mary, you have been baptized and joined the church. That means you have chosen to submit to the *Ordnung* and the *Gmay*."

Mary gulped a ragged breath. "Bishop, I know, but I have done nothing wrong."

He shook his head. "Do not allow this *Englischer* to court you. He attended church, but other than that, he has given no indication that he wants to join our Order."

"I work with Noah. We picked up supplies for our kitchen, and Susan asked us to bring back a few things for her." Mary kept her attention on the pie, picking at it with her fork, except for a quick glance at the bishop's face.

"Listen to me, Mary." He tapped his hand softly on the edge of the table. "I think you have told yourself that. At your baptism, you promised to obey the regulations. Has that changed?"

A streak of pain tore through her and dropped to the pit of her stomach. "You're right, Bishop. I have been letting my heart overrule my head and what I have professed with my lips. I will move out of Noah's store next week. By then, Sweet Delights will be far enough along. I can work inside and get it ready to open."

The bishop stood. "*Jah*, I don't believe we will need to have this conversation again. I will let you finish your pie in peace and in prayer."

What was she thinking? She should have kept her distance from Noah.

She'd only be at his store for a few more days. Tomorrow was Thursday and the day her first contest entry was due. She and Noah were competitors once again. This time she needed to keep her focus on the prize, otherwise Noah, or someone else, would win the $20,000.

Chapter Eighteen

Thursday morning, Mary hitched King at 4:00 a.m. and headed to Noah's store.

Lord Gott, all that I do is to serve You. If I fail in any way, please lead my feet back on the right path so that my work glorifies Your name. I hope that my will is in line with Your will for me and Sweet Delights. But truly, Father, I don't know what I'd do if I lost the bakery, but Your will be done.

She reached for the doorknob and noticed the light shining through the parted curtain. Noah was already here. He thought like her, the first entry might require repeat making until they turned out perfect.

She gulped a breath and opened the door. Noah was busy at work and didn't look up, but Amanda was also in the kitchen, setting a pan of bread in the oven.

"*Danki*, Amanda, for getting here early."

Amanda tossed her a smile and winked. "I knew you would be busy all day. I'll do our baking, and you worry about getting your entry perfect."

After stowing her bag, Mary pulled eggs from the cooler and beat them until light and fluffy. She added the yeast and milk mixture, stirred and turned it out onto a floured board and began kneading the dough until it was elastic. She plopped it in a bowl, covered it and set the dough aside to rise.

She glanced over at Noah just as he raised his head from mashing bananas. He nodded and went right back to work. Strange he had said nothing to her. He was usually very talkative. Had Bishop Yoder said something to him?

Mary brushed that thought aside. She grabbed fresh strawberries, cleaned them, added sugar, a little water, and cooked the fruit down into a thick syrup. *Ach*, she forgot to add the lemon juice. She turned the fire down and hurried to the refrigerator.

A scorching aroma filled the kitchen as she slammed the fridge door closed and ran back to the stove. She jerked the pan off the burner and noticed she'd turned the flame up instead of down. Burnt!

She glanced at Noah. He didn't acknowledge the mistake. Any other time, he would have teased her. She missed his verbal quips. They broke up the day and made standing on her feet fun…because it was with him.

Grabbing another bag of strawberries, she started over. Her hand was shaking as she stirred the sauce over a low heat.

Amanda patted her on the back. "You've got this. Relax!"

When the sauce was at the right temperature and thickened, Mary removed it from the heat and set it to cool. She started the cream cheese filling and whipped it until it was light and fluffy.

She rolled out the dough into a flat rectangle, added her filling, rolled it into a log and cut the rolls into one-inch slices. When they had finished rising, Mary popped them in the oven. This had to win…it just had to.

Fifteen minutes later, she pulled the rolls from the oven and set them on a rack to cool. After a few minutes, she eased a roll off the jellyroll pan with a spatula, set it on a plate and handed it to Amanda.

Amanda took a bite and then another. "*Ach.* This is so delicious I could eat the whole pan. P-e-r-f-e-c-t." She waved her fork. "This should put you in the finalist category."

Mary heaved a sigh. *"Danki."*

"Congratulations," Noah said as he walked past them and out the swinging door to the front of the store.

Amanda peered over her shoulder at the door. "What happened? Did you two get into a fight?"

"Nein. Yesterday, we dropped off some supplies at Lazy Susan's. We had a piece of pie, and Bishop Yoder walked in and interrupted us. Noah left, and the bishop told me since I had been baptized and joined church, I shouldn't be dating an *Englischer.* Or what appeared that way."

"Mary, I'm sorry."

"Nein, it's for the best. We were getting too close, and it was going to lead to someone getting hurt. The bishop was right."

"What? I never thought I'd ever hear you say the bishop's advice was right. Did he say something to Noah, too? He's acting strange," Amanda whispered.

"Not that I know of. But I think by the look the bishop gave Noah, he got the idea I was in big trouble, and he should stay away. I'm moving the bakery out next week so it shouldn't be a problem."

"Okay, so we need to get busy. What time do you have to take the rolls over?"

"They have to be there by 2:00 p.m. So I need to get going." Mary carefully boxed up a dozen of her strawberry rolls. When she closed the kitchen door behind her, she paused.

Dear Heavenly Father, please bless my offering. I pray that it is a worthy entry and part of Your plan for me. Amen.

Noah rushed into the kitchen and looked around. Amanda stood at the sink, her back to him washing pans. "Where's Mary?" His words jumped out a bit too demanding.

Amanda jerked around. "She left to take her rolls over to be judged."

"When did she leave?"

"She just walked out the door. She had to hitch King, so she might still be at the corral. Why? Something wrong?"

"Jenny got a ride home from school to spend the weekend, but she borrowed the SUV to go visit friends. And I just noticed that I misread the judging time—it's not 3:00 p.m., it's 2:00 p.m. In fifteen minutes."

Amanda dried her hands and yelled. "Get your entry, and I'll run out and see if I can stop her."

He ran to the pantry, pulled a box off the shelf and set his banana cake inside. He darted out the door and headed across the street to the corral.

Mary was still waiting. "Hurry, Noah!" He climbed in, and before he could sit, she tapped the reins against King's back. The horse shot off down the street and threw Noah against the back of the seat. He righted himself and settled back, his hand still grasping the box. "Thanks for waiting."

Silence stretched across the buggy.

Finally, Mary glanced at him. "Yesterday, the bishop reminded me that I was a baptized member of the church. That means I have an obligation to my vow."

He nodded. "I understand."

Mary turned the buggy, set King at a fast trot down Ninth Street, pulled on the reins and stopped King by the contest booth. Noah jumped down, and Mary followed, grasping her entry.

When they reached the sidewalk next to the judging tent, Bishop Yoder was standing there watching them as they approached. Mary nodded to him and entered the tent behind Noah. They joined the registration line just as a contest worker closed the tent flap.

One glance at Mary's ashen face told Noah he'd gotten her into some serious trouble. "Thanks for the ride. I'll stay a while and find my own way home."

She nodded. "*Danki.* I'm sorry."

"No need to be. I understand." He regretted having to ask her for a ride.

On his way out of the tent, he spied Mary talking to the bishop.

The bishop glanced over Mary's shoulder at Noah with a stare that spoke volumes. Yes, he understood. He needed to stay away from her.

Early Friday morning, Mary unlocked the back door of the store and hung her bag. The kitchen had a strangeness hanging in the air. Noah stood at the counter stirring up something, and Amanda was at the sink washing dishes. Neither one greeted her. What was going on? As she headed to the pantry, Mary noticed the open newspaper on a chair. She glanced at it and stopped. The bold headline popped out.

Finalists Announced for the Kalona Fall Apple Festival Baking Contest

Her hand shook as she reached for the paper. The kitchen went silent. Mary drew in a deep breath as her eyes searched the column for the list of categories and winners.

1) Breads, rolls, scones:
   Lilly Wiggs
   Mary Brenneman
   Timothy Jenkins

2) Pies, strudels, cakes:
   Don Thompson
   Noah Miller
   Theresa Vogel

3) Cookies, cupcakes, bars:
   Carlos Vegas
   Clara Schnowsky
   Cynthia Návar

Mary gasped. "Oh, no!"

"What's wrong, didn't you see your name?" Amanda hurried to her side.

"Yes, I see it, but one of the other finalists is Cynthia Návar. She's a pastry chef from Chicago, and she won the contest last year. Clara Schnowsky is a well-known chef from Des Moines."

Mary read the whole article then laid the paper back

on the chair. "What are you making for the second round, Noah?"

"Apple strudel." He glanced up at her as he worked.

"*Gut*, I'm making apple bars."

"Don't worry." Amanda patted her shoulder. "You're a fabulous baker, and you can compete with the best of them."

"I hate dumping all the work on you."

"Nonsense. If you lose the bakery, I'm out of a job. I came in early because I knew you'd be a finalist in your category. So get baking, that cake will need to be perfect to take you to the final round."

"*Danki*, Amanda."

Noah opened the oven door, pulled out two dishes of apple strudel and set them in a corner to cool. "Amanda, I made two. When they cool, would you taste one and tell me what you think?"

"Of course, but aren't you afraid I might be biased?"

"That never occurred to me. Would you rather not do it since Mary is entering?"

"I'm only kidding. I'd love to taste yours. It smells *gut*, and I'll give you my honest opinion."

Heavy footfalls approached the kitchen from the grocery and Ethan poked his head around the doorway. "Here you are, Amanda. I thought you might be out front working." He sauntered up to her side, "Would you like to go to the festival with me tonight?"

Amanda smiled. "*Jah*, that would be nice."

"I'll stop back when you get off work."

"I'll be ready."

Ethan turned to leave but paused. "Noah, I thought you'd be out at your *grossdaddi*'s farm."

Noah lifted his head for a second but worked while he

talked. "I've got a lot to do with all the festival baking, and I'm entered in the baking contest. What made you think I'd be at my grandpa's farm?"

Ethan's eyes widened. "I thought you knew. A cow was stuck in the mud. Your grandpa was out in the lot by himself and tried to help the old girl. The bossy lost her footing and fell on him. He lay there a long time. The bishop was called, and he told my *daed*."

Noah dropped the pan he was holding. "Is he dead?"

"*Nein*, but he's hurt bad. They think he broke his back. Your grandma went to look for him. When she found him, she called for help. He's in the hospital in Iowa City last I heard."

Noah tore off his apron and washed his hands. "Thanks for letting me know. When did it happen?"

"Yesterday, I think."

"Mary, I'm going to see my grandfather." His voice strained with concern.

"Okay, but what about your entry?"

He tossed her a glance. "When you go, would you mind entering it for me?" He grabbed his hat and keys off the hook that held them and headed for the back door.

"*Jah*, I can do that and pray." His sad eyes nearly squeezed the breath from her.

"*Danki* for stopping, Ethan. I'll see you later." Amanda patted his shoulder as he, too, headed for the back door.

"*Danki*, for bringing the news, Ethan. I know Noah really appreciated it." Mary recognized the look on Noah's face when he left. Sarah had a rough time having the twins and scared them all. Jah, she'd pray and keep her hands busy until he returned with the update on his *grossdaddi*.

She pulled the ingredients and stirred up two pans of

apple bars. While they baked, she cleaned up the kitchen and whipped cinnamon into the cream.

Amanda watched as the cream foamed nice and high. "Won't that melt before they get it judged?"

"I asked, and they said I can take the whipped cream in a small cooler, set it by the bars and add a note asking the judges to add the topping."

"You're taking a big chance with that idea." Amanda's voice held a skeptical warning.

"I know, but it's delicious. Have you tried Noah's strudel yet?"

"No. I'll try it right now." She sliced a piece and sat it on a plate. "It smells *gut*." She took a bite, blinked then took another bite. Amanda looked at the strudel as if it had an odd taste.

"What's wrong? Isn't it fully baked?"

Amanda looked at Mary, her eyes as wide as if she'd seen a bear. "It tastes as delicious as your apple strudel. In fact, it tastes like yours. Maybe better."

Chapter Nineteen

Noah asked at the hospital's front desk for the room number of Thomas Miller. He found the room, knocked on the door and entered when his grandmother called, "Come in."

He slowly walked to his grandfather's bed. Cyrus and Judith were sitting in chairs off to the side by the window. Grandpa's eyes were open slightly, but his parted lips indicated he was ready for sleep.

Noah stood by the bed rail. "How do you feel? What happened? Ethan said a cow fell on you."

The old man looked frail. Days ago, when Noah had visited, he'd looked healthy, strong, and even ten years younger. Now, just a few days later, age had caught up with him.

Grandpa's eyelids popped opened. "The cow's hooves had sunk in the mud, and she couldn't lift them out. When I tried to push her, she rocked back, slipped in the mud and pushed me down. She managed to get up off me, but I couldn't stand. My back hurt too badly. I managed to pull myself over to the gate and crawled through it, but I lay on the ground until Anna came." His eyes fluttered closed as if the talking had expended all his energy.

Noah sat in the chair beside his grandmother so he'd be close to the bed. He leaned toward her. "What's wrong with him? Did he break his back?"

"*Nein*, he was blessed. The Lord was with him and saw to it that he could maneuver out of the pen. He cracked three ribs. It hurts him to take deep breaths and move. They said six weeks to mend, but he will have restrictions on his activities. They're going to give him respiratory therapy to teach him breathing techniques to reduce the pain."

Noah leaned closer to the bed. "Grandpa, I'll come out and help you farm until you get healed."

Thomas tried to rise, then winced and fell back down. He gritted his teeth, gulped a breath and blew it out slowly. "Jeremiah never bothered to do his duty. You don't need to help me, either."

The words hit Noah like a wrecking ball, stunning him for a second. "I can't help what my dad did or how he treated you. That was between you and him."

Cyrus walked over to the bed. "Noah, I think it's time you left. He doesn't need all this stress and strain. You're not wanted here."

Noah scanned his grandfather's face. "I love you and want to help no matter what you think. I don't know why Dad left you to do the work by yourself, but it doesn't sound like him. Dad worked day and night in the store. He was a dedicated, hardworking man." Noah swallowed hard. "The man you talk about wasn't the man I knew. Maybe he matured over the years. But I loved him, and I'm willing to forgive as God says I must do. Everyone says you Amish are gentle and forgiving, but I don't see it. You're vindictive, spiteful and unforgiving."

Cyrus moved a step closer to Noah. "I think it's time you left." He pointed to the door.

"I want to talk to Noah. Sit down, Cyrus, and don't interfere." Grandpa glanced up and put one hand on the bed railing. "The family jumped to conclusions the day your father left. Except, he didn't just leave. I threw him off the property and told him never to come back. Jeremiah had been working with my father at his bakery. The bakery that Joshua Lapp, Sarah Brenneman's *daed*, and my father owned for a short time together. Jeremiah told me that morning on the barn roof that he didn't want to farm with me. He wanted to own a store and bakery. He said Cyrus and I could farm together. Cyrus and I have never seen eye to eye on anything."

Cyrus let out a loud huff but never said a word.

Grandpa gripped the railing and took another breath. "I told Jeremiah to get off the farm and never come back. He did just that. I never saw him again. I'm ashamed of myself." His voice trailed off, and tears streamed down the old man's cheek. He finally brushed them away with a trembling hand.

Noah stood and strolled closer to the old man's bed. His grandpa's eyelids fluttered shut then opened and shut again. "Grandpa," he said quietly, "I'm going to go so you can sleep, but I'll be back tomorrow."

The old man's head nodded slightly.

Closing the door, Noah rested his back against it for a few seconds, trying to absorb a new truth. He pushed himself away, his knees trembling, but he managed the distance to his vehicle.

Noah rested his hands on the steering wheel, letting

the amazement of his grandfather's confession wash over him. He slid the gearshift to Drive, hit the gas and eased out into traffic. He thanked God all the way back to Kalona for finally lifting the veil and revealing the truth.

He squeezed the steering wheel as another truth swirled around in his heart. He should have been Amish instead of *Englisch*. Everything that he was familiar and comfortable with his whole life was a lie.

Mary rushed to drop off her bars and Noah's strudel at the judging tent and raced back to get started practicing for the last round, in case she won this round. Her hands shook as she pulled her pie out of the oven. Amanda said Noah's strudel was better than hers and that made her nervous.

Amanda stepped back. "Be careful you don't drop that. Is something wrong?"

"I'm afraid my pie won't have an exceptional enough taste to win the contest."

"*Nein*. Stop doubting yourself. You are every bit as *gut* as Noah. You can do this." Amanda cheered as she dried a plate.

Ethan burst through the kitchen door. "Sorry, I'm late, Amanda, I got held up doing chores. The buggy is waiting out back."

"I'll be there in a minute."

Mary's gaze shifted from the door to Amanda. "Ethan really is taking you to the festival then?"

"*Nein*, he's not taking me, we're just going together."

"I heard him ask you. It sounded like a date to me."

Amanda finished drying dishes and putting them away. "He's never really called me a *freundin*, but I'll soon be twenty-one, an old maid. He might just be hanging around waiting for Jenny to show up so he can talk to her." Her voice quaked.

Mary cocked her head at her friend. "How do you feel about that?"

"It hurts if I let myself think about it. It hurts a lot. But the only reason it hurts is because I like him."

"Maybe you should ask him about your relationship and where it's going."

Amanda headed for the door and stopped. "Because I'm scared of the answer."

"So you're hoping that if you go out enough, you'll grow on him?"

"*Jah*, but it sounded better when I first thought of it."

Mary rushed across the kitchen and gave Amanda a hug. "Don't get hurt."

"*Nein*, I'm tough, and in spite of the situation, we have a *gut* time together. Do you want to go with us?"

"*Danki*, but I'll catch up with you and Ethan in a little while."

Mary finished cleaning the kitchen then glanced at the clock. 5:45 p.m. It was almost time for them to read the names of the winners of the second round. The winners of each category would compete tomorrow for the grand prize.

She gathered her bag, locked the front door of the store and stepped to the sidewalk just as Noah pulled his SUV up to the curb and rolled down the window. "Need a lift to the festival?"

"*Danki*." She opened the door and slid onto the seat. "How's your *grossdaddi*?"

"He's got three cracked ribs. He can't do much for the next six weeks, but he'll heal. Are you excited about hearing who won?"

"I'm nervous. Cynthia Návar, the chef from Chicago, won last year, and she's here again this year."

"You're a wonderful baker, Mary. Don't let Cynthia intimidate you. Keep your eye on your goal. Don't let anyone steal your vision."

"You're right. Let's change the subject. Who is going to do Thomas's farming?"

"Since you, Amanda and Jean do such a good job watching the store, I thought I could go out to the farm for a while each day and help. It's the end of September, tourism will start to slow down, and that will give me time to help my grandpa. I thought sometimes Emily could come along and help grandma."

"Of course we can do that for you and Thomas."

Noah pulled up by the curb and stopped. "I'll let you off here and go park."

Mary slid out of the vehicle and gazed at all the festivalgoers, tents, game booths, activities, and food wagons. There were more in attendance this year than ever before. Maybe the feuding and the increased prize for the baking contest had drawn more people. She pushed her way through the crowd and walked straight into Bishop Yoder.

"*Gut* day, Mary."

A swarm of butterflies rampaged her stomach. "*Hallo*, Bishop. A *wunderbaar* festival, *jah*?"

He nodded. "Mary, can I have a word with you?"

"Of course. Is something wrong?"

He walked her to the edge of the sidewalk. "Some members of the *Gmay* have contacted me regarding all this commotion about the feud between you and Noah Miller. It's causing attention and drawing this huge crowd here to see who will win the prize of $20,000, a trophy and a trip to New York. You have made a spectacle of the Amish people. Your name appeared in the newspaper along with the mention of our Plain community. Only we don't seem so Plain when you have all those fancy pastries in your bakery and on display in a contest. The *Gmay* has decided to forbid you to participate any further in this contest."

Mary gasped. "Bishop, they can't do that."

Daed and *Mamm*, holding the twins, walked up behind the bishop and stood off to the side. "What's going on here?" *Daed* asked, his gaze flinging from Mary to the bishop.

"Your *tochter* will tell you, Caleb. It's time she acted like she is Plain." Bishop Yoder turned and stomped off down the sidewalk.

Mary clutched her quilted bag and twisted the straps around her hand. *Jah*, she knew what the bishop meant. Not only did she have to give up the contest and maybe the chance to save the bakery, but he was expecting her to give up her relationship with Noah. She hadn't wanted to admit it before, but she loved Noah.

Chapter Twenty

Mary walked beside her *stiefmutter*, delaying any lecture from *Daed*, as her gaze scanned the area for Noah.

"What's going on, Mary, why was the bishop so upset?" Sarah waved her hand in the direction of the bishop storming off then wrapped her arm back around Liza.

Daed walked up on Mary's other side. "What did you do? No doubt it has something to do with Noah. As soon as the festival is over, it's time for you to move back to Sweet Delights. It should be ready to open in a couple of weeks."

Sarah nodded in agreement. "Mayor Conrad told us that this year the festival has broken an all-time attendance record. He said it's because of the publicized feud between you and Noah, which was also the reason why they raised the prize money to $20,000. Is that what's bothering the bishop?"

Mary lowered her head as Sarah's words galloped over her like a runaway horse. She gulped a breath. "*Jah*, but it sounds like the town should be thanking us."

"The town is praising you and Noah, but the bishop

is upset with all the notoriety and attention a member is bringing to his Community. We are a Plain, quiet people. Having the news media say an Amish woman has an opportunity to win money, a trophy and a trip to New York City doesn't sound Plain or quiet," her vater chided.

"You can't accept a *trophy*. The bishop is looking out for our church," *Mamm* softly chastised.

"I know, it was never supposed to blow up into this big of a deal." Mary threw her arms open and gestured to the park bursting with tents and festivalgoers.

"What's going on between you and the store owner?" *Daed* tilted his head toward Noah standing at the contest tent motioning for her to come over there.

"Nothing. I work at his store. That's all. You two are imagining things." Mary slipped her arm around her *mamm* and pulled her over to the quilt tent.

She walked beside *mamm* up and down aisles while *Daed* followed behind with Lena squirming in his arms wanting to get down.

Mary turned to look at a quilt behind her and noticed Amanda and Ethan hurrying toward her.

Amanda caught Mary's arm. "Come, they are getting ready to read the names of the finalists."

"*Ach*, I didn't realize the time." She turned to Sarah. "They are going to read the names of the finalists. I'm going with Amanda to the contest tent."

Mamm nodded. "Go, we'll see you there."

Mary followed Amanda and Ethan and as she approached the contest tent, she watched for a glimpse of Noah but couldn't find him.

Inside the contest tent, Amanda weaved her way through the throng of people to the front by the podium. Mary searched the faces of the crowd. Off in the corner, Noah stood talking to Cynthia Návar, the chef from Chicago.

The loud speaker squawked. "Good afternoon, everyone, I'm Connie Goodnight. We are so pleased to see such a great turnout for our festival and participation in the baking contest. Just a refresher of the rules before I announce the names. It is mandatory that all three, category winners bake their final entry in front of the judges. They will evaluate and assign points on degree of difficulty, originality, presentation and taste."

Whispers and shuffling of feet sounded throughout the tent. Connie tapped on the microphone for quiet. "The names I read will be the finalists, who will meet tomorrow at 10:00 a.m. at Lazy Susan's. The contestants must bring everything they need to make their dessert. They will receive the use of the restaurant's stoves, ovens and refrigerators. Good baking to you all and please hold your applause until all three names are announced. Category one, Mary Brenneman. Category two, Noah Miller. Category three, Cynthia Návar."

The tent erupted into applause.

Amanda grabbed Mary and squeezed her in a hug. "You did it, but I knew you would."

Ethan patted her shoulder. "Congrats, Mary. You deserve it. I'll be rooting for you."

"*Danki*, Ethan." A rush of excitement soared through her, and tears clouded her vision as she blinked them away. She drew a choked breath. "I'm so excited I'm going back to the store right now to get my supplies ready to take to Lazy Susan's. I don't want to forget a thing." *I'll deal with the bishop later.*

"Amanda and I'll give you a ride back," Ethan offered.

"*Danki* but you two stay. It's only a few blocks, and I want to walk off this energy and clear my head."

Mamm and *Daed* had waited for her by the tent opening. "Congratulations, *honig*. We are so happy for you." *Mamm* patted her cheek.

"*Danki* but the bishop isn't. He said the *Gmay* has forbidden me from competing any further in the contest. What will they do if I continue?"

Mamm looked at *Daed*, then leveled her gaze back on Mary. "He will probably discipline you. You may have to apologize in front of the congregation."

"Is that all?"

Daed placed a hand on Sarah's shoulder. "Mary, if the bishop has warned you, he will take action. If they find you in violation of a biblical teaching, you may have to go before the *Gmay* to confess or explain your behavior. Be careful, *tochter*, it's a serious matter."

"I asked permission to enter, and the bishop said I could. Now that the news media has made a story out of Noah and me, and they printed my name in the paper, our community is upset. I can't control that."

Sarah's voice turned dire. "Mary, you need to talk to the bishop and the *Gmay*. They don't like the attention that's being given to the Plain community."

"*Mamm*, the final contest is tomorrow. There isn't time to ask permission. Just because my name was mentioned in the newspaper, it doesn't go against biblical teaching or the *Ordnung*. Gossiping and bringing false accusation against another member is also a biblical teaching."

"Be careful, Mary. You need to think about your actions." *Daed* pressed his hand on Sarah's back and guided her down the sidewalk. "We'll see you at home."

"Congratulations, Mary." Noah tapped her shoulder.

She jerked and whirled around. "*Jah*, to you, too. We did it. I can hardly believe we made it into the final contest." She caught control of her wavering voice.

"Is everything all right?"

"I—I'm not sure. The bishop told me our *Gmay* is concerned about all the publicity I've been receiving. They said it looks bad for the Plain community and have forbidden me to bake tomorrow."

Noah laughed. "Really, who is saying that? I was over at the Amish wood-crafting shop, and they told me business is booming with all the tourist and festivalgoers in town this week. They also said the Plain community bakery in the country is doing very well."

"Are you teasing me, Noah?"

"No, that's what they said. Did he say the names of those complaining?"

"*Nein*, but I'll ask next time and repeat what you told me."

"Are you going back to the bakery? I can give you a ride." He motioned to his vehicle parked a few hundred feet away.

"*Danki*, but I'm in enough trouble. Besides, I want to walk and think though this mess before I make a decision." She crossed the street and headed down the sidewalk.

Maybe someone was jealous of her chance to win $20,000. Jealousy and envy were also against biblical teachings.

Mary unlocked the back door of the store and was surprised not to see Noah. She hung her bag and found his note. "I'll let you work alone, and I'll pack later. N."

She pulled a box out of the pantry for her supplies to take to Lazy Susan's. As she practiced making a pie, she washed and placed each bowl, measuring spoon, whisk and ingredients in the box. She made a copy of her recipe and placed that in. When the pie cooled, she sat down, drew a deep breath and took a big bite… Perfect.

Mary grabbed her box out of Noah's store on Saturday morning and hurried to Lazy Susan's. After a sleepless night, she was running late and Amanda said Noah had already left for the restaurant.

When she knocked, Simone opened the door and led her to the kitchen. Noah and Cynthia had already arrived and set up their workstations.

Mary nodded as she passed them, following Simone to her area. She set her box down, and laid out all her utensils and ingredients on her station as Chef Simone André instructed.

Simone watched the clock. "Five minutes, chefs."

Mary blotted her hands on her apron, drew a deep breath and prayed.

"It's ten o'clock. You have four hours. Go!" Simone yelled.

Mary simmered fresh spices in apple juice, added the sugar, and thickened it. She made the crust, peeled and sliced the apples. She arranged them piled high in the shell then poured the spice mixture over top. She set the pie in the warmed oven and set the timer. While that baked, she made the caramel sauce. When the pie came out of the oven, she set it to cool then added the warm caramel sauce.

Simone called a thirty-minute warning, then ten. "Stop. Please bring your desserts to the judges' table in the restaurant area."

Mary led the way into the restaurant, set her dish down

in front of the judges, took a step back and waited for Noah and Cynthia to follow suite.

"Thank you, contestants, your jobs are done. You may go and enjoy the festival. The winner to the baking contest winner will be announced at four o'clock." Simone smiled and waved her hand toward the door.

Mary stepped out the door, her heart pounding like a sledgehammer, and drew a deep breath. "I'm glad that's over."

Noah and Cynthia followed her out, stopped and heaved big sighs.

"Would you two ladies like me to give you a ride back to the festival?" Noah's gaze bounced from Mary to Cynthia.

"Thank you, but my husband, Brian, is waiting for me." Cynthia slipped her cell phone back in her pocket as she approached the car at the curb. She turned back to Mary and Noah. "See you at the announcement."

Noah fell into step beside Mary. "It seems we're always together, and I get the impression your family doesn't like it."

"I'm going to meet Amanda and Ethan at the festival, but I'll walk. My family is protective of me. They don't want to see me get hurt again by someone who doesn't have my best interests at heart."

Her words walloped Noah's chest. He fought to take a deep breath. Seth had hurt Mary deeply, that was obvious. While she walked back to the festival, he hurried to the store and entered the backdoor to the kitchen. The steamy heat of fresh-baked peanut butter bars wafted through the air. "Mmm, the bars smell good."

Emily held up a plate. "They're all ready for the contest. Jenny helped me."

"Well, sort of." Jenny hugged her little sister. "Emily really knew what she was doing. I was impressed. Amanda and Mary did a great job of teaching our little girl how to bake." Jenny beamed with pride.

Emily set her plate down and covered it with plastic wrap. "Thanks for coming home, Jenny, to watch me compete in the contest, Noah, are you going over to the festival with Jenny and me?"

"I wouldn't miss it, little sister, but we need to get going." Noah stopped at the checkout counter in the front of the store. "Jean, if I'm not back by six o'clock, go ahead and lock up."

She nodded. "Have fun."

At the park, Jenny excused herself to find friends, and Noah guided Emily to the judging tent and helped her register her entry. "Shall we walk around and come back later for the contest results?"

"Yes, but I'm really nervous, Noah. All the other entries looked yummy."

But Emily forgot about her entry by the time they reached the first game booth. She tried to knock over bottles with a tennis ball to win a prize. "I'm not a good ball thrower."

"I'm not either, Emily. I spend my time baking, not throwing a ball."

Noah followed his sister around the festival from booth to booth. At the next booth, she caught a plastic, floating duck and won a hair barrette. While she picked out her prize, Noah glanced at his watch. "Let's hurry back to the judging tent and find chairs before they're all gone."

They found their seats. Five minutes later, Noah watched Emily squirm around on her chair. She jumped up and stood then flopped back down. When Goodnight walked to the podium and tapped on the microphone, Noah grabbed Emily's hand and squeezed. She glanced up at him and smiled. Their mom would have been so proud of her little girl so grown up and baking.

"We will announce the three finalists' names to the children's bakeoff in no particular order. You can all come forward, but audience, please hold your applause until all the names are read." Connie glanced at her paper. "Roger Ferguson, Summer Conway, Emily Miller."

Emily flew off the chair and ran to the front. Noah smiled and blotted a tear at the corner of his eye as the tent erupted into applause.

Finally, Connie raised her hand for quiet. "Again, please hold your applause until all names and places have been read, they receive their certificates and first place gets their pink backpack. In third place, Summer Conway. Second place winner, Roger Ferguson. And first place winner, Emily Miller."

The tent roared with clapping and cheers. Noah jumped from his seat, pushed his way to the front, grabbed Emily and hugged her. "I'm so proud of you."

"Noah, I didn't think I could do it! I would have been happy winning third place. I can't believe I actually got first place. Now I want to start working for you in the bakery. I could make my peanut butter bars and cookies and—"

"Slow down." Noah laughed. "You can make a few things, but don't forget you're still in school."

"I know, I'm just so excited!"

"Emily!" Kate, Emily's friend, squealed as she ran up

and hugged her. "You won. I'm so proud of you. Now you can teach me to bake better. My folks are waiting for me, do you want to come and walk around the festival with us?"

Noah nodded his approval. "If you can't find me when you're done, go back to the store, and I'll be there at six when Jean leaves."

"Okay, Noah." Emily grabbed Kate's hand, and they ran off through the crowd.

The microphone squawked, and Connie held her hand up. "Please take your seats. We need to make the presentation for the main baking contest." She waited for the tent to quiet down.

Noah found his seat and looked around for Mary. He saw Cynthia sitting next to the tent wall on the opposite side with her husband. She waved and gave Noah a thumbs-up.

Mary pushed her way past a couple of people waiting for chairs. "Is this seat taken?" she asked him.

Noah moved his arm from the back of the chair. "I was saving it for you. Did you see Emily win?"

She slid around Noah and sat down. "Yes, Amanda, Ethan and I were in the back with Jenny. I caught Emily on her way out. She's ecstatic over her win. I'm so happy for her. It gave her a boost of confidence."

"I'll say. Now she wants to bake for me."

"She's old enough to help. I baked at her age."

Connie put her hand in the air, motioning for quiet. When the crowd finally simmered down, she glanced down at the paper in her hand. After a few seconds, she leveled her gaze at the audience. "This year's contest has turned out to have a very unusual result." She waved her hand toward the table with the desserts from the three finalists.

"But first, let me introduce our panel of judges. Magdalena Morgan from Magdalena's Pastry Shop, Chicago, Illinois. Joel Bélanger from Bélanger French Cuisine, Des Moines, Iowa. And Simone André from MyBaking Channel.

A round of applause acknowledged the judges.

A voice directly behind Mary broke through the noise. "Hope one of you two show them how it's done in Iowa."

Mary smiled. "*Danki*, Frank."

Connie motioned for the crowd to simmer down. "Next, let's have our three finalists come up front. I will call names in no particular order. Cynthia Návar, Mary Brenneman and Noah Miller."

She held up a hand for the clapping to stop. "According to the rules, the judges were to select a finalist based on degree of difficulty, originality, presentation and taste. However, the judges have told me there is a clear third place, but two of the dishes met all the criteria and their numbers added up to the same score."

Murmurs from the crowd grew louder as she tried to talk. Connie raised her voice. "Please, just give me a few more minutes to explain. Two desserts were so close in taste that it was impossible to tell which was best. In fact, the tastes seem identical. It was brought to our attention that these two dishes are from contestants who are friends and who work together."

Mary gasped and turned toward Noah. "You stole my recipe?"

Her words flamed across the space between them and seared into Noah's gut.

Chapter Twenty-One

$\sim$

Mary whirled to her side and faced Noah. "Did you use my recipe without asking? I trusted you." Her heart nearly fell to the floor.

Noah gasped. "I didn't take your recipe. I used mine."

"Please," Connie interrupted, "can either of you explain how this happened?"

Whispers and voices hummed throughout the tent.

Connie tapped the mic. "We need quiet."

Mary's legs froze to the spot as humiliation raised bile to her throat. She spotted her *stiefmutter* and *daed* with red tinging their faces.

"I didn't steal your recipe," Noah went on. "It's in my family recipe book. I don't make it often because it's time-consuming, although delicious. It's been in my family for at least four generations, maybe longer."

Old Bishop Ropp pushed his way to the front. He stomped up to the dessert table, picked up a spoon and tasted both of the dishes. "Mary, this is the pie I was telling you about that Sarah's vater used to make when he was in partnership with Miller."

Sarah Brenneman rushed up to the front. "What are

you talking about, Bishop? My father never had a partner."

"Yes, he did when he first opened before you were born. The partnership didn't last very long, and the two men weren't friends after that."

Sarah gasped. "My *daed* never told me any story like that."

Anna Miller stepped forward. "Yes, I remember hearing my father-in-law talking about those days. Remember, Noah, Thomas told you yesterday that his *daed* had a partnership with Joshua Lapp, and that Sweet Delights was the bakery they owned together?"

Sarah shook her head. "That's funny because *daed* never mentioned it. How long were they in business, and why did they split up?

Anna placed a finger to her temple. "They had some sort of a disagreement. They couldn't work it out so they split up. Sweet Delights is the bakery they started together. Thomas might know more of the details."

"So," Connie broke in, "am I to understand that these two desserts are from the same recipe?"

"It appears they are." Mary glanced at Noah.

Noah nodded. "It seems the recipes are the same."

Connie grabbed the microphone. "To state it for the audience and the news media, there is no stipulation against two people entering the same baked good, although it is usually done as one entry. Do you two want to count your entries as one so we can declare a winner? Otherwise, I'm not sure how we would declare a winner."

Noah whispered to Mary, and she nodded.

Mary stammered and cleared her throat. "Under these unusual circumstances, Noah and I agree to combine are entries as one and accept the check together, but we would like to give Cynthia the trophy and the spot on the cable channel."

Connie looked at Simone, who nodded. "Simone agrees to that. Cynthia, if you'll come forward."

Cynthia thanked Mary and Noah as she strolled over and stood by Connie.

Connie lifted the trophy from the stand and handed it to Cynthia. "The Kalona Fall Apple Festival baking contest presents you with this trophy," and the invitation to appear on the Simone André Show on MyBaking Channel."

After the applauding quieted, Connie motioned to Mary and Noah. "Please come forward."

Mary glanced at Noah as they took a step forward.

"As the winner of the first place entry, I want to award you this check for $20,000." The tent erupted into a commotion. Connie let it continue for a while then tapped the mic. "I want to thank all who participated in the baking contest and hope to see you next year."

Mary grabbed Noah's arm. "Let's get Sarah and Anna and go outside and talk."

He nodded. "I'll get Anna and meet you on the sidewalk."

When he approached with his grandmother outside, Mary faced him. "So you knew about the joint business all along?"

He stopped so fast he stubbed his toe on the sidewalk. "I knew that my great-grandfather co-owned a bakery in the beginning. I didn't find out it was Sarah's dad until yesterday at the hospital when my grandpa told me. I didn't have a chance to tell you." He looked at Anna. "Can you explain more about the bakeries?"

"*Jah,* after they had their disagreement, Sarah's *daed*

bought out Thomas's father. He didn't feel there was enough business in Kalona for two bakeries and moved to Iowa City and established his bakery there." Anna shrugged. "That's all I know. You could ask Thomas. He might remember."

"Why is it that I never knew all this, Anna? No one ever talked about it," Sarah pressed.

"It was before you were born and most have probably forgotten about it. Aaron Miller moved his bakery to Iowa City and was in a different district than us, so you probably never saw him, Sarah. It's funny your *daed* never had an occasion to bring it up." Anna raised a brow.

Sarah shook her head. "I can't believe Daed never told me."

Noah interrupted. "But, Grandma, if my dad learned baking from Aaron, how did he travel that distance to work in his bakery?"

"After your great-grandfather's wife died, he fell and broke his leg, and Jeremiah moved in with him in Iowa City for about a year. He actually didn't want to go home, but Thomas made him because he wanted Jeremiah to take over the farm. Then Aaron died. After your daed left home, he started his own bakery."

Sarah put her arm around Mary. "Congratulations, *honig*. I'm going to go find your *vater* and *bruder* and walk around the festival with them for a while. We'll see you at home."

"I'm going back to the festival, too, Noah, unless you have more questions." Anna turned toward the park.

"Thanks, Grandma. You were very helpful. Do you need a ride home?"

"*Nein*, Cyrus and Lois are here, they'll take me home.

And I have just enough time to visit the quilt tent." Anna smiled as she headed that way.

"Noah, I want to apologize for not trusting you." Mary's heart ached with regret.

"No, Mary, it's I who should be apologizing to you. Trust is a two-way street. It was an important piece of information that you didn't know, and I didn't take the time to tell you. I'm sorry. I was busy and going to tell you later. To be honest, I never thought anything like this could happen." His amber eyes sparkled at her.

"Yes, it was a total surprise for me, too."

He motioned to his SUV parked nearby. "Do you want a ride back to the store to get your buggy?"

"That would be nice. I'm still shaking from all the excitement."

As Mary turned toward Noah's SUV, Bishop Yoder and Rebecca strolled by on the sidewalk toward their buggy. *Jah*, he'd be paying her a visit tomorrow and would probably want her confession. But she had his approval to enter for the chance of winning $10,000 and that's all she won.

But what would she say about Noah? She'd told the bishop that she knew what her baptism meant. Yet how could she confess from her heart when that meant staying away from Noah? Could she keep that promise?

She had to, and that meant choosing a man from her faith. No doubt, the bishop would mention Seth again.

Tears filled her eyes as fast as she could blink them away.

Gott, You said You would bless me with joy and You would lead my feet on the right path, but where are You? My heart is breaking, and my joy is spilling out. Noah

is my joy. I can't be Englisch, *and he's not willing to become Amish. Where is Your healing balm for my breaking heart?*

Noah walked Mary to his vehicle, opened the door and
helped her in. As she passed by, he drew a deep breath
of her honeysuckle hair. Her fragrance nearly melted
his heart.

He drove to the corral and parked. "I'll help you hitch
King. Then I'm going to Iowa City to pick up my grandpa
and take him home."

"Are they releasing him?"

"Yes, but he has to be careful. I told him I'd be out
to help him so he didn't have to worry about the farm."

"That's nice of you. I can hitch King. You can get
going."

"Nonsense, it'll only take a few minutes."

Noah tightened the girth and finished hitching King
feeling Mary's eyes on his back as he worked.

"Noah, I can tell you've been working at your
grandpa's farm. You hitched King a lot faster than I
thought you would." She stepped into the buggy. "*Danki.*
Just so you know… I'm going to terminate my temporary shop at your store so you can get the space back to
normal. Sweet Delights is ready for interior work, and
I want to be there and help. Also, the bishop seeing us
at lunch and together in your store gives the impression
that we have some kind of relationship. I'm a baptized
member of our church." Her voice wobbled before she
gained control. "I have pledged my devotion to Jesus
and to my community, and it doesn't look right for me
to spend so much time with an *Englischer.*" She shook
the reins. "Giddyap, King."

Noah stepped away from the buggy and watched as the only woman he'd ever loved drove out of sight and out of his heart. His stomach did flips when she was near and felt as empty as a rain gauge in the middle of July when she left.

He swiped his hand down the side of his vehicle. What would make a man give up this type of automation and turn to driving a horse and buggy?

Staring down the road after Mary, he let a smile stretch across his face. One fine woman that he knew his life would never be the same without. But she wasn't the only reason.

Noah started his SUV and headed in the direction of Bishop Yoder's house. He turned in the driveway, parked and gripped the steering wheel while he said a prayer. Since he had met Mary, he'd relied on prayer and trusted God a lot more.

Enough stalling. He pushed himself out, marched to the bishop's front door and knocked. No answer. He knocked again. Were they still at the fall festival? He turned to leave just as the door opened.

The bishop glared at Noah with a puzzled look on his face.

"Bishop Yoder, may I speak to you?"

"What is this regarding?" His words had a tart sound.

"I understand it is up to you to decide if I'm sincere in my request to become Amish, and I ask for your permission."

The bishop's eyes widened. His back straightened with a startled jerk. "Come in." He stepped back. "We just returned from the festival and my feet are tired, so I hope this won't take long." He led the way to his office, closed the door and motioned to a chair. "So what is this all about?"

"I want to join the Amish church." Noah firmed his shoulders and spoke decisively.

Bishop Yoder fell back into his chair and stared at Noah. "Why do you want to join our community? Is it because you want to wed Mary?

"We aren't seeing each other, no matter what you think. I do love her and would like to court her. Whether she says yes or no, I still want to join and be part of my family's community."

The bishop leaned back in his chair. "You would need to study the church rules, learn Pennsylvania Dutch and dress like the members of our community." He nodded. "I have some clothes here that might fit you. Tomorrow is Church Sunday, your *grossdaddi* and his family are hosting."

The bishop stood and walked briskly to the door. He opened it and stepped into the hall. "Rebecca, would you bring that extra suit from the closet?" His voice lowered. "The one that fits me a little snug. There is someone here who needs to borrow it."

With suit in hand, Noah followed the bishop down the hall to the front door.

"We'll talk later, after you've had time to see if this is what you really want. There will also be classes. And don't forget, you'll need a horse and buggy." His tone at the end told Noah he enjoyed saying that immensely.

Noah turned, smiled at the bishop and nodded. Yes, it would be worth it to be part of his Amish family and try for the chance to win Mary's heart.

He certainly hadn't expected this turn of events. But weren't God's surprises the best kind? Had God told him

His plan earlier, Noah might never have come to Kalona. But he was sure glad God had set his feet on Route 218.

Mary followed her *stiefmutter* into Thomas Miller's new barn on Church Sunday, and slid onto the bench next to Sarah. She caught sight of a man entering the building. He walked to the men's side and found a spot on the bench. He looked familiar, but his hat shaded his face.

When the singing started, the man took off his hat, leaned over, placed it under the bench and straightened back up. Mary gasped and threw her hand over her mouth.

"What's wrong, Mary?" Sarah whispered.

"Look straight across, last row. It's Noah Miller."

Sarah glanced over and smiled. "He's been seeing quite a lot of his grandparents and helping Thomas on the farm, *jah*?"

"Did you know about this, *Mamm*?"

"*Nein*, but Anna did say how helpful and *wunderbaar* the *bu* was and said they were becoming fond of him."

Mary's mind wandered to Noah during the introductory message, but when the preacher started the main sermon, he dwelled on two points, the ones they often emphasized for a new member.

The first, "be not conformed to this world," Romans 12:2; and the second, "be ye not unequally yoked together with unbelievers," 2 Corinthians 6:14. This one, the preacher explained, forbade an Amish person from marrying or entering a business partnership with a non-Amish person.

Mary's throat welled with a lump. She'd hadn't expected to see Noah in Amish clothing. What had made him decide to take such a big step?

She looked for Noah after service but couldn't find him. She'd caught sight of him at the table but there wasn't time to talk. After the common-meal cleanup, Mary started across the lawn to meet her parents at their buggy. When she crossed the driveway, there sat Noah under the tree sitting on a swing. He stood and met her halfway.

"Hello, Mary."

"Noah, what a surprise. What changed your mind?"

"Emily has been going out to our grandparents' farm with me. She has met several Amish girl cousins, and they have become friends. Together, we made the decision."

Mary glanced at her *daed* waiting in the buggy. "I need to go."

"Mary, I have one thing to ask." He paused. "I would like to court you. You'll probably want to think about it."

Tears blurred her eyes. She pressed a fingertip against each one. "*Nein*, I don't need to think about it." A smile brewed deep in her stomach and burst across her face. "*Jah*, I would like that very much."

"I borrowed Ethan's buggy. Can I give you a ride home?"

"I'll run and tell *Daed*."

When she returned, Noah walked her to his buggy. She settled on the seat a foot from the man she wanted to marry. She could feel his warmth just inches from her. Noah reached across the expanse and took her hand in his, her heart beating faster by the moment.

She turned toward Noah as he shook the reins and turned the buggy down the drive and out onto the road.

Noah winked. "I was worried you wouldn't say yes." He guided the buggy to the side of the road and stopped.

He pulled her into his arms, his face bathed in a smile so *wunderbaar* it stole her heart.

He lowered his lips to hers for a tender kiss. "I love you, Mary, with all my heart. I never want to let you out of my arms."

"*Ich liebe dich*, I love you, Noah Miller." She drew in a deep, shuddering breath as his lips touched hers once again. *Jah*, he was the man she wanted to marry, and she'd spend the rest of her life making him forget the *Englisch* ways.

Epilogue

One year later

After returning with Noah from their twenty-minute premarital talk with the ministers, Mary sat next to her attendants, sidesitters Amanda and Nettie. Heat burning her cheeks remembering the ministers' words as they explained what it meant to be a *frau* and *ehemann*.

Her heart pulsed with an overwhelming love for Noah, sitting on the bench parallel to hers. His attendants Ethan and Jacob, sitting next to him. She'd always remember this moment, and how her love bubbled over for this man.

The three-hour service focused on marital relationship, the obstacles, the joys, and working together to raise a family. The bishop gave examples of biblical marriages and walking the road of a *frau that* were inspirational.

Her heart raced and her throat tightened as the time to take her vow drew near. She blotted her hands together.

"Mary, calm down. You look like you're ready to faint," Amanda whispered.

She winked at Amanda and her cousin Nettie. "I'm fine, just nervous."

Bishop Yoder rose and walked to the front of her daed's barn. "Noah and Mary, will you please join me?"

Mary rose and walked beside Noah to stand before the bishop.

"Will you join hands?" the bishop said with a soft voice.

"Are you willing to enter into wedlock as God ordained?" the bishop asked.

"Yes," they replied in unison.

"Noah, do you believe *Gott* has ordained Mary to be your wedded *frau*?"

"Yes."

"Mary, do you believe *Gott* has ordained Noah to be your wedded *ehemann*?"

Her throat grew dry and tight as tears teetered at the edges of her eyelids. "Yes."

The bishop placed a warm palm over her and Noah's clasped hands. The bishop's voice was rich and reverent. "May the *Gott* of Abraham, the *Gott* of Isaac and the *Gott* of Jacob be with you and bless you abundantly through Jesus Christ. I now pronounce you *ehemann* and *frau*."

After the service, Noah grabbed her hands and pulled her close. "Now you are all mine for the rest of our lives," then he smiled. "But right now, my lovely frau, we must greet our guests."

Jenny and Emily threw their arms around Mary. "Welcome to the family, Mary. You look lovely." Jenny crushed her new sister-in-law to her then stepped back and let Emily hug Mary.

"We're sisters now, Mary." Emily beamed. "Jenny helped me make a cake for the *Eck,* the bridal table. It's the tall vanilla one with lots of frosting."

"*Danki*, I'm so proud of you. I will make sure I have

a piece of it. I'm going to enjoy having sisters to talk to and share my secrets with." Mary squeezed Emily again.

Jenny grabbed Emily's hand and tugged her away. "We'll go get our places and see you at dinner."

As wedding guests started to drift toward the dinner tables, Noah leaned close to her ear and whispered, "Come, Mary. I have something to show you." He tightened his grip on her hand, pulling her across the lawn over the driveway and toward his buggy.

"Stop, Noah! We can't leave our own wedding."

He laughed. "Mrs. Miller, I would sure like to, but instead, I have a wedding gift for you. Stand right here, close your eyes and hold your hands out. Wait just a minute." There was a rustling sound from his buggy, and then something soft and heavy was laid in her arms. "Okay, open your eyes."

Mary blinked and dropped her jaw. Tears filled her eyes. It was the quilt her real *mamm* had made her. "Where did you get it?"

"Sarah saw it sticking out of your bag after she told you they couldn't afford to give you the thousand dollars for an espresso machine. She figured you took it to the consignment shop. It upset her. And when she stopped into my store to see what you were competing against, she told me."

Mary wrapped her arms around him, squeezing the quilt between them. "*Danki*, Noah. You'll never know how much my heart hurt that day or how much it is filled today knowing you are my *ehemann*."

A man huffed and puffed as he ran toward them, his feet scuffing the stones on the driveway. Noah released his hold on Mary and turned.

"Oh, no you don't. You're not leaving your own wedding just yet." Bishop Yoder heaved out the words with a lot of gasping and gulping.

Noah laughed. "Bishop, did you run across the yard? We're not going to leave. I was giving Mary her wedding gift."

The bishop plunged his hand in his waistband, pulled out a handkerchief and patted his forehead. "I didn't want you escaping before the guests could actually see you two were married."

Mary shook a finger at the old man. "*Ach*, Bishop Yoder, it's a wonder we were ever married the way you were always trying to push me toward Seth."

The bishop laid his right hand on his heart. "Mary, you know I only want what's right for you. As you'll recall, I only relayed Seth's request to you. I never insisted you marry him. And what better way to get you to not marry Seth then to nudge you toward him? You are Sarah's *tochter* for sure and for certain. She, too, always went her own way. Sometimes *Gott* takes away so He can give you something that's right for you."

"*Mamm* was right, Bishop." Mary nodded. "You are an old softy."

The bishop jerked his chin in the air. "No one will ever believe that, and don't you repeat it. I have an image to uphold. So, Mary," Bishop Yoder changed the subject, "what will you do with Sweet Delights now?"

She glanced at Noah, and he raised a brow. "Noah is going to continue to help his *grossdaddi*, and I'm going to combine Sweet Delights with Noah's store, so to speak. We'll sell all the baked goods at Sweet Delights. Sarah plans to run the bakery with me, so we're combining the two families back into one bakery as it had been long ago. Did you see the sign that Noah hung in both our shops?

'Food nourishes the body on its journey, but it's love that gives the real taste to life.'"

The bishop nodded at Noah. "And will Jenny be joining the Amish as well?"

"*Nein*, Bishop, I don't think so. Jenny wasn't brought up in the Amish church and doesn't have the same urge to live among a family she doesn't know. She has picked a church that suits her. I was angry with God for taking our parents, and He was taking me on a journey to reconcile my heart back to Him." Noah squeezed Mary's hand. "And that led me straight to Mary."

"*Jah*, and what did you learn on this journey?"

"That God doesn't cause car accidents, men do. But God used the situation to bring my heart home to where it was meant to be."

Bishop Yoder patted Noah on the back. "*Jah*, but you had to find the right path. *Willkommen* to our community." He turned and headed back across the drive. "And don't be too long, you two. You have the rest of your lives together."

Noah pulled Mary back into his arms and pressed a long-overdue, tender kiss against her lips. "I love you, Mary."

"*Ich liebe dich*. I love you, Noah, with all my heart."

* * * * *

She leaned back, watching him.

Curiosity about this man who could make the best of a difficult childhood—and who actually owned a garlic press—flashed through her, warm and intense. She didn't want to be nosy, shouldn't be. His childhood wasn't her business, and she ought to be polite and drop the subject.

But this man and his son tugged at her. The more she learned about them, the more she felt for them. And maybe part of it was to do with Landon, with his being the same age her son would have been, but that wasn't all of it. They were a fascinating pair. They'd come through some challenges, Dev with his childhood and both of them with a divorce, and yet they were still positive. She really wanted to know how, what their secret was. "Did you grow up in the Denver area or all over?"

"Denver and the farm country around it." He slid the bread into the oven. "How about you?"

"Just a few towns over on the other side of the mountain." Indeed, she'd spent most of her life, including her married life, in this part of the state.

He didn't volunteer any more information about himself and Landon, so she didn't press. Instead, she leaned down and showed Landon Lady's favorite spot to be scratched, right behind the ears. Now that they weren't working anymore, he was talkative and happy, asking her a million questions about the dog.

It was hard to leave the kitchen, cozy and warm, infused with the fragrances of garlic and tomato and bread. Her quiet home and the can of soup she'd likely heat up for dinner both seemed lonely after being here. But she had her own life and couldn't mooch off theirs. "I'd better let you men get on with your dinner," she said and started gathering up her books.

"You want to stay?" Dev asked.

The question, hanging in the air, ignited danger flares in her mind.

The answer was obvious: yes, she did want to stay. But an Unwise! Unwise! warning message seemed to flash in her head.

Spending even more time with Dev and Landon was no way to keep the distance she knew she had to keep. As appealing as this pair was, she couldn't risk getting closer. Her heart might not survive the wrenching away that would have to happen, sooner rather than later.

Don't miss
Her Easter Prayer *by Lee Tobin McClain,*
available April 2022 wherever
Love Inspired books and ebooks are sold.

LoveInspired.com

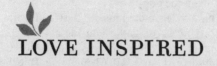

LOVE INSPIRED

Stories to uplift and inspire

Fall in love with Love Inspired—
inspirational and uplifting stories of faith
and hope. Find strength and comfort in
the bonds of friendship and community.
Revel in the warmth of possibility and the
promise of new beginnings.

Sign up for the Love Inspired newsletter
at **LoveInspired.com** to be the first
to find out about upcoming titles,
special promotions and exclusive content.

Get 4 FREE REWARDS!

We'll send you 2 FREE Books plus 2 FREE Mystery Gifts.

Both the **Love Inspired**® and **Love Inspired**® Suspense series feature compelling novels filled with inspirational romance, faith, forgiveness, and hope.

YES! Please send me 2 FREE novels from the Love Inspired or Love Inspired Suspense series and my 2 FREE gifts (gifts are worth about $10 retail). After receiving them, if I don't wish to receive any more books, I can return the shipping statement marked "cancel." If I don't cancel, I will receive 6 brand-new Love Inspired Larger-Print books or Love Inspired Suspense Larger-Print books every month and be billed just $5.99 each in the U.S. or $6.24 each in Canada. That is a savings of at least 17% off the cover price. It's quite a bargain! Shipping and handling is just 50¢ per book in the U.S. and $1.25 per book in Canada.* I understand that accepting the 2 free books and gifts places me under no obligation to buy anything. I can always return a shipment and cancel at any time. The free books and gifts are mine to keep no matter what I decide.

Choose one: ☐ **Love Inspired**
Larger-Print
(122/322 IDN GNWC)

☐ **Love Inspired Suspense**
Larger-Print
(107/307 IDN GNWN)

Name (please print)

Address   Apt. #

City   State/Province   Zip/Postal Code

Email: Please check this box ☐ if you would like to receive newsletters and promotional emails from Harlequin Enterprises ULC and its affiliates. You can unsubscribe anytime.

Mail to the **Harlequin Reader Service:**
IN U.S.A.: P.O. Box 1341, Buffalo, NY 14240-8531
IN CANADA: P.O. Box 603, Fort Erie, Ontario L2A 5X3

Want to try 2 free books from another series? Call 1-800-873-8635 or visit www.ReaderService.com.

*Terms and prices subject to change without notice. Prices do not include sales taxes, which will be charged (if applicable) based on your state or country of residence. Canadian residents will be charged applicable taxes. Offer not valid in Quebec. This offer is limited to one order per household. Books received may not be as shown. Not valid for current subscribers to the Love Inspired or Love Inspired Suspense series. All orders subject to approval. Credit or debit balances in a customer's account(s) may be offset by any other outstanding balance owed by or to the customer. Please allow 4 to 6 weeks for delivery. Offer available while quantities last.

Your Privacy—Your information is being collected by Harlequin Enterprises ULC, operating as Harlequin Reader Service. For a complete summary of the information we collect, how we use this information and to whom it is disclosed, please visit our privacy notice located at corporate.harlequin.com/privacy-notice. From time to time we may also exchange your personal information with reputable third parties. If you wish to opt out of this sharing of your personal information, please visit readerservice.com/consumerschoice or call 1-800-873-8635. **Notice to California Residents**—Under California law, you have specific rights to control and access your data. For more information on these rights and how to exercise them, visit corporate.harlequin.com/california-privacy.

LIRLIS22